Come Sunday Morning Saga

Come Sunday Morning Saga

Terry E. Hill

www.urbanbooks.net

Urban Books, LLC
97 N18th Street
Wyandanch, NY 11798

Come Sunday Morning Saga Copyright © 2015 Terry E. Hill

ISBN 13: 978-1-62286-706-6
ISBN 10: 1-62286-706-8

First Trade Paperback Printing July 2015
Printed in the United States of America

10 9 8 7 6 5 4 3 2 1

This is a work of fiction. Any references or similarities to actual events, real people, living or dead, or to real locales are intended to give the novel a sense of reality. Any similarity in other names, characters, places, and incidents is entirely coincidental.

Distributed by Kensington Publishing Corp.
Submit Orders to:
Customer Service
400 Hahn Road
Westminster, MD 21157-4627
Phone: 1-800-733-3000
Fax: 1-800-659-2436

1
Sunday Morning

Cynthia Pryce scanned the pages of the Sunday paper. A silk robe sloped gracefully around the calves of her slender legs. Hair, the color of burnt caramel, curved leisurely over cheekbones that most women would gladly pay thousands to replicate. Cynthia looked perfect even with no one there to impress. She had no choice.

It was six o'clock on Sunday morning. The city lay at her feet as she looked from the twenty-third floor of the rooftop condominium. Morning light drifted into the penthouse while floating clouds peeked through the windows for a glimpse of the beautiful woman.

Crystal vases and glass tables throughout the condominium sparkled from the light flowing through the floor-to-ceiling windows. Soft beige carpet served as a lush backdrop for Cynthia's expensive and eclectic taste in furniture.

Scandinavian leather sofas and chairs stood in the center of the living room, and a Louis XV armoire held a state-of-the-art sound system and music collection that ranged from classical to gospel and included every genre in between.

Original paintings by Bearden, Barnes, and Motley hung in places of honor above the fireplace, behind the sofa, and at the head of the dining-room table. Freshly cut flowers, magenta, mauve, and pink, arranged by the skillful and nimble fingers of Cynthia's favorite florist, were poised to greet visitors in the large foyer, as well as the dining and living rooms.

Hands and fingernails that never went a day without special attention lifted a second cup of coffee to her lips as she searched for mention of her pastor, Hezekiah T. Cleaveland, in the paper.

Cynthia slammed the paper to the coffee table when the last page was turned, rattling her coffee cup and plate, which held the remains of a half-eaten poppy seed muffin. The story she had waited for was not there, as had been promised. She looked again to the front page. The headline read: FATHER KILLS FAMILY AND SELF, DESPONDENT OVER FINANCIAL LOSSES.

Cynthia pushed the paper to the floor. *Who gives a fuck?* she thought while reaching for the cell phone on the dining-room table.

She entered the number that had been called frequently in the last month. "Hello," a raspy voice answered. "What do you want? It's six o'clock in the morning."

"Lance, it's Cynthia. Where's the story? You told me it would be in this morning's edition."

"My editor won't run it until I give Hezekiah a chance to respond. I tried to convince him the evidence stands on its own, but he wouldn't budge."

Lance Savage sat up in bed and rubbed his squinting eyes. "I've got a meeting with Hezekiah tomorrow. He thinks I'm doing a story on the new cathedral. I can't wait to see his face when I drop this bomb on him."

"He'll deny everything," she said. "When you meet with him, make sure Naomi isn't there."

"Naomi isn't available for the interview. I think Catherine will probably sit in, though." Cynthia laughed. "That's fine. You'll certainly get a reaction from Catherine if you can't get one from Hezekiah."

"That's what I'm hoping. Does she know anything about this?"

"I doubt it. As far as Catherine is concerned, Hezekiah walks on water. If she does, let me know and I'll deal with her later."

The joy in the Sunday morning church service at New Testament Cathedral was palpable. Brass instruments, drums, violins, guitars, and pianos caused the auditorium to pulsate with rhythmic music. Images on the twenty-foot-high Jumbotron screen alternated rapidly between sweeping images of the 15,000-member congregation standing, clapping, and singing, to the 200-member choir and orchestra performing songs of inspiration.

Shots of Hezekiah and Samantha Cleaveland standing at the front row, smiling and waving their hands in the air, filled the screen throughout the morning. The captions below their images read, "Visit our Web site at www.New TestamentCathedral.com to make your love offering today!"

On cue, the pace of the music gradually shifted to a more melodic and reverent tone. A soprano sang a hypnotic tune and the audience obediently chimed in. A billowing hum from the crowd rolled from the front of the church to the top rear row and filled the room as congregants softly sang in unison and looked upward to heaven.

The camera followed Hezekiah as he walked up the steps to the center of the stage. Behind the pulpit to his left and right were waterfalls made of a series of stacked boulders, greenery, and gently flowing ribbons of water.

The stage backdrop was an electric wall of light that periodically changed from blue to green, lavender, and a hazy yellow to accompany the desired mood of each moment during the service.

"Good morning, New Testament Cathedral," Hezekiah said when the music began to subside and the audience settled into their seats.

The room replied in unison, "Good morning, Pastor Cleaveland."

Hezekiah was well over six feet tall. He wore a crisp white shirt and a sleek tailored black suit that was stitched to perfection around his muscular frame. A cranberry-colored necktie complemented perfectly his flawless skin, which seemed to glow under the bright lights.

Hezekiah flashed his radiant signature smile approvingly in acknowledgment and continued, "This is the day the Lord hath made. I will rejoice and be glad in it."

For the next fifteen minutes the jumbo screen was filled with the image of Hezekiah Cleaveland delivering the Sunday sermon, interspersed with shots of members of the audience reading a verse in their Bible that he had referenced, nodding their head in agreement to a word of wisdom just shared, and his wife, Samantha, looking lovingly up at her husband and pastor. The sermon ended on a euphoric note that had all the attendees up on their feet, clapping, and Hezekiah looking pleased and exuberant at the podium.

After a final uplifting song from the choir and orchestra, Samantha joined Hezekiah on the stage. The last shot that appeared on the screen was that of the beautiful couple waving to the camera with a caption that read: ALWAYS REMEMBER, GOD LOVES YOU AND SO DO WE! TO MAKE A LOVE OFFERING, CALL US TOLL FREE AT 1(800) 555-4455 OR VISIT OUR WEB SITE AT: WWW.NEWTESTAMENTCATHEDRAL.COM.

The service had ended and members of New Testament Cathedral gathered in the Fellowship Hall. The cavernous room was filled to capacity. It served as the meeting place for thousands of congregants after the morning service.

Sunday hats, which seemed to defy gravity, dotted the room: swirling turbans, perfectly erect feathers, fluttering satins, and wilting silks crowned freshly coiffed heads and made-up faces. Colorful dresses and well-constructed suits filled every inch of the room.

The space vibrated from the roar of laughter and gossip. Words of encouragement were exchanged, assignations planned, schemes plotted, and reputations ruined.

The multiple conversations fused into an indecipherable buzz above their heads.

"Pastor Cleaveland outdid himself this morning," came a comment from a cluster of women in the center of the room.

"Jason got laid off last week. I don't know what we're going to do now," was heard from two women huddled near the entrance.

"I can't believe she wore that to church. Looks like she should be at a cocktail party," a woman said while rolling her eyes and shielding her mouth.

"She should have left him years ago. He's slept with half the women here," was observed simultaneously by three different sets of women referring to three different men in the hall.

"Look at him over there in the gray suit. Girl, that man is fine. All he would have to do is smile at me and I'd give him whatever he wanted and a little more just to make sure he came back for seconds," said a woman as she peeked from behind her leather-bound Bible.

Children balancing cookies on paper plates and spilling fruit punch from plastic cups wove through a forest of high heels and freshly shined leather shoes. The elder women of the church had taken seats against the rear wall of the hall, beneath a stained-glass window. Parishioners took breaks between animated conversations to kiss the church mothers weathered cheeks and tell them, "You're looking good this morning, dear," and that they were praying for them.

Reverend Willie Mitchell stood in his usual spot in the center of the room. His bulging stomach made it impossible for him to button the coat of his favorite cream-colored suit.

A red necktie formed a puddle on the top of his belly and then sloped down like a neon arrow advertising his oversized gold belt buckle. The thick hand in his pocket unconsciously caressed and massaged keys to a new appliance-white Mercedes-Benz. He threw his head back and laughed as Reverend Pryce's wife, Cynthia, commented on the abrupt ending of the morning sermon.

"I guess Samantha was afraid she'd be late for her afternoon manicure," she said, checking to ensure no one other than Reverend Mitchell had heard her. The silk flowers on her hat shook as she spoke.

"I'm glad he cut it short. I could hardly stay awake,"

Reverend Mitchell responded. Unlike Cynthia, the reverend didn't look over his shoulder.

He wanted everyone to hear his harsh critique of the morning service.

Hattie Williams graciously accepted kisses from the younger members. She sat embraced in the glow from the window and soothed by the warmth on her shoulders.

Hattie was the senior mother of New Testament Cathedral. She had been a member since the first service held in the little storefront building ten years earlier.

Hattie was eighty-two years old. She was a stately and imposing woman, but her warm smile could melt away the fears of any troubled soul fortunate enough to be in her presence. Her silver upswept hair was held in place by a row of well-positioned black bobby pins. A shiny patent leather purse filled with tissues and peppermints matched her sensible Sunday shoes perfectly. Hattie wore a simple lavender floral-print dress with a white ruffled collar which she had made herself. In one hand she held a handkerchief used to occasionally dab perspiration from upper lip and in the

other, the smooth curved handle of a wooden cane for maneu-
vering the steps in the church.

A barrage of emotions suddenly pulsed through Hattie as she
clutched the handle of the cane leaning against her swollen knee.
She knew the feelings were not her own but instead belonged to
others in the room. Sifting through the hidden passions and pain
of others each Sunday morning had almost become a game for her.
She inherited the empathic gift from her grandmother. Once she
thought it a curse, but now she considered it a blessing.

Silent prayers were said for the more desperate cases and stern
rebukes issued to those with nefarious intentions.

She immediately recognized the pool of jealousy surrounding
Willie Mitchell. *That man's going to have a heart attack worrying
about how much money Pastor Cleaveland has,* she thought.

Hattie looked to her left and saw Scarlet Shackelford handing
a cup of red punch to a little boy in a black suit with his crumpled
white shirttail hanging from the rear.

Scarlet's chiseled face resembled a tormented angel imagined
only in the mind of an artist. Her pastel silk dress twirled gracefully around the calves of her slender legs.

Hattie preferred to keep a safe distance from the young woman.
The pain she experienced in her presence was sometimes even too
much for her to bear. That girl needs to forgive herself for having
the pastor's baby, she observed as she fought to block the still raw
emotions pouring from Scarlet. It's been over five years and still
nobody knows anything about it.

Hattie suddenly felt Samantha Cleaveland enter the hall.Only
Samantha carried with her such extreme feelings of anger and
hate and only Samantha could so skillfully conceal it from others.
The hate, however, was transported in a body that rivaled the
beauty of a marble statue intricately carved by the hand of a master.

Shoulder-length glimmering black hair surrounded her flawless
pampered skin. The mint linen suit she wore had been designed
to accentuate her sensuous curves. The heels of her elegant shoes
were the exact height to contort her calves into the perfect feminine silhouette.

Proud, commanding, and in control, her body moved through the room as though carried on a horse-drawn chariot.

She's going to hurt somebody one day. Lord, you better keep an eye on that one, Hattie thought as Samantha passed. Hattie acknowledged her only with a slight nod of her head.

The few remaining worshippers said their final good-byes in the parking lot.

Reverend Mitchell honked the horn of his lumbering Mercedes and waved to the security guard at the gate as he turned onto Hezekiah T. Cleaveland Avenue. The street had been named in Hezekiah's honor the year he broke ground for the senior citizen housing complex behind the church. If there were any other exit from the parking lot Reverend Mitchell would have taken it. He often wondered why his backroom lobbying against the street name change had failed. *Maybe I should have made a bigger contribution to the mayor for his reelection campaign,* he thought while plunging the car into oncoming traffic.

Samantha Cleaveland waited patiently in the rear of the black limousine and watched as Hezekiah handed a twenty-dollar bill to a young man wearing a wrinkled shirt and pants too short for his long legs.

"Who was that?" she asked as Hezekiah folded his body in next to her.

"That was Melanie Jackson's son, Virgil. He used to play drums for the youth choir. I had to fire him after the police caught him trying to break into the church. He was released from jail a couple of months ago. He said he's been off drugs for over a year. You remember him."

"Yes, I do remember him. He doesn't appear to be off drugs. Don't get involved with him, Hezekiah. He looks like he could be trouble," Samantha said with contempt as the limousine turned onto Cleaveland Avenue.

She prayed the driver would go faster and turn quickly off the street that bore her husband's name. The sooner she was off that road the better she would feel. She regretted all the campaign contributions she had made and the luncheons she'd hosted to get the street named in his honor. *Now I've got to look at those damned signs every time I come to church,* she thought as the car idled at a missed red light. Maybe I should pay that thug Virgil to knock them all down. It would take the city years to replace them in this neighborhood.

"What did you think of my sermon?" Hezekiah asked. "I think I should have spent more time on the Twenty-third Psalm. People hear it their whole lives but never really understand its true meaning."

"It was fine, Hezekiah," she said. The tiresome chore of reassuring him of his oratory prowess had been part of their Sunday-sermon debriefing for the last ten years. "I'm sure everyone enjoyed it very much."

"Next time I think I'll do a sermon on the entire chapter." Hezekiah looked pensively out the window and continued. "Willie Mitchell slept through my entire sermon. At least he pretended to be asleep. Why doesn't he go to another church if he dislikes me so much?"

"I've told you before, we need him here. He's already donated a million dollars toward construction of the cathedral and he's hinted that he might double that. Just smile, shake his hand on Sunday mornings, and let me handle him."

"I know you like him, Samantha, but sometimes I'm not sure if the money is worth the trouble."

"That's where you're wrong. I don't like him either, but we need him."

"One day he's going to push me too far and . . ."

"And what, Hezekiah? You'll kill him?" Hezekiah laughed. "No, something worse. I'll sic you on him."

Samantha quickly changed the subject. "You should use the cordless microphone more often. You look stiff standing behind the podium for the entire sermon. I wish you'd move around more. The audience and the cameras would love it."

"I'll try to remember next Sunday," he said as he laid his head on the headrest. Without looking in her direction, Hezekiah continued to speak. "Do you want to preach next Sunday? I think I could use a break."

Samantha's heart fluttered when she heard the words. She was rarely offered the opportunity to preach at the coveted Sunday-morning service. She had earned her doctorate in theology six years earlier and was a gifted and inspiring ordained minister, but her more frequent role was that of the expensively dressed mannequin smiling at Hezekiah's side on their weekly television program.

The 15,000-seat sanctuary had always been filled to capacity on the rare occasions she had been given the opportunity to preach. Television ratings would skyrocket, primarily due to channel surfers forced to pause by the striking and charismatic woman who flashed on their screens.

Men loved Samantha for one reason. She was beautiful. At thirty-five she commanded the adoring attention of deacons, cameramen, lighting technicians, and every heterosexual male within range of her seductive voice.

She never flaunted her looks. Everyone in her presence took notice of them without any effort on her part. Instead, she focused her energy on perfecting the image of a sacrificing wife and mother who stood by her man, come what may.

Women had the predictable love-hate reaction to Samantha Cleaveland. They loved her devotion to the man they admired, but envied the command she had over every inch of her body. No part of her was unattended, unnoticed, or unappreciated.

She only wore clothes designed especially for her voluptuous figure or those from her favorite boutiques in Beverly Hills, New York, and Paris. Even if other women could afford the clothes and accessories she took for granted, they could never assemble them as masterfully as she. It took years to perfect the look and most people didn't have her patience, skills, or her means.

"Why didn't you ask me earlier?" she hissed. "I won't have time to prepare a sermon by next Sunday. I've got a busy week." Anger took over after the initial shock from the unfortunate timing of his request. Titles of the dozens of sermons she'd written but never had the opportunity to deliver flashed through her mind.

"You don't have to do anything new. How about preaching the one on wives supporting their husbands?"

Samantha marveled at the arrogance of her husband.

His one-dimensional view of her caused her blood to run cold. She had spent their entire marriage in the shadow of Hezekiah's greatness. Her beauty and talents only served to propel him higher.

She responded sharply, "I've got more important things to say than to remind women of how great their husbands are."

"I know you do, honey. I just thought it was a good sermon."

"Drop it, Hezekiah. I won't be able to preach next Sunday."

"All right, baby, maybe the following Sunday," he said while rubbing her knee. "I think I've got at least one more good sermon in me."

Hezekiah stared out the tinted limousine window. He braced himself and hoped that the next exchange would be quick and painless. "Reverend Duncan is in town," he said, closing his eyes.

"Who's Reverend Duncan?" Samantha asked with a hint of suspicion.

"He's from Shiloh Church of God in Detroit. I'm having dinner with him today."

"I wish you would have told me this morning. Etta has been home all day preparing dinner for us." She knew there was no Reverend Duncan.

"I didn't know about it then," Hezekiah snapped defensively.

"He called before this morning's service. Where was Jasmine? I didn't see her at church."

"She wasn't feeling well." Samantha had no intention of allowing him to use their daughter as a diversion for his lies. "I can go to dinner with you."

"He wants to talk to me alone. I think he's having marriage problems."

Samantha was almost embarrassed by the perverse pleasure she took in his obvious discomfort. "Then he might benefit from a woman's perspective," she said looking directly at him.

"Damn it, Samantha, he said he wanted to talk to me alone." Hezekiah knew he had overreacted as his words reverberated through the car.

"Hezekiah, I know you're seeing someone. You haven't been yourself for months now. The least you can do is come up with more original lies."

"Can I have dinner with a fellow pastor without you thinking I'm sleeping with another woman?" he snapped.

"Your paranoia is getting out of control."

"It's not just dinner, Hezekiah. You've been sulking around the house for weeks now. You could never hide your feelings from me."

"Maybe if you had a life of your own I wouldn't have to hide my feelings."

Samantha sat erect in the plush leather seat. "A life of my own? You wouldn't have a life if it weren't for me.

You'd still be in that storefront preaching to neighborhood kids and old ladies. Everyone knows I made you and without me you'd be nothing."

"I don't want to argue with you, Samantha."

"I'm not arguing. I simply want you to tell me the truth for once. I can't keep pretending not to know something is wrong. I deserve better than this."

"I'm not seeing anyone, Samantha. I've just had a lot on my mind. You can believe it or not. I don't care anymore." The intersections rushed by in a blur. Samantha's mind raced as she thought. *When this is done, I should send his body to whoever the bitch is and let her bury him.*

The car turned onto Sunset Boulevard, toward the whitewashed towers at the West Gate of Bel Air, and began the familiar ascent up the hill. Rolling estates quickly replaced the grime and congestion of the city streets below.

Lush trees on each side of the winding road tilted inward and formed a green lace canopy over the street. The center median was filled with vibrant flowers and cement fountains poured water from the mouths of lions at each intersection. Pristine terra-cotta-tiled roofs peeked over the tops of densely clustered shrubs and waving palm trees. Couples wearing matching jogging suits strolled leisurely along the paved sidewalks with their sprightly Lhasa Apsos and prancing Irish setters in tow.

Samantha's thoughts shifted to her daughter, Jasmine.

She remembered the therapist's recommendation to admit their only child into a drug rehabilitation program. Her stomach tensed at the thought of the public scandal it would cause. The daughter of a prominent pastor spending the tithes given by grandmothers on pensions to support her addiction to Ecstasy and alcohol.

No further words were exchanged until the car turned into the driveway of the Cleaveland estate. Hezekiah never liked the enormous house that overlooked Los Angeles but Samantha felt it appropriate for a family of their prominence. An eight-foot white stucco fence surrounded the grounds. Lower points in the rolling fence allowed passersby brief glimpses of the magnificent home. A wrought-iron gate emblazoned with the initials "HC" quietly parted at the sight of the car and gently closed behind it. Palm trees that lined the winding driveway quivered gently as the car drove past. Meticulously manicured grounds surrounded the home and seemed to spill down the hill into the skyline. To the left was a freshly painted green tennis court with sharp white lines. A whitewashed gazebo stood to the right, overlooking the Pacific Ocean, and a two-story guesthouse could be seen tucked behind a grove of trees. At the final curve of the driveway, the trees unfurled like a stage curtain and the house could finally be seen. It was an off-white Mediterranean villa, nestled behind pine and oak trees, sitting on a sloped crest with spectacular views of the city and Pacific Ocean.

Double stone stairways ascended to the grand main entrance under a covered porch, which was held by four twenty-foot-high white carved pillars. Each window on the front of the home was topped by cream-colored arches and flanked by stone columns. Branches dripping with lavender and white wisteria spilled from a deck on the second floor.

The car stopped at the foot of the stairway.

"Are you coming in?" she asked coldly.

"No," came the abrupt reply.

"What time will you be home?"

"I won't be gone long."

Samantha slammed the car door and walked up the steps to the house without turning to see her husband being driven back down the hill.

Etta Washington, the Cleavelands' housekeeper and cook, opened the massive double wooden doors as Samantha approached. Etta had been with the Cleavelands for five years. She was forty-eight years old but appeared much older. She wore a white apron, knotted at the waist, over a simple black dress which fell just below her knees. Samantha insisted she wear the uniform at all times. Etta had never married and had no children. To Etta, the Cleavelands were her family, but to Samantha, Etta had never risen above the rank of hired help.

The opulent exterior of the house was mirrored in its interior. Sunlight poured through a skylight in the two-story foyer and coated the oval-shaped room in a warm glow. Double living-room and dining-room doors framed in oak were to the right and to the left. A round marble table holding a massive floral arrangement sat in the center of the room and on each side symmetrical stairways molded into the curve of the walls and climbed to a second-floor landing which overlooked the room. Black wrought-iron banisters provided a stark contrast in the bright room. Directly ahead hung the first of two original Picassos in the Cleaveland home. The painting was in the center of the foyer rear wall and the first thing seen when entering the home. The dreaming woman's hands rested suggestively in her lap. Her head was slightly tilted to the right and her closed eyes hinted of erotic sweet dreams. Parts of her deconstructed face provided a glimpse of the thoughts that seemed to give her such serene pleasure.

Antique furniture and European oil masterpieces were skillfully displayed throughout. A well-thought-out floor plan of wing-backed chairs, marble and glass-topped tea tables, and satin-swathed couches created the optimum setting to impress and entertain the rich, the pious, and the famous. Crystal chandeliers and Lalique vases glittered throughout, while plush pastel carpets softened the hard edges of each room. A sleek black baby grand rested in front of a wall of glass which overlooked the grounds and a shimmering cobalt blue infinity edge swimming pool. The second Picasso hung over the fireplace in the living room. The five women of Les Demoiselles d'Avignon looked approvingly over the elegant room. Their faces resembled primitive tribal masks and the jagged edges of their pink flesh formed sharp angles that pointed in every direction.

An oil painting of Hezekiah and Samantha was on the opposite wall. The two smiling faces countered the seductive and horrifying image of the five women across the room. Hezekiah's and Samantha's smiles in the painting absorbed all the light that streamed through the room's many windows. As lovely and masterfully executed as the dueling paintings were, their beauty was eclipsed when Samantha entered the room.

"Good afternoon, Mrs. Cleaveland." Etta took her coat and hung it neatly over her arm. "How was church today?"

"It was fine, Etta. I'm sorry you had to miss it."

"Will Pastor be home for dinner?" Etta asked.

"No," Samantha said. "He's having dinner with a pastor from out of state. How's Jasmine? Has she been out of her room today?"

"No, ma'am, she's been up there all day. I knocked on the door a few times but, she told me to go away." Etta knew an addict when she saw one but had been sternly warned by Samantha not to get involved in Cleaveland family matters. "Will you be having dinner in the dining room, ma'am?"

"No. I think I'll have it in my study. I'm going to check on Jasmine first. I'll ask if she wants dinner."

"Yes, ma'am."

From birth Jasmine had two strikes against her: she was an only child and a pastor's kid. To others her life was a fantasy: two loving parents, a beautiful home, the finest private schools, a new convertible BMW on her sixteenth birthday, and lots of attention from the many people who loved her parents. But it was a nightmare for her. She often referred to herself as "a theater prop" used by her parents to illustrate their idyllic Christian life.

Years of being "the perfect little angel" had taken their toll on her. She ran away from home for the first time at thirteen. Her first abortion was at fourteen and the second at fifteen. She added the use of Ecstasy to her already nagging alcohol problem at the exclusive Catholic high school. Jasmine ran with the most privileged kids in the school, and soon she even ran them. The drug use turned from recreation to abuse. Now, at sixteen, she was rapidly heading for what appeared to be a tragic ending, but only her mother was able to see the signs.

Samantha put her black patent leather Gucci clutch under her arm as she climbed the staircase. At the top she looked over the banister into the vestibule below to ensure Etta had gone back to the kitchen.

"Jasmine, honey, open the door," she said, accompanied by a gentle tap. "Jasmine, it's Mommy."

"Go away," came the hostile reply from a hoarse voice behind the door.

"Young lady, open this door right now."

Jasmine crawled out of bed and abruptly swung open the door. "What do you want?" she moaned as she crawled back into bed.

Samantha, with determination, stepped into the room.

It was dark and musty. The room still looked as it did when it was designed especially for Jasmine when she was ten years old. Pink was the dominant color. A dusty pink floral paper covered the walls and a pile of satin and silk pink pillows lay jumbled beneath a brass headboard.

Cherubic faces of the favorite boy bands from her innocent years still hung on the walls. A collection of over one hundred dolls from exotic lands she and her parents had traveled stared down on the groggy teen from shelves around the room. Pink shades were drawn and designer clothes were strewn on the bed and floor. Samantha immediately pulled up the blinds and began picking up clothes.

"Why are you still in bed?" she asked. "Get up this minute, take a shower, and get dressed. Dinner is ready, and I want you downstairs."

Jasmine shielded her eyes from the light and asked,

"Where's Daddy?"

"He's having dinner with a minister from Detroit."

"Then why do I have to come downstairs?"

"Because you don't need to be in this dark room all Sunday."

"I'm not hungry. I still feel sick. Just leave me alone, please."

Samantha threw her purse onto an overstuffed pink chair under the window and sat down on the edge of the bed, which was partially covered by a satin pink down comforter. She pulled the comforter back to reveal Jasmine's tired face. She was a young and beautiful female version of Hezekiah Cleaveland. Her skin was still taut and clear, but her eyes told of the troubles she had seen.

"Honey, you've got to let me help you with this problem."

Jasmine recited her well-rehearsed denial. "I've told you, I don't have a problem. I was just out too late last night. I'll be fine if you would leave me alone."

She knew well the fine line between her mother's love and rage. Jasmine skillfully stopped short of pushing her to the edge.

"Jasmine, I'm not stupid. You smell of alcohol. Your eyes are red and you've been in this room all day. I won't have this in my house. You're going to have to get some help, or else . . ."

"Or else what?" Jasmine blurted out. "You'll throw me out? How would that look? The daughter of the perfect Samantha Cleaveland living on the streets and begging for food. Maybe I could sit on the steps of the church with a sign that says, *Pastor's daughter—will work for food*."

Samantha's eyes tightened. "You know that's not what I was going to say. Why are you doing this to me? I love you and it's killing me to watch you destroy yourself like this."

Jasmine turned to avoid her mother's eyes. "I'm not destroying myself. I told you I'm just tired. Now please leave me alone."

"I won't put up with this much longer." Samantha stood and picked up her purse from the chair. "I'm not going to let you embarrass this family with your behavior."

She slammed the door of her daughter's room and stood for a moment to compose herself before walking back down the stairs.

Samantha took keys from her purse and unlocked the door to her private study. Hezekiah had never understood why she needed a private study, but he didn't protest when the locksmith came and installed the dead bolt. The room provided a startling contrast to the décor of the other rooms in the house. A sleek Swedish couch and two modern leather chairs, too perfect and erect for comfort, floated on a bloodred island rug in the center of the room.

Samantha locked the door behind her. Sitting at her desk, she opened the purse and removed her BlackBerry.

Next she removed a pack of cigarettes and then a small black revolver. She found the weight and cold steel of the pistol strangely erotic as she held it in her hand. A sudden knock on the door startled her and she quickly placed the gun back into the purse.

"Mrs. Cleaveland," Etta called through the locked door,

"I have your dinner, ma'am."

2

Monday Morning

Muted light filled the large conference room at New Testament Cathedral. The ministry's staff looked as rested and eager as possible considering it was nine o'clock on a Monday morning.

The room bulged with a mix of young technology whiz kids, religious zealots, ministers, accountants, administrators, and wide-eyed interns who were clueless to the gravity of their role in running the renowned megachurch and television ministry. Hands clung to coffee cups. Expensive leather attaché cases and purses littered the floral-print carpet.

Five to six bodies sat at tables placed around the room in no particular order. Pastor Hezekiah Cleaveland stood at the front of the room and addressed the gathering of sixty-two employees.

"Good morning, everyone," he said with enthusiasm.

"I'm sure you've all heard by now, Sunday's broadcast was seen by a record number of viewers. This is largely due to the great new marketing campaign launched by our PR department."

Everyone applauded to acknowledge the good news.

"We've got a busy week ahead of us," Hezekiah continued.

"We officially entered the final phase of the capital campaign for the new cathedral and media center. To date, twenty-five million dollars have been raised and, as a result of the recent jump in viewership, contributions are still pouring in. We are going to need each of you to double your fund-raising efforts. We've got twenty million more to raise in the next six months."

The rear door opened and Samantha Cleaveland walked in as he spoke. She sat down at a table near the door. Her beige pantsuit was constructed with skilled precision to complement her body. A silk scarf, knotted to perfection, hung over her shoulder, revealing the subtle red tones in her unblemished skin.

Hezekiah paused midsentence and greeted Samantha.

"Good morning, honey," he said. "I was just reminding everyone that we have to increase our fund-raising efforts over the next six months. . . ."

"Correction, Hezekiah," Samantha interrupted. "Everyone who expects to keep his or her job will have to double the amount of contributions, publicity, and the number of new members they bring to the church in the next month."

Hezekiah attempted to change the subject. "Thank you, Samantha. We received more good news last week. The Trinity Broadcasting Network has asked us to allow them to air the opening ceremony for the new cathedral."

Samantha ignored Hezekiah and stood abruptly. She walked to the front of the room and peered into the now mortified crowd.

"Some of you don't seem to realize this job is not just a paycheck. It's a calling. People all over the country depend on this ministry to fill the empty void in their lives. Every Sunday morning New Testament Cathedral gives hope to millions of viewers who, without us, would have no reason to live.

"Let me remind you that you represent Hezekiah and Samantha Cleaveland, and if you don't do your jobs and raise more money the ministry suffers and if the ministry suffers, so will each of you."

Everyone sat frozen as all eyes in the room searched each other's faces for the humiliation they all now shared.

Samantha exited the room through the door she had entered without further comment. The staff meeting continued for the next half hour. Several brave staff members asked pointless questions in attempts to appear unfazed by the thrashing delivered by Samantha.

Bodies retrieved briefcases and coffee cups and filed solemnly through the double doors into the cavernous hall and retreated to their designated cubicles and offices.

Catherine Birdsong, New Testament Cathedral's chief operations officer, gathered her belongings and darted through the crowd behind Hezekiah. Public relations director Naomi Preston followed closely behind. Both women ignored comments and questions from staff members as they passed through the crowd.

They focused on catching up with Hezekiah who had exited the room and now moved rapidly toward the elevators.

Naomi was a tall woman who, regardless of the season, always wore two-piece monotone suits. Her stiff hair bobbed like a straw hat as she maneuvered around people whose names she never felt the need to remember. A costume bracelet rattled with each step she took.

The two women caught up with Hezekiah and together they fell quickly into step as if they had been at his side the entire length of the hall. Lesser staff members moved to the side as Catherine and Naomi took their rightful places beside the pastor. Hezekiah stared directly ahead.

"What time am I scheduled to be interviewed by Lance Savage and what's the article he's writing about us?"

Naomi's throat dried as she strained to respond.

"Eleven o'clock, Pastor Cleaveland. I believe he wants to get an update on the cathedral construction."

The three stepped into an elevator heading up to the fifth floor. The doors closed and Hezekiah's firm body slumped against the back wall with a thud.

"Catherine, get me the most recent construction figures," he said, peering directly at the doors ahead as if a face were looking back at him. "How much we've spent and how much we've raised. I want to be ready for Lance."

Catherine scribbled the pastor's instructions and answered, "Yes, Pastor Cleaveland," as the elevator doors slid open.

Hezekiah, Catherine, and Naomi exited the elevator and walked directly toward the pastor's suite of offices. Floor-to-ceiling glass double doors stood before them.

Naomi took a double step ahead of the pastor and opened the door. Hezekiah entered the suite without altering his stride as she stepped aside.

The outer office now held many of the same faces from the staff meeting. Attractive young women shuttled important-looking documents from one side of the room to the other. Handsome men wearing cheap suits and expensive neckties huddled in various corners of the office as they conferred on urgent church business.

Lush burgundy carpets muffled the sound of multiple conversations. Mahogany panels covered the walls from which architectural renderings of the new towering 25,000-seat glass cathedral hung.

Hezekiah scanned the room. His eyes rested on no one in particular. They were all just bodies. Empty faces serving at his whim. The people he and Samantha surrounded themselves with were there simply to do their bidding—not to think, analyze, or make decisions.

A lanky man with wavy black hair approached him. Associate Pastor, Rev. Kenneth Davis was the only staff member brave enough to break bad news to Hezekiah so early in the morning.

"Good morning, Pastor Cleaveland," Kenneth said as Hezekiah looked up from a stack of telephone messages.

"Sorry to start your week like this, but there is another protest going on in front of the church." Kenneth pointed toward open French doors along the rear wall.

"What is it now?" Hezekiah asked sharply.

"It seems another group of homeless advocates are angry about the amount of money we're spending on the construction of the new cathedral. They think we should be spending the money on the homeless instead."

The sound of a man speaking through a megaphone met Hezekiah's ears as he looked from the third floor onto the grounds of New Testament Cathedral.

A group of over 200 people waved protest signs that read: LOS ANGELES NEEDS MORE AFFORDABLE HOUSING, NOT SHRINES TO GREEDY PASTORS and HEZEKIAH CLEAVELAND DOESN'T CARE ABOUT POOR PEOPLE.

New Testament Cathedral was a two-block-long, five-story stucco structure with a row of stained-glass windows lining each side of the building. Park like settings wrapped around its perimeter. Cobblestone paths dotted with benches, curved brick walls, gurgling rock fountains, and lush greenery provided parishioners with aesthetic justification for the millions of dollars they gave to the Cleavelands each year.

Worshippers were greeted by a sweeping flight of steps that spanned the width of the building and led up to a two-story-high glass wall containing six sets of double doors.

Through the windows a massive crystal chandelier could be seen dangling in the sun-drenched lobby. A twenty-foot sapphire blue cross was the centerpiece of the stainedglass window that dominated much of the front of the building. Massive birds were on each side of the cross.

Their outstretched glass wings were made of blue, red, yellow, lavender, and white opaque panels, and they held olive branches in their powerful beaks. Visual proclamations proudly declaring the edifice to be the home of New Testament Cathedral and presided over by Dr. Hezekiah T. Cleaveland, pastor sat above the stained-glass centerpiece.

"Hezekiah Cleaveland is spending forty-five million dollars to build a shrine to himself while homeless people, sick people, and mentally ill people are living and dying on the streets all around him," the megaphone-toting man below shouted to the crowd. "New Testament Cathedral and Hezekiah Cleaveland should be spending that money to build affordable housing, shelters, and clinics for the poor in this community!"

The crowd cheered, and the grounds of New Testament Cathedral were alive with the sounds of boos, whistles, and clapping hands. Burly men hoisting television cameras on their shoulders captured the scenes for the evening news.

Hezekiah could see the construction site of the new cathedral directly across the street, on Imperial Highway. Bulldozers kicked up dust as they moved dirt to clear a space for the new parking structure. Men in yellow hard hats and wagging tool belts walked around the site carrying blueprints, lumber, and power tools. Cranes carefully positioned steel beams onto the rising structure. The new site was twice the size of the one the church now occupied.

It included a 25,000-seat sanctuary to hold even more generous congregants each Sunday morning, three thirty-two by eighteen–foot Jumbotron screens, the Hezekiah T. Cleaveland elementary, middle, and high schools, a theological seminary complete with dorms to house future missionaries, a sprawling park with two restaurants, a bookstore and gift shop, and a 5,000-seat amphitheater for outdoor summer concerts. The new campus also included a fitness center and an automotive repair complex.

Hezekiah spotted the *Los Angeles Chronicle* reporter Lance Savage talking to a man wrapped in a trench coat that looked like he had slept in it for months.

"Maybe you should go down there and address them," Naomi said, walking up behind Hezekiah and Kenneth.

"Since there are so many reporters, maybe this would be a good opportunity to tell the public how we already help the homeless."

Hezekiah's smile quickly vanished. His shoulders tensed as he stared directly into her eyes. "Are you crazy? Do you want me to be on the six o'clock news, being yelled at by a bunch of bums?"

"I didn't mean . . ."

"That's your problem. You don't seem to know what you mean most of the time." Hezekiah spun on his heels and stormed through the door leading to his private office suite.

Everyone present pretended not to have heard the lashing Naomi had just received. Nervous hands throughout the office frantically groped for telephones on the first ring; papers were shuffled and feet darted toward the nearest exits when she turned from the window.

Kenneth looked at Naomi with a sympathetic eye and said, "He's in one of his moods today. What is going on?"

"He's been like this for weeks now and it seems to be getting worse," replied Naomi as the crimson hue slowly drained from her face.

Hezekiah retrieved more telephone messages from an assistant positioned outside his office.

The scheduling secretary greeted Hezekiah as he approached. "Good morning, Pastor Cleaveland," she said. "Senator Swanson's office is on the line. The senator will be in town next week and wants to know if you're available for lunch."

Hezekiah looked unimpressed as he retrieved more telephone messages from her neatly appointed desk.

"That's fine," he said. "Go ahead and set it up." When he entered his office, the private telephone rang.

After dropping the stack of telephone messages on the desk, he picked up the receiver. "Hello. This is Hezekiah Cleaveland."

"Good morning, handsome," said the voice on the line.

The tension in Hezekiah's shoulders slowly dissolved.

"Good morning, baby," he said in a whisper.

"I'm driving down Imperial Highway past your church.

I'm on my way to give out condoms and socks to a group of homeless guys at an encampment under the freeway near your church and I just wanted to hear your voice."

"Condoms?" Hezekiah asked, laughing. "Why do homeless people need condoms? They shouldn't be having sex under the freeways."

The voice on the phone laughed with him.

Hezekiah lowered his body into his huge black leather chair and said, "I loved being with you last night. I miss you already."

"I miss you too."

"Do me a favor?" Hezekiah said. "Drive in front of the church and tell those protesters to get off my property. I think they might be friends of yours."

"Friends? What are you talking about?"

Hezekiah could hear the blaring horn of a city bus through the receiver. "It's those homeless advocates who've got nothing better to do on a Monday morning than harass me."

The voice on the line began to laugh again. "Don't let them get to you, Hezekiah. Everyone knows you do a lot for the homeless."

"I've got a meeting in a few minutes," Hezekiah said as he spun around in his chair to watch the protest escalating outside his window. "When am I going to see you this week? I miss you."

"How about tonight?"

"I can't tonight. I think I'm free tomorrow evening. I've got to meet with my attorneys at six, but I should be free by seven."

"Sounds good. I can hold out until then."

Hezekiah whispered seductively, "You know I love you. Be careful out there and tell those guys to stop having sex near my church."

The voice laughed again and said, "I'll give them the message. I love you too, Hezekiah. See you tomorrow night."

3

One Year Earlier

Hezekiah first saw the young man kneeling at a corner on skid row. His green canvas backpack lay on the sidewalk beside him, filled with the daily rations of vitamins, warm socks, and condoms for homeless people he encountered on his rounds of the city.

The sounds of horns honking and public-transit bus engines revving echoed off glass towers and graffiti-marred hotel facades. The block was cluttered with wobbly shopping carts filled with plastic trash bags, aluminum cans, plastic bottles, soiled clothes, and half-eaten cans of beans and sardines. Cyclone fences served as the only barriers between the human debris and parking lots filled with BMWs, Jaguars, and other nondescript silver foreign automobiles.

The pungent smell of urine and human feces was everywhere. Emaciated dogs foraged through piles of trash, looking for the morsel that, for them, stood between life and death. Drivers sped by, making extra efforts to avoid looking to the left or the right. The human misery was too painful to witness, and the filth too disgusting to stomach.

One man lay sleeping in the middle of the sidewalk. His limbs were twisted and his face was pressed into the cement. His blue denim jeans were stained from being worn for over two months. Alcohol fumes were almost visible as he breathed. He looked as though he had been dropped from the roof of a five-story building.

A woman sat on the curb with her legs spread to the street. She wore a dirty pink scarf wrapped around her matted hair, a dingy, tattered yellow sweater, and no shoes. Her feet were covered with scabs and open wounds. "I told you ta stop bring'n dose peopo in'ta my mothafuck'n house. I'm mo kill that mothafucka if he do dat ta me again," she cursed to the air as it breezed by.

Other men and women lay coiled and hidden under oily, lice-ridden blankets and behind cardboard fortresses.

When Hezekiah first saw Danny St. John, he was speaking to a homeless man named Old Joe, who was sitting on the curb, rattling a paper cup filled with coins. Everyone who lived in or walked through the shopping cart shantytown knew Old Joe. He was a tall man with matted black hair, wearing oil-stained clothes.

Brakes screeched, a car barely missing elderly pedestrians, as Danny and Old Joe talked below on the sidewalk. Lights flashed green, yellow, and red, and pigeons danced amid the remains of half-eaten burgers and discarded French fries. The two men spoke of warm places for Joe to sleep when the cold returned for the night.

Danny reached into his bag for a clean hypodermic needle sealed in cellophane. He searched in the bag around packages of alcohol wipes, a tin canister filled with condoms, bottles of Purell hand sanitizer, and bundles of clean socks until he found the syringes. He looked over his shoulder to ensure a private moment for the exchange and found himself staring into the eyes of Hezekiah Cleaveland.

The pastor was watching him intently from the driver's seat of a silver Mercedes-Benz. Before Danny could look away, Hezekiah called out, "Excuse me. Are you a city employee? May I speak to you for a moment? I have a question for you."

Danny recognized the handsome face immediately. He excused himself from Old Joe and walked to the car.

"No, I don't work for the city," Danny said bending to the window. "I work for a nonprofit homeless-outreach agency downtown."

Hezekiah's brain went uncharacteristically blank as the tall, attractive young man looked into the car. He hadn't expected to see such a beautiful face or hear so gentle a voice come from a man who worked so closely with the outcasts of the city.

At twenty-eight Danny looked as though he had never had a difficult day in his life. He was a handsome man, with smooth almond-brown skin, who attracted admiring glances from both men and women. Just over six feet tall, his slender body was modestly hidden under a baggy T-shirt and green army fatigues.

Hezekiah quickly regained his composure and introduced himself. "My name is Pastor Hezekiah Cleaveland. There's a homeless woman who sleeps near my church on Cleaveland Avenue at Imperial Highway," he said. "She's obviously mentally ill and has a dog in a shopping cart. You can't miss her. She's always there. Can you go over and talk to her?"

"I know her. Everyone in my agency knows her but she has a long history of refusing services from our agency."

As Danny spoke, Hezekiah became distracted again by a glimmer in the beautiful young man's eyes.

There was an awkward silence after Danny finished his sentence. Then Hezekiah replied, "I would appreciate it if you would speak with her again."

Danny looked surprised. He never thought Hezekiah Cleaveland had any interest in people who couldn't send him a donation.

"I'm glad to hear you're concerned Rev. Cleaveland. When I've seen you and your wife on television it seemed you were only interested in people who could make large contributions to your church."

"Don't believe everything you see on television," Hezekiah said, smiling. "I was poor once myself and I've never forgotten it."

As Danny walked back to Old Joe he heard Hezekiah call out again. "After you talk to her would you mind stopping by my office at the church? Just to let me know how it goes," the minister explained.

"I'll stop by and see her this afternoon."

"Thank you," Hezekiah replied with an odd sense of relief.

"By the way, what's your name?"

"Danny. Danny St. John."

4

Monday

It was 10:50 a.m. Catherine Birdsong rushed to gather the information Hezekiah had requested. Her office was small compared to others in the administrative wing. There were no pictures on the walls. Newspapers, magazines, and press releases occupied every available surface. A silver frame on the desk held a picture of her seven-year-old daughter, Sarah.

Catherine jumped when the telephone rang.

"Yes, Pastor Cleaveland. I'm on my way," she said before the voice on the line could speak. She hurried through the winding halls to Hezekiah's office.

Without stopping at the receptionist's desk in front of Hezekiah's door, Catherine snapped over her shoulder, "He's expecting me."

Hezekiah was laughing on the telephone when she entered the room. He concluded the conversation with, "Don't worry, Barry. Just let me know if you need me to call him. He's good for at least another hundred thousand."

Hezekiah hung up the telephone. "Where have you been? It's almost eleven o'clock."

Catherine did not respond while handing him the reports. She stood over his shoulder and attempted to explain the numbers as Hezekiah studied the pages.

"Pastor, no one seems to have an accurate number on how much the project has cost to date. The figures range from twenty to twenty-five million. That would mean we have between twenty and twenty-five million more to raise. I recommend going with the lower number because of all the controversy surrounding the building project."

Catherine continued quickly before Hezekiah could ask a question. "The second page is a geographic breakdown of contributions to date. As you can see, the majority of our contributions are coming from the southern states. The Midwest is coming in at a strong second. It looks like we need to put more emphasis on the East Coast, though. For example, donations from Maryland, Rhode Island, and D.C. are falling short of what we projected for this final phase of fund-raising.

"The last page shows the donor demographics. Of course, women between twenty-five and sixty-five years of age are our most prolific donors. Followed by men thirty-five to sixty-five. The number of single white female donors has increased significantly in the last two months." Catherine refrained from offering further explanations as Hezekiah continued to scan the reports.

The intercom on his desk cut through the silence.

"Pastor Cleaveland," said the receptionist, "Mr. Lance Savage is here for your eleven o'clock."

"I'll be out in a minute," Hezekiah said sharply.

Moments later Hezekiah and Catherine emerged from the office and Lance Savage jumped to his feet. Lance was a tall man of thirty-five years who never left home without a slightly wrinkled sport coat, thick corduroy pants, and a pair of well-worn suede shoes. His pale yellow shirt had gone several wearings without benefit of dry cleaning.

"Hello, Lance," Catherine said as she approached him.

"I'm going to join you in this meeting if you don't mind."

"No, I don't mind. I've just got a few questions for Pastor Cleaveland."

Hezekiah approached Lance with a welcoming grin.

"Lance," he said, extending his hand. "You here to rake me over the coals again?"

Lance laughed and shook Hezekiah's hand.

Hezekiah directed Lance and Catherine to attractive, yet uncomfortable, chairs in front of his desk. He sat behind the desk surrounded by plaques, awards, and framed magazine covers with pictures of the perfect Cleaveland couple which served to remind all who entered the room that he was one of the most famous ministers in the country.

Hezekiah spoke before Lance could settle into the chair. "Lance, I've pulled together some information on the new sanctuary and media center building project. The community is going to benefit greatly from the expansion of our ministry."

"I'm sure the project is very impressive, Pastor Cleaveland, but I'm not here to talk about the new cathedral."

Lance retrieved a small notepad from his breast pocket and continued. "Pastor Cleaveland, are you familiar with a man named Danny St. John?"

With no discernible signs of surprise, Hezekiah responded, "The name doesn't sound familiar."

Lance continued his questioning. "Is that so? Would it jog your memory if I told you Mr. St. John is a homeless-outreach worker with whom, my sources tell me, you've spent a considerable amount of time over the last year?"

Hezekiah's face hardened as he felt the muscles contract in his shoulders. "I'm sorry, but I don't know of anyone by that name. My ministry, however, is very concerned about the growing number of homeless people in Los Angeles."

"Pastor Cleaveland, I have been given information by a reliable source that you and Mr. St. John have a relationship that . . . How can I put this? A relationship that goes beyond your mutual concern for the well-being of Los Angeles's indigent population."

"I'm a busy man, Lance," Hezekiah said impatiently. "What is this about?"

"All right, sir. Would you care to comment on the fact that we have information which suggests that for the past year you've been involved in a homosexual relationship with Danny St. John?"

The chair bumped the bulletproof window behind the desk as Hezekiah leaped to his feet. "What are you talking about? This is ridiculous! Who told you that?"

"I'm sorry, sir, but I am not at liberty to say."

"How dare you come into my church and make a libelous claim like that? I'll sue you and the *Los Angeles Chronicle* if any word of this lie appears in it."

Lance stood to his feet. "Pastor Cleaveland, there's really no point in denying it. My source's proof is irrefutable. I'm here to give you the opportunity to respond, even if that response is simply 'No comment.'"

"I won't dignify this nonsense with a response. Now get out of my office."

"That is your choice, Pastor Cleaveland. However, please know that we will run this story within a week, with or without a quote from you."

Hezekiah rushed from behind the desk to Lance and pointed to the door. "Get out."

Catherine stood. "Lance, this is outrageous. Pastor Cleaveland said he never met this Danny St. John person!"

"Shut up, Catherine." Hezekiah turned his anger to her shrieking face. "Stay out of this."

As Lance walked to the door, he turned and said, "If you change your mind, you know how to reach me."

Catherine collapsed into the chair after Lance left the room. "Pastor, a story like this could ruin you. Would you like me to call our attorneys?"

Hezekiah's eyes glazed over. He stood in front of her and slammed an open palm on the desk.

"No," he snapped. "Don't say a word about this to anyone, and especially not Samantha."

5

Associate Pastor Kenneth Davis sat alone in his office on the second floor. His was one of the largest offices in the church, second only to the pastor's. The size of his space reflected the tremendous influence he wielded in the ministry. His power came from his shameless tendency to flaunt his close association with Hezekiah Cleaveland.

Kenneth paced the floor. *Stupid idiot*, he thought angrily, not of Lance Savage but of Hezekiah Cleaveland. So close to completing a multimillion-dollar construction project and he pulls a stunt like this.

The framed picture of his twelve-year-old son from a failed attempt at marriage stared helplessly at him each time he walked past the desk. His mind was awash with thoughts of private school tuition, braces for the crooked bright smile, monthly child support, his car note, and mortgage payments for the Tudor mini-mansion he had purchased behind the gated walls of Hancock Park only a year earlier.

His clenched fists slammed together repeatedly as he continued his silent assault on Hezekiah. "All the work that went into this fundraising campaign, down the drain," he muttered. His steps grew more agitated as he silently tabulated his monthly bills.

"I've got to stop that story," he said loudly. "There's no way I'm going to let him screw up all I've worked for. I'm not going out like this."

Kenneth had first heard the name Danny St. John two weeks earlier at a gay bar in West Hollywood. He had always taken painstaking efforts at church to conceal his predilection toward men, but the idea of being spotted in a gay bar by some other "closeted queen" seemed a risk worth taking in exchange for the camaraderie he felt with others who had similar tastes in companions. He was having a drink with Larry Kennedy, a fellow closeted minister from another congregation.

The small neighborhood bar was filled with men who looked like they had just returned from long weekends in Palm Springs. Toned, tanned, and well-dressed bodies packed the room. Music blared from below, above, and everywhere in between. The two men had just ordered their second round of beers.

"So what's up with the latest gossip going around about Hezekiah?" Larry asked while reaching for his drink.

"Why? What have you heard? Who's he supposed to be sleeping with this time?"

"Everybody's been talking about it. I'm surprised you haven't heard. I hear it's some guy who works with the homeless downtown. Danny something. A buddy of mine who works for the same agency told me he is gorgeous."

Kenneth laughed loud enough to be heard over the pulsating music. "A guy?" he said dismissively. "You're joking. What else have you heard?"

"Well," Larry said, leaning forward, "supposedly it's been going on for about a year now, but I don't know how true that is."

"Larry, if you're dumb enough to believe a story like that, then you deserve to be an assistant pastor for the rest of your life."

Larry smiled. "Yeah, I know. It sounded ridiculous to me when I first heard about it, but what if it's true? Can you imagine the fallout? The gay community would be pissed because he's a closeted high-profile minister. The black community would feel betrayed and embarrassed, and God only knows what the evangelicals would do."

"Nobody is ever going to find out, Larry, because there's nothing to this. Hezekiah's not dumb enough to sneak around banging some guy in the middle of a forty-five-million-dollar capital campaign."

"For his sake and yours, I hope you're right. By the way, who's Lance Savage?"

"He's a reporter with the *Los Angeles Chronicle*. Why?" Kenneth asked.

"Because he's been asking questions around town lately. Apparently, he's working on a tell-all story."

Now sitting alone in his office, Kenneth recalled the conversation with Larry Kennedy. He began to wonder if the gossip could be true. He hoped the possibility of Hezekiah being gay or even bisexual was too far-fetched to be real.

If it is true, he thought, *he can kiss his church good-bye. This country isn't ready for a powerful gay black preacher, and especially not one who cheats on a woman like Samantha.*

Collard green stalks peeked over the pink brick fence surrounding Hattie Williams's garden. Green tomatoes waited for the day Hattie would say, "You're just right for picking." Green beans on the vine protected their precious contents from the sun, and bright yellow squash provided a beautiful contrast in the emerald sea.

The neat stucco house was quiet except for the gospel hymns playing on the radio. Hattie sat at her kitchen table, which overlooked the garden.

Her Bible was open to John 3:16.

She read aloud, "For God so loved the world, that he gave his only begotten Son, that whosoever believeth in him should not perish, but have everlasting life."

As she pondered the words and gazed out the window, the image of Hezekiah Cleaveland flashed before her. His face expressionless and his eyes hollow. He wasn't looking at her, but rather looking at himself.

All she could hear, see, and feel at that moment was the battle of emotions that raged in his soul. The pastor's conflicting feelings of torment and relief, anger and fear, drowned out the crackling of the radio. She sat motionless and silently watched the battle that played out in the reflection of her garden window.

"Lord, what has the pastor got himself into now?" she asked aloud as the melee in her window raged on.

She had never seen so many warriors on the battlefield of one man's soul before. Fear violently thrashed his sword at the breastplate of peace. Contentment protected his head from the deadly blows of confusion. Love cowered under the pounding leveled by a white horse whose rider was death.

The image of the equestrian made Hattie shiver. She had seen him before: at the bedside of her mother and in the hospital room of her late husband. On each occasion she pleaded that he ride away and allow her just one more day with her loved ones. Each time he did not hear her.

She knew he would not hear her today.

Hattie had learned to separate her emotions from those of others. But today she sat helplessly and succumbed to the tears that welled in her eyes as the horseman delivered the lethal blow to the man lying on the ground.

"Oh Lord, not the pastor. Not Pastor Cleaveland!" she cried out as the scene faded from her window.

Catherine Birdsong instructed her secretary to hold all calls after the startling meeting with Lance Savage. Her body trembled as she reached for the small flask of bourbon tucked beneath an even smaller bottle of minty green mouthwash, tissue, and a silver makeup compact.

The office was quiet. Only the muffled white noise of traffic passing below her window could be heard. Cool pale light hovered around oil canvases and ceramic vases filled with yellow and white lilies. With shaking hands, she took the first sip of the brown tonic, then a second, and third.

Catherine had been with Hezekiah Cleaveland for over ten years, throughout his various business and religious incarnations. She was thirty-three years old and always impeccably dressed, accomplished by frequent and extended-lunch shopping excursions throughout Beverly Hills.

Her expensive tastes in clothes and jewelry far exceeded her salary as a chief operations officer. That of her husband, however, generously supplemented her own. He was a prominent real estate developer who sold New Testament Cathedral the property across the street for the new church. This deal had bordered precariously on a conflict of interest for Catherine. She naively believed that her position in the church never influenced her husband's sweetheart deal, but silent observers knew otherwise.

A knock on the door shattered the private moment between her and the bottle. Catherine returned the now half empty bottle to the safety of her purse. It was Kenneth Davis.

"Kenneth, this isn't a good time for me. Is this something that can wait?"

"Catherine," he said, "I want to know what's going on. He's been snapping at everyone for weeks now. There are rumors going around that Pastor Cleaveland is gay and supposedly a Lance Savage is working on a story about it. Do you know anything about this?"

The alcohol had temporarily sharpened her defensive skills. Catherine bolted to her feet. "Kenneth, I said now is not a good time."

Kenneth's long legs made light work of the distance between the door and her desk.

"Catherine, you need to tell me what's going on. We need to do damage control. You can't hide in this office and pretend this will go away. The entire ministry might be at stake. If Hezekiah is destroyed, we'll all be destroyed with him."

Catherine's knees buckled under the weight of his statement causing her to wilt back into the soft leather chair. Her eyes filled with tears as she scrambled for the tissue in her purse. There was a tense silence shared between the two while she stared vacantly out the window.

Reverend Davis held his gaze firmly on her quivering face.

Then, through mounting sobs, Catherine said, "Close the door, Kenneth. I don't want anyone to hear this."

Kenneth closed the office door and sat in front of her desk.

"So what is this all about?"

"Kenneth, you've got to promise me you won't repeat this to anyone. He'd kill me if he knew I spoke to you."

"Who am I going to talk to? Now tell me."

Catherine took a deep breath and proceeded to recount the amazing confrontation she had just witnessed between Hezekiah and Lance Savage.

"Savage claims to have proof that Pastor Cleaveland is having an affair with a man."

Catherine looked away to avoid Kenneth's bulging eyes. Her lips longed for another encounter with the flask in her purse.

"His name is Danny, Danny St. John. He's a homeless-outreach worker."

"Catherine, that's crazy," Kenneth said. "A gay rumor surfaces about Hezekiah every few years, but no one has ever proved anything."

"I know, Kenneth. I've heard them too, but . . . but it was the way he reacted when Lance said it. I've never seen him that angry before. He snapped. I thought he was going to attack him. It was horrible."

"So what makes you think he can prove it? Did he identify his source?"

"No. Pastor Cleaveland didn't give him a chance to. He exploded and threw him out. Lance would have never confronted him the way he did unless he knew something. He was so cocky and bold."

Kenneth stood and walked abruptly to the door.

"I'm going to call Savage. We'll sue that paper for slander if they print the story, even if it is true."

Catherine sprang from her desk. She grabbed Kenneth by the arm as he reached for the door handle. "Kenneth," she said through tears, "you said you wouldn't repeat this to anyone. You promised."

Kenneth pushed her away. The force of his thrust, and the alcohol, caused her to lose her footing and stumble backward.

"You're crazy, Catherine, if you think I'm going to sit by and allow Lance Savage to destroy this ministry."

"You bastard," Catherine said as the reverend darted down the hallway. "You liar. You're going to make him even angrier. Stay out of this, Kenneth."

Her words echoed without reception, through the hall as Reverend Davis vanished from sight.

6

Monday Afternoon

Fortunately for Hezekiah, the protest on the grounds had ended before he left the church. A group of smiling tourists stopped him and requested photos with him as he walked through the first-floor lobby.

Always gracious to visitors, he shook their hands and posed for pictures. Hezekiah spoke kindly to the small group. "You should all move to Los Angeles," he said. "We could use more dedicated Christians like you in our city."

The group laughed and snapped more pictures as he walked through the doors.

It was a crisp clear day in the city. The grounds were now filled with office workers from the surrounding buildings leisurely reading newspapers and eating homemade lunches.

Dino Goodman stood next to the black Lincoln at the foot of the church steps. He was to drive Hezekiah to his standing Monday lunch with three of his oldest friends.

Dino was perfectly suited for the roles of muscular bodyguard, driver, and loyal keeper of all things secret.

His brown trench coat wafted in the breeze, revealing a revolver nestled in a leather shoulder holster as Hezekiah approached.

Dino was the one person in the church who consistently saw the vulnerable Hezekiah Cleaveland from the unobstructed vantage of his rearview mirror. What would have shocked his flock the most were the countless hours Dino had spent late at night waiting in the limo outside the old converted Victorian in the Adams District.

Hezekiah was already ten minutes late when they arrived at the restaurant. It had taken him more energy than expected to recover from the confrontation with Lance Savage. His hand shook as he steadied himself to step from the rear of the car.

He heard a man yell out as he walked to the entrance, "Hey, it's Hezekiah Cleaveland!"

Hezekiah looked to his right and saw a wiry little black man with disheveled hair approaching. He wore ragged pants and walked with a limp.

Hezekiah waved, hoping the gesture would provide ample fodder for the little man to recount future stories of "the day I met Pastor Hezekiah Cleaveland."

The tattered man was not satisfied. Dino saw the rapid pace at which he advanced and stepped in front of the man.

"Hey, Pastor Cleaveland!" the man blurted out as he tried in vain to walk around Dino. "You ought to be helping poor people in this city instead of building that megachurch."

A lengthy barrage of insults from the scraggly man caused Hezekiah to halt in his tracks. He placed his hand firmly on Dino's shoulder and moved him to one side allowing the little man clear passage and said, "Maybe you should go back to wherever it is you came from?" With that, Hezekiah took a one-hundred-dollar bill from his wallet and threw it at the stunned man's feet. "That should be enough for a bus ticket out of town."

The little vagrant stood speechless as Hezekiah disappeared through the restaurant door.

Hezekiah's first inclination had been to cancel the lunch with his three buddies. After anguished deliberation, he decided to meet with them to learn just how far rumors of his affair had spread.

Franco, the maître d' at Petro's Steak House, greeted his most famous customer. "Pastor Cleaveland," he said, "good to see you, sir. Your party is waiting for you at your usual booth."

Reverend Jonathon Copperfield, a ruddy-faced pastor from Anaheim, was the first to see Hezekiah walking to the table. Hector Ramirez, the mayor of Los Angeles, was sitting next to him, and Phillip Thornton, the owner of the *Los Angeles Chronicle*, sat across the table.

All three men were natives of the city. If there was a secret worth telling in Los Angeles, one, if not all, of these men knew it.

Hezekiah was immediately struck by the absence of boisterous chatter that normally greeted him.

"Hello, gentlemen," he said as he placed a linen napkin on his lap. "What's going on here? Who died?"

The three men exchanged momentary glances. Jonathon Copperfield was the first to speak.

"Nobody died, Hezekiah. We were just talking about some gossip Phillip heard last week."

"All right, boys. Who's going to fill me in, or are we just going to change the subject to one you feel won't offend my delicate sensibilities?"

A heavyset waiter wearing a black vest, which barely concealed his bulging belly, came to the table and handed Hezekiah a menu.

"Good afternoon, Pastor Cleaveland," he said jovially in a thick Italian accent. "Will you be having your usual or would you like to try something different today?"

Hezekiah placed his order and the waiter left the table.

"All right, Phillip," Hezekiah said. "Who's trying to screw me over now? Come on, spill it."

Phillip drank the last of his red wine.

"It's not about who's screwing you, Hezekiah," he said.

"It's more about who it is you're screwing."

Hezekiah sat silent. There was a hush at the table when the waiter returned with a basket of steaming bread.

"I'll have another drink, Luigi," Phillip said as the waiter walked away.

"I don't know what you're talking about," Hezekiah said.

"Come on, Hezekiah," Hector said. "You know what this is about. Don't try to bullshit us. We've known each other too long for that. We all get our share of pussy in this town." He leaned in and lowered his voice. "But a man? That's just sick. This country will never tolerate a faggot as the pastor of one of its largest churches."

Hezekiah looked to the source of the information.

"Phillip, this is all a lie. It's Lance Savage at your newspaper. He's been trying to dig something up on me ever since I broke ground on the new cathedral."

"You say it's a lie," said Phillip. "But, Lance says he has proof and can back up the entire story. Hezekiah, he's going to bury you with this one and there's nothing I can do about it."

Hezekiah grew agitated. "What do you mean, nothing? It's your newspaper, Phillip. Stop the story. Fire him. Transfer him to Idaho. You could get him off my back if you wanted."

"You know I don't have any editorial control, and besides, he's not the only one at the paper who knows about it. Lance has already briefed the managing editor and I understand he's just about finished with the final copy."

There was a long pause and then Phillip continued.

"How'd you let it get this far, Hezekiah? I thought your people were supposed to be out there making sure things like this never leaked out. You've dug your own grave this time and I can't pull you out."

"You can do something about it," Hezekiah said, throwing his napkin on the table. "You just won't. Your bottom line is selling that paper, and if it's at my expense, then so be it."

"Hezekiah, wait a minute. That's not fair," Jonathon Copperfield interjected. "This isn't Phillip's fault. You've only got yourself to blame for this one. If you just had to get your cock sucked by a man, you could have gone anywhere in the world. Instead, you chose to do it in your own backyard." Jonathon stood from the table. "I can't take this anymore. This is just sick. Sick and stupid. I'm out of here."

Jonathon wove through the neighboring tables and disappeared out the door. The remaining men sat in silence for what seemed like hours. Hezekiah, with his right hand over his mouth, stared blankly at the untouched basket of bread. Hector tapped his fingers on the bare wooden table and Phillip gulped down the remains of his second glass of wine.

The quiet was finally broken. "So what am I going to do?" Hezekiah said with his hand still cupped over his mouth. The torment in his voice was deafening. "If that story runs I'm through. I could kill that bastard—"

Hector cut him off. "Take it easy, Hezekiah. Look, you haven't denied it so I assume it's true."

Hezekiah's silence served as confirmation.

"Oh, shit. This is crazy," Hector said. "You throw away your whole ministry for a dick. How could you let this happen? You're too smart for this, Hezekiah." There was a pause. Then, "I don't think you have any choice other than to step down."

Hezekiah sat astonished, unable to speak. At that moment life slowly began to seep from his body.

7
Tuesday

Samantha Cleaveland lay awake in the massive oak bed as Hezekiah slept at her side. It was 7:10 on Tuesday morning. She'd been awake since 5:30 a.m., staring out the window, watching the sun rise over the city. The bed headboard loomed above their heads like the facade of an Italian cathedral with peaks that almost reached the ceiling. Ornately carved mahogany pillars stood at the foot of the massive structure.

The bed had belonged to her deceased mother, Florence Weaver. A few porcelain figurines and the bed were the only items belonging to Florence that Samantha felt worthy of occupying space in her home after her mother died.

Samantha often wondered how Mama Flo, as everyone called her, could have afforded the magnificent piece of furniture. She wished her mother could have seen the bed in its opulent new home. Samantha knew that Mama Flo would have been very impressed.

A vanity with a large oval etched mirror was perfectly positioned to catch the light from the window. The surface held expensive perfumes, which provided more evidence for discerning noses that Samantha wore only the finest of everything. Fresh flowers sat on a table between two overstuffed chairs. The mantel over the fireplace held more gold-framed pictures of the Cleavelands.

Hezekiah jerked as he grudgingly emerged from a fitful sleep. Silk pajamas stroked his skin with each twist of his body. For a brief luxurious moment he could feel Danny nuzzling his ear and stroking his thick black hair. He slowly entered the reality of his true location as his eyes adjusted to the light and saw the oak posts standing guard at his feet.

"What time is it?" he asked, sitting up abruptly.

Samantha looked up and then rolled onto her side with her back to him "Seven-ten," she curtly replied.

"Why didn't you wake me? You know I have to meet with the contractor this morning."

"Where were you last night?"

"Don't start, Samantha. I don't have time for your paranoia this morning," he snapped, and stormed into the adjoining master bathroom.

"You're not going to put me through this again!" she shouted, jumping from the bed and throwing a pillow behind him. "I won't stand by and let you humiliate me again!" Her rage was legendary behind closed doors in the Cleaveland house, but this time it was different.

The image of the pistol in her purse flashed as she continued to scream and burst through the bathroom door.

"You can't do this to me again!"

Hezekiah had already removed his pajamas and was stepping into the shower when she entered. His long, muscular body gave no hint of his divine calling. Without his clothes he didn't look like the elegant clergyman most knew, but rather like a man who could satisfy the most carnal of desires.

On most mornings Hezekiah would meditate under the flow of hot water, but this morning his ritual was interrupted by the attack escalating beyond the glass shower door.

"Who is she?" Samantha demanded. "Is she from church? Is it Catherine? I should have never let you hire that bitch!"

"Leave Catherine out of this," he sternly shouted over the shower door. "She doesn't have anything to do with this."

"Then who is it? You've already fucked half the staff. Who's left?"

Exhausted and broken by a long year of lying, and now her tirade, Hezekiah placed his hands against the tile above his head and shouted, "It's nobody from church, all right?"

He began to sob into the stream of water flowing on his face as the words fell without consent from his wet lips.

"I knew it. You fucking bastard. How could you do this to me again? Who the fuck is she?"

Samantha violently swung open the shower door. She reached in through the stream of water and grabbed one hand from his face. "I want to know who she is."

Hezekiah tried to pull away, but her grip was too firm. His face, dripping with water and tears, turned away from her gaze.

Samantha stepped into the shower and pushed Hezekiah against the marble-tiled wall. Water from the gushing nozzle drenched her nightgown and caused her hair to flop and dangle over her eyes. Hezekiah backed away to the rear of the space but she matched him step for step. "Hezekiah, you can't do this to me again," she said, pulling his head toward her. "I can't go through this again with you."

Hezekiah jerked his hand from her grasp and leaned against the wall. "You're making a fool of yourself, Samantha. Get out of here. We can talk about this later."

Samantha then pulled Hezekiah's body from the shower.

"We'll talk about it now," she said, blocking his reflection in the mirror. "What if someone finds out? Everything we've worked for will be destroyed."

"I don't want to talk about it right now. I'm already late for an appointment," he snapped.

Samantha jerked his head up and looked him in the eye.

"Fuck your appointment. There is nothing more important than this right now. You have to talk about it. I'm not going to let you ruin me. I'm not going to let you destroy everything we've built. Now tell me who she is."

Hezekiah did not respond.

"You're leaving me no choice, Hezekiah. I won't be humiliated. If you don't tell me I'm going to expose you. I'm not going down with you."

Hezekiah looked her in the eyes and grabbed her shoulders and held her steady.

"Don't threaten me, Samantha."

Samantha winced from his tight grip and demanded, "Let go of me, Hezekiah."

"Don't ever threaten me. This is my life and my ministry."

"It's not your life. It's our life and I made this ministry what it is. I'm not going to let you destroy it and me as well."

Samantha broke free and ran to the bedroom. Hezekiah ran behind and grabbed her bobbing wet hair. With one forceful yank he pulled her backward, causing her knees to buckle. She groped for a chair to maintain balance, but he pulled harder, sending her tumbling to the carpet.

Hezekiah straddled her chest, pinning her body to the floor. He jerked her head up and said, "If you tell anyone about this, I'll . . ."

Samantha thrashed beneath the full weight of his body.

Her flailing legs toppled a table, sending a vase filled with flowers, and two of her mother's porcelain figurines crashing to the floor. Hezekiah grabbed her wrists to restrain her. Her hips bucked upward and from side to side. She twisted and turned, but Hezekiah's weight held her pinned on her back.

"You'll what?" she screamed, clawing at his face. "Kill me?"

Blood flowed from the scratches on Hezekiah's face and dripped onto Samantha's as she yelled obscenities and clawed viciously. "Get the fuck off me!"

Samantha finally was able to squirm from beneath him and scrambled to her feet. Her wet, tangled, and tossed hair flew in every direction. The straps of her nightgown flopped from her shoulders, exposing her breast. Years of suppressed rage exploded onto her bloodstained face.

"You're pathetic!" she raved as she backed away from him. She picked up a book which was sitting on a table near the window and threw it at Hezekiah. "I can't wait for the whole world to find out exactly who you are. I hope the bitch is worth it because she just cost you every fucking thing you ever worked for."

Hezekiah looked up in amazement. He had never seen the woman who stood howling before him. He didn't recognize the rage nor had he ever encountered such unbridled anger from another human being.

Samantha picked up a silver dish from a nearby table and flung it at Hezekiah. He ducked, causing the dish to whiz over his head and crash into the wall with a loud metallic clank.

"Break it off with her now or I'll tell everyone the truth about the great Hezekiah T. Cleaveland. You'll end up like all those other redneck ministers crying like idiots on television, begging the world to forgive you because you can't keep your dick in your pants."

Hezekiah stared blankly for moments at the raging woman; then he began to sob again.

"I can't break it off with her," he finally said.

"Oh my God, is she pregnant?"

"No," he said through mounting tears.

"Then why not, you coward?"

"Because . . . it's not a woman."

Samantha froze in place. Her heaving chest was the only thing moving on her body. Each breath she took caused her still exposed breast to rise up and down. She looked at him with a puzzled expression and asked through deep, gasping breaths, "What do you mean it's not a woman?"

"Just what I said. It's not a woman. It's a man."

Hezekiah came downstairs and was greeted by Etta. His eyes, behind dark sunglasses, were red and his face was puffy.

"Good morning, Pastor," Etta said as she wiped her hands on her apron. "Are you all right? I hope you're not coming down with that flu that's going around. Let me feel your head."

Hezekiah moved away from her like a frightened child.

"I'm all right, Etta. My allergies are acting up again." He turned his back to her and walked toward the door.

"Aren't you having breakfast this morning? I made your favorite—eggs Benedict, blueberry muffins, and a strong pot of coffee."

"Not today. I'm running late." With that, he picked up his keys from the table in the foyer and left the house.

Samantha sat, still moist from the shower, curled on the sofa in the living room. Her silk robe held tight around her waist and legs under her body. Etta looked at the figure of the woman and knew something was seriously wrong. Samantha hadn't given the pastor her usual litany of directives before he left the house. She quietly withdrew to the safety of her kitchen.

Under normal circumstances Samantha would also have provided him with a better cover story for his unusual behavior. However, this morning she just sat and continued looking out the window. She no longer had the desire or strength to use her well-honed skills of deception.

"Sammy. Open the door, honey. It's me, Sandra," Sandra Kelly said, ringing the bell and pounding on the front door.

Sandra Kelly was one of Samantha's closest confidantes. They had gone to college together and over the years had remained friends and mutually supportive.

Samantha had comforted Sandra through her first and second divorces, a series of abusive boyfriends, and the meteoric rise of her law career. In turn, Sandra had nursed Samantha through Hezekiah's many affairs and coached her through the political and social labyrinth that was the lot of every powerful pastor's wife.

Sandra was one of the most sought-after attorneys in California and represented only high-profile clients who could guarantee her prime-time coverage on CNN, or an interview with Anderson Cooper. They were sisters, but the only common blood they shared was the pain endured at the hands of the men they loved.

Samantha looked through the beveled-glass windowpane of the double front door to ensure that Sandra was alone, and then hurriedly unlatched the locks.

Sandra was an attractive woman with a slight masculine air about her. She frequently wore navy blue pantsuits with the lapel of a white silk blouse framing her full and deep cleavage. Today was no exception. "Sammy, are you okay? I came as soon as I got your message. Is he still here? Did he hurt you, honey?"

Samantha collapsed sobbing into Sandra's arms. The silk robe draped off her bare shoulder. "Oh, Sandra," she cried. "I thought he was going to kill me. I've never seen him like that before."

"Where is Etta?" Sandra asked.

"I don't know. As usual she disappeared after Hezekiah left."

"Stop crying, honey, and tell me what happened."

Sandra led her to the living-room sofa. As Sandra sat, she saw drops of blood on Samantha's face.

"Oh my God, Samantha. You're bleeding. What did that son of a bitch do to you?" Samantha wiped the blood from her cheek with a shaking hand.

"This isn't my blood. It's Hezekiah's. I confronted him about having another affair. We got into an argument and he went berserk. He attacked me. He jumped on top of me, choking me, and I scratched his face." She began to sob again. "It was horrible, Sandra. I swear he was trying to kill me."

Sandra retrieved a hand towel from a powder room off the entry hall and handed it to Samantha.

"All right, honey, it's over now. Everything is going to be fine. That cheating bastard will get what's coming to him one day, I promise you. When are you going to wise up and leave that asshole?"

The question registered slowly. *I won't have to leave him*, Samantha thought. Soon Hezekiah Cleaveland would be out of her life for good. She would be free from the man whom she now loathed. A smile, ever so slight, crept across her blood-smeared face.

The telephone on a side table rang and Samantha jumped. "I don't want to answer that. It might be him. Would you get it, Sandra?"

"Hello," Sandra said calmly. "Cleaveland residence."

"Who is this?" Hezekiah growled from the rear of the limousine.

"Oh, hello, Hezekiah. This is Sandra. Samantha can't come to the phone right now. She's busy wiping your blood off her face."

Sandra sat on the sofa and crossed her legs. Her face contorted into that of an attorney preparing for a fierce courtroom battle.

As Dino maneuvered the winding hills away from the Cleaveland estate, Hezekiah pressed the button to raise the window that separated the rear cabin of the car from the driver's section. He put the phone on speaker and calmly replied, "Don't start with me this morning, Sandra. I'm not in the mood. Put her on the phone."

"Hezekiah, do you need a building to fall on you to realize how much you're hurting Samantha?"

"This is none of your business. This is between me and my wife."

"It becomes my business when you hurt someone I love. If you're not careful, she might accidentally talk to the media about how you physically assaulted your loving wife and have been cheating on her since the day you married. You'd be a laughingstock, the butt of every joke on late-night talk shows."

There was a brief pause, then, "Are you threatening me? It all makes sense to me now. You're a lesbian. I always thought you were after Samantha, but I never figured you'd stoop this low. You would encourage her to do something stupid so you could run to her rescue and . . ."

Sandra put her hand over the mouthpiece and whispered to Samantha, "He's saying he's going to kick my ass the next time he sees me."

Hezekiah continued on the other end. "Does she know, Sandra? Have you told Samantha you're in love with her yet?"

Sandra looked stunned for a brief moment, and then whispered again to Samantha, "He's saying you're lying and that he never touched you. He said you attacked him."

"Well, I've got news for you," Hezekiah continued.

"Samantha likes dick—the bigger the better."

Sandra laughed into the telephone. "Speaking of dicks," she said sarcastically, "you should try keeping yours in your pants."

Hezekiah slammed the leather car seat with three rapid strikes, and then yelled, "You can't talk to me that way!"

"He said I can't talk to him like that," Sandra said, mimicking Hezekiah's baritone indignation. "He's Hezekiah Cleaveland."

Hezekiah could hear Samantha's familiar laugh in the background. It was the same laugh he had heard when he told a bad joke on the night of their first date. The same laugh that teased him when he fell off the bed the night they made love in their first apartment together.

Sandra quickly grew impatient. She held the receiver away from her ear as Hezekiah spewed a flurry of accusations.

"Hezekiah," she interjected, "you're fucking with the wrong person. I'm not impressed or intimidated by your holier-than-thou bullshit. If you don't watch your step, I will take matters into my own hands and believe me, I have more than enough shit on you to make your life a living hell."

Hezekiah stopped mid-insult when he heard the words. "Shit? What are you talking about? You don't know anything about me. I told you, Sandra, I didn't touch her. Now stay out of this. Samantha and I will work this out without your interference."

"I know more than you think, and you'll find out soon enough. Brace yourself. Things are about to get even worse for you."

Sandra hung up the telephone. Within seconds the telephone rang again. "Don't answer it, Sammy," she said.

"He's livid and screaming like a madman."

Samantha looked at Sandra with a puzzled expression.

"What dirt are you talking about?"

"Nothing for you to concern yourself about right now, Sammy."

Samantha stepped dripping from the shower when she heard a knock on her bathroom door.

"Are you all right in there?" Sandra called out.

"I'm fine," she responded, startled by the intrusion. "I'll be out in a minute. Wait for me downstairs."

When Samantha came downstairs, Sandra greeted her in the living room with a steaming cup of chamomile tea.

"I feel much better now," Samantha said, sitting on the sofa. "I don't know if I could have got through this without you. I'm so lucky to have a friend like you."

"I'm the lucky one, Samantha. You've helped me through so much bullshit in my life. This is the least I can do for you. Sammy, can I ask you a question? Why do you stay with him? He ignores you unless the cameras are rolling. He's never cared about your career, or even acknowledged that you have one apart from him."

Samantha was silent for a moment. She laid her head on the back of the sofa. "I've asked myself the same question a thousand times," she finally said. "He used to make me so happy. But the larger the church grew, and the more famous we became, he seemed to change. The only time I think he notices me is when he thinks someone was watching. I honestly don't believe that he loves me anymore."

Samantha took a sip of the tea. "Now it's your turn. Why do you hate Hezekiah? You've never said it to me, but I can tell by the way you look at him sometimes. He has always been so good to you. He got you your first job out of law school. Loaned you money to set up your law practice."

Without hesitation Sandra responded, "It's because of you."

"But—"

"Wait a minute, Samantha. Let me finish." Sandra set her cup on the table and turned to Samantha. "It's because I see how miserable your life is in his shadow. My heart aches every time I see you smiling dutifully behind him while people heap praise on him. I see how he went chasing after his dreams and left you to struggle through seminary alone.

"I didn't tell you this earlier, but when I spoke to Hezekiah, he accused me of . . . Well, I won't say exactly what he accused me of . . . but in essence he said I was in love with you. At first I was shocked and embarrassed. But the more I thought about it the more I knew he was right."

Samantha showed no reaction.

"I am in love with you," Sandra continued. "But, not in the way he meant it. I love you like a sister. He accused me of being a lesbian. That's where his bruised ego caused him to miss the point completely. He'll be disappointed to learn that I'm just your average run-of-the-mill heterosexual. But I'm a woman who's blessed enough to have another woman in my life whose friend-ship, happiness, and well-being are as important to me as my own. If that makes me a lesbian, then fine . . . call me a dyke and sign me up for the standard-issue blue flannel shirt and Birkenstocks. At least I won't have to shave my legs anymore.

"I won't apologize or be ashamed of caring for you and for doing anything in my power to ensure that you have every opportunity to realize your dreams. The same thing you've always done for me."

A tear fell from Samantha's eye. For moments the two sat in silence.

Samantha turned to her with a smile and said, "So, does that mean you don't want to sleep with me?"

They laughed out loud together, and Sandra replied, "Sorry, girlfriend, but I like dick way too much."

Hattie Williams sat down in her favorite floral-print wing-back chair in her living room. She placed a round wicker sewing kit, which had belonged to her mother, on the tea table next to her. Hattie had raised three children in the house. Her husband died four years earlier and she now lived alone. The newest piece of furniture in the entire house was a small ottoman her husband had purchased twenty years earlier so she could elevate her leg and take the pressure off her arthritic knee. Every other piece of furniture in the house had decades of stories to tell. A pot of greens simmered on the stove, filling the small house with the smell of smoked neck bones and onions.

Hattie turned on a ceramic lamp to provide the extra light she would need to mend the tear in her favorite housecoat. As she searched the sewing kit for just the right thread, the image of a man in flight flashed before her.

It is Pastor Cleaveland. Hattie leans back in the chair with a look of cautious curiosity and watches Hezekiah, wearing a meticulously tailored suit that flaps with each twist of his flailing limbs, as he plummets through the air in the sanctuary at New Testament Cathedral.

Hattie dropped the sewing basket in her lap and it tumbled to the floor, spreading bobbins, pins, and needles over the thick green carpet. She gasped and covered her mouth in disbelief.

Hezekiah is falling and she cannot save him. Hideous flying gargoyles accompany him as he spirals downward. They dance rhapsodically in the air around him, cheering him on to his final destination below. Their wings flap in delight as Hezekiah tries in vain to find some hint of sympathy in their grotesque faces.

"Oh Lord, please don't let him fall," Hattie cries out loud. "Please catch him." But the harder she prays, the faster he falls. Then their eyes meet for a brief moment.

Although he does not speak, she knows what he is saying to her. "Help me, Hattie. I can't stop. Help me."

She hears a chorus of screams echoing through the sanctuary as he continues his glide like a hawk toward its prey on the canyon floor below.

"Oh my God," comes as a howl from the balcony.

Other shrieks of horror reverberate through the chamber.

"It's the pastor. He's falling!"

Women in fashionable heels drop helplessly to their knees, unable to fathom the event unfolding before them.

Men leave skid marks on the balcony floors, from the rubber on their soles, as they dash in disbelief toward the rail for a clearer view.

"Tell me who did this, Pastor," Hattie says out loud to the falling man. "Tell me what to do."

But it's too late. The falling man becomes dimmer and dimmer until the image fades away.

Hattie cupped her hand to her mouth and sobbed into the housecoat she had planned to mend and said one last time, "Tell me what you need, Pastor. Lord, please tell me what to do."

***

Hezekiah tried calling Samantha again, but still there was no answer. He struggled helplessly in an overwhelming sense of embarrassment and guilt as Dino drove the limousine along the now flat city streets. He had dealt the ultimate blow to the woman he once loved so deeply. She wouldn't leave him, but what dismal part of her soul would survive such a devastating assault? He resisted the urge to go back and comfort her, like he had done so many times before. *How could I put my family through this?* he questioned silently.

As he rode in the rear of the limousine through the city, he painfully navigated the emotional debris that accompanied infidelity, being caught, and confession. However, at the end of his silent process, there was no trace of the remorse he thought would greet him. Instead, he felt a sense of relief that he could not explain, although at times he ached at the thought of what Samantha must have been feeling at the moment. His breath seemed to pass freely through every organ in his body and then flow out the pores of his skin. The images he saw on the street seemed more vivid than they ever had before. Streams of energy rose from his belly, up his spine, and lifted an oppressive smoky haze from his shoulders and then flowed out the top of his head. He could feel the fog leave his body and evaporate into the light.

The car turned into the construction site across the street from his church and parked next to a pickup truck.

He had been sitting for a moment when a tap on the window commanded his attention.

"Good morning, Reverend," said a jolly red-cheeked man wearing a plaid shirt and baggy denim jeans. "I didn't think you were going to make it. I was just about to leave."

"Good morning, Benny. Sorry I'm late. I had a little problem at home. The building is looking great."

Benny Winters was the general contractor for the cathedral that would soon be the new home of New Testament Cathedral and Media Center. Hezekiah never trusted the round little man, but he had a reputation for building some of the most impressive edifices in the country. As a result of his concerns, Hezekiah insisted on approving every construction change order, regardless of how small, and visited the construction site as frequently as he could.

"Thank you. We're right on schedule, too. Come with me. I've got a few things to show you," Benny replied.

The two men put on hard hats and began a tour of the grounds and skeletal tower. Trucks drove on unpaved roads and dust filled the air. Men in hard hats and construction boots waved good morning as they passed. To their left a cement truck churned as a wet gray substance poured from its bowels.

"There is where we decided to put the satellite dish. Now everyone in the world will be able to see your pretty face live every Sunday morning," Benny said with a hearty laugh and pointed to a leveled piece of ground in the distance.

Hezekiah followed Benny into the cathedral and along corridors with exposed metal beams and wires. Workers were busy drilling and moving items through the halls.

Benny pointed to a series of metal brackets along the corridor and said, "Those are where we're installing the smoke detectors and alarms. The fire inspector came by yesterday and approved the distance between each unit. He went over the building with a fine-tooth comb and said everything looked to be in order."

Images of Danny flashed through Hezekiah's mind as he walked and made him smile. He remembered bringing him to the construction site on several occasions. He always wanted Danny, more than anyone else in his world, to be proud of him. He often wondered what Danny would think of a decision he had made or a project he was considering. He never hesitated to call and ask his opinion.

Hezekiah suppressed a smile and asked, "Have you got the final bids in for the carpet and tile work yet?"

"They're in, and I think you'll be very pleased. Most of them came in under what we budgeted. It's tough out there now and all these contractors are desperate to get a job as big as this."

"I never understood the point of hiring the cost estimator. It sounds like he overestimated the market. Maybe I should underestimate his fee," Hezekiah said without humor.

Ben smiled only to appease Hezekiah. "I don't think it was his fault. No one knew the economy would end up in the toilet like this."

Hezekiah barely heard the words spoken by Benny in front of the building. All he could think about was Danny and holding him again. The pounding of hammers and the smell of freshly cut wood seemed only to remind him more of how much he was in love.

Samantha paced the floor of her study after Sandra had left the house. Her silk robe trailed behind as she retraced her steps in front of the desk.

I could survive an affair with a woman, but a man? she thought. *If I didn't have a good reason to kill him before, I sure as hell have the perfect one now.*

Her course was clearer now than it ever was before.

She could survive the affair with that bitch from the restaurant they frequented, or the scheduling secretary she had immediately fired. But a man? She would never stand by and have the power of her feminine allure called into question. He handed her the verdict and read his own sentence. Death by shooting on the stage he had built for himself.

Samantha removed a pack of cigarettes from her desk. She nervously inhaled the smoke and retrieved her cell phone.

Reverend Willie Mitchell answered. "Yeah? This is Willie."

"Willie, it's Samantha. Are you alone? Can you talk?"

Reverend Mitchell, like so many other men, worshipped Samantha Cleaveland. He had schemed to be a part of her inner circle from the first day he saw her standing next to Hezekiah at a fundraiser for a state senator.

Over the years he watched her become more confident and saw her naive good looks evolve into seductive and intoxicating beauty.

He willingly gave everything Samantha had requested of him: one million for the new cathedral, substantial contributions to the politicians of her choice, or playing the "heavy" with any misguided bureaucrat or church trustee who dared to challenge her wishes.

Years earlier, he had bravely confessed his true feelings for her. She was repulsed by his proposition but kept her sentiments private. Instead, she used his adoration as a leash to keep him securely within her reach. The unspoken agreement was that if he acted upon her every wish, then maybe someday she would return his affection.

Willie quickly sat up on the edge of his couch and turned down the volume of the television with a remote control. Striped boxer shorts bunched between his legs and a tight white T-shirt stretched around his belly. "Yes, I can talk. What's up?"

"Have you found someone to do it yet?"

"What's the rush? The guy I've got in mind won't get out of jail for at least three more months."

"I don't have three months. It has to be done this Sunday."

"This Sunday? Are you fucking crazy? How the hell am I going to find anyone to do it in less than a week?"

"If you can't handle it, then I'll find someone else who can."

Willie rubbed his eyes and released a heavy sigh. "Wait a minute. I didn't say I couldn't do it. You just caught me off guard. Where do you want it done? Inside the house? A drive-by?"

"No. I want it done at church. Hezekiah always said he wanted to die in the pulpit. I want him killed this Sunday morning while he's giving the sermon. That's the least I can do for him."

"Where the fuck am I going to find someone stupid enough to kill him in front of the whole damn church and broadcast live all over the fucking country?"

"I know of someone who I think will be perfect for the job."

"Who?" Willie asked suspiciously.

"Virgil Jackson. He used to play drums for the youth choir. Now he's a crackhead living on the streets. He just got out of jail and I'm sure he's desperate. He bummed twenty dollars from Hezekiah this past Sunday."

"Yeah, I know him, but that's kind of close to home, don't you think?" Willie asked. "I don't know, Samantha. This seems unnecessarily risky. What if he gets caught?"

"That's why he's perfect. Hezekiah fired him a year ago, when he was caught trying to break into the church. That's what he was in jail for. People will think he was just settling a score."

"What if—"

"No more 'what-ifs.' Just talk to him and make sure he says yes and offer him enough money to leave Los Angeles permanently. I'll make sure the church balcony is empty. He can sneak up there at about eleven thirty. If he stays low behind the seats, no one will see him, and he'll be out of the range of the cameras up there."

Unable to deny the woman he had loved for years, Willie responded, "I still say this is fucking crazy, but I'll talk to him."

"Get back to me as soon as you've spoken to him," Samantha concluded.

Samantha disconnected without saying good-bye. She took one final drag from a cigarette and dropped the almost extinguished butt into a tepid cup of tea.

Willie adjusted his body on the sofa to relieve the pinching from the tight boxers. He reached for his bottle of Mylanta sitting on a cluttered coffee table. Samantha's sudden need to speed up the murder of Hezekiah concerned him.

Why the rush now? he thought. *We've planned this for almost a year, but now she wants it done within a week.*

He worried that her haste would cause mistakes. His stomach growled as he tensed his body to force the release of a trapped air bubble. She had never been that terse with him before. In the past she had convinced him to do her bidding by dangling the hope of sex in front of him. This time, however, was different.

His thoughts continued to whirl. *If she could do this to her own husband, what would she do if I disappoint her?* Would she ever allow him to touch her, or was it just another game? He feared she would shun him and his life would change dramatically if he disappointed her. The source of much of his power in the city came largely from his relationship with her. She made him worth talking to.

Her association with him prompted others to look past his portly and crass exterior and tolerate his company.

His mind turned to Hezekiah. The man who embodied everything Willie ever wanted in life: looks, wealth, fame and, most important, Samantha. Only Willie truly knew the depth of his hatred for Hezekiah Cleaveland. His stomach continued to rumble after he drank the last of the medicine. He pictured Samantha running to him for comfort and protection after Hezekiah was gone.

He would be her hero and those who laughed behind his back would then clamor for his attention.

8

One Year Earlier

The first time Danny had ever been in the church, and also the first time the two men had ever been alone together, had been one year earlier. Hezekiah had asked him to come by after he talked with the homeless woman near the church. Danny was nervous about speaking for the second time in one day with the pastor of New Testament Cathedral.

Danny sat with his backpack at his feet in Hezekiah's outer office. A dark-haired young woman opened envelopes at a desk near Hezekiah's door. Danny thought her face was exceptionally attractive for a church employee.

After reading the content of a letter, she looked in Danny's direction and smiled. "I'm sure he'll only be a few more minutes," she said as her hands reached for the next envelope. "He's running behind schedule today."

As he thumbed through a religious periodical, the door opened and three expensively dressed people walked out, with Hezekiah close behind. The first was a woman wearing a blue suit. She smiled from ear to ear as Hezekiah shook her hand. The two men accompanying her waited their turn to shake the pastor's hand.

"Thank you for your generous contributions," Hezekiah said to the three. "I'm going to have my staff contact you to work out the details. It's good to know the corporate community is also concerned about spreading the gospel."

"It's our pleasure. I only wish we could do more," came the eager reply from the youngest man.

Hezekiah saw Danny as the three spouted their support.

His mind became blank for the second time that day.

Each lapse had been prompted by the sight of the attractive young man. The three executives assessed that their fifteen minutes of face time had expired and politely exited the room.

"It's Danny St. John, right?" Hezekiah asked without moving forward. "Thank you for stopping by. Please come in."

"Pastor Cleaveland," the receptionist reminded him, "your next appointment is on his way. You're running a little behind schedule."

"This will only take a few minutes," Hezekiah replied without removing his eyes from Danny.

Hezekiah sat with Danny in chairs in front of his desk.

"So, did you have a chance to speak with that woman? What's her name? Is she mentally ill?" Hezekiah asked as Danny placed his backpack on the floor.

"I'm sorry, sir, but I can't say too much about her without breaching her confidentiality. As I said to you earlier, she refuses to accept any assistance. She said she makes enough money pan-handling to survive without our help."

"For God's sake, she's homeless. That's no way to live. Can't you at least talk her into going into a shelter?"

"I've tried. She thinks they're too dangerous. Her belongings were stolen a few years ago at a shelter. Now she refuses to go back. Women are exceptionally vulnerable in shelters, especially women with mental disorders. They often feel safer out in public, where there are other people around, and they can keep all their belongings with them."

Hezekiah found himself lost once again in the melodic tone of Danny's voice. His full lips were forming words, but Hezekiah could hear only music.

Why does this kid have such an effect on me? Hezekiah thought. *God, he's beautiful.*

"Danny, what exactly is it that you do on the outreach team? It must be very difficult to see human misery on a daily basis."

The intercom sounded before Danny could answer.

"Pastor Cleaveland your four o'clock is here. He said he has a plane to catch in forty-five minutes and will only take a few minutes of your time."

"Excuse me, Danny," Hezekiah said as he picked up the tele-phone. "Why did he schedule a four o'clock appointment with me if he had a four forty-five flight? Tell him I'll be right out."

Hezekiah returned his focus to Danny. "I'm sorry I have to cut this short, Danny." The two men stood up and walked toward the door. Hezekiah put his hand on the doorknob. He hesitated for a moment and then said, "I've got a proposal for you. If it wouldn't be too much trouble, I'd like to go with you one afternoon on your rounds." The words escaped effortlessly from his mouth. "I'd like to see firsthand how people live on the streets."

Danny raised his eyebrows at the suggestion. "I think you will be surprised if you've never seen it before. I'd be glad to take you around to a few shelters."

"I've been to shelters before," Hezekiah said. "No, I want to see where people live on the streets, under the freeways, in the parks. I'll put on some jeans, tennis shoes, and a baseball cap. No one will recognize me."

"Sir, I think people would recognize you even if you went in drag."

Hezekiah laughed out loud. "In drag? I won't go that far. I don't think my congregation would like that."

"Well, they'd love it in West Hollywood," Danny said, laughing along with Hezekiah.

"Maybe, but I think I'll stick with jeans. Do we have a date, then?" Hezekiah asked as his laughter subsided.

Danny picked up his backpack and shook Hezekiah's hand.

"Anytime you'd like, Pastor Cleaveland," he said as the two walked to the door.

"Good, then. I'll have my secretary set it up. And, Danny?"

"Yes, sir."

"Please call me Hezekiah."

It happened exactly one week after the first day they met. Hezekiah and Danny stood on a corner in skid row talking to a homeless man.

"Hey, ain't you Pastor Hezekiah Cleaveland?" the man said, tucking a half-empty beer can in his coat pocket.

"What are you doing out here on skid row?"

"I came out with Danny so I could talk to homeless people like you and ask what more my church can do to help."

The scraggly old man in dirty short pants struggled to his feet. "The first thing you can do is build more motherfucking—excuse my French, Reverend—more affordable housing. They're always full, so me and my buddies have to sleep out here in the streets like dogs."

"When was the last time you stayed in a shelter?" Danny asked, goading the man to tell Hezekiah more.

"It's been months now. I gave up a long time ago. Every time I tried, some young son of a bitch would tell me they're all full. After a while you just get tired of trying."

"You know it's illegal to sleep on the streets, don't you?" Hezekiah asked, restraining his irritation with the wobbling vagrant.

"Hell yeah, I know. The fucking cops won't let me forget it, but where the hell else am I supposed to go?"

Hezekiah looked to Danny. "Can't you get him into a program somewhere?"

"I can certainly try, but he's right. The shelters are usually full."

Hezekiah quickly grew impatient with the dirty man and his slurred speech.

"Danny, I should be getting back now," he said, dismissing the vagabond's observations. "Sir, it was nice meeting you. Good luck and keep trying to get into a shelter. I'm sure something will eventually open up for you."

As Danny and Hezekiah walked away and said, "That's my bus coming. I'm going to have to leave you now. I hope this has helped."

Hezekiah looked up and spoke quickly. "My car is around the corner. Let me give you a ride home."

Danny hesitated. "I'll be fine. I drove here too."

"Please, Danny, it's the least I can do. You've been very kind to me."

The ride to Danny's home was filled with animated conversation and laughter. Hezekiah sat cramped but inexplicably comfortable in the passenger seat of Danny's florescent orange 1973 Volkswagen Beetle as they hurled through the city streets. Danny skillfully shifted the grinding gears and the engine sputtered as Hezekiah's head jerked from side-to-side, back-and-forth with every shift of the transmission. After reaching Danny's apartment, they continued to talk for another fifteen minutes while the car engine was still running.

Danny finally said, "If we talk out here any longer I'm going to run out of gas. I'd better let you go."

Hezekiah looked at this watch. "I have two hours before my next appointment. Would you mind if I hung out with you for a while longer? I can have my driver pick me up here in an hour or so."

The floors of Danny's small apartment were covered with old rugs, dull from the afternoon sun. A burgundy couch from the local furniture outlet sat beneath arched windows looking onto the street. A computer sat on a large wooden desk which was covered with papers and open books. No art hung on the beige stucco walls.

A snow-white cat with one blue eye and one green greeted Danny as he and Hezekiah entered.

"This is Parker," Danny said as he stooped down to rub Parker's back.

"Why did you name him Parker?" Hezekiah asked.

"I was on my way to the market one day and I saw him walking down Park Street. It was a hot day and the pavement was burning his paws. I came back home and couldn't get the poor little guy out of my mind. He was so cute and he looked so helpless. So I got a bottle of water and a bowl and went to look for him. He was still there and he's been my best buddy ever since."

"From what I've seen today, that makes sense."

"What do you mean?"

"You've obviously dedicated your entire life to taking care of strays," Hezekiah said gently. "I feel like we have that in common."

"I would hardly call the members of your church 'strays.' From what I've heard, your church is full of celebrities, professional athletes, doctors, and lawyers."

"Some of them are, but not all. It doesn't matter how much money or education they have. That's not what I meant. People come to church because they are searching for something that money can't buy. Some are looking for peace, others for something larger than themselves to believe in. But the one thing they all have in common is they're looking for someone who cares about them, just like Parker and the homeless people you work with."

"The difference between you and me is that I don't charge these people for my services and I'm not paid nearly as much as I assume you are."

Hezekiah laughed. "Regardless of what you've heard, Danny, I don't charge either. People give to the church because the Bible instructs them to do so. I would still do exactly what I do even if no one ever gave me a dime." His tone turned somber as he continued. "For some reason it's very important to me that you understand that I do what I do because I believe deeply in the message and the good it does for so many lonely and lost people. It's not about money, Danny. In that way I think we are very much alike. Does that make sense to you?"

"I didn't mean to offend you, but I'm glad to hear you say that. I'll be honest with you. The Hezekiah Cleaveland I saw today is nothing like what I expected."

Hezekiah laughed again. "I'm almost afraid to ask, but what were you expecting?"

"I thought you'd be the person I've seen on television. All smiles and spewing a string of quotable quotes from the Bible. But, instead, I saw a very kind and vulnerable man. I think you're searching for something yourself."

"And what do you think that is?"

"I don't know yet. But I can see it in your eyes. I saw it the first day I met you on the street. There was something very sad about you that day. I kind of felt the same way about you as I did when I saw Parker for first time wandering the streets alone."

Hezekiah did not respond. He, instead, walked to the sofa and stared out the arched windows at the traffic passing below.

Danny changed the subject. "What do you think of my place? It's not much, but it's home," Danny said as he turned on the lights and laid his mail and keys on the cluttered but clean desk.

"It's very nice, Danny. It feels so comfortable and warm. It feels like a very loving and special person lives here."

"Would you like a cup of coffee?"

"That would be nice, if it's not too much trouble," Hezekiah replied.

Hezekiah felt strangely at ease in the little apartment, even though he had not been in a home that sparse in years. He sat down on the couch and thumbed through a magazine that lay on an old wooden coffee table.

"How do you take your coffee?" came a voice from the kitchen.
"Black is fine."

In a few moments Danny returned with two large mugs and set them on the coffee table. He flopped down on the sofa at a respectable distance from the pastor.

"Do you live here alone?" Hezekiah asked.

"Yes. I had a roommate, but he moved in with his boyfriend about a year ago." Danny chose this route of subtle disclosure rather than directly declaring that he was gay.

They talked and laughed for thirty minutes when Hezekiah said, "I hope I'm not keeping you from anything. I know you must be tired after such a long day."

"Not at all. I'm enjoying your company."

As they spoke, Hezekiah looked at his watch. "I should leave. I really enjoyed this afternoon. It was the most relaxed I've felt in years."

While saying the words, he squeezed Danny's hand tightly and looked intently into his eyes. They stood and studied each other's faces for silent moments. The exchange between their clasped hands and locked eyes spoke more than any words they could have spoke. For each, the extended gaze served as confirmation of their shared feelings. Then in a moment of mutual consent, they simultaneously pressed their bodies together and kissed long, deep, and hard. Hezekiah's soft, full lips enveloped Danny's mouth. The kiss was slow and passionate.

Thoughts were shared with each breath they exchanged.

Hezekiah took off his baseball cap and tossed it onto a nearby console without looking. His erection stretched the leg of his jeans as he probed the rear of Danny's faded army fatigues with one hand and pressed his face closer with the other.

They made love for the first time that afternoon.

Hezekiah and Danny both knew that it would not be the last time they would be in each other's arms. Over the next year they had "coffee" together often.

9
Six Months Earlier

The alliance between Cynthia Pryce and Sandra Kelly had been forged six month earlier. Though their motivations for outing Hezekiah Cleaveland were different, the means served each of their purposes well. Sandra had introduced Cynthia to Phillip Thornton, the *Los Angeles Chronicle* publisher, after Cynthia told her about the e-mails between Hezekiah and Danny St. John during a dinner party at the Cleaveland estate.

The table in the dining room had been set to perfection. An elaborate floral arrangement in the center of the table was illuminated by the massive crystal chandelier above. Eight place settings held so many utensils, plates, bowls, and goblets that even the most sophisticated diner would have been at a loss determining what their specific uses were.

Hezekiah sat at the head of the table. To his right and left were Hector Ramirez, the mayor of Los Angeles, and his wife, Miranda. Then came Percy and Cynthia Pryce, and next to them Sandra Kelly and Kenneth Davis.

Samantha sat facing Hezekiah at the opposite end of the table.

"I've lived in Los Angeles my entire life and I've never seen as many homeless people living on the streets and in the parks as there are today," Cynthia said to the mayor.

"Can't the city do more to help them?"

"I was downtown at a meeting yesterday and I was amazed at how aggressive panhandlers have become," Kenneth chimed in. "Two to three people on every block stopped me to ask for money. I like to think I'm a compassionate man, but that was a bit overwhelming for me."

"I don't feel that way at all," Percy said. "I always carry extra cash so I can give it to people when they ask."

"I think that does more harm than good, Reverend Pryce," Sandra said between sips of white wine. "Most homeless people are either addicted to drugs and alcohol or mentally ill. Giving them cash only perpetuates their addiction."

"Nonsense," Percy said defensively. "I'd rather give a dollar directly to a homeless person than to some of these so-called 'nonprofit agencies' that take forty cents off the top of every dollar they collect."

"That's a gross generalization," Hector said, leaning forward in his seat. "Many of the organizations that the city funds to serve the homeless are doing amazing work and are fiscally responsible."

Hezekiah finally spoke. "I agree. I know of an outreach worker who works for an agency downtown"—Hezekiah contained his passion and spoke cautiously—"He is a selfless and compassionate guy. He does amazing work with some of the most destitute people in this city."

Cynthia's ears perked up. She could not believe Hezekiah had the audacity to talk about his lover in such glowing terms in front of everyone. "He sounds like a wonderful person, Pastor. What's his name?" she asked slyly.

Hezekiah looked at her with an innocent expression and said, "I can't remember offhand, but I know he does good work."

"Don't get me wrong. I'm not saying there aren't any good social service agencies out there," Percy said before he could swallow his most recent bite of quail. "The point I'm trying to make is if I give the money myself, I know it won't end up in the pockets of some overpaid administrator."

"Since I've taken office, the city has doubled its budget for social service programs. We've built three new shelters and two new community clinics," Hector replied defensively. "But it's still not enough. The reality is governments can only do so much to address the social ills that face this city. We need to develop more public and private partnerships with the corporate and faith communities."

Hector looked to Hezekiah. "We need churches like yours to step up to the plate and help us."

Hezekiah smiled and said, "Don't you start on me too. New Testament Cathedral has been on the front line in the fight against poverty. We have clothes and food drives. Our members volunteer at shelters, and we make generous contributions to several agencies around the city."

"That doesn't sound like the front to me," Sandra said.

"Sounds more like the tail." The table fell silent. "Homeless people don't need more hand-me-down clothes or dented cans of tuna. They need affordable housing. They need affordable health care and drug rehabilitation programs."

"Is that so?" Hezekiah asked. "Then why don't you tell us how much you give to the homeless? And I don't mean giving them your doggie bag after you've dined at Spago."

"Hezekiah, you shouldn't ask her a personal question like that," Samantha interjected. "Sandra, ignore him. He's just being provocative."

"No, I think it's a fair question," Sandra said, laying her fork gently on her plate. "First of all, I haven't eaten at Spago in years, Hezekiah," Sandra said, leaning back in her chair. "I didn't know anyone other than tourists still went there. And as for your second question, last year alone my law firm worked over one thousand hours pro bono on discrimination cases involving low-income housing. And, before you ask, I personally have donated a substantial portion of my own income to multiple charities in Los Angeles and New York."

Hezekiah looked coldly at Sandra and said, "That's admirable, Sandra, but I don't think that places you in a morally superior position, nor does it give you the right to criticize what we do at New Testament Cathedral."

"I hadn't intended for it to. I simply wanted to answer your question."

There was an uneasy tension at the table. The easy chatter that had preceded the most recent exchange was now replaced with awkward glances and a preoccupation with bread crumbs that had fallen on the table. The servers' pace slowed a notch as the tone of the party shifted.

There was a brief silence, and then Percy spoke. "Sandra, Hezekiah is right. I don't think that is a thorough or fair depiction of the significant impact New Testament Cathedral has had on the lives of poor people in this city," he said diplomatically. "Hezekiah gives something more important than housing. He gives them hope with his message. He feeds their soul."

Sandra rolled her eyes but did not respond, and Cynthia coughed as if choking on the words her husband just spoke.

"That is very important," Miranda said, "but with all due respect to Hezekiah, and all other ministers in this city, a sermon doesn't keep a person warm and dry at night when they are sleeping under a bush in Griffith Park."

Hector looked at his wife sharply. "Miranda," he rebuked.

"I'm sure Hezekiah is doing his best. As you can see, Miranda is very passionate about this issue."

"That's all right, Hector," Hezekiah said. "Miranda is right. The church should be doing more. Samantha and I have been thinking of ways we can get more involved in the issue."

Hezekiah looked to Samantha for support, but instead, she placed her napkin on the table and said, "Why don't we all go into the living room? We can have our coffee and after dinner liqueur, if you'd like, in there."

The guests filed in pairs from the dining room into the living room. They were greeted by the sound of a Mozart sonata played by a pianist on the baby grand in a corner of the room. A lavish silver coffee setting had been placed on a table behind the sofa, and a server stood near another table, which held a full brandy decanter and matching Baccarat glasses.

Miranda and Samantha sat chatting in chairs that faced the floor-to-ceiling window overlooking the Pacific Ocean.

"I hope I didn't offend you with my comment earlier," Miranda said. "I get so upset when people criticize Hector on his homeless policies."

"I wasn't offended. I'm glad you said it. Hezekiah needed to hear that," Samantha replied. "I tried to convince him that we should have built an affordable housing complex instead of the new cathedral, but you know how men are. It's all about ego and power."

"The same could be said about Hector. Sometimes I think if he could marry his ego, he would have no use for me at all."

The two women laughed in unison.

"Behind Hector's painted-on smiles and expensive suits, there really is a man who cares about people," Miranda continued. "It hurts him to see so many people living on the streets in this city. I think, if he could, he would build a shelter in every neighborhood, but people won't let him."

"I wish I could say the same for Hezekiah," Samantha said, "but he only has himself to blame for doing so little to help the homeless. It was his idea to build the cathedral, and once his mind is set, there is no changing it."

Hezekiah and Hector stood near the fireplace, sipping brandy. "I'm sorry about what Miranda said earlier," Hector said. "Sometimes she says things without thinking first."

"Not a problem, Hector. Samantha is the same way. I've had to apologize for inappropriate things she's said in public more times than I'd care to remember."

"The real problem this city faces in addressing homelessness is its lack of coordination of services," Hector continued. "There are five different departments that fund and monitor programs for the homeless and none of them know what the other is doing."

"You should hire Samantha," Hezekiah said with a smile. "She knows what every department in the church is doing and where every dime is spent."

Kenneth and Percy accepted cups of coffee from the server. "Sandra was completely out of line," Percy said quietly. "She took shots at Hezekiah every chance she got."

"I think the rumors are true about her," Kenneth said while stirring his coffee and clinking the inside of the cup with a silver spoon. "Did you notice the way she looks at Samantha?"

Cynthia and Sandra were huddled in a remote corner of the living room, having their own discussion.

"It's so sad how he cheats on her. I don't know why she puts up with it," Cynthia observed.

"I guess she loves him enough to ignore the other women," Sandra said in defense of her friend.

"All the other women he's had affairs with are bad enough, but . . ." Cynthia stopped midsentence.

"But what?" Sandra inquired.

Cynthia looked over her shoulder to ensure the other guests at the party were preoccupied and said, "Let's just say, I know for a fact that Hezekiah has recently expanded his horizons."

Sandra led Cynthia into the foyer. "You know something, don't you?" she inquired forcefully. "Spill it, girl. What's he done now?"

"I don't like to gossip, but I hate to see a wonderful woman like Samantha get hurt," Cynthia replied sheepishly.

"I found out, purely by accident, mind you, that Hezekiah is having an affair. . . ." She paused, and then whispered quietly, "With a man this time."

Sandra quickly covered her mouth to prevent a gasp from reverberating through the room. "Cynthia, you must be mistaken. Hezekiah is a lot of things, but I don't think he's gay."

"I know, girl. I was just as shocked as you are."

On the last word Samantha walked up behind them.

"There you two are. Why aren't you circulating? I'll be glad when this is over. I want to get this over with as soon as possible. What are you two talking about?"

Sandra was still in shock and could not respond, so Cynthia quickly interjected, "Sandra was telling me about the new case she's working on."

10

Tuesday

Cynthia Pryce greeted guests in the banquet hall of the Bonaventure Hotel. Her vanilla linen pantsuit followed perfectly each elegant gesture of her body.

It was the fifth annual Los Angeles Women in Business Awards Luncheon at the Bonaventure Hotel and Cynthia was the honorary chair. Due to time constraints Samantha Cleaveland had not been able to accept the honor, so the organizing committee viewed Cynthia as a suitable alternative.

Cynthia shook manicured hands and air kissed taut rosy cheeks as the powerful, the beautiful, and the wellheeled filed past her. Sandra Kelly was the next in line to greet Cynthia.

"Cynthia," Sandra said, approaching with a glass of champagne in one hand and a cell phone in the other.

Sandra leaned in, kissed Cynthia on the cheek, and whispered, "These old divas look like they belong on a poster in a plastic surgeon's office."

"Sandra, you made it," said Cynthia. "I called your office, but they said you'd be in Sacramento until this evening. How's your new case going? I hear the surrogate mother wants to claim her parental rights now."

"It's turning into a nightmare," said Sandra. "Never mind that. What's happening with the story?"

Cynthia took Sandra by the arm and led her to an unoccupied section of the ballroom in the Bonaventure.

"Lance had to delay the story. He said he needed a quote from Hezekiah before the editor would approve it for publication."

"Has he got it yet?" Sandra asked.

"I don't know. He had a meeting with Hezekiah on Monday, but I haven't heard anything."

"I hope he didn't tell Hezekiah we're the source," Sandra said. "Our hands have to stay clean in order for this to work."

"He won't. Our agreement was that we anonymously provide him with the proof of the affair, and he keeps our names out of it." There was a long pause; then Cynthia said, "I hope Hezekiah's ego doesn't stop him from stepping down."

"Trust me, Cynthia, he'll resign," Sandra said, placing her now empty champagne glass on a vacant surface nearby. "Hezekiah's ego may be out of control, but he's not an idiot. Besides, if he doesn't, there is no way the board of trustees will accept a gay man as pastor, even if that man is the great Hezekiah Cleaveland."

Cynthia waved at an anonymous face across the room and then continued, "Does Samantha know anything about this?"

"She knows Hezekiah is having an affair, but she didn't tell me it's with a man."

"Not that. I mean, does she know anything about the article Lance is writing?"

"I don't think so. If she did, she would have told me." Sandra waved off the question and continued. "I've set up a meeting tomorrow night at my home with Phillip Thornton. He wants to talk to you face-to-face."

"Why?" Cynthia asked nervously.

"He doesn't want to face Hezekiah's wrath if we get cold feet on this. He needs assurances that we'll stand behind the story in case Hezekiah pursues legal action against the *Los Angeles Chronicle*."

"Okay," Cynthia agreed hesitantly. "I'll be there, but I don't trust Phillip. He and Hezekiah go way back."

"I don't either, but it's a risk we have to take."

The two women embraced and walked arm in arm to the front of the ballroom.

It was three o'clock and Cynthia still had not heard from Lance. The luncheon at the Bonaventure Hotel had ended and throngs of admiring women had heaped praise upon her for hosting the successful event.

"Where is he? Why hasn't he called yet?" Cynthia said as she and Sandra Kelly drove out of the circular driveway of the hotel.

"Hezekiah must have scared him off the story," Cynthia said. "We're screwed if he drops the ball on this."

Sandra veered her hunter green Jaguar into the flow of cars on the street and drove toward Cynthia's penthouse.

"Lance can take care of himself, Cynthia. This is the biggest story of his career. If he brings down Hezekiah, he'll be able to work for any major newspaper in the country. He won't screw this up."

"What if he buckled and told Hezekiah that we're the ones who leaked the story?"

"Cynthia, you're getting paranoid. Slow down, honey. Call Lance now, if it'll make you feel better." Sandra handed her a cell phone. "I'm sure he's at his dingy little desk at the Chronicle right now, finishing up the story."

Cynthia dialed Lance's number.

"Hello, this is Lance Savage," came the recorded message. "I'm not available to take your call. Please leave a message at the tone and I will contact you as soon as possible."

The familiar beep sent a jolt through Cynthia's body.

"Damn it, Lance. This is Cynthia," she said into the wireless void. "Where are you? Have you interviewed Hezekiah yet? Call me as soon as you get this message."

Cynthia disconnected the line and threw the sleek black telephone onto the seat of the car.

"Cynthia, you need to relax. We've come this far, right? This is no time to panic." While driving with one hand, Sandra reached into her pocket and handed Cynthia a vial filled with white pills. "Here, honey," she said, "take one of these. It'll calm you down."

"What are they?" Cynthia asked, reaching for the little brown bottle.

"It's Xanax. Just take one, honey. You'll feel better."

Cynthia eagerly consumed the tablet. "I could use a joint right now, too. This is driving me crazy."

Sandra looked cautiously in her rearview mirror, then reached into the glove compartment and produced the leafy prescription Cynthia had desired.

"I shouldn't be doing this, but you look like you could really use this right now," Sandra said nervously, looking in her rearview mirror and from side to side. The two women passed the joint between them as they drove along Wilshire Boulevard.

A woman driving beside them recognized Cynthia from the luncheon and waved while waiting at a red light. Cynthia clamped her smiling red lips shut to prevent a stream of smoke from escaping and dutifully waved back. Cynthia burst into a combination of laughter and coughs that filled the car with billowing white smoke after the woman had proceeded to a safe distance ahead.

"That bitch almost killed me." She laughed while coughing out more smoke. "I thought I was going to pass out."

Cynthia considered what her next move would be as the Xanax and marijuana mixed in her brain. "I don't know what we're going to do if this doesn't work."

"It is going to work, and you're going to do just what we've planned for the last three months," Sandra said impatiently.

As Sandra turned the car into the covered carport of her high-rise building, Cynthia tossed the remains of the marijuana cigarette out the window of the rolling vehicle.

The women embraced and an attendant rushed to open the car door for Cynthia.

"Good afternoon, Mrs. Pryce," a round-faced man, clad in a red uniform, said as Cynthia extended her leg to the pavement. "Reverend Pryce just arrived only a few minutes ago. He should be in your apartment by now."

Cynthia hesitated for a moment and looked to Sandra.

"Do you want me to come up with you? Are you going to be all right?" Sandra asked.

"I'm fine now. I'll call you as soon as I've heard from . . ." Cynthia stopped when she realized the doorman was listening. "I'll call you."

Cynthia walked toward the double glass doors of the luxury building. Two rows of potted palm trees lining the carpeted path bristled from a slight breeze under the massive blue awning. The attendant sped past her to the glass doors and flung them open.

"Thank you," she said without looking at the man's anxious face.

The foyer sparkled from the afternoon sun. Classical music played as several residents retrieved mail from boxes partially hidden behind another cluster of potted plants.

Cynthia walked quickly toward the elevator doors, hoping to avoid the inevitable greetings from omnipresent neighbors.

As she pressed the button, she heard, "Hello, Mrs. Pryce. The reverend went up a few minutes ago. You just missed him."

When she turned, she saw Carl, the building security guard. He moved toward her as he spoke.

"Seems like he's in a pretty bad mood today. Nearly bit the head off poor Mrs. Nussbaum in Seventeen-D. She was complaining about the homeless guys who have been urinating behind the building. Said she walked up on one of them this morning as he was taking a leak. 'Nearly scared me to death,' she told the reverend, and before she could even finish her sentence, Reverend Pryce lit into her like there was no tomorrow."

Cynthia listened intently to the account from the overly familiar guard.

"He said to her, 'You wouldn't have seen him taking a piss if you weren't always lurking around the building. Maybe that'll teach you to mind your own business.' I thought she was going to cry after he got through with her."

"I'm sure he didn't mean to offend her," Cynthia said while pressing the elevator button again, hoping to speed its arrival. "He probably has a lot on his mind today. You know how he gets sometimes."

Carl gave her a knowing smile. "I sure do, ma'am. I've been on the receiving end of his sharp tongue a few times myself."

The elevator doors glided open.

"I will apologize to Mrs. Nussbaum the next time I see her," Cynthia said as the doors closed between them.

She pressed the button, causing the elevator to rise with a jerk.

The ding of the elevator alert told her it had reached its final destination and could ascend no farther through the artery of the building. As the doors slid open, Cynthia took a deep breath, then another, before stepping into the empty hallway. They shared the top floor with a reclusive tenant, a neighbor whom she had not seen or even heard through the walls in over five years. The double doors to her apartment seemed to throb as she walked toward them. She could hear footsteps from behind the doors when she turned the key.

"Percy," she called out, stepping into the empty foyer.

"Honey, are you home?"

***

The two senior ministers of New Testament Cathedral sat around a large table in the conference room of the church. Hezekiah entered the room with his usual flare.

"Good afternoon, Brothers," he said. "Let's get this meeting started."

Each man had his Bible placed on the table in front of him. Although no one wore black robes, the air still smacked of reverence and piety. Hezekiah sat at the head of the table with Reverend Percy Pryce to his right and Rev. Kenneth Davis to his left.

After a short prayer Hezekiah began the meeting. "The first thing on the agenda is the funeral for Mabel Smith. It's scheduled for this Friday and I'm going to be out of town for the weekend. Reverend Pryce, are you available that day?"

Percy retrieved his BlackBerry from his breast pocket.

"Yes, I can officiate."

"Good. Next item."

Both men at the table shifted slightly in their seats and exchanged curious glances in response to the curt manner in which the pastor conducted the meeting.

"Someone needs to represent the church at the thirtyfifth anniversary of Mount Zion AME on the twenty-sixth," Hezekiah continued. "Neither Samantha nor I will be able to attend."

Reverend Pryce cleared his throat. "I can do it, Pastor. I'm very close to the pastor at Mount Zion."

Hezekiah looked up and said, "Thank you, Percy, but I was hoping Reverend Davis would cover this one."

"I can represent us. I had planned on attending, anyway," said Reverend Davis while looking sympathetically at Percy. "You can attend with me, if you'd like, Reverend Pryce."

Percy did not respond.

Hezekiah pressed forward. "I'll be here this Sunday, but Samantha will be preaching on the following Sunday. I won't be there, so I expect each of you to be present to support her."

The tension in the room grew thicker. The two men could sense Hezekiah was preoccupied. When the last agenda item had been discussed, Hezekiah placed his hands on the table and said,

"Gentlemen, I have a question for you. What would the two of you do if I were no longer able to serve as pastor?"

The room was silent for a chilling moment as the question hung in the air. They all had thought about the possibility from time to time, but no one expected Hezekiah to raise that subject.

Confusion rushed through the head of Reverend Davis.

He could not imagine New Testament Cathedral without Pastor Hezekiah T. Cleaveland.

Reverend Pryce spoke first. "Pastor, I'm not sure what you mean. Is something wrong?"

"No, but it is part of your responsibility as senior ministers of this church to think in these terms. I could die at any time and then what would you do? Who would replace me? How would you select him?"

Reverend Pryce leaned in closer. "Pastor, as you know, the decision of who will serve as pastor in the event of your departure does not fall within the authority of this body. It is the responsibility of the board of trustees to select your replacement, should the need arise."

Hezekiah gave him a sharp look. "I know what the bylaws say. I wrote them. But the trustees will look to you for counsel. They'll want to know what you recommend and you all need to be prepared to answer. Not as individuals but as the team of senior ministers."

The two men looked anxiously into each other's faces, searching for answers that they knew were not there.

Then in unison they returned their gaze to Hezekiah, and Kenneth spoke.

"What would you want to see happen?"

"The bylaws state that I cannot select my replacement, and I still think that is appropriate. You, meaning the members of the church, should have the right to select who your shepherd will be if I am forced to resign. The only thing I do want and expect from you is that you select someone who shares my vision for this ministry. And if you don't know what that is by now, you should not be here. I'd expect you to support whoever the new pastor would be in the same manner you have supported me. I also want you to make sure that he respects the heritage and traditions of this ministry and not allow him to make any sweeping changes to everything we've built over the years."

The clarity and force of Hezekiah's statements had a paralyzing effect on the ministers.

"This is your assignment, gentlemen," Hezekiah continued. "Think carefully on these questions and come to some definite conclusions. You don't have to share them with me, but make sure you have the answers if the situation should ever arise. I don't want my church to be left unprepared and end up like all those others, with bitter infighting that always leads to fracturing into smaller pathetic storefront ministries." After a short pause Hezekiah said, "Good day, gentlemen. I'll see you on Sunday morning."

No further words were said. The two men gathered their belongings and left the room in silence. Hezekiah remained at the conference table with his hands clasped in his lap. He was too tired to think anymore and too afraid to cry. The swirl of the wood grain on the conference table occupied his thoughts for the next suspended moments.

He then slowly picked up his belongings, turned out the light, and left the room.

Steel slammed against steel as men in shorts strained to complete their next set. Bodies stretched and treadmills churned from stationary workouts. Hezekiah started his next set of repetitions on the weight machine.

Hezekiah and Percy had met for their weekly workout.

"Thirteen, fourteen, come on, Pastor, you can do it. Fifteen," Percy counted as he squatted at Hezekiah's side.

"You still got it, old man. I think you should add another ten pounds next time."

Hezekiah lay panting on the bench, with his arms spread at his side. "You're trying to give me a heart attack."

He got up from the bench and wiped sweat from his brow. "Okay Reverend, let's see what you got."

With that, Percy sat down and began his repetitions with the same weights. He gripped the steel rod above his head and lowered the weights to his chest.

"Push. Come on, man, push. Give me three more. Thirteen, fourteen, fifteen." Hezekiah helped Percy from the bench.

"That's it for me, man," Percy said between breaths.

"I'm going to hit the showers. Are you coming?"

Hezekiah welcomed the words signaling the end of their work-out. Percy led the way to the locker room. It was a large open space with orange lockers. Used towels were scattered on the floor and the doors of empty lockers hung open. The two men dialed the combinations to their locks and sat on a thin wooden bench to remove their shoes.

"What's going on with you, Hezekiah?" Percy asked as the two men stood naked under the steaming shower.

"What do you mean? I've never been in better shape."

"We've worked together for years now. Not only are you my pastor, but you're also my friend, and I'd like to think you feel the same. I know when something is troubling you. That whole thing about us thinking about your replacement—what's going on?"

"I can't talk about it right now, but I'm not sure if I'll be able to continue as pastor for much longer."

Percy stood naked and shocked before the pastor. "Are you sick?"

Hezekiah turned his back to Percy and continued to soap his body. He was not prepared to have this conversation.

"No, it's nothing like that. I'm fine. I'll be honest with you, Percy. I'm struggling with a moral dilemma that I don't think I'll ever be able to resolve."

"Hezekiah, nothing could be that bad. Maybe you should talk about it with someone. Have you considered seeing a therapist? I know several ministers who are seeing a guy in Anaheim who's supposed to be excellent."

Hezekiah had never considered seeing a therapist, although he had made the recommendation to many members whose problems required more time than he was willing or able to give. "I don't think he could help me with this," Hezekiah said with a resolute expression on his face. "Everything is more complicated than you could ever imagine."

"No problem you could have on earth is too complicated for God. Let me get you the therapist's number. Give him a call. Whatever is going on might not be as bad as you think."

"Okay, Percy. I'll call him. But if I should leave, I want you to take over as pastor. You're a good man and you're the only person I would trust with New Testament."

"Don't even think in those terms yet, Hezekiah. You know I'm honored, but I hope it doesn't come to that."

The two men showered in silence, only the sound of drops echoed through the tiled room.

11

Ten Months Earlier

The year of secrecy had been difficult for Danny. He wanted to tell someone, everyone, about his love for Hezekiah. However, the cost of such a revelation was too high. He had cursed himself on many occasions for loving a man who was a prisoner of public opinion. Why had he allowed himself to love a man whose existence, life, and livelihood depended on receiving daily approval from thousands of nameless, faceless people?

Hezekiah had warned him of the perils of their union on the day they first exchanged the words "I love you," exactly two months after they met.

"Are you sure you know what you're getting into?"

Hezekiah questioned while they lay naked under the covers in Danny's bed. "I'm a pastor and I can't change that. It means a lot of sacrifice on both our parts."

"I didn't mean to fall in love with you, Hezekiah," Danny said as he laid his head on Hezekiah's chest, "but since I have, I'll have to live with the consequences."

"I didn't know I was going to fall in love with you, either, but I'm glad I did. I just don't want you to get hurt. I love you too much. If someone, anyone, finds out about us, your life will never be the same. You'll become a public figure. The media will be brutal. They'll try to destroy us both, and they'll probably succeed. I've seen it happen to other pastors."

"Then why are you willing to take that kind of a risk?"

Hezekiah answered without pause. He had asked himself the same question on many occasions. "Because I need you. I've never loved anyone, or even myself, as much as I love you. No one has ever forced me to look beyond myself and my own needs or my own ego." He sat up in the bed and placed Danny's head in his lap and looked earnestly into his deep brown eyes. "You've made me realize I've never really cared for anyone and didn't think I had the capacity to. My world has always been about me, and what I desired more than life itself. I wanted power and all that came with it—fame, wealth, and respect. It has consumed my every thought for as long as I can remember. Every word I spoke, and every step I took, was taken only to move me closer to my goals.

"Well, I've done it. I have it all, and when I got it, I began to hate myself more than I had ever hated my worst enemy. All I could see staring back at me in the mirror was a hollow, lonely man who had traded his soul just to be recognized when he walked down the street.

"I had actually thought about committing suicide on the day I first saw you helping that man downtown. I wanted to punish myself for being a fool, for forcing myself to waste an entire life chasing something that left me vacant and alone. And then I met you."

Hezekiah gently placed his hand on Danny's chest. "I don't know what happened, but when I first looked in your eyes, I had an overwhelming desire to have you know me deep down inside. I thought you might be able to understand me and maybe even help me understand myself. And you have."

The two then lay silently in bed, sharing hidden places in their hearts without words and with gentle, caring hands.

12
Tuesday

No response came to Etta's announcement of arrival at the Cleaveland estate. She called out again, "Pastor Cleaveland, Mrs. Cleaveland, are you home?"

Hezekiah's coat had been tossed over the back of a chair in the living room. This was the first clue that all was not well in the Cleaveland household. Hezekiah's fastidious and controlling nature had always prevented him from leaving clothes scattered about the house.

She began the long walk down the hallway toward Hezekiah's study. She could hear the telephone ringing in the room. Etta stood with her ear near the door. The ringing telephone went unanswered. Clue number two.

Hezekiah never passed up the opportunity to talk on the telephone.

Etta tapped on the door and entered the dark room.

The only light came from a glowing computer screen on the desk at which Hezekiah sat with his back to the door. Bookshelves filled with awards and mementos covered the walls of the study. Deep forest green carpet absorbed the remains of light that peeked through the drawn shades at the windows.

Etta could only see the back of Hezekiah's head above the high-backed leather chair.

"Aren't you going to answer the phone?" she asked softly. But there was no response. "Pastor Cleaveland, is everything all right?"

The leather chair spun around. From the computer light she could see his hollow eyes. A silk tie hung loosely from his neck and unfastened cuffs dangled around his wrists. His expressionless face peered through the darkness.

He spoke after several agonizing seconds. "No, I'm afraid that everything isn't all right."

Etta's face contorted into an expression of concern as she approached the desk. "Pastor Cleaveland, you're scaring me. What's wrong?"

"Someone is trying to destroy everything I've . . ." He paused and swallowed deeply. "Everything Samantha and I have worked all these years for," he finished.

Etta sat slowly in a chair near the desk and asked, "Who?"

Hezekiah waved his hands in a sign of bewilderment and replied, "That's the problem. I don't know who it is. I only know it's someone intent on bringing down my ministry, and this time it just might work."

Etta looked puzzled as her heart pounded in her chest.

She could clearly see the fear and despair on Hezekiah's face.

"What do you mean you don't know who?" she asked.

Hezekiah avoided her concerned gaze. He spun the chair around until his back faced her.

"I don't want to talk about it right now, Etta. I just need to think. Maybe I'm making too much out of this."

Etta stood and softly said, "All right, Pastor Cleaveland, but you know we all love you, and no matter how bad this is, everyone will always stand behind you." She placed a hand on his shoulder. "I'm sure you'll figure something out. You always do. I'll be in the kitchen if you need me."

Chimes of the doorbell echoed through the house as she exited the room. Hezekiah turned his back to the door and said, "Whoever that is, tell them I'm not here."

Etta looked through the peephole and saw the head of Kenneth Davis.

"Pastor Cleaveland, it's me, Kenneth. Open the door. I need to talk to you," he said from the porch.

She opened the door. "Hello, Reverend Davis. Come in, but Pastor Cleaveland said he doesn't want to be disturbed."

"Hello, Etta," he said. "I'm sorry to come by unannounced, but I need to speak with Pastor Cleaveland. It's very important. Is he in his study?"

"Yes, but . . ."

Kenneth walked through the house toward the study before she could stop him. "This will take only a minute," he said over his shoulder.

Hezekiah heard the door open, and before he could see Kenneth, he shouted, "I said I don't want . . . Oh, it's you. What do you want?"

Kenneth entered and turned on the lights to reveal the crumpled man behind the desk. "Who is Danny St. John, and why didn't you tell me about him yourself?"

Hezekiah looked sternly at the towering man. "Because it's not your concern."

Kenneth closed the door and walked toward the desk.

"When you talk about stepping down and ask me to think about who your replacement will be, it is my concern. Now, please tell me what is going on."

"It sounds like you've already heard everything. Who told you? Catherine?"

"Yes, she told me, but this isn't about Catherine."

"Yes, I know. Like everything else in this church, it's about me," Hezekiah said sternly. "Well, I wish I could tell you it's all a lie, but I can't. I've been with Danny for a year now and somehow Lance Savage found out about it."

"Who told him? Who else knows about this?"

"It looks like quite a few people know. Phillip, Hector, and Jonathon had a nice little surprise for me at lunch. Catherine, and now you."

Kenneth collapsed into a chair and threw his hands into the air.

"Do you realize how serious this is? If the public finds out, they're going to crucify you in the media."

"So that's your opinion? I pay you a fortune, and all you can do is predict my demise? That's the best you can come up with? Then maybe you should resign." Hezekiah waved his hands in disgust.

"This is just like you, Hezekiah. You screw up and then blame someone else. Well, this time you can't blame anyone but yourself. I hope he was worth it, because he is going to cost you your ministry."

Hezekiah jumped from behind the desk and stood directly in front of Kenneth, who bolted to his feet. The two men stood nose to nose.

"Who do you think you are speaking to?" Hezekiah said, poking a finger into Kenneth's chest. "I'm still the pastor, and you still work for me. No one talks to me that way."

Kenneth did not demur.

"You can get angry at me if you want, but that's not going to solve anything. I'm just being honest with you. You don't seem to realize the damage a story like this can do."

Hezekiah took a step backward. "You're wrong. I do know the damage it can do. It's all I've been able to think about ever since I met him, and for some reason, I just couldn't stop seeing him."

The two men sat as the tension in the room slowly dissolved.

"It wasn't just sex," Hezekiah said, looking into Kenneth's eyes. "I actually do love him." He placed his face in his hands and said, "Oh God. What am I going to do?"

Without pausing to ponder the question, Kenneth spoke authoritatively. "The first thing you're going to do is break it off with him. And then you're going to deny everything."

Hezekiah looked up. "I can't do that," he said with deep emotion. "It'll destroy him. You just don't understand."

Kenneth grabbed Hezekiah's shoulders. "No one in the world is that important. You've had your fun with this Danny kid. Now you've got to move on. It's either him or your ministry."

Etta stood silently outside the office door with her ear pressed against the wood. She prayed Hezekiah had finally found a love strong enough to draw him away from Samantha Cleaveland.

"What sides do you want with that? We've got macaroni and cheese, pinto beans, rice, cabbage, and candied yams.

We're out of greens today," the waitress said, holding a pencil over a grease-stained order pad.

Reverend Willie Mitchell scowled. "You're always out of greens. I'll have the macaroni and cheese and cabbage. And give me a Diet Coke with that."

Willie sat in the soul food restaurant with Virgil Jackson.

The slight smell of mildew filled the air of the crowded room. Momma Lee, the restaurant's owner, sat on a stool behind the cash register, where she pretended not to look at every bite each customer took. She never trusted anyone to run the register; so after twenty years of having sat on that stool, her stomach fit perfectly into the ninety-degree angle of the counter.

The waitress looked suspiciously at Reverend Mitchell's companion. "What will you have?" She knew a crackhead when she saw one. The yellow on his fingertips and the pink scars on his lips from sucking a hot glass pipe were the first things she noticed about him.

"Get whatever you want. This is on me," Willie said.

"Then I'll have the short ribs with beans and candied yams and a Coke. Does corn bread come with that?"

The waitress nodded yes, took their menus, and abruptly left the table.

Willie rolled up the sleeves of his shirt. The paper napkin tucked into his collar was moist from the perspiration dripping down his neck. His cell phone sat on the table next to an arrangement of Louisiana hot sauce, ketchup, salt, pepper, and a jar of peppers in vinegar.

"I hear you just got out of jail. What were you in for?"

"Burglary, but I've been straight ever since."

"That's good. Where are you working at?"

Virgil knew the caliber of men like Reverend Willie Mitchell. A shallow facade of respectability and Southern charm, under which lay the heart of a man who would kill his brother, if there was something worthwhile to be gained. He played along, anyway. "Nobody's going to hire an ex-con these days. I've been looking for two months now."

"Where do you live? With your mother?"

"No. She put me out a month ago. I've been living here and there. I have a social worker at the Los Angeles Community Center. He's been trying to find a rehab program for me, but every place is full. I've been on a waiting list for over a month."

Willie snorted. "You need to get off that shit. Fucks up your brain and then dumps you in the gutter. You're too smart for that. Man, all I need is plenty of tight pussy, a good suit, and new car every year, and I'm fine." He laughed out loud at his own wit. "Don't need no shit that's going to fuck me up and take all my money."

"I haven't had any pussy in almost a year. I almost forgot what it feels like."

"I got a job for you that'll pay enough to buy all the pussy you want."

Virgil could tell by the sudden change in the reverend's demeanor that the "job" entailed something illegal. But in his current state of desperation, he was willing to do anything.

"What kind of job?" he asked suspiciously.

"I'll get to that soon enough."

The waitress returned to the table with their orders balanced on her arms. "All right. Who had the fried chicken with cabbage and macaroni and cheese?"

"Right here." The reverend moved his cell phone to the side.

"And you had the short ribs, pinto beans, and candied yams." She placed the orders on the crammed little table.

"I'll be back in a minute with your Cokes."

"Diet Coke," the reverend called out as she walked away. "And bring more butter with you." The food required their full attention for the next few minutes. Hot sauce was sprinkled liberally over all of the reverend's food. Salt and pepper seasoned his meat and everything within six inches of his plate. His corn bread crumbled as he spread on a cold pat of butter.

The waitress returned with their sodas. Virgil immediately tore open six packets of sugar and poured them into his drink.

"What the hell are you doing?" the reverend asked, with the flesh of the chicken dangling from his slippery lips.

"I have a sweet tooth."

The conversation progressed too slowly for Virgil, so he decided to give the reverend a hand. "So what kind of work are you talking about? I'm desperate. I'll do fucking anything."

"I need someone taken care of."

"What do you mean, 'taken care of'?" Virgil asked, setting the fork on his plate.

"You know what the fuck I mean. Gotten rid of. Smoked. Eliminated."

"Hey, look, old man. I can't get involved in no shit like that. The next one is my third strike. My ass would be in jail for the rest of my fucking life."

Reverend Mitchell saw the fear in Virgil's eyes. He held up his grease-smeared hands and said, "Slow down, boy. Take it easy. I'm not talking about doing anything that's going to get you caught. I'm not as stupid as I look."

He didn't want to lose him and disappoint Samantha, so he quickly introduced what he hoped would be ample incentive.

"You're a smart kid. I'm a smart man. You won't get caught. It pays ten thousand dollars. Part up front and the rest when the job is done."

Virgil heard the glass pipe calling his name. A familiar pang cramped his stomach. His lips became dry, and his eyes glazed over with a smoky film. He grabbed the Coke and took a long swallow. "It's not worth it," he said, nervously clutching the edges of the table.

Willie decided to up the ante. "All right. Twenty thousand and a plane ticket to anywhere in the fucking world you want to go."

"You're shit'n me, right? Who is it?"

"What difference does it make? Are you fucking in or not? Let me know so I can move on."

There was a long pause. Neither of the men ate. Virgil shifted from side to side in his chair while a fly buzzed over the corn bread. He pushed his plate away and asked,

"When do you want it done?"

Reverend Mitchell started eating again. He felt he had regained control. Now it was just a matter of closing the deal. His stomach churned as he recalled the urgency in Samantha's voice earlier that day. "Sunday," he said in a whisper.

"This Sunday?"

Willie looked nervously over his shoulders and whispered, "Keep your voice down, boy. You want the whole fucking place to hear? Yes, this Sunday."

Virgil stared out the window at the cars moving past the restaurant. "When would I get the money?"

"Like I said. Part up front and the rest after it's done."

"I'd want half up front."

"You think I'm fucking stupid? You'd smoke it up before you got to the corner, and I'd never see your ass again. I'll give you one thousand on Sunday morning and then meet you somewhere later and give you the rest. So what's your answer? Are you in or not?"

Virgil thought of his mother, and what he could buy her with $20,000. He also naively thought of how he could get his life on the right track with that kind of money.

"Do you have a gun?" he asked the reverend.

"Yes."

"You know if you don't pay me, I'll fucking kill you," Virgil said, looking directly into his eyes.

Under the tough, seasoned facade, Willie Mitchell was a coward. The stomach ulcer kicked with such force that the flow of sweat on his brow doubled. "You don't have to worry about that. You'll get your money."

"All right. I'm in. So who is it?"

"Hezekiah Cleaveland."

Virgil jumped up from the table and said, "You're fucking crazy. Do it yourself." He immediately walked to the door and left the restaurant.

Willie pulled the napkin from under his chin and bolted for the door past Momma Lee. She struggled to her feet and yelled, "Hey, wait a minute. You better pay for that."

Without slowing his stride, Willie shouted, "I'll be back. You'll get your fucking money."

By the time Reverend Mitchell reached the sidewalk, Virgil was a half block away and preparing to cross in the middle of the street. Traffic was heavy as he waited for a clearing. Willie caught up with him. He was winded and his shirt flap came out of his pants from the run. He grabbed Virgil's arm and said, "Wait a minute, Virgil. Hear me out. I know you need the money. What about your mother? I hear she's about to get evicted from her apartment. You don't give a shit about her?"

Virgil snatched his arm away. "Leave my mother out of this. I told you no. Now, get out of my fucking way, before I slam your fat ass into the fucking sidewalk."

Virgil had just started to step into the street when he heard Willie shout, "All right, thirty thousand dollars. Cash."

Even though the street was now clear, Virgil stopped with one foot still on the curb. He looked at Willie and asked, "Man, what is this all about? Why do you want this guy dead? What did he do to you?"

Reverend Mitchell caught his breath and said, "It's not for me. I've got a powerful associate whom he crossed and they asked me to take care of it."

"What are you getting out of it?"

Willie laughed nervously. "Nothing. At least not yet. If I do this for them, I'll get what I want soon enough."

Though he tried, Virgil could not turn away. The two men struck a deal and discussed the details as the cars whizzed by. Willie would pick up Virgil on Sunday morning in front of the Los Angeles Community Center. From there they would drive two blocks from the church, where Virgil would wait until exactly 11:30 a.m. The balcony of the church would be empty and all Virgil would have to do was get through the foyer of the church unnoticed, fire two shots, and escape as quickly as possible down Hezekiah T. Cleaveland Avenue.

"I'll meet you downtown that night with the rest of the money and drop you at the bus depot."

"Remember what I said, Reverend. If I don't get my money . . ."

"I know, I know. You don't have to say it again."

13

Eight Months Earlier

Patrons filled the lively restaurant on the waterfront in the marina. Men in light blue shirts and Bermuda shorts shared hearty laughs with their wives and companions.

Casually dressed women with windblown hair chatted while sipping steaming flavored coffees.

"Good afternoon, gentlemen. Welcome to Shutters," said the maître d' through a studied French accent. "Table for two?"

"Yes, and somewhere quiet if you have it," Hezekiah replied.

"Would you prefer the deck? It is a lovely day for the sun."

Hezekiah looked at Danny, who nodded approval, and then said, "That would be fine."

The two men followed the maître d' to the sunny deck at the rear of the restaurant. It was the sixth month of their relation-ship. Danny's khaki pants and blue buttondown shirt provided ample cover for the truth, that he was the younger man who held the heart of his elegant companion in his neatly pressed rear pocket. Together the couple struck the most innocent of poses. Maybe they were brothers, or mentor and protégé. Only one with the most sensitive radar could possibly have detected the truth about the two men.

Hezekiah hung his jacket on the back of his chair as they sat down.

"Enjoy your meal, gentlemen," said the maître d' as he bowed slightly and exited the deck.

Dark blue umbrellas shielded glass tables from the bright noonday sun. Polished silver utensils, lush linen napkins, and sparkling water goblets stood at the ready in their appointed places. Although the deck was filled with similar faces to those in the dining room, the tables were positioned farther apart, offering their occupants additional privacy. Large potted plants danced gently to music felt but not heard. The deck overlooked a glassy ocean, where sailboats drifted by lazily.

Hezekiah and Danny laughed together as they ate, obviously pleased to be in each other's company. They were not only lovers, but also the closest of friends. When they looked into each other's eyes, they saw themselves. Little lost boys searching for their reflection in the face of someone who cared.

They talked of politics, not religion. They talked about the Dodgers' chances at making it to the World Series. They talked about life, and they talked about love.

After lunch they walked along a boardwalk lined with shops selling souvenirs to the tourists that filled the cobbled path. Four pelicans lounged in the sun on a landing near the water.

After moments of silence Hezekiah said, "I want us to be together someday, Danny."

Not comprehending the gravity of the statement, Danny smiled and replied, "We are together."

"You know what I mean . . . permanently. I want us to live together. Meeting for a few hours here and there is so frustrating for me. I want us to build a life together."

"What about Samantha?"

"My relationship with Samantha is over. We're not in love, and if I stay around much longer, I'll end up hating her. I don't want that."

"So you want me to be the new Samantha? I'm sorry, Hezekiah, I can't fill those . . ."

Hezekiah moved in closer. "What are you talking about? My wanting to be with you has nothing to do with how I feel about her. Even if I did love her, I would still want us to be together."

"I don't want to be the person you run to because you suddenly realize who your wife really is. This may sound silly, but I want to be the person you come to because this is where you want to be, because it's right, not just convenient."

"I've called you a lot of things, sexy, smart, stubborn, even naive, but never convenient. Do you think these last six months have been 'convenient' for me—sneaking around, lying to cover up lies, juggling two relationships with two very demanding people? It's been hell for me, and you, of all people, should—"

"Should what? Be grateful that the great Hezekiah Cleaveland picked me. Well, I'm not grateful. You're not doing me a favor by being with me. If you're not with me because this is where you want to be, then we've both wasted our time."

"I was going to say, you of all people should understand. Why are you twisting my words around? I don't know how many other ways to say 'I love you.' If I did love Samantha, I would still love you. I've never felt about her, or anyone else, the way I feel about you. I wouldn't jeopardize my entire ministry if I didn't feel this way. You can twist my words, but I know exactly what I'm saying."

Danny stared out into the ocean. The wind gently propelled little boats past.

"I'm sorry. I've waited my whole life for someone like you, and now that you're here, I'm afraid I'll wake up one morning and you'll be gone. Sometimes I find myself pushing you away to keep from getting hurt."

Hezekiah smiled. "I thought I was the only one who felt that way."

"What about your church? Samantha will try to ruin you if she ever finds out. She'll never let you go. Her ego won't allow it."

"You let me worry about Samantha."

"This won't work, Hezekiah. You've got too much to lose."

"You don't want to be with me?"

"You know I do. It's all I ever think about. I just don't see how it could work."

At that moment walking in the sun with Danny made the risks seem worthwhile.

Their marriage had begun like so many others. Hezekiah met Samantha at the Bible Institute of Los Angeles.

He was a senior and she a sophomore. He was the intense, smart boy on campus, president of the Black Student Union, number one on the dean's list, and editor of the school newspaper. She was the attractive and popular girl whom all the boys pursued, member of the debate team, the girls' track team, and volunteer tutor for the neighborhood children.

From the beginning they were a power couple, protesting at city hall when funds were cut for social services in poor neighborhoods. If there was a cause that affected disenfranchised people, of any race, Samantha and Hezekiah could be seen on the front lines of the struggle.

Ironically, the things that attracted Samantha to Hezekiah were the same that prevented her from ever feeling she truly knew him. There was always another mistress—not a woman, but his ferocious and insatiable ambition.

Since their first year of marriage Hezekiah's obsessive and all-consuming desire to succeed in life was his first and only love. Yes, he showered her with outward affection, but still something was missing.

He skillfully concealed parts of himself from Samantha.

She could see it simmering behind his smoldering brown eyes. She could hear it lurking just beneath the words he spoke, taunting her from behind his beguiling smile.

Samantha didn't know what "it" was and couldn't be sure if he knew either. Hezekiah's secret gradually formed a chasm between them, which stretched wider as his ministry reached higher.

Samantha soon grew bitter and weary from years of foraging for the secret that Hezekiah hid so well. She began to sublimate her energy, instead, into regaining the goals she had abandoned on the day they married.

Samantha completed her doctorate in theology, but only after much personal sacrifice and constant accusations of neglect from Hezekiah.

Still, their combined outward personas were dazzling and commanding. He, the handsome pastor who could do no wrong in the eyes of the public, and she, the strikingly beautiful wife who could sway and mesmerize even Hezekiah's most fanatic critics. Their smiling faces on the front page of any magazine would double its circulation.

Their presence at a charity fundraiser would guarantee its success. The Cleavelands were Los Angeles's cherished and much loved ecumenical dynasty.

However, in the sheltered darkness of their limousine, or in the cocoon of the gated mansion, their golden smiles turned to stone. Hezekiah's secret had eclipsed even the places in his heart that he had once shared with Samantha.

The only part of him that remained for her to touch was the veneer that could be seen on the home page of their Web site, or in the pulpit of New Testament Cathedral every Sunday morning.

Rumors of Hezekiah's affairs with other women had haunted their marriage for years. The distance between them served as a sufficient buffer to protect Samantha's ego and heart. The influence and prestige she had accumulated over the years soon replaced the love Samantha once had for Hezekiah. It comforted her when she was lonely and held her at night, until she drifted into sleep.

As Hezekiah withdrew deeper into his dark, veiled world, she relied more and more on public accolades and praise to fill the void created by their hollow union.

Dino had only seen Danny St. John once. Danny and Hezekiah had already been seeing each other for five months. It was well after 1:00 a.m. on a Thursday. Hezekiah had just completed an exceptionally long negotiation session with the building contractor. When Hezekiah settled into the rear of the car it was apparent he was emotionally spent. Dino instinctively headed toward the pastor's estate.

"I'm not going home yet, Dino," Hezekiah said as his blurry eyes adjusted to the street signs. "Take me to the Adams District. I'm going to have a cup of coffee with a friend."

Dino had heard the command on many occasions before that evening. Usually, the directive came late at night when no other engagements were scheduled. Dino came to assume that "having coffee with a friend" actually meant, "I'm going to get laid."

Dino drove to the familiar apartment on the corner of Adams Boulevard and Hillcrest Avenue. Until that night Dino had never seen its occupant, although he had been to the house on many occasions before. He parked in the red zone, knowing that no police officer would dare harass him, once they learned of his distinguished passenger.

It was a large faded beige Victorian-style house that had been divided into five smaller units. Perennials lined the brick walkway leading to a steep flight of stairs. Magnolia and pine trees illuminated by antique streetlamps bristled from a gentle breeze.

The front door of the first-floor unit swung open before Hezekiah could reach the top step. An attractive young black man in his twenties, wearing baggy green pants and no shirt, stepped from a pool of darkness in the threshold. The partially clad figure immediately embraced Hezekiah and kissed him directly on the lips.

Even through the heavy cashmere overcoat Hezekiah wore that evening, Dino could see Hezekiah's body stiffen. Hezekiah sternly, yet with gentle familiarity, pushed the young man away. As he did, he turned and looked Dino directly in the eyes. The message Hezekiah sent was very clear despite the distance between the car and the man's front door. This was an assignation that must be added to the already-lengthy list of those not to be discussed with anyone, including the pastor himself.

Four months after they met, Hezekiah flew Danny, in his private jet, to San Francisco for the opening night of Porgy and Bess at the War Memorial Opera House. The two arrived in San Francisco and rode in a waiting limousine to the Fairmont Hotel.

As the bellman placed their bags neatly in the parlor, he asked Hezekiah, "Will there be anything else, Mr. Radcliff?"

"No, thank you. We can take it from here," Hezekiah responded.

Their suite had breathtaking views of the city, framed by large picture windows that wrapped around the twenty-second floor. To the right they could see the pointed tip of the Transamerica Pyramid peeking through the fog and the sparkling towers of the Golden Gate Bridge. To the left were Grace Cathedral, the Flood Mansion, and Coit Tower, with the San Francisco Bay and Alcatraz Island as the backdrop. The suite had a parquet-floor entrance that led to a paneled parlor, cream-hued French Provincial furniture, a fireplace, and wet bar.

After unpacking their bags Hezekiah and Danny made love under cascading water in the marble shower.

"I love you, Danny," Hezekiah said as he caressed Danny's glistening body in the pulsating waterfall.

Through breathless panting Danny responded, "I love you too, Hezekiah."

They took a cab to the opera house. Ticket holders wearing their finest evening dresses and black suits were beginning to arrive. As the two men exited the cab, Hezekiah gave the driver an extra twenty dollars in appreciation for getting them there on time for their dinner reservations.

The hostess in the restaurant on the bottom floor of the opera house tried her best not to look impressed as the two handsome men walked toward her. "Good evening, Reverend Cleaveland. Welcome to Patina's Cafe," said the attractive woman standing behind a well-lit podium.

"Good evening," Hezekiah responded. "I'm afraid you've mistaken me for someone else. We have reservations for two."

"I'm sorry, but you look just like . . . Yes, sir. Under what name?" she asked apologetically.

"Radcliff. Michael Radcliff," Hezekiah said, smiling at Danny.

After scanning her list she replied, "Very good, sir. Please follow me."

At their table a flurry of waiters attended their needs in rapid succession. Waters, wines, breads, and appetizers were followed by their meals. A well-dressed couple approached the table as the two laughed and recalled previous performances of Porgy and Bess they each had seen before they met.

"Excuse me," said the man shyly, "we hate to interrupt your dinner, but aren't you Hezekiah Cleaveland? My wife and I watch you every Sunday. Would it be possible for us to take a picture with you? We're here visiting from Chicago."

Hezekiah looked up with a smile and said, "I'm sorry, I'm not Hezekiah Cleaveland, but whoever he is, he must be a very handsome guy."

The couple looked disappointed. "Are you sure?" the wife asked. "I would know that face anywhere. Is Samantha with you tonight? I love her. I've read her autobiography twice. She is such an inspiration."

Hezekiah kindly responded, "I really do hate to disappoint you, but—"

Danny looked up at the couple and interrupted, "This is Hezekiah Cleaveland. He's just feeling a little shy this evening. Give me your camera and I'll be happy to take the picture for you."

Hezekiah tensed. "Danny?" he said questioningly.

"It's all right, Hezekiah," Danny reassured him.

Hezekiah stood up and the couple flanked his sides.

Danny took the picture, and the couple left smiling and apologizing profusely for disturbing their dinner, but only after asking Hezekiah to sign a menu they had taken from their table.

"Danny, I don't think that was a good idea. Pictures like that end up on the Internet."

"I realized that. That's why I took the picture so I wouldn't be in the photo. If you hadn't allowed them, they probably would have taken one of you from a distance, and I would have been in it too."

"Sounds like you've done this before. Are you sure I'm the only famous person you've dated?"

They both laughed and Danny replied, "I'm sure. And, believe me, you'll also be the last."

In the grand gold-gilded theater a bronze diva on the stage passionately sang the aria to her man: "I loves you, Porgy, don't let him take me. Don't let him handle me and drive me mad. If you can keep me, I wanna stay here with you forever, and I'll be glad."

She pleaded and wept to the rapt delight of the audience.

"Yes, I loves you, Porgy, don't let him take me. Don't let him handle me with his hot hands. If you can keep me, I wants to stay here with you forever. I've got my man."

Hezekiah affectionately brushed Danny's shoulder with his. Their knees touched as the songbird so graciously provided the prophetic soundtrack to their lives.

14
Wednesday

Catherine functioned as if it were a typical day at New Testament Cathedral. Telephone calls were returned, decisions made, and problems were solved.

Who could have leaked the story to the press? she thought while laboriously attending to the daily chores ascribed to a chief operations officer. Everyone was suspect.

Maybe it's the secretary who screens Hezekiah's calls, or maybe Dino Goodman, the pastor's driver. I've never trusted him. He must have known something was going on. Maybe he's being paid to sabotage Hezekiah.

The list of suspects grew and rationales for betrayal abounded as five o'clock drew near.

"Ms. Birdsong," came a voice from the intercom in her office. "Reverend Pryce is here for your five-fifteen appointment."

"Give me two minutes and then tell him to come in," was the instruction that followed.

Catherine quickly looked into a mirror behind her desk to check the remains of makeup under her puffy eyes. Once again she swallowed mouthwash and returned the little bottle to her purse under the desk.

"Hello, Catherine. Sorry I'm late."

From across the room Percy honed in on Catherine's troubled face.

"You look terrible. Is there something wrong? Have you been crying?" he asked, approaching her with an outstretched hand. "What has Hezekiah done to you now?"

The comment was initially said in jest, but as he walked closer, he detected the faint remnant of a tear in the corner of her eye.

Catherine extended her hand and allowed it to be enveloped by Percy's hearty grip.

"I'm fine, Reverend Pryce," she said, pointing to the chair in front of her desk and inviting him to sit. "What did you want to see me about?"

"Catherine, you can't fool me. I know something is wrong. We've known each other a long time. I think of you as a friend, and I hope you feel the same about me. Has Hezekiah done something to upset you?"

Catherine looked away, avoiding his sympathetic gaze.

There was silence for a moment and then she spoke, "Percy, something terrible has happened and I don't know what to do about it."

"Then tell me about it, maybe we can figure it out together."

"It's about Hezekiah, but he told me not to discuss it with anyone."

Percy threw his head back and laughed aloud.

"How many times have we both heard that over the years? We each know sometimes it's necessary to discuss our concerns with others we trust to make sure our perspectives are clear and unclouded by fear. Now tell me. What's going on? Maybe it's not as bad as you think."

Catherine proceeded to recount the antagonistic meeting with the reporter. It was a relief for her to tell the story to a man as wise as Percy. If anyone would know what to do, it would be Percy.

He listened attentively, shifting several times in the seat and occasionally interrupting to ask questions.

"What did Hezekiah say?" and "When is the story supposed to run?"

Catherine concluded her tale by saying, "I've never been this worried about anything in my life. I think I'm going to have a breakdown."

Percy's last question was "Who else knows about this?"

"I made the mistake of telling Kenneth. He's threatened to call Lance Savage and sue the *Chronicle*."

"Don't worry, I'll talk to Kenneth." Percy then flashed a comforting smile and said, "Catherine, it doesn't sound all that bad. You know these crazies come out of the woodwork every few years. This St. John person is probably some nut who's obsessed with

Hezekiah. I'll bet if I put a little scare into him, he'll stop spreading these lies."

"That's just it, Percy. I'm not convinced it's a lie.

Hezekiah never denied it and swore me to secrecy. Why would he do that if it weren't true?"

"What kind of mood was Hezekiah in this afternoon?"

"I have no idea," she said fretfully. "He canceled all his appointments. I haven't seen or heard from him all day."

"That's not like him. I'll see if I can reach him on his cell later this evening."

"Please don't tell him you spoke to me. Tell him you ran into Lance in the hall and he told you."

"Don't worry about that. I won't even mention your name. In the meantime we should meet with Naomi and Reverend Davis to see if we can come up with a plan for damage control, just in case the story does eventually run. Will you set that up?"

"Are you sure they can be trusted? How do we know one of them didn't leak the story in the first place?"

"Why would they do something as stupid as that? If Hezekiah is ousted, they'll both be out of a job."

"I know, but I just don't trust anyone," Catherine said.

"Right now we don't have a choice."

The two walked toward the door and embraced.

"Oh my God," Catherine said. "You wanted to talk to me about something. I'm sorry, Percy. This has got me so distracted."

"Don't worry about that. We can talk about it later. This is much more important."

Catherine had called together key staff members to decide how to address the impending scandal. Percy took the seat of power at the head of the table in the conference room. Catherine and Naomi sat to his left, with Reverend Kenneth Davis to his right.

Naomi broke the silence at the table and asked, "Where is Hezekiah? Shouldn't he be here to talk about this?"

"I thought the whole discussion might make him uncomfortable," Catherine replied. "He doesn't know we're meeting."

"I think that was a mistake," Naomi said nervously. "If he finds out we discussed this behind his back, he'll be furious."

As she spoke, she began to gather her belongings from the floor. "I don't want any part of this."

Reverend Pryce leaned forward. "Wait a minute, Naomi. There's no reason for him to find out. I just wanted us to put our heads together and come up with a plan. This meeting never took place, as far as anyone outside this room is concerned."

Naomi searched the faces in the room for signs of agreement. Everyone signified yes by nodding.

"All right, I'll stay. But if he finds out about this meeting, I'll deny I was ever here."

"Good, then," Percy said with relief. "I tried to reach Hezekiah all last night, but he didn't answer his phone. Has anyone talked to him about the alleged affair?"

Kenneth Davis then spoke. "I spoke with Hezekiah, and it's not alleged. He confirmed the whole story. There is, in fact, a Danny St. John, and they are involved in a sexual relationship."

"How long has it been going on?" Percy asked.

"He said for about a year."

Percy threw his hands into the air in disbelief. "I don't believe this," he said. "If that story is printed, all hell is going to break loose."

"We're all aware of that, Percy, but there just might be some way to convince Lance Savage to kill the story."

Kenneth looked at Naomi. "You know Lance better than all of us. What do you think? Can he be bribed, frightened off?"

Naomi shook her head. "I don't think there's any way he's going to let this slide. I've seen him in action. He's relentless once he gets his hands on anything sensational, and he stands to build a national reputation on this."

"Come on, there's got to be some way," Percy interjected.

"Every man has a price. We just have to find out what his is."

"The construction budget has one million dollars in discretionary funds," Reverend Davis said to no one in particular. "I think we should offer to buy his silence. That's the only way."

Catherine sat silently while the three debated the plan's merits. The conversation progressed more rapidly than she had wished.

She finally spoke. "I think we're getting ahead of ourselves here. What I'd like to know is who leaked the story in the first place. That's what's most important."

Naomi looked at her impatiently and said, "That's irrelevant. It's out, and now we have to deal with the consequences."

"I disagree," Catherine protested. "Let's say we are able to silence Lance. Whoever the source is could easily find another reporter to pick it up. We'll eventually have to buy off every reporter in the city."

Reverend Davis leaned back in his chair and said, "She's right. Whoever this person is, he or she is obviously very close to Hezekiah and has something to gain by him not being the pastor. Any ideas?"

"It could be anyone," Catherine said. "Even one of us."

Catherine's last words unleashed a flurry of retorts.

Naomi bolted to her feet. "If you're suggesting I'm responsible, you're crazy. I'll be out of a job if this ever gets out."

Percy raised his voice. "I take personal offense at your accusations, Catherine. I've devoted the last five years of my life to this church and I deserve better than that."

Kenneth held up his hands in an appeal for calm. "Hold on, everybody. No one is accusing anyone, but we do have to look at every possibility. Who else could have got that close to Hezekiah to know about this?"

"How about Dino, his driver?" Catherine asked. "He must have known about it. Even though I don't trust him, I think he would rather take a bullet in the head than see any harm come to Pastor Cleaveland."

Everyone nodded in consensus. Puzzled expressions formed on their faces as they pondered who might be the Judas.

Catherine, with great caution, broke the silence.

"I know this might sound crazy, but I'm going to say it, anyway. What about Samantha?"

The puzzled looks quickly changed to shock and horror.

"Catherine, how could you even think something that horrible?" they all chanted. "Samantha worships the ground Hezekiah walks on. She would rather die than see him publicly humiliated."

Catherine recoiled into her chair.

"I know, you're right. I just wanted to put it out there."

"Well, please don't ever say anything like that again," Reverend Pryce said passionately. "She's going to be hurt enough when she learns about the affair. I'd hate to see her hurt even more if a rumor like that started circulating."

Catherine sat chastised. "I'm sorry. I'm not suggesting she did it, but we have to look at all possibilities."

"Look, this idle speculation isn't getting us anywhere," Kenneth said with his hands clasped in front of his face.

"We could be here all day trying to figure out who did this. I say we go back to our original plan and offer Lance money. If the story resurfaces again later, then maybe we'll have more time to flush out the source. Not now, though. We don't have the time."

"Kenneth is right," said Naomi. "If we're going to act, we have to do it quickly."

"Are we all in agreement?" Kenneth asked.

Naomi and Percy both said yes, but Catherine simply stared out the window.

"Catherine, what about you? Do you agree or not?" Naomi asked.

"I don't think it's going to work, but if that's our only option, then yes, I agree."

Kenneth clapped his hands and said, "All right, then. I'll meet with Lance this afternoon and make the offer, and hopefully—"

"Wait a minute, Kenneth," Percy said. "I want to come with you. I'd like to have a few words with him myself."

"You don't want to upset Lance," Naomi said. "He's in control. If you threaten him, he'll turn you down flat."

"I won't threaten him. I just think we should hedge our bet with a little intimidation. Let him know if he reneges on the agreement, there will be serious consequences."

"It's risky, but it might help in the long run," said Kenneth.

"Okay, Percy, as soon as I set up a time for the meeting, I'll call you." Kenneth stood and said, "Wish us luck, everybody. We're going to need it."

Hezekiah sat and read a magazine in the waiting room of Dr. Joseph Canton. The room was bright, and light reflected off the many chrome and glass surfaces. A piano concerto by Mozart played almost undetected in the background.

Hezekiah made the trip to the Anaheim therapist not for absolution but rather to somehow relieve his apprehension through an unorthodox form of confession. He did not expect to hear words of encouragement. No Christian psychiatrist would condone his behavior, but maybe he could understand it.

Dr. Canton had served as psychiatrist and confidant to some of the most influential clergy in the country. When he explained to the receptionist that he was about to make a decision that would affect thousands of people and change his life drastically, Hezekiah was scheduled promptly for a session.

"Reverend Cleaveland," the receptionist said after returning from the doctor's inner chamber. "Dr. Canton is ready for you now."

Hezekiah entered the office and shut the door behind him before he focused on the figure standing behind the desk.

Dr. Canton was a tall, lean man with shiny white hair. His gray suit hung loosely on his body, and wire-rimmed glasses sat on the tip of his pointed nose. He walked toward Hezekiah, extended his hand, and said, "Hello, Pastor Cleaveland. I'm Dr. Joseph Canton. Please come in and sit down."

"Thank you for seeing me at such short notice. Your secretary was very kind."

"How can I help you? Of course everything we discuss within this room will be kept in the strictest of confidence."

The two men sat at angles to each other in slick leather chairs facing the front of the desk. "Of course. That's why I selected a psychiatrist and not my gardener," Hezekiah replied with a smile.

Dr. Canton laughed as Hezekiah continued speaking.

"I'm not sure where to start. By all outward appearances my life is perfect. My ministry is growing faster than I can keep up with. We're building a new state-of-the-art sanctuary and media center. I have a beautiful wife and daughter. It all looks great."

"Well, Hezekiah. May I call you Hezekiah? If everything is great, I can't imagine why you would be here today."

Hezekiah looked out the window and saw a sea of silver high-rise buildings. He felt like a child confessing to his father that he had stolen sweets from the cookie jar. A wave of shame and embarrassment filled his chest.

"Maybe this wasn't a good idea."

"I'm not saying I can help you with whatever it is that's troubling you, but we'll never know unless you tell me what it is. There is nothing that you can tell me that will embarrass or shock me. Like you, I've pretty much heard it all."

Hezekiah took a deep breath and slouched in the chair. "Okay. To start with, my marriage is over."

The doctor nodded for him to continue.

"We've done and said things that we'll never be able to undo, and I'm not sure that I want to. When we first married and were building the ministry, I appreciated and even relied on her take-charge personality. Now I feel like it's choking the life out of me. She is a very beautiful woman—smart, creative—but she treats me like an employee. Telling me where I should go, whom I should talk to, what I should preach about."

"Have you talked to her about how you feel?"

"I've tried, but . . ."

"You've tried, but what?"

"She doesn't listen."

The doctor looked pensively at Hezekiah. "Is this about your wife or is this about you? What is really causing you to have such negative feelings toward her?"

"All right, Doctor, I'm just going to say it. The bottom line is I'm in love with someone else. I didn't mean for it to happen. It just . . ." Hezekiah clasped his hands together as if contemplating a difficult task. The doctor's face showed no sign of reaction.

Hezekiah continued to talk. "I've know him . . ." He paused and looked as though he had delivered a punch line to a joke. "Did I forget to mention it was a man?"

"Yes, you did. Have you always had homosexual tendencies?"

Hezekiah looked embarrassed. "I suppose maybe I have. But I never acted on them."

"Hezekiah, if you want me to help, you have to be honest with me. I'm not here to judge you. I'm here to listen and, if I can, to help you."

Hezekiah looked out the window and said softly, "There was another man a few years ago. He was a dancer I met in New York. I went to a play he was performing in on Broadway and a mutual friend introduced us backstage."

"Why did it end?"

"It was primarily a physical relationship. And the distance made it difficult for us to see each other that often. He eventually met someone else and we lost contact after a while."

"So now there's . . . What is the new person's name?"

"Danny."

"So now there is Danny. Tell me about him," Dr. Canton said as he removed his glasses and leaned farther back in his chair.

"He works with the homeless in downtown Los Angeles. I saw him on a corner about a year ago and asked him if he would speak to a homeless woman living near my church. When I approached him, my intention was only to help that woman."

"I don't doubt that. Please go on."

"But when I looked in his eyes, something just clicked in my brain. He was so handsome and his voice was so gentle. There was something so vulnerable about him. I still see that in him to this day."

"How else is this different from the man you were involved with in New York?"

"Like I said, that was just physical. With Danny it's . . ."

"It's what?" Dr. Canton prompted.

"It's more. Yes, it's physical, of course, but it's also emotional and even spiritual. Sometimes I feel like we are connected on a deeper level. It's very difficult to describe."

"Are you in love with him?" Dr. Canton asked delicately.

"Isn't that rather obvious?"

"Yes, but I didn't want to assume."

Hezekiah shrugged his shoulders. "I've known him for almost a year now, and I've decided to leave my wife to be with him."

Still no reaction from the doctor.

"He's the most beautiful person I have ever met. I've never been this happy before in my life. I know this sounds crazy. It sounds ridiculous to me every time I say it, but I've pretty much made up my mind. When I'm with him, nothing else in the world matters. He doesn't judge me. He doesn't expect anything from me. I can just relax and be myself."

"Hezekiah, that implies that you are not yourself at other times."

"Maybe that's true. Maybe everything else is just an act. Everyone around me has expectations of how I should behave, what I should wear, say, and think. But he doesn't. He accepts me for who I am at the moment. And to be honest, I think he's helped me to discover who I am for myself, for the first time in my life."

"He sounds perfect. So why have you come to me?"

"I really don't know. I think I wanted someone to hear me say the words, to see the reaction on someone's face so I could gauge what to expect from the rest of the world. I just needed to say it to someone."

"Have you told your wife?"

"I told her this week about Danny. She said she knew I was seeing someone, but she didn't know it was a man. I haven't told her about leaving yet."

"Why have you hesitated?"

"I just decided this week. I plan on telling her after this Sunday." Hezekiah went on to recount the inner struggles he faced.

Dr. Canton gave no indication of emotion. He only asked questions that he knew Hezekiah had already asked himself. The doctor was very familiar with the subject.

Ministers from around the country had sat in the same chair and shared almost identical stories. Some spoke of female lovers. Others spoke of men. Regardless of the gender of the object of their affection, the pain was the same.

"Hezekiah," the doctor said after the details of the saga were exhausted. "I'm not here to judge you. I'm here to help you sort through your feelings. I would imagine they run very deep right now. You seem like an exposed bundle of nerves, sensitive to every word, every move, and every gesture, which is understandable under the circumstances."

Hezekiah rested his head on the back of the chair and spoke. "I don't expect you to understand, Doctor. I just needed you to listen, and you've done a good job. I'm very grateful. I've searched my heart and prayed more about this than anything in my life. I always end up at the same place."

"And where is that?"

"Back in a place where I'm happy, where I don't feel guilty, and where I'm not ashamed about who it is I love. It's a good place, and I don't want to leave."

The level of resolve in his voice surprised the doctor.

"I'd like to help you with this problem," he said. "We, of course, won't be able to solve it today, but I would like for you to come back next week before you talk to your wife about it. I'd like to help you figure out how to save your marriage and your ministry. Would you allow me to do that?"

"I think it's too late, Doctor."

"It's never too late to do the right thing." They exchanged a few more words when a gentle reminder sounded on the desk. The two men stood and shook hands.

"I hope to see you next week, Hezekiah."

"I'll think about it. Thank you for listening."

As Hezekiah pressed the button summoning the elevator, he knew that this would be the last time he would ever see Dr. Joseph Canton again.

Danny sat alone as he sipped a frothy latte at the coffee shop a block from his home on Crenshaw Boulevard. The smell of freshly brewed coffee filled the space, and the compact disc "Pick of the Day" was playing over the shop's sound system. It was a funky little café with overstuffed secondhand sofas and chairs placed in positions that allowed customers varying degrees of privacy while they leisurely enjoyed exotic blends and overpriced pastries.

Customers stood three deep at the counter ordering subtly nuanced variations of the traditional steaming cup of joe. Other patrons sat in chairs and sofas and read the morning newspaper, or busily tapped away on laptop computers. Danny was lucky enough to get his favorite table in an alcove at the front window. Here he could be assured that no one would sit close enough to subject him to an irritating one-sided cell phone conversation consisting of, "Who will be at the meeting today? Why was she invited?" or, "Where would you like to have dinner? I hear the food there is lousy. Okay, that sounds like a good idea."

Danny was reading the local section of the paper, when he felt the familiar vibration of his telephone in his pocket.

The caller ID indicated it was his friend Kay Braisden, who had recently moved to Washington, D.C.

"Hello, Kay," he said. "How are you?"

Danny and Kay had been friends since college. She was the same age as Danny, a devout Christian, and the daughter of a pastor. By all outward appearances they seemed an unlikely pair. But the reality was they were very much alike. She was pretty, prim, and proper, and he was the soulful poet who preferred staying home on Saturday night over dancing the night away out at the hottest new nightclub with the beautiful, young, and gay crowd.

"Don't 'how are you' me, Danny St. John," Kay answered snippily. "I've been trying to reach you for two weeks now. Why haven't you returned my calls?"

"I know. I'm sorry. I haven't been a very good friend to you lately, but I've been really busy here. What is going on with you in D.C.? Have you found an apartment yet?"

"I couldn't find one in Washington, but I finally got a cute brownstone just over the bridge in Virginia. I can't wait for you to see it. It has the coziest fireplace and original fixtures. It's two stories and I actually like my neighbors. It's a bit pricey, so I had to get two roommates. One is a writer and the other a buyer for a boutique in DC. You'll like them. When are you going to come and see me? I can't wait to show you around."

Danny hesitated. "I'm not sure when I'll be able to get away."

"All right, Danny. Who is he?"

"What do you mean?" Danny asked shyly.

"I know you very well. Whenever you disappear like this, I know you're seeing someone. Now tell me who it is this time."

Danny paused and then said, "You're right. I am seeing someone, but—"

"I knew it." Kay interjected and continued with a flurry of questions. "I want to know everything. Who is he? Where did you meet him? How old is he? What does he look like? What does he do for a living?"

"Slow down, Kay. I can't say who it is. You would know him."

"Why? Is he famous? Did you snag yourself one of the Lakers?"

"No, he's not an athlete," Danny replied with a hint of exasperation in his voice. "I really don't want to talk about it. Can we please change the subject? I saw your sister last week at the market. She said your father is thinking about retiring."

"Danny, I thought I was your best friend. Why are you afraid to tell me his name? Do you think I'm going to blab it to the newspapers?"

"Don't be ridiculous. That never crossed my mind. To be honest, I'm concerned that you might judge me."

"I didn't overreact when you told me you were gay, did I?" she asked defensively.

"As a matter of fact, you did. You didn't speak to me for a week after I told you."

"I apologized for that. It just took me some time to get used to the idea."

"I know, and I accepted your apology. But for that whole week I thought I had lost my best friend. I don't want to go through that again. What you think of me is very important, and I don't want to risk our friendship."

"Why would you think this would upset me?"

"Because he's a married man." Danny took a deep breath and continued. "And a minister."

Kay did not respond. There was a long moment when no words were exchanged. Then Danny said, "You see. I knew this would upset you. That's why I haven't told you about him. I've never done anything like this before, but I love him."

To Danny's relief Kay finally spoke. "Who is he?" she asked with no expression in her tone.

"Hezekiah Cleaveland."

Danny could hear a slight gasp escape from her lips.

"Danny," she said with great hesitation in her voice, "I don't believe this. Honey, you know I love you, but this is wrong. He's a married man."

"I don't need you to tell me that. I've gone over this a thousand times in my head. I've wanted to break it off with him, but I just can't."

"Danny, I accepted the fact that you are gay, even though I never told you it broke my heart. I even held my tongue when you were dating that horrible egomaniac from San Francisco. But this . . ."

Danny did not interrupt, and allowed Kay's words to continue their painful course.

"Danny, I have to pray about this. I don't know what to say."

"I understand, Kay."

"I love you, Danny."

"I know you do."

"I'll call you in a few days."

"Good-bye, Kay."

Danny stared out the window of the café. The morning traffic had begun to subside, and the paper no longer held stories of interest to him. He knew this would be the last time he would receive a call from Kay Braisden.

15

Hattie had not slept well the night before. Exhausted and still a bit groggy, she made a strong pot of coffee, sat under the bird lamp, and turned her weathered brown leather Bible, with King James Version embossed in gold on the cover, to the Twenty-third Psalm. The dates of her mother's and father's births and deaths were recorded on the front pages of the Bible. The marriages, births, baptisms, and deaths of the Williams and Fisher, Hattie's maiden name, families were all chronicled within the pages of the Bible. Yellow highlighter striped passages on every page, and all the margins contained Hattie's handwritten notes in black, red, blue, and graphite.

Hezekiah had appeared in her dream again the night before. Hattie clearly saw Hezekiah's body falling through the sanctuary at New Testament Cathedral with a force that would ensure death. Members of the congregation scrambled frantically to clear a space on the sanctuary floor. Feathered and flowered hats scurried around the room like brightly colored marbles that had been spilled from a schoolgirl's sack onto the pavement. Choir members in flowing robes and sashes ran to safety and screamed, "Pastor Cleaveland is falling!"

Mothers shielded the eyes of their small children from the scene that would surely scar their young minds for life, while old ladies in sensible shoes hobbled away from the inevitable point of impact.

Hezekiah could see the look of horror and fear in the eyes of his beloved members even at the pace that his body fell. Women whose powdered cheeks he had kissed and men whose hands he had firmly shaken now ran with abandon from the one they once called pastor, shepherd, and friend.

The dream had faded as quickly as it had appeared.

Hattie now pondered the scene that had played like a movie in her dream. Was the pedestal they had placed him on too high and unstable? Everyone knew a fall from so high was inevitable, but still they had insisted Hezekiah take the place of honor above their heads and beyond their reach. What mortal could survive at such heights? she thought. How could his soul find peace at elevations so dangerously close to the sun?

Hattie sat still under the glow of the lamp with her feet planted firmly on the floor and hands resting on the open pages of the Bible.

"Hold on, Pastor Cleaveland," she said softly. "I'm praying for you."

Samantha drove her car into the parking lot of the church. She retrieved her purse from the seat and walked briskly through the corridors toward Catherine's office.

Catherine Birdsong was sitting behind her desk. She wore a green skirt and a white ruffled blouse with a floral scarf around her neck. She looked like a woman who wrestled daily in front of her mirror to find a look befitting her station in life as chief operations officer to a prominent church.

A large, curved desk surrounded Catherine. The walls were covered with plaques that the church and pastor had received over the years. A fax machine and copier sat in the corner, and Catherine's desk held a computer, telephone, and pad.

"Good morning, Mrs. Cleaveland," she said to Samantha, who was standing in her doorway. "Pastor Cleaveland hasn't arrived yet. He called earlier and said he would be late."

"I'm not here to see Hezekiah. I'm here to see you."

Catherine saw the familiar hint of anger in Samantha's eyes. She adjusted her chair in preparation to stand. "Is there something I can do for you?"

"Yes." Her voice began to escalate. "You can tell me why you've been covering for Hezekiah when I call and he's not here. Why you've never mentioned to me that he's been unable to account for his whereabouts lately, and why do you think it's in your job description to interfere in my marriage?"

Catherine's eyes widened. Her knees shook as she braced herself on the desk and stood. "I'm not sure what you're talking about. I—"

Samantha cut her off. "Don't lie to me. You know exactly what I'm talking about. You are not to decide what information I should and should not have about my husband or this church. I knew this wasn't going to work out when I first met you. I knew you wouldn't fit in here."

Catherine could not speak. She found her throat was contracting as she tried to sputter out her defense. "I . . . I never . . ."

"Don't bother. I don't want to hear anything you have to say. It's over. You're fired. I want you out of here by the end of the day, and you better leave every stapler, paper clip, and pen, or I'll have the police at your door to get them back." Samantha clutched the purse under her arm and stormed out of the office.

Catherine sat down as the telephone rang. It was impossible for her to contain her tears. She felt as though breath had been snatched from her lungs by an incubus that had descended from the steeple of the church. The ringing of her unanswered telephone echoed through the empty halls of the building.

The *Los Angeles Chronicle* newsroom was busy as usual. Loud conversations mingled into an indecipherable buzz through the long, windowless room. Sounds of clanging computer keyboards, whirring copy machines, and ringing telephones flooded the space. The anonymous faces behind the stories that chronicled life in the city worked furiously to meet yet another deadline.

Lance Savage sat at a corner desk with his eyes on a glowing computer screen. His fingers tapped furiously at the keyboard, making the final revisions to the article he had toiled over for the last six months:

> When confronted in his office at New Testament Cathedral, Pastor Cleaveland refused to comment on the allegations of the one-year affair with Mr. St. John.
>
> Sources close to Pastor Cleaveland have confirmed that he has been seen on numerous occasions going into St. John's home in the Adams District. St. John has not returned calls to the *Los Angeles Chronicle*.

Lance paused as he read the last line on the computer screen. He had, in fact, never attempted to contact Danny.

Hezekiah's shouting face flashed in his mind. He had denied the allegations so adamantly that a trace of doubt prevented Lance from further typing. *What if Cynthia is lying?* he thought. *What if this Danny person is just a cousin or a family friend?*

There had been no doubt concerning the relationship with the young outreach worker until the explosive confrontation with Hezekiah. But the look in Hezekiah's eyes, the indignation in his voice, caused Lance to hesitate. Had he overlooked some important piece of evidence?

Lance had questioned Cynthia Pryce's motives when she first contacted him with the unbelievable story six months earlier.

"Mrs. Pryce," he had asked when they spoke on the telephone months earlier. "Why are you coming forward with this story? You know if this is true, Hezekiah will be forced to step down as pastor."

"I know," she replied. "But I can't sit by any longer and watch the Cleavelands waste so much of God's money building that horrible shrine to themselves. That money could be used to do so much good in the world. It's time someone exposed them for the immoral and greedy people they are."

"So what is his alleged lover's name, and how did you find out about him?" Lance asked, making no attempt to conceal his skepticism.

"His name is Danny," she answered confidently. "He's a homeless-outreach worker. I found out about it by accident."

"By accident?" Lance asked.

"Yes, by accident. I was in a meeting with Hezekiah and several other people in the church conference room, and Hezekiah needed a document he had left on his desk and asked me if I wouldn't mind getting it for him. When I went into his office, his computer was on. There was a half-written love letter to Danny on the screen. I did a search for other e-mails sent to that address and found dozens of disgusting messages they had sent to each other. I printed as many as I could. I didn't have time to print them all because Hezekiah was waiting for me to return to the meeting. You can see them, if you don't believe me."

Lance had thoroughly investigated the story after the conversation with Cynthia. He reviewed all the e-mails between Hezekiah and Danny. Several telephone calls to agencies that serve the homeless in Los Angeles led him directly to Danny St. John. He even followed Hezekiah's limousine one evening to the house in the Adams District and saw Danny for the first time as he greeted his illustrious guest at the door.

Lance had also secretly followed Danny on his rounds for two weeks. Through the parks, under freeway passes, to homeless shelters, and to the emergency room at Los Angeles General Hospital, where the young man had accompanied a woman who later died from an overdose of heroin.

From a safe distance, ducking behind buildings, cars, and lurking in the shadows, Lance marveled at Danny's gentle manner. Without fail, he held the scab-covered hands and patted the weary backs of disheveled men and women whose singular existence was never acknowledged by housed residents of the city. They were simply called "the homeless," a lumbering beast roaming the city.

Danny was the embodiment of the compassion that the creature craved so desperately.

Lance could not bring himself to confront Danny after all he had witnessed. He didn't want to disturb the gentle spirit he'd seen wandering the streets with the green backpack on his back, bending down to touch the weary shoulders of so many destitute people. Lance grew surprisingly fond and, against his better judgment, protective of the Danny he had come to know during those two weeks.

Moisture began to accumulate in the palms of his hands. The toxic words begged for closure as his eyes focused again on the computer screen. *I don't have a choice*, he thought. *I've got to interview Danny or I don't have a story.*

Danny's weekly outreach schedule was predictable. He arrived at the homeless center on Central Avenue. There he would encourage members of the large crowd to visit the city's free clinic, where their myriad wounds and infections could be treated.

The large, open space was busy with activity. Men in tattered clothes and worn-out shoes sat transfixed in front of a large television screen, watching the *Today Show*. In the facility's shower area, women made futile attempts at washing away the streets' grime, while others slept in crumpled heaps on the floor, preparing for another night of aimless wandering through the city.

He walked through the room, searching for those in obvious need of medical attention: the man nursing a swollen foot, the woman cradling a bruised arm, or the old lady cowering in a corner with an open wound on her emaciated and frightened face. There was never a shortage of candidates for his services.

Danny spotted a man limping through the crowd. His pant leg was torn, exposing a deep gash on his right leg.

"Excuse me, sir," Danny said, approaching the man. "That cut looks pretty bad. You should have a doctor look at it at the free clinic."

The man turned around slowly, attempting to maintain his balance. His white hair pointed in every direction from beneath a red bandanna. A scraggly yellow-stained mustache dipped in and out of his mouth as he spoke.

"Who are you?" he asked in a raspy voice.

The smell of alcohol and stale breath met Danny's nose immediately. "My name is Danny." He smiled disarmingly.

"I work for the Homeless-Outreach Team. I can make an appointment for you with a doctor, if you would like."

The man steadied himself on his good leg. "Some strung-out junkies jumped me last night. I was drinking with them out in Griffith Park and all of a sudden they just started beat'n the shit outta me. Took my last two dollars, too, fucking assholes." He leaned over to show Danny the wound on his leg.

"Cut me with a knife here," he said. Then, standing erect again, he raised his shirt to reveal yet another gash on the side of his torso. "And here," he said. "I'da gave 'em the fucking two dollars if they'd just asked for it."

Danny escorted the man to the only vacant seat in the lobby. "You really shouldn't be walking around with those wounds. You might have some internal damage. I'm going to have our outreach van come and pick you up and take you to the clinic. What's your name?"

"Nathanial Ford. Folks call me Nate."

"All right, Nate. Just wait here. I'll be back in a moment."

Danny made his way to the receptionist counter. "Hi, Chris," he said to an attractive Asian woman with wide brown eyes behind the counter. "Can I use your telephone? I have to call for a van to pick up Mr. Ford and take him to the clinic, and the battery on my cell phone is almost dead."

"Hello, Danny," she responded with a smile. "Looks like Nate got beat up pretty bad again last night."

Danny nodded in affirmation as the woman handed him the telephone.

"Hi, Emma. It's Danny. Could you send the van to the drop-in center on Central? I need to have someone transported to the clinic."

After completing the arrangement, Danny thanked the receptionist and headed back to the old man in the lobby.

As he made his way through the crowd, he felt a light tap on his shoulder. When he turned, he saw the clean-shaven face of a man who looked out of place in the room filled with homeless people.

"Excuse me. May I speak with you for a moment?" he said. "My name is Lance Savage. I work for the *Los Angeles Chronicle*."

"I'm sorry. I'm not authorized to speak to the media," Danny said, turning to walk away. "It's against agency policy. You'll have to call my supervisor."

"This isn't about the homeless, Mr. St. John," Lance said with a hint of regret in his voice. "Is there somewhere we can speak in private?"

The sound of his name spoken by the stranger startled him.

"How do you know my name?" he asked.

"I know a lot about you, Danny. May I call you Danny? This is about Hezekiah Cleaveland."

Danny began to walk away.

"I've never met him."

"I know all about you two," Lance said as he followed Danny through the crowd. "And I've already spoken to Pastor Cleaveland."

Danny stopped in the center of the room when he heard the words. He fought off the urge to run to the nearest exit.

Lance stood behind Danny and spoke in a whisper. "If it's not true, Danny, you can deny it. This is the only chance I'm going to give you."

Danny did not respond. It was clear that the stranger in the wrinkled sport coat knew something of his relationship with Hezekiah. But how had he found out?

"This will only take a minute, Danny," Lance said in a soft and reassuring tone.

The sound of Lance's voice jarred Danny from his silent contemplation. His eyes focused again on the whirl of activity around him.

"Meet me in front of the building in five minutes," he said without looking at Lance. "I have to finish helping someone."

Lance stood on the busy street in front of the center and took the last puff from a cigarette. Noise from traffic streaming by drowned out the loud conversations and blaring television set from the room he had just left.

Through the windows he could see Danny bending over to speak to the weathered old man in the lobby. After a few moments Danny approached him on the street.

"Thanks for agreeing to talk with me, Danny. I know this is difficult for you."

Danny did not respond.

"Would you like to comment on your relationship with Pastor Cleaveland?"

"Who told you about that? Did Hezekiah say something?"

"I'll be honest with you, Danny. Hezekiah didn't confirm your relationship."

"Then what makes you think it's true?"

"I have a source who is very close to Hezekiah who can prove that you two are involved."

"Who?"

"I can't say. I can tell you, though, that I have been given a substantial amount of evidence that proves it."

"Why are you doing this to him? Do you hate him that much?"

"I'm not doing anything other than my job. This is a significant story, and people have a right to know about it."

"Why do they have a right to know something so private about him?" Danny asked. "He has rights too. He has the right to have some part of his life to keep to himself."

"I'm sorry, Danny, but he doesn't. When Hezekiah became a public figure, he gave up the right to privacy. Every part of his life is fair game and subject to public scrutiny. He must have told you that."

"He's told me a lot of things, but that doesn't make them right."

"So you admit that you do know him," Lance said gently, as though speaking to a small child.

Danny's eyes drifted wearily to the procession of cars that sped by. "Is there any way I can convince you not to pursue this? You're going to hurt a lot of innocent people."

"I'm not trying to hurt anyone. I just want the truth, and I want to give you a chance to tell your side of the story," Lance said innocently.

Danny looked sharply back at Lance. "You don't give a fuck about all the good Hezekiah has done for this city. What's important to you is furthering your career, and if someone gets hurt, or a few lives are ruined in the process, you justify it by saying, 'I'm just doing my job.' Well, you've come to the wrong person. I'm not going to help you do your job."

Danny peered deeply into Lance's widening eyes and continued his tirade. "For the record, Mr. Savage, I have never met Hezekiah Cleaveland. I have no desire to meet Hezekiah Cleaveland, and if my name appears in your paper in relation to this lie, I will contact my father's law firm in New York and they will be happy to sue the *Los Angeles Chronicle*, and you personally, for slander and defamation of character."

With these final words Danny adjusted the backpack on his shoulder, tipped his head in a gesture of farewell, and fell into step with the flow of pedestrians.

Lance stood astonished as Danny disappeared into the moving crowd. He had severely miscalculated the cunning of his prey.

Hezekiah has schooled him well, he thought while fumbling anxiously for the package of cigarettes. *Cynthia had better be right about this.*

16

Thursday

Samantha and Hezekiah still had an undeniable physical attraction, despite the chasm that had developed between them. Hezekiah was a man who found refuge and peace in the pleasure that physical contact gave him.

Samantha, however, viewed erotic pleasure as simply another means by which to possess the body and soul of her prey, if only for a few brief moments.

The further apart they had grown over the years, the more intense their lovemaking had become. Hezekiah and Samantha woke together to find their bodies entwined, as they had on so many mornings before. As Hezekiah slowly emerged from his sleep, he felt his morning erection pressing against Samantha's soft thigh. Gentle brushing from the satin of Samantha's nightgown made her nipples stand firm.

By the time they had gained full consciousness, there was no turning back. Hezekiah grabbed the hair on the back of her head and pressed her lips to his. Their nightclothes provided ample shields for raw emotions, and their bodies did what seemed only natural. Hezekiah pinned her arms above her head as she twisted violently beneath the weight of his body. Her hands broke free and she plunged her fingernails into his back. He refused to allow her to squirm from beneath him, and she refused to be released.

"Fuck me. Hezekiah, please fuck me," Samantha whispered as she held him close.

Blankets and sheets lay in a bundle at the foot of the bed. Hezekiah entered her with such force that her head, cushioned only by the pillows, rocked the huge headboard.

After moments of intense rhythmic pounding, Samantha forced her body on top, with Hezekiah still deep inside her. Her straddled legs held him like a vise beneath her silk nightgown. Her breast broke free from the garment as she moaned with each downward plunge. He slapped her face and grabbed her neck as if to choke her. In time he released her, not to spare her life but to slap her buttocks as though encouraging a horse to run faster.

Hezekiah groped for the side of the mattress when he knew the end was near. The edges of the large bed extended beyond his reach, so he gripped the sheets and braced himself for the reward of the pounding he had endured.

For the brief moments of climactic pleasure, the two could only hear, see, smell, and feel the overpowering sensations rushing through their bodies. There was no hate, no jealousy, and no remorse. There was only ecstasy.

Samantha collapsed, spent, on her side of the bed. She brushed the hair from her face with her last bit of energy.

Hezekiah's chest continued to heave in attempts to regain the breath he had lost. Slowly their eyes focused on the light surrounding their bed. The feelings they had just shared began to dissolve and were replaced with remorse. Remorse for succumbing to desires they thought were no longer shared. Desires that only complicated their journey. The course of which was now irreversible.

No words were exchanged. They had none left. All that had to be said from that point on required no response.

There were no more questions. There were only answers.

Hezekiah got out of bed, nightclothes still intact, and went into the bathroom. Samantha lay with her back to him, hoping he would be quick and leave her to wash from her body and memory what would be the last time he was in her, and she in him. Still in a daze she angrily kicked the bedcovers to the floor and checked the clock on her nightstand. Why had she done it? She searched for the answer in the light of the window and fought back tears when there was no response.

***

Danny stood at his living-room window looking out into the busy street below. The tidy apartment was filled with flea market and garage sale finds. His bare feet were planted firmly on an Asian-print rug he'd found abandoned at a curb, and a tea table bought at a thrift shop held his morning cup of coffee.

Female joggers, with ponytails bouncing behind, ran along the sidewalk. From his window he could see four homeless men bundled in sleeping bags at a bus stop across the street. He had never offered his services to the group of regulars, fearing that if he had, they would discover where he lived and return for additional kindness.

The little apartment was his only refuge, and even he could not share it with the needy people to whom he had dedicated his life.

There had been no rest for him the night before. He tossed in bed and watched infomercials on television. Twice during the course of the restless evening, Danny had picked up the telephone to dial Hezekiah's cell phone, but each time he resisted. The next conversation would surely mark the end of their relationship.

Through his twenties Danny had searched for the one man willing to look in his eyes and tell him honestly what he saw. Did he see a kind man with a loving heart, or a hideous monster intent on destroying all in its path? Was there a child playing behind his brown eyes, or a weary old man eager to share all that his life had taught?

But no one had stayed long enough or looked deeply enough to explore the depths of Danny's heart. No one, until Hezekiah.

Hezekiah offered himself as a mirror, reflecting images that Danny had never seen before. When they were together, Danny saw his own countenance for the first time in Hezekiah's comforting smile. He felt his own warmth in Hezekiah's embrace. He heard his joy in Hezekiah's laugh and tasted his fears in his kiss. Without him the light in his soul would be dim once again, and the Danny he had come to know would be lost forever.

Danny's cat, Parker, purred around his feet, waiting for the morning tummy rub that was long overdue. Footsteps from the neighbors above leaving for the day could be heard on the stairs near his door. Danny asked himself, over and over again, the same questions in his mind. *Is Lance Savage bluffing and really has no proof? How did he find me? Who could have known? How can I continue living in this city once everyone finds out?*

The questions were unending, and no answers came to provide refuge from his fears. Fear had prevented him from going to work that morning, and also from scratching Parker's fuzzy gray belly. His life was ending; yet the joggers continued to run, smiling news anchors continued reporting tragedy after tragedy on television, and steam continued to rise from his coffee cup.

As the cat's purring grew more insistent, Danny, without moving his feet, bent down and gently scratched his stomach. Parker rolled blissfully onto his back, and then the telephone rang.

Hezekiah's strained voice came through the black box.

"Hello, Danny," Hezekiah said softly. "I called your cell, and I called your office this morning, but they said you were out sick. I hope it's nothing serious. Look, baby, something pretty serious is going on and I need to talk to you as soon as possible. You know I love you. I'll try again later."

A tear rolled down Danny's cheek as he continued to comfort the little rescued cat at his feet. There was no longer a need to remain at the window. There was no safe place for him to stand. The world had forced open his front door and barged in without invitation. The books on the shelves, magazines on the coffee table, and the chipped plates in the cupboard no longer belonged to him.

He looked around the room. The pale walls had lost their warm glow. The voices on television seemed louder than before. Had the walls inched in closer? Did someone rearrange the furniture? Were the leaves on the potted plants suddenly wilting, and had Parker stopped purring at his feet? Nothing in the room seemed familiar anymore.

On that morning Danny found the world to be lonelier and more frightening than he had ever imagined possible.

Hezekiah sat quietly in the rear of the limousine as Dino drove toward the church. He thought about how much he loved sex with Danny and compared it to the regrettable physical encounter he had just had with Samantha.

They both were wildly passionate and tinged with the slightest hint of abuse. But at this point in Hezekiah's life, Danny was now his companion of choice.

Although Samantha had been silent for much of the previous evening and the morning, she seemed to handle his startling revelation with a surprising amount of restraint.

They had exchanged no further words on the subject, which led him to believe she had resigned herself to the situation.

He thought of her beauty and knew she could have any man she selected. He would leave her wanting for nothing.

She can have that awful house. He would continue to pay for her extravagant lifestyle. Samantha had never worked a day in her life and the only line on her résumé would read, "Dutifully served as the wife of Pastor Dr. Hezekiah T. Cleaveland."

She was nineteen years old when they met. Tall and skinny, but mature for her age. While other girls were throwing themselves at the feet of the handsome young man, Samantha ignored him. She considered him incapable of providing her with the life she knew she deserved.

Nonetheless, he pursued her relentlessly, taking her for walks on campus and bringing her mother flowers every time he came to visit.

Samantha gradually began to see in him what he had always seen in himself. A man that could stir the souls of anyone he came in contact with. A man whose magnificent future was as apparent as his striking good looks. He knew he was handsome, but he had never relied on his looks to get ahead. He had something more important, sincerity. When he spoke to you, even if only to say hello, it was as though no one else in the world existed. You had his full attention, and whatever you had on your mind was important to him.

The limousine turned into the parking lot of the church.

As he walked toward Catherine's office, he heard the telephone ringing. At the door he could see Catherine crying, with her head on the desk.

"Catherine," he shouted and entered the room. "Catherine, what's wrong?" He lifted her by the shoulders. "Stop crying and tell me what happened."

She looked as if she had been physically assaulted.

Mascara ran down her cheeks and a scarf was twisted around her neck like a hangman's noose.

"Samantha was just here. She fired me."

"Fired you. Why? What did she say?"

"She accused me of covering for you. I didn't even have a chance to defend myself. She just stormed in, fired me, and left."

Hezekiah could hear his heart pounding in his ears. He had learned to tolerate the sometimes volatile behavior of his wife, but he could never stand by and allow her to attack innocent people. "She crossed the line this time. You didn't deserve to be treated that way."

"Now what am I going to do?" she asked through sobs.

"Come on, stop crying. This entire thing is my fault. You had nothing to do with it."

"Pastor Cleaveland, you've got to tell her. She wouldn't listen to me."

"Don't worry, Catherine. She can't fire you. I hired you and I'm the only one who can fire you. Everything is going to be fine," he said, hugging her. She rested her head on his chest. "I'm so sorry you had to go through this, Catherine."

"I've never seen her that angry before. I thought she was going to throw something at me. I was frightened. Why does she treat people like that? She has no right."

When her sobs began to subside, Hezekiah said, "You let me worry about Samantha. Now go to the ladies' room and clean yourself up," he said, smiling. "Remember, we've got twenty million dollars to raise."

The intoxication from thoughts of Danny mingled in his head with rage at Samantha and pity for the trauma-stricken Catherine. He now knew what he had to do.

Leave Samantha, move in with Danny, and accomplish this feat while maintaining the ministry he had dedicated his life to.

He could tell people that Danny was his housekeeper, or maybe the son of a dear friend in Texas. *There has to be a way to make this work*, he thought.

Particulars of the complicated process raced through his mind. The church was not big enough for the both of them. Samantha would have to leave it and join another one. There was no way he could look at her each Sunday in the audience with venom darting from her eyes. He could pay her to leave the church. Promise her something, anything she wanted, to let him go and allow him to start a new life.

Hezekiah, Samantha, and Jasmine sat at their dining-room table having dinner. Etta busily set platters and bowls of food around the well-appointed table. No one spoke and eye contact was avoided.

Over the years Etta had seen the Cleavelands at their best and at their worst. This night was unprecedented, as far as she could recall. She could not begin to imagine how the evening would end, but she hoped she would have the opportunity to retire to her quarters before things got out of control. Her heart went out to Hezekiah as he sat at the head of the table with Jasmine to his right and Samantha to his left. She often wondered why he stayed with her. Why did he put up with her lavish spending and her often unpredictable temper?

"I hope the meat is cooked the way you like it, Pastor," she said as she placed the last dish on the table.

"I'm sure it's fine, Etta. Thank you."

"If you need anything else, I'll be in the kitchen." Etta said a silent prayer for the Cleavelands as she retreated from the room.

Jasmine shuffled food around her plate with her fork.

She had grown to hate the dinner ritual. Her mind jumped from remembering the wild events of the previous evening to anticipating the ones scheduled for that night.

She tried to ignore the tension between her parents as she prepared an excuse for leaving the house.

"Daddy," she said innocently, "I need a hundred dollars. I'm going out this evening."

Before Hezekiah could answer, Samantha stepped in.

"Where are you going?"

"I was talking to Daddy."

Hezekiah sat and barely listened to the exchange. He had a rule not to get involved in arguments between his wife and daughter. He felt the relationship between a mother and daughter was far too complicated for any man to understand.

Samantha abruptly dropped her fork on the plate. "I don't care who you were talking to. I asked where you are planning on going."

Not wanting to tangle with her mother while she was teetering on one of her terrible moods, Jasmine snapped, "Never mind. Just drop it."

"Don't talk to your mother that way, young lady." Hezekiah finally spoke while reaching for his wallet. "Where are you going?"

Jasmine welcomed the intervention of her father. She could always count on him to look beyond her condition, regardless of how chaotic, and only see his bright-eyed little girl. "Kelly and I are going to a movie."

Hezekiah reached into his wallet and handed her a hundred-dollar bill. Whenever he looked at Jasmine, he could only see the little girl in a white lace dress with yellow ribbons in her hair who ran into his arms every time he entered a room. He couldn't see the rapidly deteriorating young woman who drank too much and had sex in the back of cars with men she barely knew.

"What are you doing, Hezekiah? She's lying. Don't give her that!" Samantha shrieked.

"Don't tell me what to do," Hezekiah said calmly.

"Why do you indulge her like this? It only makes things worse. Can't you see what's happening to her?"

"You're making things worse by blowing this out of proportion. If, for once in your life, you could stop and think of how your tantrums and manipulation affect others, maybe we wouldn't be in this mess."

"So it's my fault that you can't control yourself, and that our marriage is falling apart. The fact that you can't keep your . . ." Acknowledging Jasmine, Samantha had the presence of mind to censor her words.

"Yes, Samantha, much of this is your fault. You want to control everything and everyone around you. This is not the church, damn it. It's our home. You can't even tell the difference anymore. People have their own lives. People have a right to private thoughts—thoughts that even you can't control."

"Save your sermon for Sunday morning. I'm not one of your sheep that needs you to tell them when to sing and when to pray."

Samantha snatched the cloth napkin from her lap and threw it onto the table. The china shook as she stood and a glass of water almost tipped over.

"If you could pull your head out of the sand for once, you'd see that your daughter is killing herself and needs our help. But you've got more important people on your mind these days."

"Don't involve Jasmine in our problems. Jasmine, you should leave. Your mother and I have to talk."

Jasmine stood up from the table. "Are you going to be all right, Daddy?"

"I'll be fine, honey. Don't stay out too late. I want you home at a decent hour."

"I will be, Daddy." Jasmine kissed her father on the forehead and made a hasty exit.

From the kitchen Etta heard the loud voices and pressed her ear against the door.

Hezekiah waited to hear Jasmine close the front door before he spoke. "I want to talk to you about Catherine. You had no right to fire her. You crossed the line and you owe her an apology."

"Crossed the line? You must be joking. I'm not the one fucking men in alleys, or park bathrooms, or wherever the hell it is that you go."

Etta gasped behind the kitchen door.

Hezekiah stood up quickly and took a physically threatening stance. Samantha looked him in the eye and said, "What are you going to do, hit me?"

Hezekiah rushed toward her and slapped her hard on the cheek. Samantha's long hair swirled as she rebounded from the blow.

The force of the impact caused her to knock her plate off the table. After gaining her footing she stood upright and said, "So now you want to be a man. After seventeen fucking years, you want to be in charge now. I've got news for you, Reverend. It's too late! You never were a man and now you've proved it by letting some faggot fuck you in the ass."

Hezekiah slapped her again. This time, before his hand completely cleared her face, she lunged at him and wrestled him to the floor. Dishes and glasses crashed to the carpet. The flower centerpiece toppled over and water splashed against the wall.

"I'll kill you, you fucking bastard. I'll kill you." She pounded his head with her open palms. Hezekiah grabbed her neck and rolled her to her back. He straddled her chest while she continued to scream and claw at his face.

Etta burst through the kitchen door, screaming, "Pastor, no! Don't hit her." She ran behind him and tried to pull him away from Samantha's thrashing body. "Pastor, no. You're going to kill her."

When he heard Etta's voice, his hands froze. His eyes focused on Samantha's distorted face as she continued to spew obscenities. He pushed Etta aside and stood up.

Panting, Samantha moved away from him and scrambled to her knees, shouting through disheveled hair,

"What's wrong—you not man enough to put me in my place?"

Hezekiah coldly stared at her and said nothing. He looked at Etta cowering next to the wall and yelled, "Don't just stand there. Clean this mess up!" He then gestured toward Samantha, still on her knees. "And get her out of here."

Hezekiah turned and walked out of the room. Etta bent down to Samantha and tried to help her up.

Samantha snapped, "Don't touch me. And if you ever mention this to anyone, I swear I'll kill you."

17

Danny St. John stood beneath the freeway overpass, next to a pile of clothes, soiled blankets, and soggy newspapers. He was one block from the sprawling construction site of New Testament Cathedral. The smell of urine and human waste assaulted his nose.

Sounds from cars speeding overhead filled the air. Remains of a campfire burned in the distance, and a mother with two small children gathered a large stuffed plastic bag and dashed from the area before he could approach.

As Danny walked toward two men sitting next to a cement pillar, which vibrated from the traffic above, the mud squished beneath his feet. Their foggy eyes became alert as he approached. One man struggled to his feet and tried to walk away.

"Wait a minute, guys," Danny called out. "I'm not the police. My name is Danny. I'm an outreach worker."

The two men seemed to relax and turn themselves over once again to their alcohol-induced haze.

"Hey, man," one said, "you got any vitamins? I got a cold that I ain't been able to shake for weeks."

They each wore blue jeans covered with mud. One was a Native American, and the other's thick drawl told of his deep Southern roots. Their shirts were torn and missing several buttons. Hair that had once been their crowns was matted and covered with unidentifiable white flecks. Danny rustled through his backpack and found two small bottles of vitamin C. "Here you go, guys," he said, handing them the bottles. "I've also got clean socks if you need them."

The Indian's words were slurred from three days of nonstop drinking. "Man, I been trying to get an affordable apartment for three years now, but they always tell me there ain't none available."

"They told me I had to be sober before I could get an apartment," the Southerner chimed in. "What kinda shit is that? If I could get sober by myself, I wouldn't need their motherfucking charity."

Both men laughed in unison and leaned toward each other in a gesture of camaraderie. Danny had heard the story many times before.

"I know it's tough, guys, but if you come to my office, I can make a few calls for you and maybe get you in somewhere."

The two men seemed startled by Danny's proposal.

"Man, I got an appointment at the welfare office this afternoon. Can I come in some other time?" came the response from the Southerner.

The Native American held up his hand, signifying his rejection of the offer.

Danny handed them his business card.

"My office hours are on the back. You can come in anytime. If I don't hear from you by next week, I'll check back here, if that's okay."

"You guys oughta build more affordable housing," said the Indian. "Somebody should tell the fucking pastor of that church over there that instead of building that fucking forty-five-million-dollar piece of shit, he oughta be building housing for poor people."

As Danny walked to his car, he made a mental note of the conversation with the two men and the squalor in which they lived. He wanted to recount it to Hezekiah the next time he saw him.

Something was not quite right at New Testament Cathedral. Staff members speculated about the strange behavior of those closest to the pastor. Why had Hezekiah canceled all his afternoon appointments? Why had Catherine barricaded herself in her office?

"Hold all my calls" was the only instruction to the baffled secretary.

Why had Naomi suddenly dropped a wall of silence via an "urgent" e-mail sent to all department heads? It read: Until further notice, all communications with members of the press are to be cleared by me first. Violation of this directive will result in disciplinary actions by the pastor's office.

"I heard the pastor collapsed last night and had to be rushed to the hospital" was the rumor whirling through the carpeted cubicles of the finance office.

"Naomi finally stood up for herself and told the pastor to get off her back" emerged as the top theory with the maintenance crew.

"Hezekiah caught Percy Pryce in bed with Samantha. They had a fight and Percy punched Hezekiah in the jaw. Didn't you see the scar on his face this morning?" The scintillation of this rumor made it the top choice for staff in the cafeteria.

New Testament Cathedral still looked the same. Mail room staff, on their usual morning rounds, delivered stacks of envelopes stuffed with cash and checks. This morning, however, the air was thick with a tension that caused conversations to halt suddenly when unfamiliar faces entered a room, or when a member of the pastor's inner circle walked by.

"Good morning, Naomi," a brave staff member said as Naomi passed her in the hall. "Is everything all right with Pastor Cleaveland?"

Naomi recognized the woman's face, but couldn't remember her name. "Why? What have you heard?" Naomi asked, slowing her pace only slightly.

"Someone said that he looked sick."

Naomi turned her head to the woman, but her feet continued to move forward. "I just saw the pastor this morning. He looked fine to me. Only idiots believe the gossip they hear around here. What's your name?"

"Sarah," said the startled woman.

"Sarah," Naomi said, as if making a mental note. "I'll mention what you said to the pastor the next time I see him. I'm sure he'll want to know who said it."

"I didn't mean . . . It was just something I heard from someone," the panicked woman said to Naomi's back. "I would never gossip about the pastor."

Naomi said over her shoulder, "Have a nice day, Sarah."

Hattie Williams squirmed in her favorite chair as she dozed. An old gospel hymn crackled on the radio. She intermittently thrashed her head from side to side. "No, don't do it," she mumbled in her sleep. "Look out, Pastor. Don't listen to them."

The dream was so vivid, Hattie thought she was awake.

The church floor ripples to the rhythm of Hezekiah's beating heart as he falls in the sanctuary. From the top to the bottom, each pew ebbs and flows, mimicking the motion of an ocean wave.

Frightened people on the billowing pews ride the waves in horror as Hezekiah's body spirals downward.

Women, wearing clothing inappropriate for such a turbulent sea, lose their footing as they look upward at the flying pastor. They tumble to the floor. Some hit the solid ground with a thud, while others scurry on hands and knees to avoid being crushed.

Chords of music screech from the pipe organ. The chandeliers flicker and shrieks of horror can be heard from every corner of the room. Suddenly the glass birds and cherubs in the stained-glass windows come to life and join Hezekiah in his flight. Beams of light reach through glass panels, trying to catch Hezekiah as he falls, but his twirling body eludes their grasp. He tumbles in the air like a leaf falling to the earth, which heralds the end of a long, hot summer, or a snowflake foretelling the cold winter to come. The fall seems endless.

Laws of gravity have ceased and have left him suspended in air, unable to touch the ground below. He is a wounded bird in flight for all to see and pity.

Hezekiah looks down and suddenly sees the faces of his beloved members have contorted into hideous shapes, spewing bile and contempt.

"You lied to us, Hezekiah Cleaveland!" they shout.

"If God loved you so much, then why has he let you fall?" they challenge, mocking and laughing.

The chorus of truths causes Hezekiah's body to slow its descent. "Fall, Hezekiah Cleaveland," they chant.

"Fall!"

"God doesn't love you anymore!"

The bulging eyes and distorted face of Samantha Cleaveland appears on the balcony of the auditorium. A diamond bracelet on her wrist sparkles as she extends her long, deformed hands toward the falling Hezekiah, not to break his fall, but to speed it.

Hezekiah's plunge continues mercilessly as familiar faces, dreaded confrontations, and painful events flash in rapid succession through his mind. This is it. His life has been condensed into the eight seconds it took to fall to the earth.

"Please tick faster." His eyes are pleading. "I don't want to see any more of my life. Please, God . . . let this end."

Hattie violently jerked her head one last time and bolted upright in the chair. She was shaking and her brow was doused with perspiration. She gasped for breath as she gripped the cushioned arms of the chair.

Through anguished gasps Hattie cried out loud, "She's going to do it. Lord, you've got to stop her."

Lance typed revisions to the article after his interview with Danny:

Pastor Hezekiah Cleaveland has been involved in a homosexual affair with Mr. Danny St. John, a resident of the Adams District. St. John is an employee of the Los Angeles Homeless-Outreach Team.

Cleaveland and St. John met for the first time in June of last year. It is not clear if they are still together, but e-mail messages obtained by this reporter show that their last correspondence occurred as recently as last week.

In one such e-mail Cleaveland wrote, "I can't meet you tonight, baby, because there is a planning commission hearing I have to attend. They're finally deciding tonight whether to grant the conditional use permit for the new sanctuary. Wish me luck. I am free tomorrow evening. I love you, Danny, and can't wait to hold you again. Love, Hezekiah." *The e-mail was dated April 17.*

Parties close to Cleaveland have confirmed that the relationship was sexual in nature, and that the two have met a minimum of once per week over the last twelve months. Our source, who requested anonymity, is quoted as saying, "His driver takes him to Mr. St. John's house usually after dark. He stays there for at least two or three hours. I only know of one occasion when he actually spent the night."

Colleagues at the Los Angeles Homeless-Outreach Team have confirmed that Cleaveland has called personally on many occasions inquiring as to the whereabouts of St. John.

A Los Angeles Homeless-Outreach Team employee is quoted as saying, "We all thought it was strange that Hezekiah Cleaveland would call personally. He never said why he was looking for him, but just to tell him to call back as soon as he got the message."

A total of 173 e-mail messages have been legally obtained by the Los Angeles Chronicle. The majority attests to both a physical and emotional bond between the two men. One such correspondence reads as follows:

"Dear Danny, Thank you for being in my life.

You have given me more joy than I ever thought I deserved. My wife loves me, but I don't think she ever actually knew who I really am, or even wants to. If only she had taken the time to look a little deeper, she would have seen that I'm just a guy. A guy that wants to be loved and cared for, just like everybody else in this lonely world.

I love you because I didn't have to tell you this. Somehow you already knew. My biggest dream is that someday you and I will live together. I often think of what it will be like to wake up every morning with you in my arms. One day, Danny. One day soon. Love you with all that I am, Hezekiah."

St. John has denied knowing or ever meeting Cleaveland.

The telephone rang as he typed the final line. "Lance, I've been trying to reach you all week," Cynthia Pryce said, sitting on her bed and removing her shoes. "What happened in the interview with Hezekiah?"

"It went as expected. He denied the affair." Lance pressed the save button on his computer and continued speaking. "I talked to Danny St. John today."

"What did he have to say for himself?"

"He denied it all as well. Said he never met Hezekiah Cleaveland. It was obvious he was lying, but it doesn't matter. The e-mail messages are enough to nail them both."

"So what's next? When does the story run?"

"I just finished the revisions. Now I have to get my editor's approval, and that's it. It should be on the stands this Sunday morning." Lance paused for a moment and then said, "I just have one more question for you, Cynthia."

"What's that?"

"Why are you doing this to Hezekiah and Samantha?"

"I've already told you. Someone has to hold the Cleavelands accountable for his actions."

"That is certainly understandable, but I feel like there's something you're not telling me. It's making me nervous about the whole story."

"Nervous?" Cynthia countered. "This is the biggest story of your career. How can you even think about passing it up?"

"This isn't just about my career, Mrs. Pryce," he said curtly. "It's about New Testament Cathedral, Hezekiah and Samantha Cleaveland, and Danny St John. It's about causing a lot of suffering for people in that church and around the country. It's about hurting a seemingly nice young guy who just got involved with the wrong person."

"You don't have to tell me what's at stake."

"That's what's confusing me. I get the feeling that you will actually gain more than anyone else if this story comes out."

"That's ridiculous," Cynthia said nervously. "What could I possibly gain from having my pastor exposed as a homosexual?"

"That's the exact question I need answered. And I think until I get that answer, I'm going to have to put the story on hold."

It was risky, but Lance felt it was necessary to ensure the information Cynthia had provided was legitimate.

Cynthia felt trapped by the reporter who, until then, had gobbled hungrily every morsel she had laid before him.

"All right, Lance. I'll be honest with you. I do have ambitions of my own."

"What does your ambition have to do with outing Hezekiah?"

"Come on. You can figure it out, can't you? What do you think will happen to my husband, Percy, if this comes out?"

"I don't know. What?" Lance asked.

"You're really going to make me say it, aren't you?" Cynthia paused in an agonizing plea for clemency, but there was no response.

She continued. "Hezekiah and Samantha are publicly humiliated and vanish into obscurity. My husband is second in command. He'll be called on to hold the church together through a devastating and embarrassing scandal, and then . . ."

The cloud lifted and all became suddenly clear. Lance snapped his fingers and said, "And then you and your husband take over New Testament Cathedral."

"Exactly."

"You must really hate them to do something like this."

"This isn't about hate or love—it's about power and doing God's work."

"Why did you pick me to do your dirty work? Any reporter in the city would have jumped at the chance to investigate a story this hot."

"I didn't pick you, Lance."

"What do you mean?"

"I mean that someone else selected you for the story."

"But I thought—"

Cynthia cut him off. "I know what you thought, but I didn't just call you out of the blue."

Sweat began to accumulate in the palm of Lance's hands. "Then who decided I would be the lucky guy?"

"Phillip Thornton selected you personally. He said you were the only one at his paper who had the balls to take on Hezekiah."

Lance stood up and nervously brushed the hair from his face. "Phillip Thornton knew about this? He has nothing to do with the day-to-day running of this paper. I've never even met him."

"I had no idea you were so naive."

Lance calculated his next move as she spoke.

"Cynthia," he said with an exaggerated twang of ambivalence, "I'm suddenly not sure if I can go through with this. I don't like the idea of being a pawn in your little game."

Cynthia stood and began to pace the room. "Don't fuck with me, Lance. Just run the story and this will all be over."

Lance leaned on his desk and lowered his voice. "Now, now," he said teasingly, "let's not rush things. I think I'd like to see you in person before sending this to my editor."

"See me for what?"

"Oh, I don't know. Maybe you could be more persuasive in person. You're such a beautiful woman, Mrs. Pryce. Maybe seeing you would give me the extra push I need."

Cynthia writhed helplessly in the vulnerable position she now found herself: the woman possessing the final bargaining tool necessary to close a deal. She stepped back into her shoes while silently cursing her misguided candor.

"Where are you?" she asked. "Maybe a face-to-face meeting would be a good idea."

"I'm in my office."

"Meet me in front of the building. I'll pick you up in fifteen minutes," she instructed, and hung up the phone.

Cynthia left the condominium unnoticed and retrieved her car in the building's subterranean parking structure.

A loathing for Lance Savage, and what she was about to do, crept through her body as she drove toward the *Los Angeles Chronicle*'s building.

The sun had set, and the swarm of commuters had mercifully left the city virtually empty. She saw homeless men bedding down for the night in front of train entrances and at bus shelters as she drove. Steam rose from street grates at each intersection as she searched the sidewalks for Lance Savage.

Then she saw him. He paced at the entrance of the brick building, clutching a laptop computer case and waving to her as she approached.

"That was quick," he said, climbing breathlessly into the passenger seat. "Thanks for agreeing to meet me."

"I didn't know I had a choice," Cynthia said, restraining the anger she felt toward the unkempt man. "So why did you want to see me?"

Lance patted the computer carrier he held in his lap.

"I've got the story right here, but I didn't want to send it until I had a few minutes alone with you."

Lance found it hard to resist the woman sitting next to him. She was more beautiful than he had imagined. A beauty most men found irresistible. Her hair seemed to glow in the moonlight. The silk of her stockings bristled as she manipulated the pedals of the car. In that moment her scent was enough to cause his sharp mind to drift in a haze of lust and desire.

Almost involuntarily Lance reached over and caressed her knee as she drove.

"I think you can guess what will . . . let's just say, inspire me to send this to my editor." The words surprised and embarrassed him as they escaped his lips.

Cynthia pushed the accelerator hard as they raced through downtown.

"I knew I couldn't trust you. This is extortion."

"Now hold on, Mrs. Pryce," he said playfully. "I wouldn't call it extortion. It's more like quid pro quo. You do something for me and . . . Well, I make you the first lady of New Testament Cathedral."

Cynthia turned the car onto Third Street. She silently reasoned, *A few minutes with this cretin is a small price to pay to get Hezekiah and Samantha out of the way permanently.*

She looked Lance in the eye and said, "I'll do this on one condition."

Lance looked at her guardedly and asked, "What's that?"

"That when we're done, you'll let me send the article."

Lance laughed loudly. "Hell, when we're done, I'll probably be too tired to push the key myself. It's a deal."

"Where can we go? I, of course, can't be seen in public with you."

"We could go to my place. I live on the canals."

"That's too far. I don't have much time," she replied shortly.

Lance thought for a minute and then said, "The construction site is near here. We can park there and no one will disturb us. Turn left at the next light."

In a few short blocks Cynthia could see large mounds of dirt piled next to the skeletal structure of New Testament Cathedral. Lance instructed her to drive behind the building and turn off the car. He placed the computer in the rear seat and said, "Kind of poetic, don't you think?"

He removed his jacket and loosened his tie; Cynthia watched his every move.

Without hesitation Lance leaned toward Cynthia and kissed her hard on the lips. His breathing became intense as he kissed her neck and caressed her breasts. "Mrs. Pryce," he panted, "you are such a beautiful woman."

Cynthia saw flashes of herself standing behind her husband, Pastor Percy Pryce, on the television screen while Lance fumbled awkwardly to unbutton her blouse.

The intoxication of possible fame and power slowly overrode her initial feelings of repulsion for the man stroking her partially naked body. Cynthia felt Lance's lips gently circling her exposed nipples as the vision faded.

The sounds of cold wind whirring at the base of the building and the distant hum of the freeway could be heard through the car's darkly tinted windows.

Cynthia lifted Lance's head to hers and kissed him passionately.

Her panting now matched his, breath for breath. She skillfully undid his belt buckle and pants and firmly gripped his erect member.

"Fuck me," she moaned. "I want you to fuck me, Lance."

Lance fumbled with levers and pushed buttons until he found the one to recline the driver's seat. Their writhing bodies descended in unison into the depths of the vehicle as the seat glided into a fully prone position.

Lance lifted Cynthia's skirt, slid her panties around her ankles, and lowered his trousers. He then climbed on top of her to explore her waiting mouth once again.

"Hurry," she said in a whisper. "Fuck me and then we'll send it together."

Lance moaned as he thrust his hips against hers. "I'm going to fuck you first, and then we'll both fuck the Cleavelands."

Cynthia lifted her knees toward the roof of the car and in the process turned on the windshield wipers. Lance entered her with great force and pounded double time to the beat of the whooshing rubber blades. Cynthia held him tightly and raised her hips to meet each thrust. The two reveled in passion heightened by the euphoric prospect of the Cleavelands' demise. The car bounced uncontrollably until they reached a fevered climax, then lay spent and breathless in each other's arms.

Cynthia was the first to speak. "It's time. Get your computer."

Lance rolled, exhausted, back to the passenger seat.

"Wow," he panted. "You don't waste any time, do you?"

"That was the agreement, wasn't it? Are you planning to back out again?"

"No, no," he protested. "I'm a man of my word." With his trousers still around his ankles, Lance reached behind and retrieved the case. He turned on the computer and the glowing screen lit up the car. As he waited for the article to appear, he said, "You're quite a woman, Mrs. Pryce. New Testament is in for one hell of a ride."

The headline flashed onto the screen: PASTOR HEZEKIAH T. CLEAVELAND INVOLVED IN SECRET GAY AFFAIR.

"There it is," Lance said. "This is what you've been waiting for."

"That's exactly what I've been waiting for," Cynthia said with a smile. "Now stop wasting time. Let's send it."

"Okay, Mrs. Pryce. Just press ENTER and you'll be one step closer to being queen of the empire."

Cynthia returned her seat to its upright position. She pressed the key without saying a word.

After a message appeared on the screen confirming that the article had been sent, Cynthia looked at Lance and firmly said, "Now, would you please pull your pants up and get the fuck out of my car?"

18

Friday

Richard Harrison, the editor of the *Los Angeles Chronicle*, stood behind his desk.

"Calm down, would you," he said as Lance Savage paced the floor. "Phillip thought it better that you not know. He felt the fewer people who knew about the arrangement with Cynthia, the better. He just didn't want to take any unnecessary chances."

"It's none of my business that he sold this paper's soul to Cynthia Pryce. It doesn't even bother me that you wasted six months of my life digging up information that you already had. What does piss me off is that you didn't trust me enough to tell me. I don't give a shit about Phillip Thornton or Hezekiah Cleaveland, but you, Richard. How could you have kept this from me?"

"I know, I know," Richard said with arms raised. "I wanted to tell you, but Phillip—"

"Fuck Phillip. This is about you and me."

"Whether you like it or not, Lance, Phillip owns this paper. He calls the shots."

"Why did he pick me? He's never met me."

"Because he knows your reputation. He knows that you are the only reporter on staff who's not impressed or intimidated by Hezekiah."

"But that doesn't explain why he's stabbing Hezekiah in the back. They've been friends for years."

"Don't be naive, Lance. Stories like this sell papers. We're facing layoffs, fighting off hostile takeovers. Papers all around the country are going under. This will save the *Chronicle*."

Lance prepared to ask another question, when the intercom buzzed.

"Sorry to interrupt, Mr. Harrison," came the secretary's voice, "but Reverend Hezekiah Cleaveland is on the line for you. He said it's important. Would you like to take the call?"

Richard looked into Lance's eyes and said, "Yes, Carol, I'll take it. Put him through."

Richard sat down at the desk and pushed the speaker button.

"Hello, Hezekiah. I was wondering when you were going to get around to calling me. How are you?"

The speakerphone made Hezekiah's voice sound as though he were calling from a barrel or a tunnel. "How do you think I am?" Hezekiah said bitterly. "Lance Savage has crossed the line with this one, Richard. I swear if—"

Richard cut him off. "Excuse me, Hezekiah. I think you should know that Lance is here with me now. You're on the speakerphone."

"Hello, Pastor. This is Lance Savage. Nice to hear your voice again."

Hezekiah's body shifted with each turn of the limousine.

The city streets whizzed by as he spoke.

"Richard, if you believe him on this one, then that sad excuse for a reporter is going to cost you your paper."

"So, Reverend Cleaveland, you're saying this is all fabricated?" asked Richard.

"You're damn right that's what I'm saying."

"Then how do you explain the numerous e-mails between you and Mr. St. John that we now have in our possession?"

"How did you get those?" Hezekiah shouted. "That's invasion of my fucking privacy. I could have you both arrested for hacking into my computer." Hezekiah's hands began to shake uncontrollably. "Why do you need to make me look like a fool, Richard? I got you that job."

"It's about the news, and unfortunately for you, this is an incredibly important story. It's my responsibility to report relevant news that affects this city."

"Don't give me that bullshit, Richard. Nobody gives a damn about tabloid crap like this. You know you could bury this right now, if you wanted to."

Lance leaned anxiously forward in his chair to respond, but Richard held up his hand to silence him.

"You're right, I could," Richard replied. "But why should I? Why would anyone in my position suppress the fact that one of the most influential pastors in the country is a closeted homosexual?"

"Because it's not true, goddamn it," Hezekiah screeched. "I'm not gay!"

"Maybe that was a poor choice of words, Richard," Lance said. "Reverend Cleaveland, would it be more accurate if he had said, 'The pastor of New Testament Cathedral is on the down low'?"

Richard stifled a laugh. No response came from the speakerphone. "Reverend Cleaveland, would that be more accurate?" Richard asked cynically. "Hello, Hezekiah, are you still there?"

The last words Hezekiah could manage through his rage were "Fuck both of you assholes!" He then slammed his cell phone shut.

Lance and Richard each flinched from the sound of the crash, followed by the dial tone. They sat breathless from the heated exchange.

"You did well, Lance," Richard finally said. "Phillip was right about you."

It was eleven o'clock when Danny locked his apartment door. A light fog met him on the porch and flowed between the cars and around the sycamore trees. He walked upstairs to his neighbor's front door, holding a note containing instructions for the care and feeding of Parker:

> *Dear Mr. and Mrs. Somner,*
> *I will be away for a while and am not sure exactly how long. I know how much you both like Parker, and I ask that you will take him into your home until I return. I left a bag of dry cat food under the sink, along with several cans.*
> *Thank you for watching him for me.*
> *Sincerely,*
> *Danny*

Danny slipped the folded paper under the Somners' front door and proceeded back down the steps toward his car.

As he walked, he could not see the lush green grounds of the park across the street from his home. He didn't hear dogs barking as their masters threw tennis balls into the distance. The joggers with bouncing ponytails and aching muscles were mere dashes of color in the corner of his eye. Formerly fond images of rolling lawns and trees gently quivering in the breeze now served only to remind him of the love and the city that had been snatched from his tenuous grasp.

There were four messages on his answering machine from Hezekiah that morning. The last came at 10:30 a.m.:

"Danny, baby, I'm so sorry," the trembling voice said.

"Since you haven't returned my calls, I assume Lance Savage has found you. I never wanted you to get hurt, and I did everything I could to protect you . . . to protect us, but . . ." There was a long pause. "I guess I failed. I know you're hurting right now. Believe me, this is eating me up inside too, but they've got me trapped. They're determined to destroy me over this. I think it best that we . . ."

He stopped. An anguished sigh could be heard. "Danny, I don't want to do this in a telephone message. Please call me. I love you."

Rush hour traffic had given way to a light stream of motorists attending to their midday errands. Danny drove along Santa Monica Boulevard toward the Pacific Ocean.

The homeless shelter, where he spent every Thursday afternoon giving out warm socks and medical referrals, went by without a glance from Danny. The Department of Motor Vehicles building, where he had recently paid fines for a collection of overdue parking tickets, passed without Danny's usual sneer of disdain.

There was no longer a reason to look at the city he loved. As Danny neared Ocean Park Boulevard, traffic began to slow. A toothless man sat on a white plastic bucket in the street's median. His left foot was wrapped in soiled gauze, while his other wiggled through a worn-out tennis shoe. Stains of dried blood dotted his ruddy cheeks, and his salty white hair whirled in the wind. He refused to make eye contact with drivers waiting at the red light.

Instead, his tattered cardboard sign pleaded his case: VIETNAM VETERAN WILL WORK FOR FOOD. THANK YOU AND GOD BLESS.

When the light turned green, Danny removed the last twenty-seven dollars from his wallet. Driving forward slowly, he handed the man the wrinkled bills through the car window.

The man looked suspicious at first but then eagerly accepted the generous gift.

"God bless you, sir," he said with a toothless grin.

"Thank you, sir. God bless you."

Danny merged his small car into the next lane and began the slow ascent up the winding ramp to the Santa Monica Pier. The lush green shrubbery along the side of the road was littered with the remains of human inhabitants.

To his right he could see a bundle of blue blankets, soggy from water and mud. An abandoned shopping cart rested on its side, with the few remaining contents of plastic bags and newspapers scattered about. A poorly concealed man stood urinating behind a tree, while another searched the muddy ground for cigarette butts and a stray pebble of crack cocaine.

The pain that Danny had once felt upon viewing such human despair was nowhere to be found. There was no outrage toward an uncaring society. No sorrow for the discarded lives wallowing in the mud and debris. The numbing realization that his life would never be the same again was all that remained. He crept forward as if guided by fate.

The world had crossed an invisible line and boldly stepped into the space he had so carefully protected. He could have no more secrets. No more private moments.

His life would soon be on the front page of every newspaper in town. The sorrow that welled in his heart would serve as fodder for gossip at restaurant tables and park benches in every part of the city.

How could he mourn the loss of Hezekiah with the media exploring every pore of his existence under the microscope of public opinion? It would be impossible to start again without Hezekiah. Impossible to heal while his life was being delivered daily to front porches and sold for seventy-five cents on every corner.

The crush of traffic eased as he approached the parking lot for the Santa Monica Pier. Danny maneuvered the car into the lot and parked in the nearest available space. A cool sea breeze raced past him as he walked along the creaking wharf. Couples strolled by, hand in hand, and a massive Ferris wheel clanked and churned to the delight of a few small children as their parents waved from the dock below.

Once at the tip of the pier, Danny stood and stared out into the ocean. Waves crashed into the pylons below, causing sprays of mist to dampen his face and mingle with the tear that rolled down his cheek. Danny could hear the sea calling his name. He thought frantically for a reason not to respond.

Sympathetic tourists avoided eye contact with the seemingly distraught young man as he inched closer to the railing. Danny looked out and could see the sprawling mountains of Malibu, the high-rise condominiums along Pacific Coast Highway, and the hills of Santa Monica.

Without hesitation he hoisted his body onto the railing and dangled his legs over the edge. At that point the few pedestrians walking nearby began to watch him more attentively.

"Don't jump!" he heard a woman yell.

"Oh my God! Hey, wait, buddy, it can't be that bad!" came a husky, concerned cry.

"Go for it, guy! Fuck this place!" another man exclaimed.

Then Danny heard a little girl crying behind him. He looked over his shoulder and saw a little brown girl wearing a pink polka-dot bathing suit and holding a melting red snow cone. Danny climbed down and knelt beside her and asked, "Are you okay? Why are you crying?"

She looked up through her sobs and replied, "I can't find my mommy. She left me here. I want my mommy."

"Don't cry," Danny said, brushing a tear from her cheek.

"I'm sure your mommy didn't leave you. Come on, let's go and find her together."

With that, Danny stood up and took the little girl by her sticky little hand and together they walked away from the edge of the pier to find the ones who could stop their tears from falling.

Hezekiah sat at his desk with pen in hand, suspended above the closing line of a form thank-you letter: *Yours Truly, Pastor Hezekiah T. Cleaveland*

A stack of white papers adorned with the embossed seal of the New Testament Cathedral lay before him. All were waiting for the ink from his pen to breathe life into the hollow words each contained.

Hezekiah didn't know the content of the official correspondence.

Perhaps they were thank-you notes for $50,000 contributions toward the construction of the new cathedral or complimentary VIP tickets to the next big political fundraiser. Their purpose and the protocol that dictated each line were of no interest to him.

He had dialed Danny's number four times that morning, but the only reply was the generic greeting on the answering machine.

Hezekiah had instinctively known when Danny was troubled throughout their year together. Days would pass without a word between them, when suddenly a "feeling" would come over him that something was wrong with the man he loved. Hezekiah would then call Danny, and inevitably he would be right. On one occasion Danny's mother had suffered a heart attack and died. Another time Danny's landlord had threatened to evict him.

Hezekiah was now having one such haunting premonition.

As the pen, without prompting, glided across the first letter in the stack, a jolt suddenly kicked inside his stomach. He grabbed his belly and buckled from the pain.

It was unbearable—what he imagined a heart attack must feel like. Droplets of perspiration formed on his brow, and the room began to spin around him. Then came another strike followed by yet another.

Hezekiah braced himself and stood with agonizing effort.

He staggered toward the private bathroom at the rear of the office. Nausea overtook him as he stumbled across the floor. He gagged violently, clamping his lips shut to contain the bile that threatened to spew onto the freshly shampooed carpet.

An intangible yet familiar force was being yanked from the depths of his body. Hezekiah fought to maintain his grasp on the elusive energy that now thrashed violently for release. Without turning on the lights in the little bathroom, Hezekiah dropped to his knees and positioned his gaping mouth over the porcelain toilet. Vomit gushed out with each brutal contraction of his stomach. Troubling thoughts raced through his mind as his kneeling body heaved. *Something is happening to . . .* The thoughts stopped to accommodate yet another convulsion. Then again they came. *Danny. Where is Danny? Please don't do this. I won't leave you.*

After a series of painful spasms and agonizing groans, the heaving in his stomach gradually subsided, but feelings of fright and dread continued. "Danny, where are you?" he said out loud. "Don't leave me like this."

Hezekiah's body was drenched in sweat as he collapsed backward onto the tiled bathroom floor. He could hear his secretary pounding from outside the office door.

"Pastor Cleaveland!" came a panicked shout through the locked door. "Are you all right, sir? Pastor Cleaveland, please open the door!"

Hezekiah's white shirt clung to his body, wet and transparent from fluids he had released. His chest heaved up and down, gasping for air, and lifeless arms stretched at his sides.

He stared at the darkened light fixture above and surrendered to the overpowering need to cry, to mourn. His body convulsed again, not from the need to reject unwanted liquid, but to acknowledge the grief that flooded his heart. To mourn the loss of an essence that had been so painfully torn from his body. Hezekiah felt a familiar emptiness, which the last year with Danny had allowed him to forget. The void that Danny had so lovingly filled, the hollow that called for no one but him. At that moment Hezekiah felt that Danny was gone, and he was alone again.

Hezekiah stepped from the rear of the double-parked limousine. The curtains to Danny's apartment were open.

He looked to the window for the familiar figure of Parker sitting on the sill. He was not there. Hezekiah rang the bell, then knocked loudly. There was no response. He leaned over the wrought-iron railing and peered into the window. The apartment was just as he had remembered, but Danny was nowhere to be seen.

Hezekiah walked to the car, when he heard, "Excuse me! Are you looking for Danny?"

Hezekiah looked up and saw an old man standing in the window above Danny's apartment. "Yes, I am. Have you seen him today?"

"Not today. But he . . . Hey, you're the pastor, Hezekiah Cleaveland." The man turned and yelled to someone in the apartment. "Norma, come here. Look, it's Hezekiah Cleaveland. I told you I saw him here the other week."

Ray looked again to Hezekiah and said, "Norma watches you and your wife on TV all the time. She even sends you money."

An equally aged Norma joined her husband in the window to gawk at Hezekiah.

"I'm sorry. She didn't believe me when I told her that I saw you here before. I'm Ray Somner, and this is my wife, Norma."

Hezekiah smiled politely. "You were about to say something about Danny."

"Oh, yeah. Strangest thing. He left a note under our door this morning asking us to take care of his cat 'cause he wouldn't be coming back soon. I hope he's okay. He's a real nice kid. Works with the homeless, you know."

Hezekiah walked up the steps toward the couple. "Yes, I know. Would you mind if I saw the note? He's a friend, and I'm a little concerned about him."

"Sure. Norma, go get the note. It's over there on the table."

Hezekiah read the shaky print as Norma and Ray vowed their support for his new cathedral.

"Do you have Parker?"

"Yeah, we used our spare key to get him. He's in the kitchen right now, eating. Do you want to see him?"

"No. That won't be necessary. Will he be able to stay with you until Danny returns? He loves that cat."

"No problem. What's going on? Maybe we ought to call the police or something. This isn't like him to leave without telling us where he's going."

"Yes, that might be a good idea. If you hear from Danny, would you please tell him I came by?"

"Of course we will, sir. I hope nothing has happened to him."

"I hope not too. It was a pleasure meeting you both."

"Likewise, Pastor."

When Hezekiah reached the car, he heard one of the two shout from the window, "Good luck with the . . ."

Dino slammed the car door before the final word could be heard.

Dino turned the car onto Crenshaw Boulevard. Hezekiah looked out the window through weary eyes and asked, "Where are you going? I just want to go home."

"Pastor Cleaveland," Dino said, holding up a sheet of paper, "your schedule says you have a meeting with a group of homeless advocates at the community center near the church in ten minutes. Would you like for me to call ahead and tell your advance man that you will not be coming?"

The muscles in Hezekiah's stomach churned again.

"No. I should go. Take me there."

All heads in the room turned to the door when Hezekiah entered the community center in the South Central part of town. Folding chairs were placed auditorium-style in the center of the hall.

Clusters of people lined the perimeter walls, and the chairs were filled with a mix of homeless people and educated young men and women—many who had used their degrees from Brown and Harvard to advocate for the rights of the city's poor and disabled.

"Oh good, the pastor has arrived," a frail-looking man with thin hair said, addressing the audience. "Hello Reverend. For a moment there we thought you were going to be a no-show."

Hezekiah nodded his head in acknowledgment and moved toward the front of the room.

"Now that Pastor Cleaveland is here I think we'll hold our other agenda items until later and give him the opportunity to speak," the meeting facilitator continued. "I know you all have a lot to ask him, but please hold your questions until he has finished." With a grand sweep of his arm, he yielded the floor to Hezekiah.

"Good evening, everyone," Hezekiah said, standing before the crowd. "Thank you all for coming out to discuss this very important issue with me. As many of you may know, I have always been very concerned about the issues faced by homeless people in Los Angeles and in this country.

"New Testament Cathedral had spent the last ten years giving money to local feeding programs and shelters. Members of my congregation volunteer their time at many social service programs around the city, and my wife and I sit on the board of several national programs whose missions are to serve homeless men, women, and children. We've held countless meetings with merchants, concerned citizens, and members of the faith community, listening to your concerns and—"

"We're tired of you just listening," a heavily bearded man interjected. "You're spending millions of dollars to build a shrine to yourself, and all you can do for the homeless is sponsor a food drive once a year so your members can drop dented cans of tuna in a box in your lobby. When are you going to do something that would help the homeless people that live on the streets all around your new church?"

The facilitator jumped to his feet. "Please, there will be plenty of time for questions after he's done."

Hezekiah proceeded with his speech. "There's no question that homelessness is a growing problem, not only here but all over the city. That is why I've recently instructed our accountants to increase the amount of money we donate annually to social service programs."

"We don't need your money. We need you to build more shelters and affordable housing instead of a massive glass church for rich people," came a shout from another part of the room.

An elderly woman near the front stood to her feet and said, "How can you justify spending forty-five million dollars on a building that will only be open on Sunday mornings when you know that every night, of every year, thousands of men, women, and children live and die on the streets of this city?"

Angry-faced people shook their heads and blurted out expressions of agreement.

Hezekiah raised his hands. "Please, please, everyone. I know this is a very difficult situation, but there are also factions in this city that believe the homeless have a constitutional right to live on the streets. You cannot force anyone to go into a shelter who does not want to go."

"That's bullshit and you know it!" shouted a homeless man near the rear. "You think I want to sleep under a bush and wash myself in park bathrooms? The problem is there's just not enough shelter beds in this city, and people like you, who could help to do something about it, prefer to ignore us and pretend it's our choice to live on the streets."

The crowd grew increasingly agitated. Random comments came from every direction:

"If you won't do anything about it, then maybe we should organize protests every Sunday morning on the steps of your church."

"You're a hypocrite. You claim to care about the homeless, but you only care about money."

"You could have built thousands of units of affordable housing with the money you're wasting on that church."

The effusive charm and quick wit that had served Hezekiah well his entire life now eluded him. He stood pummeled by the barrage of complaints and threats. Dino walked slowly toward the front of the room and positioned himself firmly a few feet from Hezekiah.

"Pastor Cleaveland," said the facilitator above the shouts. "Are you going to respond? These people are angry and frustrated. They deserve some answers."

The room fell silent. Hezekiah looked into the angry faces.

"I think I've heard enough," he said with a scowl. "For some reason you people are under the misguided impression that I need your permission to build New Testament Cathedral. Well, for your information I don't. We have every permit required by law. We own the property, and at this point no one can stop the project. I came to meet with you as a courtesy, but I'm not in the mood to tolerate your abuse and misguided anger. You should direct it at the mayor and city council, not at me."

Gasps were heard throughout, but Hezekiah continued.

"I don't pretend to have the solution to homelessness, and I don't know of anyone who does. I do know, however, that protesting and focusing your anger toward me is not the solution. It may get you on the six o'clock news, but it does nothing to help the people you claim to be advocating for."

Hezekiah turned to the stunned facilitator. "Mr. Facilitator," he said mockingly, "please do not invite me or anyone else from my church to these meetings again."

Hezekiah began to walk toward the exit. He stopped at the door and turned back to the stunned crowd and said, "Also, the next time I see any of you protesting on my property, I'm going the have the police throw you in jail for trespassing. Good night."

Hezekiah exited the room, with Dino walking protectively behind. A chorus of jeers and threats erupted.

"We're going to shut you down, Hezekiah Cleaveland."

"You've got no right to talk to us like that. We're good people."

"I've never been so insulted in my life."

The words of indignation were ignored. When they stepped into the cold night air, Dino asked, "Reverend, are you all right?"

"No, I'm not all right," Hezekiah said, turning up his collar.

"Just take me back to the Adams District."

For the second time that day Dino stopped the car in front of Danny's home. Hezekiah could see Norma and Ray peeking through the curtains of their apartment.

From the rear of the limousine Hezekiah stared into Danny's window. Nothing had changed. The lights had not been turned on. The day's mail was still in the box, and Parker was not on the sill.

Where is he? Hezekiah thought. *God, please let him be all right.*

The car was silent for several minutes, when Dino looked into the rearview mirror.

"Pastor Cleaveland, would you like me to knock on the door? Maybe he came back while we were away."

Hezekiah could see compassion and knowing in the reflection of Dino's eyes through the mirror. He simply responded, "No, Dino. I don't think he's coming back. I just want to sit here for a few more minutes. But thank you. Thank you very much."

Hezekiah's cell phone rang four times, but he did not answer it. The caller tried again. On the third ring Hezekiah picked it up. "Hello, what is it?"

"Hezekiah, it's Percy. Where are you? I've been trying to reach you all night. We have to talk."

"Now isn't a good time, Percy. Can I call you back in—"

"This will only take a minute. Now listen to me closely. I know about you and Danny St. John."

Hezekiah did not respond. He did not care.

"If that story appears in the paper, all hell is going to break loose," Percy continued. "You have to be prepared to respond. Have Naomi call a press conference for tomorrow afternoon so you can publicly deny everything. We can't afford to let this go without a statement from you. If you don't refute the accusations, everyone will assume they're true."

"I can't. I don't think I can face the public just yet. Danny is missing. No one seems to know where he is."

"You need to forget about him, Hezekiah. The rest of your career will depend on how you handle what's about to come your way over the next few days. If you mess this up, it's over. I'm going to try and talk some sense into Lance Savage. I don't know if he'll listen to reason. You should go home and get some rest. I'll call you in the morning. And by the way, make sure Samantha is standing with you in the pulpit on Sunday."

"I don't think she will, Percy."

"Why not?"

"Because she knows the story is true. What am I going to do, Percy? My life is falling apart. It's over. I don't think I can take any more."

"It's not over. We're going to fight this together, Hezekiah. It's going to be difficult, but we can get through this if you can just tough out the next few days."

Hezekiah did not hear the final words of encouragement.

He looked for the last time into Danny's window and said, "I have to go now, Percy. Just do whatever you think is necessary. I'll talk to you tomorrow."

19

Kenneth Davis had tried unsuccessfully to reach Lance Savage all afternoon. He tried Lance's number again and was greeted with, "Lance Savage here. How can I help you?"

"Mr. Savage, this is Reverend Kenneth Davis. I'm an associate pastor at New Testament—"

Lance interrupted, "I know who you are Reverend Davis. What can I do for you?"

"I'd like to meet with you to discuss the article you're working on. Would that be possible sometime today?"

"There's nothing more to discuss. Besides, it's too late." Lance looked at his watch. "I've already submitted it to my editor."

"Now, we both know it's never too late to stop a story from going to press. I have a proposition for you that might convince you to put an end to this whole unfortunate misunderstanding."

"What kind of proposition?"

"A proposition that would be mutually beneficial to all parties involved, especially for you."

Lance was intrigued. He looked at his watch again and said, "All right, Reverend Davis."

"Please, Lance, call me Kenneth."

"Okay, Kenneth, I was just about to head home. You can meet me there in one hour."

Lance gave his home address and the two men exchanged civil good-byes.

After disconnecting, Kenneth immediately called Percy Pryce.

"Percy, I finally got us a face-to-face with Lance Savage. Meet me in front of the church in thirty minutes."

"What did he say? Is he going to take the money?"

"We didn't get that far. At least he's willing to listen to what we have to offer."

Lance lived in a 1920s bungalow on the canals in Venice. Cars sped along the narrow street within ten feet of his front door. It was a small house with a permanent dampness in the air.

Lance, wearing faded jogging shorts and a wrinkled T-shirt, answered the door. "Hello, Kenneth. You didn't say you were bringing Reverend Pryce with you. Is he here in an official capacity?"

"No, he's not," Kenneth said as the two men entered the cluttered bungalow. "And neither am I. We're not here to speak on behalf of the New Testament Cathedral, or Hezekiah. We only represent ourselves."

"Have a seat, gentlemen. Can I get you a beer, or maybe something stronger?"

"No, thank you," Kenneth said. "We don't plan on staying long."

Lance retrieved a beer he had already begun and sat on a leather sofa next to Percy. Kenneth lowered his body into a chair in front of them and laid a briefcase on the floor at his feet.

Kenneth calmly began to speak. "I think it goes without saying that we would appreciate it if whatever we discuss does not leave this room. As far as anyone is concerned, this meeting never took place, and if you ever repeat anything we say, we will deny it."

"Fair enough," Lance said, setting the beer bottle on a side table.

"First of all, we'd like for you to tell us exactly what it is that you know about this affair Hezekiah is allegedly involved in, and with whom," Kenneth stated.

"All right, it will soon be public information, anyway. Your pastor has been involved with a Mr. Danny St. John for the last year. They see each other no less than twice a week. Usually, they meet at Danny's apartment in the Adams District. They also have lunch together on occasions at various restaurants around the city. Danny is an outreach worker in downtown Los Angeles. He's twenty-eight, and quite a looker, if I might add. Is there anything else you would like to know?" Lance added smugly.

"Yes," Percy said. "Everything you've just told us sounds relatively innocent. But it doesn't prove that the relationship was sexual in nature?"

"I agree," Kenneth chimed in. "There's no law against Hezekiah having a male friend. He's been to my home dozens of times and we often dine out together. That doesn't make it sexual."

Lance stood up and walked to a desk under a window overlooking the canals. He opened a drawer and retrieved a stack of
papers held together by a metal clasp. He then thumbed through
the stack, pulled a sheet out and handed it to Percy.

Percy read the e-mail silently:

> My Dearest Danny,
> Last night with you was wonderful. I love holding you in my
> arms and tasting your soft lips. Each time I kiss you feels as
> sweet as my first kiss. Feeling your body against mine gives
> me more pleasure than I ever thought possible. Caressing
> your soft skin makes me feel like the luckiest man in the
> world. I am not a poet and I know it, but I want you to know
> that I love you with all of my heart. I wish I could hold you in
> my arms forever.
> Love you always,
> Hezekiah

Percy handed the e-mail to Kenneth, who proceeded to read
as well.

"Would you like to see more? That's one of the tamer ones.
There's a few in there that give you the size of each of their
members, and one in particular that goes into great detail about
where Danny likes for Hezekiah to put his finger when he's
about to cum."

Percy quickly held up his hand and said, "No, that won't be
necessary."

"One thing I can assure you is that none of the more graphic
details of their relationship will be in the article. I don't think the
public is ready to hear what Hezekiah does when he's about to
cum," Lance said with a sly smile.

"This is so unseemly," Percy said in disgust. "I can't believe the
Los Angeles Chronicle would stoop to gutter journalism like this. It's
no better than the supermarket tabloids."

"Pathetic, isn't it?" Lance agreed sarcastically. "It's a new day in
journalism. The public craves shit like this, and if we want to stay
in business, we've got to keep up with the times. No pun intended."

"I'm glad you think this is funny," Kenneth said angrily.

"You don't seem to realize how many people will be hurt if this story is released. Hezekiah will be ruined. His wife and daughter will be devastated. The future of New Testament Cathedral will be placed in extreme jeopardy, and millions of people all over the country will lose a man they deeply love, and many will possibly also lose their faith in God."

"I'm sorry, gentlemen, but Hezekiah should have thought of all that before he, so indiscreetly, got involved with a man," Lance said as he sat back down. "I'm a reporter and I report the news. And this is definitely news."

Kenneth proceeded diplomatically with his appeal.

"You are obviously aware that the story would cause immeasurable damage to Hezekiah and New Testament Cathedral."

"I am."

"Is there any way we can appeal to your moral consciousness?" Kenneth asked passionately. "Surely, you must feel some moral obligation to your fellow man. Hezekiah made a mistake, but who among us hasn't? I'm sure you've done many things that you're not proud of. How would you like it if they were splashed all over the front page?"

"I would hate that, but you fail to recognize a few significant differences between Hezekiah and myself. I don't claim any sort of moral authority. I'm not married. I'm not the head of a multimillion-dollar empire, and even more important, I am not on television twenty-four hours a day around the country preaching about the evils of sin."

"Point taken," Kenneth conceded. "Then, let's approach this from a different angle. Needless to say, we want to put this entire ugly situation behind us all as soon, and as quietly, as possible. To that end, we are prepared to offer you one hundred seventy-five thousand dollars to forget you ever heard the name of Danny St. John."

Kenneth retrieved the briefcase from the floor and placed it on the coffee table. He opened it to reveal stacks of one-hundred-dollar bills bound by white paper strips.

Lance sat erect. "You've got to be shit'n me," he said, laughing. "You think saving your boy's ass is only worth one hundred seventy-five thousand dollars?"

"That's all we are able to come up with."

Lance stood up and walked toward the door. "You and I both know that's not true. New Testament brings in more than that just from the interest you earn on money collected in the Sunday-morning offering plate. Gentlemen," he said, "I think you've wasted enough of my time. I would appreciate it if you'd leave my home."

Percy jumped from the sofa. "You fucking piece of shit," he said, pointing his finger. "Now it's clear to me what this is all about. You're trying to get rich off the backs of Hezekiah and New Testament Cathedral. That whole speech about 'the news' was a bunch of bullshit. You don't give a fuck about the news," he said angrily. "It's all about money."

"That's some strong language for a man of God," Lance said. "I'm impressed."

"Fuck you," Percy continued. "If you have half a brain, you'll take the money and forget about this whole thing."

"It'll take a lot more than that for me to forget Danny St. John. Try half a million, and then maybe we can talk."

"You're out of your fucking mind," Percy said, "if you think we're going to give you half a million."

"I think that's a fair price, Reverend Pryce, especially considering it was your wife who got you into this sordid mess," Lance replied as he opened the front door. "Now, if you don't mind."

Percy looked stunned and then slammed the door shut.

"What are you saying? My wife isn't involved in this."

Lance walked away from the door to a nearby telephone.

"Are you trying to tell me you didn't know she is the one who leaked the story?"

Percy bolted across the room and grabbed Lance by the shoulders. "My wife had nothing to do with this. You're lying. Don't listen to him, Reverend Davis. He's trying to get more money out of us."

Reverend Davis stood and said, "Let him go, Percy. Right now it doesn't matter who leaked the story." He then looked at Lance and said, "Five hundred thousand dollars is a lot of money. It'll take me some time to come up with it, but—"

"It matters to me," Percy interrupted. He then pushed the now-shaking reporter against the wall, causing a picture to crash to the floor. "I'm not going to let this little bastard extort that kind of money out of us."

"Reverend Pryce, you would be surprised at just how low your wife had to stoop to ensure that you become the next pastor of New Testament Cathedral. Take it from me, though. She knows her way around the front seat of a car."

Lance began to walk away, but Percy grabbed his neck.

The two men struggled.

"Percy, stop it," Kenneth said, grabbing Percy by the shoulders. "Let him go. Let's go."

But their scuffle only escalated. A lamp fell from a table. Stereo equipment and CDs lurched from their shelves from bumps leveled by slamming bodies. Lance struggled for release as Percy pushed him to the ground.

When Lance fell, his head banged against the coffee table, causing the briefcase, and all its contents, to topple onto the floor. The reporter lay motionless, with bundles of money scattered around his body.

"Oh God," Kenneth said, kneeling next to Lance's limp body. "What have you done? He's not breathing."

Kenneth tried to revive the limp body of Lance Savage, while Percy panted over his shoulder.

"Wake up," Percy said through deep, anguished breaths.

"He tripped. Make him get up, Kenneth."

Kenneth shook Lance's shoulders, causing his head to flop from side to side. His arms hung limp and unresponsive to the additional abuse at the hands of such a large man.

"He's dead," Kenneth finally said. "You killed him."

"I barely touched him. You saw it. He must have tripped. Oh, shit. I don't believe this is happening. What are we going to do?"

Without responding, Kenneth carelessly dropped the mass of flesh and immediately began gathering the fallen money, returning it to the case.

"Quick," he said, "get all the money, and let's get out of here."

"We can't just leave him here. We should call the police."

"Are you crazy? You just killed a man for no reason. They'll put you in jail for the rest of your life. Let's just get out of here. Hopefully, no one saw us come in. They'll think he was killed by a burglar. Now, pull yourself together and help me pick up this money."

Kenneth scanned the room, once the case was filled.

Much of its contents lay scattered on the floor, along with the crumpled body. To his satisfaction it looked like the classic botched robbery scene he had seen so often on the evening news.

"If we pass anyone on the street, don't make eye contact with them, and try to look natural."

Percy looked again at the devastation his hands had wrought and cried out, "I don't believe this is happening!"

Kenneth ran to the kitchen at the rear of the house and retrieved a dish towel from the sink. He opened the back door of the house and stepped onto the wooden porch, wrapped his hand in the dish towel and smashed a pane of glass in the back door. With his hand still covered he closed the door and stuffed the towel into his pocket. The broken glass crackled under his feet as he quickly left the room.

The two men exited the apartment through the door they had entered. Cars raced down the busy street at speeds that permitted no more than cursory glances. No pedestrians were in sight as Kenneth drove away.

"This never happened, Percy," Kenneth said, looking directly ahead. "Do you understand? This never happened."

Percy was in shock and did not respond.

"You have to put this out of your head. We were never there."

"What if a neighbor saw us? What about Naomi and Catherine? They knew we were going to meet with him."

"No one saw us," Kenneth patiently said. "We were never in Venice. Don't ever mention this to anyone. Understand? I'll tell Naomi and Catherine that I wasn't able to contact him. If they question you, just tell them to talk to me."

"I won't mention it. I understand. I just can't get his face out of my head. Why did he make me do it? I just snapped. I don't know what happened. He shouldn't have said those lies about Cynthia. She would never do anything so cruel. She loves Hezekiah and Samantha. This would have never happened if he had just taken the money."

Kenneth deposited his shaken passenger at the main entrance of the church. It was 5:10 p.m., and a tide of fleeing employees streamed from the building.

"Are you going to be all right?" Kenneth asked as Percy exited the car. "Go directly to your office, get your things, and go home. And for God's sake, don't talk to anyone."

"I won't," Percy said, slamming the door. "But what about the story? If they don't hear from Lance, they'll just go ahead and run it."

"It's too late to worry about that now. It's out of our hands. We'll just have to brace ourselves for the worst."

Percy managed to choke out "Good night" to several familiar faces as he walked the halls to his office.

"Reverend Pryce!" came a shout from over his shoulder.

"Wait a minute. So what happened? Did you talk to Lance Savage?"

When he turned, he saw Naomi's stiff hair progressing rapidly toward him. "Did you meet with Lance?" she asked again.

"No . . . we just . . . I mean, Kenneth wasn't able to reach him."

"That's just great," Naomi said bitterly. "He always has his cell phone on. Do you have the right number?"

"No, I . . . I don't know."

Naomi glanced at her watch. "Come with me to my office, and I'll give it to you."

"It is too late." Percy's voice began to tremble. "If you had done your job in the first place and kept tabs on what Hezekiah was doing, we wouldn't be dealing with this. All we can do now is prepare for the fallout. Now just leave me alone. I'm going home."

Percy darted away, leaving Naomi standing as stiff as her hair. When he reached his office, his secretary had already gone for the day. Waiting for him on her desk was a stack of messages, including four from Catherine marked "urgent" and three from Naomi. He tossed them into the trash bin.

He entered his office and put on his trench coat without turning on the light. He gathered stacks of paper from the desk and began stuffing them into a weathered briefcase, when Catherine appeared at the door.

"I just saw Naomi," she said frantically. "Why are you guys just giving up? This is our last hope. I thought we all agreed."

Percy continued shoveling papers into the case.

"It's over, Catherine. Face it. Hezekiah has screwed us all this time."

"How can you say that? I thought—"

"Well, you thought wrong. You can pretend that there's still some way to save him, but I won't. You were the closest person to him. How could you let him do this to us?"

"I didn't know anything about it. You know how secretive he can be," she said in the form of an apology. "Percy, please try to reach Lance at least one more time." Catherine held out a scrap of paper with numbers scribbled on it. "This is his cell phone number. I got it from Naomi."

Percy shuddered and threw the last handful of documents to the floor.

"I can't, all right? I can't call him," he said, dropping into the chair behind the desk.

"You can't fall apart now. Be a man and call him. Offer him the money, like we agreed. That's all you have to do. You owe it to the pastor."

Percy rocked his head in his hands.

"I can't call him. He's dead," he said, sobbing into his hands.

Catherine closed the office door and moved in closer.

She lifted his head and saw his red eyes and tear-smeared cheeks. "What do you mean 'he's dead'? What happened?"

"I don't know what happened. We were just talking to him. He said horrible things about Cyn . . ." Percy paused and looked away. "He demanded more money. Half a million. I just lost it. Before I knew what had happened, he was lying on the floor. He tripped. I don't know how, but . . . it was an accident."

"I don't believe this. You killed him." She moved backward toward the door. "I don't want any part of this, Percy. You and Kenneth did this without my knowledge."

"Catherine, please don't say that. We just wanted to talk to him."

Catherine opened the door. "I don't want to hear any more. Stop talking. Just stop."

As she vanished through the door, Percy heard her muttering, "Oh Christ. I don't believe this."

***

Percy entered the penthouse in a flurry. "Cynthia, where are you?" he shouted as he threw his briefcase to the floor. His trench coat flapped as he ran through the house calling her name.

Cynthia emerged from the kitchen. "Percy, I'm here. What's wrong?"

Percy darted across the living room to her. "I talked to Lance Savage today. Cynthia, what have you done?"

"I don't know what you're talking about."

"Did you leak the story about Hezekiah?"

Cynthia looked puzzled. "Stop yelling. Who is Lance Savage?"

Percy grabbed her shoulders tightly. "Don't play innocent with me."

"Percy, you're out of control. Let go of me. I didn't say anything to Savage about Hezekiah."

"Do you know what you've done?"

Cynthia's face turned hard. Her body tensed, and her face exploded in rage. "I know exactly what I've done. And I did it for us. You've slaved under him all these years, and we have nothing to show for it. Now it's our turn. Look at how he and Samantha lives. We deserve to live like that too."

Percy looked at her in surprise. "You're insane. You've ruined their lives. I knew you were jealous, but I never believed you would stoop this low."

She couldn't conceal her anger any longer. Years of bottled-up rage flooded to the surface.

"I've stood by and supported you all these years. If you think I'm going to watch you let this opportunity pass us by, you are mistaken. For once, you're going to take what should be ours, even if I have to take it for you."

"Listen to yourself. You haven't once thought of Pastor Cleaveland and what he must be going through. He's my friend and—"

"He throws you crumbs from the pulpit and you grovel around like a puppy licking them up. You call that a friend? I call it a user. Those two have exploited us from the beginning, and you're not smart enough to know it. Well, I'm sick of it. He only has himself to blame for everything that is happening to him," she said.

Percy turned to walk away. Cynthia grabbed his arm and swung him around. "This is what you always do when God places an opportunity right in your lap. You turn away. This time, Percy Pryce, I'm not going to let you turn away. You are going to be the next pastor of New Testament Cathedral, even if it kills you." She pushed him aside and stormed from the room.

Percy heard the door to their bedroom slam shut. He stood shocked and embarrassed that he had not realized, until now, that he was married to a woman whose ambition would drive her to destroy a man's life.

20

"Where have you been?" Hezekiah spoke softly into the phone. "I've been trying to reach you for two days. I've been going crazy worrying about you. I thought something terrible had happened to you. Are you all right?"

Danny came from behind his desk and closed the door to his office. The room was small and cluttered. Boxes of donated clothes were piled in the corner, and stacks of files and reports cluttered his desk. "Lance Savage found me. I know about the story. I know you have to leave me," he said as he settled behind his desk.

There was a long pause and then Hezekiah spoke. "I'm not leaving you, Danny. I'll never leave you. I don't care about the article. I don't care about anything but you. I'm going to leave Samantha. And before you ask, yes, I have thought it through. It's all I've been able to think about. I can't keep on living a double life. I know that I have to make a decision, and I've made it."

Hezekiah rested his head on the back of the chair. He nervously tugged on his necktie and continued. "I talked with a therapist. He tried to talk me out of it. He's a good man."

Danny sat at his desk. He only half listened to the voice on the phone. His computer screen went blank. Flying toasters suddenly appeared and began to dance across the screen. The words were ones he had dreamed of hearing, but something prevented him from having the anticipated response.

Danny finally spoke. "I think we should talk about this, Hezekiah. Are you sure you'll be able to forgive yourself if you split up your family? A year from now, you'll be miserable and blame me. Then what?"

Hezekiah smiled and spun semicircles in his chair. "I never thought it was your responsibility to make me happy. That's something I have to figure out for myself."

"Hezekiah, I don't ever want to feel like I made you do this. Being with you is the most important thing in the world to me, but it has to be your decision alone. Not in response to pressure from anyone. You've got to know in your heart that it is the right thing for you to do."

"I don't feel any pressure from you to leave Samantha. I know it sounds half-baked to you, but you can't imagine how much I've thought about this in the last year."

"You know that whatever you decide to do, I'm still going to love you. I'll accept whatever terms you decide to define our relationship by—friends, lovers, partners. I just want the best thing for you."

"I know, baby. That's why I love you. Now, get back to work. There are hungry people waiting for you."

Danny hung up the phone. Not wanting to be alone with his thoughts, he walked back to the lobby of the homeless drop-in center. The room was filled to capacity with street refugees. Virgil Jackson quickly approached him.

"Danny, when are you going to get me into a program? I can't take this waiting any longer. You've got to get me in today, or I'm going to have to do something desperate."

Danny was startled by the aggressive tone in his voice and said, "I checked this morning and only three beds opened up. You are number eleven on the waiting list. You've got to be patient for a few more days."

Virgil's feet began to shuffle as if he were preparing to attack. He slammed his fist on the counter and shouted, "You've been saying that for over a month now!"

The reaction was to be expected from a man who had been living on the streets. It was the plea of a desperate man looking for a way out.

Danny's lips were moving, but Virgil could not hear the words. In his mind he began to rationalize what seemed to be his only option. The "system" had failed him. He had tried to do the right thing, but society wouldn't give him another chance. Who would blame him for doing what he felt he had to do to make his life better?

"There are only seven hundred detox beds in the city, and hundreds of people are waiting to get into them," Danny continued.

Before he could finish his explanation, Virgil hit the desk again, and suddenly ran out of the building.

Danny's eyes followed him as he wove through the folding chairs in the lobby and disappeared into the crowd on the street. His heart sank for the twentieth time that day.

It never got easier for him to say, "Sorry, but there's just not enough for you today."

He knew that on the day he was able to utter the words without feeling a pang in his stomach, he would have to find a new line of work.

For the remainder of the day Danny forced himself not to think about the conversations with Hezekiah or with Virgil. He didn't want to allow himself to be elated by the prospect of having the man he loved all to himself. Something would not allow him that pleasure. Something would steal his joy.

Later that day Hezekiah and Danny lay, twisted and tangled, beneath the covers of the bed. The rough surface of Danny's tongue massaged Hezekiah's engorged shaft as his head thrashed on the pillow. His muscular chest heaved upward with each stroke of Danny's mouth.

Danny's hands probed the familiar smooth surface of Hezekiah's buttocks and found the spot that would take him to the height of ecstasy. Hezekiah grabbed the sides of the bed and violently jerked his head back as he neared climax. He moaned, "I'm going to cum—you're going to make me cum!"

With a violent jolt Hezekiah succumbed to the pleasure that Danny gave so unselfishly.

The two lay motionless with legs entwined after their needs had been met. Hezekiah stroked his lover's hair, kissed the top of his head, and softly said, "I stopped by the construction site this week. That crook Benny Winters is determined to get rich off my back. I have to watch his every move."

"Then why don't you fire him?"

"It would be impossible to find another contractor at this stage of the construction." Hezekiah pulled Danny closer and continued listing his concerns. "He told me the estimates were way off. Some are coming in lower than we budgeted, but others are much higher than he expected."

"So what are you going to do?"

"I have no choice. I have to go back to my members and beg for more money."

"Don't worry about it too much, baby. You know you're doing the right thing. Just think of all those people you'll be able to reach, once this is completed. I'm very proud of you."

Danny kissed Hezekiah's temples and nestled under his chin.

"Let's take a trip together next weekend," Hezekiah said without opening his eyes.

There was no response.

He tried again. "I said, let's take a trip together."

Danny leaned on his elbows and looked into Hezekiah's eyes. "Why are you fucking with me?" He rarely cursed around Hezekiah. He did it only on the occasions when he wanted to remind Hezekiah that the "holier than thou" facade had not clouded his thinking.

"I'm not. I mean it."

"Where?" Danny asked suspiciously.

"I don't care. We could go to Paris. Have you ever been to Paris?"

Danny adjusted his body and sat on the edge of the bed, turning away from Hezekiah. "Don't fuck with me, Hezekiah. If you can go, that's fine. If you can't, that's fine too. I don't want to make plans with you, and you back out at the last minute."

"Would you stop cursing at me," Hezekiah said with an understanding smile. "I said I want to go, so we'll go. I'll make the arrangements this week."

Hezekiah rubbed Danny's back. With each stroke he grew more pensive. "I told Samantha about us." Danny jerked around to face Hezekiah. "Why?"

"She knew something was different about me and has been sensing it for weeks. She kept asking whom I was sleeping with," he said in a matter-of-fact tone.

"Did you tell her?"

Although Danny had never met Samantha, he was well aware of her wrath. He'd heard from Hezekiah how she struck terror in those who dared to cross her. While watching her at Hezekiah's side on TV, he saw the sinister glimmer that hid behind her liquid brown eyes. If anyone could convince Hezekiah to leave him, she could.

Through guilt, threats, extortion, and even violence, she could do it.

"No, I haven't told her who you are," Hezekiah replied. "And I won't. She doesn't need to know."

Danny was silent, but his eyes encouraged Hezekiah to say more.

"I'm not gay you know," Hezekiah continued. "I don't . . . I mean, I can't identify with the gay lifestyle. The banners, the bars, the parades."

"The people you see at parades in leather, drag, and feather boas don't represent or even look like most gay people," Danny responded. "Most gays and lesbians are just regular people living their lives. They go to work every day, buy homes, and raise families. They're proud men, women, mothers, fathers, sons, and daughters, first. After that, they define and express their sexuality."

Danny, without thinking, got up from the bed and paced the floor while he spoke.

Hezekiah loved watching Danny walk around in the nude, totally unselfconscious. He restrained a smile until he couldn't contain his amusement any longer and said, "Are you sure you're not a preacher? I thought you were me for a minute there."

Danny laughed and playfully jumped onto the bed. "Why do you tease me? I'm serious."

The two rolled around on the bed like puppies playing in a grassy field, and then Hezekiah gently replied, "I know you are, baby. I'm serious too."

Samantha Cleaveland sat alone in her living room and looked out the window. Muffled sounds from the city below served as background music to her racing thoughts. An antique grandfather clock chimed, alerting her that it was now 7:45 p.m. An ashtray filled with extinguished cigarettes sat on the table next to her. The house was dark and empty.

Samantha jumped when her cell phone rang. She extinguished her most recent cigarette. "Hello."

"Samantha, it's Willie."

"Where have you been? Did you talk to Virgil?"

Reverend Mitchell held his cell phone close to his ear to block the piercing siren of a passing ambulance.

"Yes," Willie said as though presenting a gift he had made in school to his mother. "He's going to do it. He's scared shitless, but he's going to do it Sunday."

A large smile appeared on Samantha's face. She held her head back and looked triumphantly up at the beamed ceiling. "Thank God," she whispered. "How much did you promise him?"

Willie had not been looking forward to delivering this bit of news. "He was getting ready to back out, so I had to offer him thirty thousand dollars. One thousand up front, and the rest after it's done."

"That's just what this city needs. A crackhead with thirty thousand dollars."

"No dealer in Los Angeles is going to see the money. Part of the deal is he's got to leave the city right after it's done."

"Good. Where did he say he was going?"

"He didn't say. I don't fucking care, and neither should you."

"I do care," she snapped. "What happens after he spends the money? He might come back for more. I could end up paying him for the rest of my life."

"Why the hell didn't you think about that before now?"

A taxi swerved in front of Willie's car, forcing him to slam on the brakes. He removed the phone from his ear and shouted, "Watch out, you fucking foreigner!"

Samantha ignored him and continued. "I have thought about it, and I assumed you had too." Samantha had withheld the second phase of her plan, until she knew it would be too late for Willie to back out. "Willie, you can't let him leave town. After he's done the job, you're going to have to kill him."

There was silence on the phone. The realization of the depth of Samantha's evil unfolded before his eyes. He blinked uncontrollably as the picture came into focus. His hands shook and beads of sweat drenched his entire body. "Samantha, you're crazy. In a month he'll probably turn up dead from an overdose in some fucking alley, anyway. Why get ourselves in any deeper?"

"We can't count on that. I don't want any loose ends. You can make it look like a drug deal gone bad. They'll write him off as just another junkie that got in over his head. You've got to do this, Willie. There's no other way."

Willie tried for the next few moments to convince her that Virgil could be trusted. The woman whom he desired so deeply inspired fear in him now. "Samantha, you're asking me to kill someone. I can't do it."

"Think about it, Willie. With Hezekiah dead and Virgil out of the way, we'll be able to do anything we want. You and I can take over New Testament without interference. I thought you wanted this more than I do." Samantha had difficulty saying the next words. "I thought you wanted me."

Willie sighed as he turned the car. Hearing her say the words clouded his thinking. "You know I want you. But we never talked about me killing anyone."

"It's the only way."

Samantha's mind raced between persuading Willie to commit murder and manipulating the trustees to appoint her pastor of New Testament Cathedral. The reverend was talking rapidly, but she did not hear him.

She would have him introduce the idea immediately after Hezekiah was dead. Very few members of the board dared to stand up to Willie Mitchell.

Again she heard his panicked ramblings. "You wanted me to hire a hit man. I did it. You want me to convince the trustees to appoint you pastor. No problem. I said I'd fucking do it. But kill a man myself?"

She stopped him midsentence and asked, "Where are you? I want to talk with you in person."

"I'm almost at my house."

"Good. I'll be there in an hour."

Samantha parked her car in front of Reverend Mitchell's home. It was a large white house that was twice the size of every other house on the block. For Willie it represented his arrival as a successful black man from Texas.

None of his family could have afforded a house like it, and he never passed up an opportunity to remind them.

Willie opened the door before Samantha pressed the bell. His face looked calmer than she had expected. His gray slacks formed a puddle at his shoes, and the everpresent beads of sweat were on his forehead.

He immediately offered her a drink when she entered the house. "I had to have one after I talked to you. My nerves are shot."

"You know I don't drink." She considered what she was about to do and changed her mind. "On second thought, I will join you. This has me nervous too."

Willie left the room to prepare Samantha's drink. When he returned, she was sitting on the couch and had removed her shoes. Her jacket was lying neatly on the back of a chair.

Willie stopped in the doorway and admired her beauty.

He handed her the drink and sat nervously beside her, causing the cushions to slant toward him. Samantha could smell his sweat-drenched body as his large stomach flopped over the gold belt buckle.

"Willie," she said before he could move closer, "have you thought any more about what I asked you to do?"

"It's all I've been able to think about. I'm glad you came. It'll help me make up my mind." A sly smile appeared on his face. "I always think clearer when a beautiful woman is nearby." He moved closer. "What are you going to do to help your daddy make the right decision?" he asked seductively.

Samantha took a sip of the drink and set it on the table.

She untied the flowered scarf around her neck and let the ends drop seductively over her breasts. No sign of the revulsion she felt was apparent on her face.

"You know the only way I can do this is if I know you're willing to kill Virgil. Otherwise, the whole thing is off, and you and I will never be together."

Willie reached his arm around her.

She could see his erection stretching the thin fabric of his pants. Samantha quickly stood up. "I need to hear you say it, Willie. Before we do anything, you need to say you'll do it."

Willie struggled off the couch and walked toward her with his arms outstretched. "Baby, you know I can never say no to you. Come on. Don't tease me like this. Let Daddy have some of that."

Samantha allowed him to nuzzle her neck and nibble her earlobes. "Don't fuck with me, Willie. Let me hear you say it."

Willie moved his tongue up and down her neck while he whispered, "I'll do it for you, baby. I'll kill Virgil Jackson for you, and any other man you want me to. Just let me have some of that. . . ."

"What else, Willie? Tell me what else you're going to do."

He couldn't remember the second thing she wanted. "I don't know. Tell me," he purred while fumbling with the buttons of her blouse.

The growing mound in his pants pressed against her leg. His stomach felt like dough on her hip.

"The trustees, Willie. What are you going to do with the trustees?"

"Oh, that," he moaned. "Don't worry about them. You'll be the pastor of New Testament by this time next week."

Samantha took a deep breath and pulled Willie's lips to hers. She kissed him as passionately as she had ever kissed Hezekiah. She could taste the remnants of alcohol and cigarettes on his tongue. With Willie's final words of consent, she frantically unbuttoned his shirt and undid his pants. She wanted it to be over as soon as possible.

She didn't want him to tear her clothes in his frenzied state, so she willingly undressed in the middle of his living room. Samantha stood naked as he groped her breasts.

As they lay on the couch, Willie's black nylon socks were the only items left on his body. Samantha flinched under the weight of his stomach. She had often wondered how men with such huge guts managed to reach a woman's vagina. She soon discovered it was at the agonizing expense of whoever was unfortunate enough to be under them. His belly flopped and slammed her stomach as he panted. Drops of sweat dripped from his brow onto her chest and neck as he pounded, oblivious to her discomfort.

For the first moments she tried to feign pleasure but quickly realized that he didn't even notice her efforts in his aroused state.

The abuse went on for what seemed an eternity, until he collapsed full weight on top of her, panting to catch his breath.

"Phew! Baby, that was amazing. The pastor doesn't know how good he had it."

Samantha sat alone in the Polo Lounge in the Beverly Hills Hotel, one of her favorite restaurant. Waiters in black vests and pants appeared at her table in rapid intervals, filling her glass with water and offering her coffee and bread, while she waited for her lunch companion to arrive. She could still feel Willie Mitchell's gut pressing into her as she occasionally she waved across the lavish room at people she recognized but preferred to keep at a distance.

She checked her watch when she heard, "Samantha, darling. Sorry I'm late. How are you?"

Samantha reached for the gloved hand of her best friend, Victoria Johnson. Victoria was the wife of Reverend Sylvester Johnson, the pastor of First Bethany Church of Los Angeles. She wore a pale peach pantsuit, which accented the beautiful curves of her body. A diamond-encrusted brooch shaped like a butterfly twinkled on her lapel. Her hands were covered in sleek buttery cream-colored leather gloves. Victoria was the only other pastor's wife with whom Samantha never competed. The women were equals in every way, and both were more ambitious than their successful husbands.

Victoria sat down and removed her gloves. "Are you okay, Sam? You look like you've been crying."

Before Samantha could speak, a waiter appeared at the table. "Good afternoon, Mrs. Johnson. May I get you something from the bar?"

"I'll have a vodka martini, thank you." The waiter left the table and Victoria continued, "Now tell me, honey, what has that bastard done this time?"

"Just more of the usual. He's having another affair. He came right out and admitted it."

"I'm so sorry. You must be devastated. Did he tell you who she is?"

Samantha picked up her napkin and caught a tear running down her cheek. Even though she shared her most intimate secrets with Victoria, she could not bring herself to confess that Hezekiah was sleeping with a man. "No, he said I didn't know her. I don't really care who it is this time."

"What do you mean you don't care? You're not going to leave him, are you?"

"No, I'm not going to leave him, but there's more. She's been calling the house at all hours and hanging up the phone. This morning I saw a car with a woman in it sitting outside the house. When he left, she followed him down the hill." Samantha dabbed her eye with the napkin and continued. "Yesterday I got a call . . . a call saying if he did not leave me, she would kill us both."

"Oh my God, Sammy. You must be frightened out of your mind." Victoria took a long swallow from the drink the waiter had delivered. "The bitch sounds crazy. Have you called the police?"

"No, I can't. I don't want to get the police involved."

"You have to. She's a psycho. I don't mean to scare you, but this is serious. What does Hezekiah have to say about it?"

"He says she's harmless. He's going to break it off with her today. Victoria, I'm so frightened." Samantha prayed Victoria's brain was not too clouded from the vodka to recall their conversation later. She had to have someone vouch for her innocence in court if the need ever arose.

Victoria drank down the remainder of her second drink and ordered another from a passing waiter. "Who cares what he thinks."

"It's not his fault, he—"

Victoria grabbed her hand across the table. "Samantha Monique Cleaveland, don't you dare defend that bastard. He doesn't deserve it. You have stood in his shadow all these years, put up with his ego, made him look better than he really is, and this is how he repays you. I swear, all men should be lined up against a wall, have their dicks cut off and shoved down their throats."

Samantha forced a laugh through her tears. "Victoria, you should do something about that mouth of yours."

"You know I'm right, girl. Sylvester has cheated on me so many times, I get suspicious when he's around too much. If he didn't have so goddamned much money, and that fucking prenup, I'd have left his ass years ago."

Samantha laughed freely. "Girl, you ought to quit."

"You're different, Sam. You could take his church and his money. Everyone knows you're a much better preacher than he is. I bet if he wasn't around, those tight-ass Holy Rollers would still follow you around like you had gold on your ass."

Samantha suppressed a hearty laugh and hoped no one could hear their conversation. "Don't say that, Victoria. I still love him. I just hope this woman doesn't hurt him."

"I hope she does, and if she doesn't, I know some guys that'll break both his and that bitch's legs for fifty dollars and a carton of Newports. You give me the word, and I'll show him just how much you love him."

"I think Hezekiah will learn his lesson this time. He'll never do this to me again."

After lunch the two women embraced on the busy street in front of the restaurant. Samantha had ended the lunch abruptly after Victoria's fourth vodka martini. She feared Victoria would get too drunk to remember they had even met that day.

"Sammy, you call me if you need anything, honey. And don't let that bitch frighten you."

They laughed and embraced one last time as the valet brought Samantha's car and held open the door.

"I just might take you up on that broken-leg offer," Samantha said as she climbed into the driver's seat. "I'll call you next week and let you know how things turn out."

As she drove away, she heard Victoria yelling to the parking attendant, "Where's my car? I've been standing on this curb so long, people are going to think I'm a hooker."

21

Saturday

Hezekiah and Danny dodged rollerbladers and couples jogging on the bike path at Santa Monica Beach. They had met earlier for breakfast at a sidewalk café, and decided to take a walk afterward. It was a beautiful morning, and the beach was already filled with tourists wearing Venice Beach T-shirts and Bermuda shorts. Children were jumping waves and sun worshippers were lying prone on colorful towels. Waves slammed against the weathered remains of the pier, which reached into the horizon.

"Heads up!" yelled a man behind them, wearing black biking shorts and a helmet. Danny and Hezekiah separated to opposite sides of the path and returned to the center when the biker had passed. Danny's shoulder brushed the arm of Hezekiah's gray jogging suit in the closest display of affection they dared in such a public place.

"I promise I'll never let a man in tight biking shorts come between us again." They both laughed as Hezekiah led the way off the paved path toward the ocean.

"I made arrangements for us to fly to Paris next weekend," Hezekiah said as he stumbled over tracks left behind by a lifeguard truck.

"I hadn't thought about that since you mentioned it. I assumed you had forgotten."

"I remember everything we've ever said to each other. Just like I've memorized every inch of your beautiful body. I know you didn't believe me. Now you can see I'm serious about this and about us."

Danny tried to switch the topic. "How did your session go with the therapist?"

"Exactly the way I expected it to. He said I should leave you and let him 'help me' save my marriage and church."

"Maybe he's right."

"Maybe. Or maybe not. It doesn't matter, though. I'm not leaving you. Sorry, but you're stuck with me. And stop trying to change the subject. My plane will be at LAX on next Friday afternoon, and a driver will be waiting for us in Paris."

Hezekiah looked at his watch. It was 11:00 a.m. "We'd better head back. I've got some work to do on my sermon for Sunday."

They walked back to the restaurant with a comfortable silence shared between them. Seagulls hunted for sand crabs while the waves erased the footprints they left behind.

Danny interrupted the silence. "Can I tell you something?"

"You can tell me anything."

"I'm afraid."

"Of what?"

"Of what I think Samantha will do if you ever leave her."

"What do you think she'll do? Kill me?" Hezekiah said with a smile.

"I'm serious, Hezekiah. I think she's capable of doing something that . . . I know you love her, but I can't shake this feeling I have about her."

"I do still have feelings for her, but not in the same way I feel about you. Yes, she has a mean streak, but she's also very pragmatic and a survivor. She'll adjust just like millions of other women do when they divorce. It's going to be difficult, but I'm sure she'll be fine."

"Just be careful, Hezekiah. I don't want anything to happen to you."

The Harbor Freeway was bumper to bumper as Samantha drove her car toward the church. Chamber music hummed from her CD. Dark sunglasses protected her eyes from the afternoon sun. As she exited onto Hezekiah Cleaveland Avenue, she saw Willie Mitchell leaning against his car in the church parking lot. Samantha pulled in next to him and got out. He looked at her silky legs as they extended from the car, and he immediately remembered why he subjected himself to the whims of the woman.

"Where's Catherine?" Samantha asked.

"She must be at lunch." He leaned in to kiss her.

Samantha pushed him away and said, "Not here, you idiot."

Samantha reached into her purse and handed Willie the gun wrapped in one of Hezekiah's handkerchiefs. She already had carefully wiped her fingerprints from it. "Put it in your pocket and give me back the handkerchief. Before you give it to Virgil, make sure you wipe your prints off, and don't let him have it until Sunday morning."

"I'm not stupid. Where'd you get this?"

"It belonged to my mother. I don't know where she got it, but I found it under her mattress when I was clearing out her house after she died. What's important is it's not registered and can't be traced back to either of us."

Willie placed the bundle into the breast pocket of his coat and removed the cloth.

"Where is Virgil?" Samantha asked in a half whisper.

"I think he's at the mission downtown. He goes there every day," he answered nervously.

"Just make sure he doesn't back out at the last minute."

"He won't." Willie looked around the parking lot and then whispered, "When am I going to get some more of that good loving?"

Samantha's eyes glazed over with disgust. "Just take care of this, and you'll get more than you can handle."

Samantha turned and walked quickly toward the church entrance. Willie rubbed his gut as he watched her legs and muttered, "Damn, that woman is fine." He then bounced into his car and drove away.

Samantha entered the church. Although no one was in sight, she could hear footsteps in the distance. As she neared the glass office, her heart began to race. It was bright from fluorescent lights, and the telephone was ringing.

She fumbled trying to put her key in the door as she heard the footsteps growing nearer.

"Good afternoon, Mrs. Cleaveland."

The voice startled her, and she dropped the keys. When she turned around, she saw Rauly Jenkins, the facility manager.

"Rauly, you scared me," she said. "I wish you wouldn't sneak up on me like that."

"I'm sorry, ma'am. I was up in the baptismal pit. I don't think they've cleaned it since I left for vacation two weeks ago."

As Rauly spoke, Samantha became concerned that he had witnessed the exchange between her and Willie Mitchell.

"Have you seen Reverend Mitchell? I thought I saw him on the street when I drove up."

"No, ma'am, I haven't seen him all day."

"I guess it's time to get my eyes checked. Rauly, please make sure the lectern is polished before this Sunday. And the stained-glass window behind the pulpit needs to be cleaned. It looked murky last Sunday morning."

"Yes, ma'am."

"Also, Pastor Cleaveland doesn't like the looks of one of the support beams under the balcony. He's concerned it could collapse if there is too much weight on it. He wants you to post CLOSED signs at the balcony entrances and set up the television monitors in Fellowship Hall for this Sunday's service," Samantha said, hoping Rauly and Hezekiah would not cross paths before the end of the day.

"That's funny. He didn't mention it earlier, when I saw him. I'll get my men on that right away. It'll be done before I leave for the weekend."

"Thank you."

Rauly returned the way he came, and Samantha entered the office. She picked up a pad from the desk and was beginning to write a note when she saw Catherine approaching.

"Hello, Catherine. I was just writing you a note. I hope you're not too upset with me about the other day. There was just so much on my mind, and I got carried away. I was completely out of line, and I hope you can forgive me."

Catherine stared at her cautiously and said, "That's all right, Mrs. Cleaveland. I understand. Pastor Cleaveland explained it to me."

A flush of blood rushed into Samantha's head. She wondered what horrible thing Hezekiah had said to the girl. "I hope he didn't say anything too terrible about me. Whatever it was, I'm sure I deserved it."

Catherine did not respond.

"Well, anyway, if there is anything I can do to make it up to you," Samantha continued, "please let me know."

Samantha had already decided that after Hezekiah was dead, the first thing she would do was fire Catherine Birdsong, again.

"Please, I just want to forget about it."

As Samantha approached the door, she turned and said, "I almost forgot. Could you order lilies, white lilies, and birds-of-paradise for the pulpit this Sunday? They're Hezekiah's favorites."

"Yes, ma'am," Catherine responded coldly. "Will there be anything else?"

"No, that's all. I'll see you on Sunday morning."

22

An attractive woman with too much makeup stood behind the counter of the beauty spa. "Mrs. Cleaveland, how nice to see you again. Andre is in with a client right now. He'll be with you in a few minutes. He asked that we start your manicure first."

"Please follow me to the changing room, and we'll get you started."

Samantha followed the young woman through white doors surrounded by carvings of grapevines and puffyfaced cherubs.

Inside, women were leisurely milling around, wearing thin blue robes with towels covering their wet hair. Some wore mint clay masks, while others had cellophane dangling from limp hair.

The buzz of hair dryers could be heard coming from an adjoining room. Samantha exchanged greetings with several women as she passed through the crowd.

"Are you having your hair colored today, Mrs. Cleaveland?" the young woman asked.

"No, just a facial and manicure."

Monique held open the door of a small dressing room for Samantha. "When you're done disrobing, Frances will start your manicure. Would you like an espresso or mineral water?"

Samantha disliked the vapid smile of the woman, and she had always refused to address her by name. "Mineral water. Thank you."

After having her hands massaged, nails treated and painted a classic clear, Samantha lay vulnerable on a padded table, with the hands of Andre gently massaging her face. A bright light pointed directly at her face, and steam sprayed to open pores. Samantha had grown fond of Andre, despite the fact that he was obviously gay. How could she not like someone that made her look five years younger than her age?

"I don't think you need a peel today. I'm just going to give you a good cleansing and facial."

Andre was a well-built man with thick dreadlocked hair, which went in every direction. He wore an African-print shirt with tight black pants and boots.

The music played softly as Andre gossiped. "Victoria was in yesterday. She nearly drank a whole bottle of champagne, and then got an attitude when we refused to serve her more. She was so drunk we had to call a cab to take her home."

Samantha smiled through the steam. "You're lucky that didn't happen five years ago. You would have had to call the police. Victoria is a lot calmer than she used to be."

"How's that gorgeous husband of yours? I saw him on television the other day. Something about a new building."

Samantha's body tensed. She instinctively reacted to a man referring to her husband as "gorgeous." She looked up at Andre standing behind her and asked, "Do you think he's gorgeous? I didn't think men noticed that kind of thing."

"Samantha, when a man looks that good, it's hard not to notice. I hope I didn't offend you."

"Not at all. Andre, may I ask you a personal question?" she inquired as he applied a gooey substance to her face.

"You can ask me anything, sweetheart. You know you're my favorite client."

"Why do you prefer men over women? We've never discussed it, but I assume you're gay."

Andre's hands froze in place for a moment, then resumed. "Why do you ask?"

"No particular reason. A friend's husband recently told her he was gay, and I guess I'm curious."

"I knew it," Andre blurted. "It's Victoria's husband, isn't it? I can tell a gay man from a mile away. The first time I saw Sylvester, I knew he was family."

"It's not Sylvester. You think he's gay? That's ridiculous. What man in his right mind would want him? He looks like a buffalo in a bad toupee. Anyway, it's not him. It's no one you would know. So tell me. What attracts a man to other men?"

"I've been attracted to men as far back as I can remember. Beyond the obvious physical stuff I guess I would say it's because a man can understand me better than any woman ever has."

"Why does that necessarily lead to sex?"

"For me they're one and the same. I can't separate my mind from my body. If I like a man, I mean his mind and how he thinks, then the physical attraction comes naturally, and that's when the fun . . ."

Andre had drifted easily into the usual salon chatter, when he suddenly remembered to whom he was talking.

"Samantha, darling. I really don't feel comfortable talking about this with you. My God, you're a minister's wife."

He laughed nervously.

Samantha reacted sternly. "What does the man I'm married to have to do with anything? You think just because I'm married to Hezekiah, I wouldn't understand."

"No, I'm not saying that. I just meant I don't want to offend you."

"Never mind. Just change the subject." Samantha sat through the rest of the facial in silence. Andre made several unsuccessful attempts to resuscitate their exchange, but Samantha would not participate beyond a curt "yes" and "no."

As he walked her to the lobby, he said, "Samantha, I'm sorry if I said something to upset you. The next time you come in, your facial will be on the house."

Without looking at him she curtly said, "That won't be necessary. I won't be back. I don't approve of your lifestyle."

Samantha quickly paid her bill and left Andre and the salon in her past.

Samantha opened the door to her closet. The lights came on automatically. Bulbs lit up around a mirror that stretched the length of the wall in the closet, which was at least half the size of her bedroom. Clothes she had acquired over the years of her marriage lined the walls. Samantha stood in the door and marveled at the items that meant so much to her. Rarely had she given any of her clothes to charity. She felt she gave enough of her life to others and drew the line at her cherished belongings.

Garments and shoes that had not been worn in years, and would probably never be worn again, stood waiting for their chance in the sunlight.

It usually took Samantha only a few hours to prepare for church, but this was going to be a special Sunday. She needed at least a day. Samantha wanted to look her most radiant, yet wear something practical that could be easily cleaned in the event it got spattered with blood. Her heels had to be just the right height for the inevitable rapid climb up the pulpit steps to cradle the body of her dead husband.

She had to select an ensemble that would not inadvertently rise and reveal too much leg if she decided to perform the "Jackie O" lunge to dodge stray bullets.

After an extended search Samantha pulled four outfits from the racks and displayed them on hooks like suits of armor in a medieval castle corridor. They all had one thing in common; they would not fly any higher than her thigh in case strenuous maneuvers were required. Two of the outfits selected were made of vibrant floral-print fabric.

One was a peach suit with a skirt designed to obediently follow the lines of her well-shaped lower half. The fourth was her favorite. It was a simple cream-colored sleeveless dress by Givenchy, and it perfectly mimicked the contours of her body. The accompanying jacket helped to partially conceal the low-cut neckline.

Over the next hour she tried on each of the dresses several times. She put each outfit through a sequence of tests that included kneeling down in front of the large mirror, walking at a quick pace across the length of the dressingroom floor, and a series of abrupt twists and turns.

She decided on the cream dress and jacket at the conclusion of the high-fashion aerobic session. The shape and easy movement suited her purposes well, and the color would serve as the perfect backdrop for his blood.

The shoes she selected were not the pair originally purchased for the ensemble. Instead, she chose a pair with a slightly lower heel and a shade darker than the dress. She did not want to risk tripping or snagging her shoe on the carpet. The accessories were the easy part. The dress would only tolerate pearls, a single strand that stopped just short of the neckline, and a matching bracelet.

Samantha stood in front of the mirror to examine her choice and was pleased. She looked like a magazine's cover model, an image that most women would never dare to try and emulate.

Hezekiah had already begun eating his dinner on Saturday evening when Jasmine rushed in and kissed him on the forehead. The smell of mouthwash surrounded her head. "Hi, Daddy. Where's Mommy?"

"She's around here somewhere. I think in her study. Where have you been all day?"

"Daddy, I'm not a little girl. I wish you would stop asking me that every time I come into the house."

Etta emerged from the kitchen and set a clean plate in front of the breathless girl. "Hello, Jasmine. I hope you're hungry."

"Not really, Etta. I think I'll just have salad tonight."

Samantha suddenly appeared below the arched entry to the dining room. "Hello. Why didn't you tell me dinner was ready?"

Hezekiah continued eating and said, "Etta knocked on your door, but you didn't answer."

"I was on the telephone."

Samantha joined them at the table. To watch the three, one would not have known what lay ahead. The conversation was polite. No mention was made of men, alcohol, or murder. Hezekiah and Samantha never made eye contact, but they did direct several inconsequential comments to each other.

The dinner went on without an argument. Etta frequently entered the room to remove dishes and fill empty glasses. She was pleased that the pastor was able to enjoy in peace the food she had prepared for him.

Before finishing her salad, Jasmine stood. "I'm going to Shelly's." She braced herself for her mother's response.

There was none.

Hezekiah broke the silence. "Honey, I expect to see you at church tomorrow."

"I'll be there, Daddy." Before reaching the door, she looked over her shoulder and said, "Good-bye, Mommy."

Samantha set her fork on her plate and said, "Good-bye, Jasmine. I love you, honey."

Samantha waited until she heard the roar of Jasmine's car passing the window. Then she looked at Hezekiah and said, "I think you should sleep in the guest room tonight."

Samantha retreated to the bedroom and was not seen again that evening.

The doorbell in Sandra's condominium rang. Cynthia walked from the kitchen, holding a fresh tray of cheeses and crackers. Lavender-scented candles had been extinguished, but remnants of their bouquet lingered in the air.

Sandra quickly turned off a languid tune sung by Nina Simone.

"Are you ready, girl?" Sandra asked, adjusting the shoulders on her black suit. "That's Phillip now."

"I'm as ready as I'll ever be. Let him in."

Sandra opened the door.

"Phillip," she said to the man at the threshold. "Thank you for coming. I know this is awkward for you. Please let me take your coat. Would you like a glass of wine?"

Phillip Thornton graciously accepted the wine and walked tentatively into the living room.

Sandra and Cynthia sat down on the couch and Phillip sat in an overstuffed chair directly in front of them. He was a handsome man with a hint of gray at each temple.

He wore a navy blue sport coat and tan khaki pants.

Sandra was the first to speak. "Let me start by saying, Phillip, that we appreciate and understand the risks you are taking by being here tonight," she said, leaning forward on the sofa. "I know that you and Hezekiah have been friends for years, and this whole ordeal must be very difficult for you."

"That's a nice speech, Sandra," said Phillip, placing his glass on the table. "You seem to be under the misguided impression that I have some reservations about running the story. Let's be clear about this. I don't. Yes, Hezekiah and I are friends, but this isn't about friendship. It's about business. This has the potential to be the biggest story in the country.

"Last year alone my paper lost fifty million dollars. I've got the unions on my ass. The fucking Internet is drawing away my readers by the thousands, and on top of that, advertisers are dropping like flies. I stand to make millions if the *Los Angeles Chronicle* breaks this story. For me it comes down to either running the story or filing bankruptcy and shutting down the entire newspaper, and shutting down is not an option I want to entertain. This paper has been in my family for three generations. My greatgrandfather started it in his father's garage when he was a teenager. I don't want to be the Thornton who ran my family's legacy into the ground. I'll leave that honor to my sons."

Cynthia sat silent as Phillip continued. "Hezekiah is going to come after us with an army of lawyers when this story breaks. Cynthia, I need some assurances that you'll stand behind your story. We'll protect your identity as long as possible, but I can't make any guarantees that at some point a judge won't insist that we reveal our source."

The room fell silent for a moment, and then Cynthia asked, "Will Chronicle attorneys represent me if a judge forces you to reveal who I am?"

"Yes. You will have full access to our legal department. I need to be honest with you about the risks. This story will be national and international news. You will be hounded by reporters for months, and possibly years, if your identity is made public. You'll also be setting yourself up for a potential civil lawsuit from Hezekiah."

"You're scaring her, Phillip," Sandra chimed in. "Cynthia, I think Phillip is overestimating the public's interest in Hezekiah. I personally think it will make a big splash in the headlines for a few weeks, and then some politician will get caught with a hooker and the public will lose interest in this. Plus, there is a strong possibility that the public will never find out who the source is."

"That is true, but she still needs to be prepared. You each know Hezekiah is loved by a lot of people. Cynthia, you will not be very popular with people who think Hezekiah walks on water. Can you handle that?"

Sandra jumped in again. "Hezekiah is also hated by just as many, if not more, people. They will see you as a hero, a woman who exposed hypocrisy at the highest level of the church."

Cynthia listened intently as the two continued to present her with the pros and cons of her actions. However, none that were mentioned came close to her own reason for outing Hezekiah.

As they talked, she saw images of her husband standing center stage at New Testament Cathedral and saying, "I am proud to be your new pastor."

She saw herself standing next him and smiling lovingly at him as cameras beamed their images to televisions all over the country. She could feel the buttery leather of the limousine caressing her body as she was being driven to luncheons, parties, and banquets in her honor. She could hear the roar of the Learjet engine as it whisked her and Percy off to the East Coast to meet with the president or some other very important person.

"All right, you two," she said. "I've heard enough. I refuse to back down because of fear. This isn't about me. It's about doing the right thing. Phillip, don't worry. I'll stand behind the story."

"Good. Then I'll give it the green light," Phillip said, clapping his hands together.

"I've told you why I'm doing this. I'm curious, ladies, why are you so eager to out Hezekiah?"

Cynthia spoke first. "This has been so difficult for me. I love Hezekiah and Samantha deeply. I would give my life for them. They've done so much for Percy and me. We wouldn't be where we are today if it weren't for them."

Both Phillip and Sandra looked skeptically at Cynthia as she continued. "I just can't sit by and not expose such a horrible abomination. Hezekiah has sinned, and it must be brought to light. It's for his own good. He has to repent before God and man and beg for forgiveness. I'm doing this to save his soul from eternal damnation."

"That is very Christian of you, Mrs. Pryce," Phillip said with a smirk. "I suppose the fact that your husband is the heir apparent to the New Testament Cathedral dynasty has had no impact on your decision."

"That never crossed my mind. This is about exposing sin and—"

Phillip interrupted, "So what about you, Sandra? Hezekiah got you your first job out of law school."

Sandra crossed her legs and said, "That's simple. I'm doing it for Samantha. She deserves better. She's too blinded by love to see how Hezekiah is destroying her life. She would never leave him. She would never do anything to hurt him, so I'm helping him leave her."

Phillip showed little interest in what he considered half-truths from the women. He could clearly see that whatever the true reasons for their betrayal, they were strong enough to ensure their full commitment to the story.

"All right, then, ladies. It looks like we're in business," he said. "The story is scheduled to run in this Sunday's paper. You had better brace yourselves because it's going to be a hell of a ride."

23

Sunday Morning

It was 1:00 a.m. Hattie Williams lay awake in her bed, staring at the ceiling. A sheer curtain quivered gently from the breeze through the open window. She hadn't slept well since viewing the images in her kitchen window days earlier. Concern for Pastor Cleaveland consumed her thoughts.

If he were already dead, someone would have called her by now. She had called Etta the day before, and everything seemed normal. Hattie prayed that the pastor would make it through the night so she could see him at least one last time. She felt helpless because there was nothing she could do to prevent it.

A tear trailed down her temple to her nightcap. "Jesus, you know what's best for the pastor. Thy will be done on earth as it is in heaven. But, Lord, let his passage be easy. Let him be surrounded by people who love him. Let him be in the place that he loves so much when you call him home."

Hezekiah's legs jerked and his hands swatted at imaginary demons as he slept. The dream that caused his brow to sweat, and his body to toss and turn, was so vivid, it felt as if he were actually awake. Hezekiah tossed in his sleep as he wrestled within the grips of another nightmare.

New Testament Cathedral is in a state of turmoil. The church grounds are filled with religious-right protesters waving placards, and gay activists demanding a full confession from Hezekiah. A squadron of broadcast news vans clogs the streets.

Hezekiah is riding in the rear of the limousine. A swarm of men and women toting cameras, lights, and microphones rush toward the car as it approaches. Dino drives slowly, and police officers clear his path. Protesters shout louder as cameras deliver their images live to homes throughout the country. Hezekiah then sees an anchorwoman standing at the foot of the church steps.

"This is Wendy Chung, with ABC News," she says crisply into the camera. "We have interrupted your regularly scheduled programming to bring you live coverage of a dramatic story unfolding in the city of Los Angeles. Pastor Hezekiah Cleaveland's car has just arrived here at New Testament Cathedral. We will try to get a statement from him on a story that broke this morning, which claims that he has been involved in a long-standing homosexual affair, but as you can see, it's a mob scene here this morning. . . . Pastor Cleaveland!" she shouts as Hezekiah sees himself stepping from the car. "Would you comment on the allegations of a homosexual affair that was reported in this morning's Los Angeles Chronicle?"

Dino steps in front of the woman as Hezekiah walks to the stairs. "Sir, these are startling claims and the American people would like to hear your response."

The reporter's pleas for attention are replaced by those of others. "Pastor Cleaveland, over here," shouts a man in the crowd. "Is it true that you refurbished a live/work loft for Danny St. John using church funds?"

Hezekiah proceeds up the stairs, but the questions continue.

"Where is Mr. St. John this morning, sir? Has he gone into hiding?"

"Are you going to divorce your wife, sir, and live openly as a same-sex couple?"

"How is this revelation going to affect your plans for the new cathedral? Will you halt construction?"

When Hezekiah reaches the top landing, the doors fling open, and Percy Pryce walks out. "The pastor has no comment at this time," he says, reaching for Hezekiah's arm. "He will make a full statement today, after this morning's church service. Now, please, let him through."

Police officers block the doors to prevent the reporters from rushing into the building.

Wendy Chung faces the camera again. "Well, you heard it. Pastor Hezekiah Cleaveland has refused to comment, but his spokesperson states that he will make a statement later today. As a result of this extramarital homosexual affair, some pundits are suggesting that Cleaveland should resign as pastor of one of the largest churches in the country.

"They say that his credibility as a spiritual leader has suffered irreparable damage. Believed by many to be one of the most powerful ministers in the United States, Pastor Hezekiah Cleaveland has served as spiritual confidant to two presidents. His future now seems to be in ruins if these startling allegations prove to be true. Also, sources close to the family have informed us that Mrs. Cleaveland intends to file for divorce and possibly mount her own campaign to replace her husband as pastor of New Testament Cathedral. We will bring you live coverage of the press conference later today. Now back to your regularly scheduled programming."

Hezekiah's body twisted and turned in bed. His legs and arms became tangled in the sheets as he fought to emerge from the dream. His mind raced forward at an alarming speed.

Hezekiah is standing on the roof of the church above the stained-glass window, looking down on the throngs of protesters and reporters. In the distance he can see the construction site of the new cathedral. It is covered in a smoky gray haze, and steel beams are falling off and crashing to the ground, causing huge plumes of dust to envelop the crowd below.

He then hears a booming voice from the clouds over his head. "Good morning, ladies and gentlemen of the press," the voice says. "Pastor Hezekiah Cleaveland has called this press conference to respond to the article that appeared in this morning's edition of the Los Angeles Chronicle. He will first make a brief statement, after which we will have a few minutes for questions. Please hold your questions until he has finished."

Hezekiah steps forward to the edge of the roof. A bright light forms a halo around him. "Good morning," he says solemnly. His booming voice echoes like thunder in clouds. "I am here to address what I consider to be a very sad day for Los Angeles and for the country. It is a tragic commentary on the state of

American journalism when a member of the media is permitted to fabricate the news without benefit of facts, truth, or credible evidence. It is a crime against the American people when a once-trusted publication appoints itself judge, juror, and executioner in matters pertaining to the lives of private citizens of this country.

"Let me say, in the most emphatic terms possible, that I have never had a sexual relationship with a man. I have never met Mr. Danny St. John in person, and I have never sent the collection of e-mail correspondence that has been falsely attributed to me. Yes, I have spoken to Mr. St. John on the telephone, but only as a citizen who is concerned about homeless people in this city. Mr. St. John has on numerous occasions responded to my requests to assist homeless people whom I encounter on a daily basis. The calls that Mr. Savage referred to were nothing more than my acting not only as a pastor but also as a citizen who is concerned about the plight of homeless women, men, and children.

"Now, as for the e-mail messages, it pains me to say that yes, the e-mails were, in fact, generated from my home computer." Hezekiah takes another step closer to the edge. *"I am sad to report to you that all the messages were written by my wife, Samantha Cleaveland."*

Gasps erupt from the crowd. Cameras flash throughout, and reporters grab for cell phones.

Hezekiah continues his statement. "She wrote and sent the letters in an attempt to further her own ambitions. Mrs. Cleaveland conspired with Mr. Danny St. John, Lance Savage, and other unscrupulous individuals."

Reporters immediately begin shouting questions, but Hezekiah holds up his hand.

"Please let me continue," he says. "I wish Mr. Savage were here so that I could ask him why he wrote a story that is based solely on lies, innuendo, and unfounded rumors, but I do not see him among you today.

"Finally, let me say to the citizens of this great city that this entire ordeal has only served to make me a better and stronger pastor. I will work even harder to earn your trust and support of my efforts to build the church of the future. Thank you."

A jumble of questions fills the air and buzzes around Hezekiah's head.

"Pastor Cleaveland, how do you account for the fact that you were seen entering Mr. St. John's apartment on numerous occasions by his upstairs neighbors, Mr. and Mrs. Somner?"

"I'm sure that the Somners are a very nice and well-intentioned couple, but I have no idea where they live, nor have I ever met them."

"Pastor Cleaveland," calls out another reporter. "Why do you think Mrs. Cleaveland did this? What did she have to gain?"

"I would imagine that some misguided person, possibly Sandra Kelly, convinced her that I was the only thing preventing her from being pastor of New Testament Cathedral. It is unfortunate. I loved, and still do love, my wife with all my heart and soul, and have dedicated my life to making her happy."

"So what's next? Are you going to file for divorce?"

"I would never divorce Samantha. She is obviously suffering through some sort of emotional crisis because that's the only way she could have been convinced to do something this horrible. Even what she did is not enough to make me leave her. I will, instead, stand by her and make sure that she receives the best psychiatric care possible."

"Did you use church funds to renovate a loft for Mr. St. John?"

"I won't even dignify that with a response," Hezekiah says sharply. "Next question, please."

"Sir, has this in any way changed your mind about building the new cathedral?"

"As I said in my statement, it has only invigorated me. My commitment to serving the people of this city is stronger than ever."

Then Hezekiah sees a woman begin to levitate above the crowd. Her lips do not move, but he can hear her speak. "Pastor Cleaveland, Sandy Gingham, from the Los Angeles Chronicle," she calls out. "The body of Mr. Danny St. John has been recovered from the ocean off Santa Monica. He apparently committed suicide by jumping from the Santa Monica Pier. Do you have any words of condolence for his family and friends?"

The mob falls silent. Hezekiah stands motionless and stares into the flashing lights. Moments pass before the reporter speaks again.

"Pastor Cleaveland, would you like to comment?"

Hezekiah does not respond, still frozen in a wash of flashing lights. Instead, he takes another step closer to the ledge.

Hezekiah puts his foot forward into the air and begins to fall. Pandemonium ensues. Reporters and cameramen begin to float up to Hezekiah and continue the line of questioning that caused him to step over the edge of the building.

"Pastor Cleaveland, would you like to comment on the apparent suicide of Mr. St. John?"

"Pastor Cleaveland, were you aware of his death prior to the press conference?"

"Sir, do you suspect foul play in the death of Mr. St. John?"

Will this fall never end? *he thinks.* Will God have mercy and release me from this torment? Can the earth stop spinning for one moment and allow me to leave this body, which is Hezekiah T. Cleaveland?

Hezekiah's plunge continues as familiar faces, dreaded confrontations, and painful events flash in rapid succession through his mind. This is it. His life condenses into the few seconds it takes to fall to the earth. It took a lifetime for Hezekiah to reach the heights of power and prestige, but only seconds to fall to the ground. When his body crashes onto the polished stone, the screaming stops and the glass birds stop flapping their wings.

The impact caused Hezekiah to bolt upright in the bed. His chest heaved as he searched the room frantically to assure himself that it was only a dream.

24

Around the city merchants jostled sleeping men in doorways. "Wake up, you bum!" they said. "It's time for me to open my shop." The morning sun readied for its first appearance over the horizon as the city grudgingly came to life. Compact cars, with headlights piercing the remains of night, scurried through neighborhoods delivering bundles of information, while vans stopped on every corner, filling news receptacles with the Sunday paper.

In the dim morning light the headline read: OUTSPOKEN NEWSMAN FOUND DEAD, SLAIN IN HOME.

The paper landed with a thud on the front porch of Kenneth Davis's home. Still in his bathrobe, he retrieved the paper and stood in his foyer in shock. He froze when he read the headline, and then quickly read the first paragraph:

> Lance Savage was found murdered late Saturday evening in his home in Venice, California. Police confirm that the cause of death was blunt trauma to the head.

Kenneth dropped the paper to the floor and poured a glass of bourbon. His hands shook as he swallowed, but the liquid offered no escape from the bold print that stared up from the carpet.

A gentle tap on Cynthia's bedroom door drew her from a fitful sleep. "Reverend and Mrs. Pryce, are you awake?"

"Come in, Carmen. What is it?" Percy responded.

A dark-haired housekeeper wearing a white apron entered. "I've brought your coffee and the morning paper," she said with a Spanish accent.

Cynthia sat up and probed the nightstand for her reading glasses. The words assaulted her eyes, causing them to blink in disbelief. She covered her mouth with a trembling hand as Percy read over her shoulder.

"Oh my God," he said, sitting upright.

"I don't believe this. It says they think he was killed by a burglar." Cynthia continued reading:

Savage was found by Richard Harrison, the editor of the Los Angeles Chronicle. According to Harrison, at the time of his death Savage was working on a very controversial story that many powerful people did not want to see printed. Harrison declined to give any details.

"In these kinds of cases we look for possible motives, financial, family, or work related," said Assistant Police Chief Michael Pincus. "We believe this was not a random killing. All indications at the crime scene are that he was targeted."

Percy got out of bed and began to pace the floor. "You see what you've done, Cynthia. If you hadn't given him those e-mails, he would still be alive."

Cynthia slammed the paper onto the bed and said, "What are you talking about? This has nothing to do with me. The article says he was being robbed. Oh God, Percy. They must have killed him shortly after you spoke with him."

Carmen spoke again. "Reverend Pryce, is there something I can do? Your hands are shaking. Can I bring you more coffee? I can put something in it to calm you."

Percy stopped pacing and sat back down on the bed and said, "No, thank you, Carmen. There's nothing anyone can do now."

The smell of coffee filled Naomi's kitchen as she summoned the courage to open the front door and retrieve the morning paper. She prayed there would be no mention of Hezekiah or New Testament Cathedral. When she opened the door, the headline greeted her as she looked down at the paper on the porch.

Naomi sat at the kitchen table with her favorite coffee mug and read:

Richard Harrison said that even though they have delayed Lance's most recent story, the Chronicle fully intends to run

it at a later date. According to Harrison, the story was
scheduled to run in today's edition, but out of respect for
Lance and his family, "we have decided to publish it at a
later date." He declined to elaborate further.

Naomi placed the paper facedown on the table and cradled the
coffee mug.

"Thank God," she said out loud. "At least we have a few more
days to figure out what to do about Hezekiah."

Sandra Kelly was already dressed for the day when the paper
arrived.

"What the fuck?" she said after reading the headline.

"Lance, you idiot. How could you do this to me?"

"We are grief stricken," said *Los Angeles Chronicle* publisher and
owner Phillip Thornton. "We've lost a family member."

Longtime associate Edward Wieland called Savage a great
reporter and very controversial. "He was persistent and would
not let people off the hook, whether he was reporting on corruption
in government, the entertainment business, or anyone else. He
ruffled a lot of feathers because of it."

Pincus said police had no motive for the killing, but that it did
not appear random. Pincus said investigators would look into
every possible connection with Savage's work.

Savage, who had been a reporter for the *Los Angeles Chronicle*
for the past three years, was killed around 8:00 p.m., Los Angeles
assistant police chief Pincus said. He said witnesses told police
they saw two men leaving the house earlier that evening.

Thornton reiterated the fact that the most recent story Savage
was working on would eventually be published. He stated that he
didn't know if the tragedy was related to it, but if it was, "those
responsible for his death should know that they cannot stop the
truth from coming out."

Sandra dropped the paper to the floor and thought, *Fortunately,*
Phillip's greed is more powerful than his conscience.

***

It was a beautiful Sunday morning at New Testament Cathedral. The parking lot was already filled with freshly washed cars. Members were soon required to park along Cleaveland Avenue. Children played on the lawn in front of the church, carefully trying to keep their flowered white dresses and little tan suits clean for as long as possible.

Women rushed their husbands up the stairs to the church to get a good seat. The lobby was filled with members waiting to be seated by the ushers. White gloves handed neatly folded powder blue bulletins to each person who entered the sanctuary.

Rauly Jenkins had dutifully placed CLOSED signs at each balcony entrance. Worshippers were directed to Fellowship Hall, where folding chairs had been assembled auditorium-style, when the sanctuary had reached capacity. No one liked viewing the service over the television monitors, but they could not refuse the only remaining option.

At 10:50 a.m. the choir lined up behind the now-closed double doors to the sanctuary. Except for choir members waiting to enter the sanctuary, the lobby was empty. They waited patiently for the first chords from the organ.

Singers nervously fastened buttons on their robes and adjusted the sashes embroidered with the name of the church.

The doors flew open and the procession began when the chord was finally struck. Parishioners stood to welcome the jubilant march.

In the quiet of his office, Pastor Cleaveland retrieved the vibrating telephone in his pocket. "I'm glad you called. I thought you had forgotten me."

"I could never forget you. How are you?" Danny asked.

"I'm okay, baby." Hezekiah spoke like a teenager in love.

"I've got you. What else could I ask for? How are you?"

"I didn't sleep too well last night. I'm still worrying about you."

"I wish I were there with you now. Maybe I should come by later and give you a back rub."

Danny smiled. "I'd like that. I'm going to the gym, but I should be back by two o'clock."

Hezekiah stood from his desk and stretched. "I'll see you then. I love you, Danny."

"I love you too, Hezekiah."

Although he was within the safe confines of his office, Hezekiah felt exposed and vulnerable to the world. A cold resolve showed in the lines of his face. His yellow necktie was neatly in place, and the pinstriped suit hung elegantly from his shoulders.

As he reached for the door, the telephone rang again. It was Percy Pryce.

"Have you read this morning's newspaper?" Percy asked.

"I never read the paper on Sunday morning. You know that," Hezekiah responded with a hint of irritation.

Percy dropped his head and propped his forehead up with his palm. "Lance Savage is . . ."

There was a pause.

"He's dead, Hezekiah. They found him yesterday in his home."

Hezekiah froze in place. "What happened to him?"

"The police don't know. From what I read, it sounded like a robbery."

"God rest his soul," Hezekiah said softly. "Did the article mention the story he was working on?"

"It did, but no details were given."

"Well, at least we can be thankful for that."

"Yes, but this is not over yet, Hezekiah. Phillip Thornton said they will run the story eventually." Percy began to sob into the telephone. "You know I would do anything for you, Hezekiah. I'm so sorry. I am so very sorry."

"This isn't your fault, Percy. You're a good friend. I know I can count on you and Cynthia."

Percy dropped his head to the dining-room table in front of his penthouse window and continued to cry as Hezekiah said, "I'll see you in the pulpit in a few minutes, my friend."

Willie Mitchell dropped Virgil three blocks away from the church. He then double-parked his car in the parking lot of the church and ran up the stairs. His seat was waiting for him in the pulpit. As he passed Samantha on the front row, he bent over to kiss her cheek and whispered, "Everything is set."

Samantha had decided against pearls for her wrist and instead chose a diamond bracelet that Hezekiah had bought her for Christmas. She listened attentively as the church secretary read announcements from the morning bulletin.

The woman at the podium had a sultry voice better suited for radio. Her glasses rested on the tip of her nose as she read, "Please mark you calendars for the first Sunday evening of next month. As you know, that is the kick off of our tenth anniversary at New Testament Cathedral."

Everyone applauded. The worship service proceeded as it had for the past ten years. The choir sang, the people rejoiced, and the cameras rolled. Pastor Cleaveland entered the sanctuary on cue. The cameras followed the precisely sculpted black suit as it floated up the steps to the pulpit. He nodded good morning to the choir as they continued their song. When the song ended, all cameras focused once again on Hezekiah. The applause subsided and Hezekiah spoke his first words of the morning.

"I know a lot of you are not going to want to hear what I have to say this morning, but, praise God, I'm going to say it, anyway.

"Brothers and Sisters, it's time for us to stop lying to ourselves. It's time we stop lying to each other, and, most important, it's time we stop lying to God. He already knows our hearts, so who is it we think we're fooling? Now, please understand, I'm preaching to myself just as much as I'm preaching to you."

A mixture of laughter and "Go ahead, Preacher" came from the far reaches of the sanctuary.

"Now, one lie is only the tip of the iceberg. Once you tell one lie, you've got to tell ten more to cover it up. Pretty soon we don't even know what the truth is ourselves. We lie about our hair color. We lie about our jobs. We stretch the truth about our income." Hezekiah extended his arms to illustrate his point. "And some of us even lie about whom we love."

Samantha looked nervously over her shoulder to the balcony. She hoped Virgil would act before Hezekiah said something that would destroy the rest of her life. She wanted to be remembered as the wife Pastor Cleaveland loved, not as the woman he had planned to divorce for a man.

Virgil Jackson entered the now-empty lobby unnoticed and quietly climbed the side stairs of the balcony. The double doors of the sanctuary were closed, and all eyes and ears were focused on Hezekiah and his cryptic sermon.

When he reached the landing at the top of the stairs, Virgil knelt down and crawled along the side aisle of the balcony. He could not see the pastor, but he heard his familiar baritone voice.

On his knees Virgil turned into the second row of pews and crawled toward the center of the gallery. He tensed as the uncarpeted floorboards creaked from his weight. The gun in his pocket accidentally banged against the leg of a pew, and Virgil froze on the wooden floor. No one seemed to have heard the noise, so he raised his head. Pastor Cleaveland was now in clear view. The tall man in the black suit was standing behind the podium. Virgil waited patiently, hoping Hezekiah would move from behind the oak structure.

Hezekiah continued his sermon. "I will be the first one to say before God and all of you that I've told my share of lies. I'm just a man, a man who must humble himself daily before God to confess my sins and to plead His forgiveness."

Hezekiah picked up the handheld microphone and walked away from the podium. "I, like you, have done some things in my life that I am not proud of."

No amens were uttered. Hattie Williams sat rocking with her Bible open and reading the Lord's Prayer. A quiet confusion began to work its way through the pews. This was a sermon like none they had ever heard from the pastor.

He had lowered himself to the level of mortal. The faces became troubled by his descent, because they needed him to be better than themselves.

Hezekiah put one foot on the steps, preparing to walk down, when two loud shots reverberated over the sanctuary.

The first shriek came from someone in the center of the church as Hezekiah fell backward into the pulpit.

Everyone was paralyzed for what seemed like minutes.

Women began ducking behind pews, while men shielded them. Screams were heard now from every part of the auditorium.

Hezekiah Cleaveland lay bleeding from bullet wounds to the head and chest. The members in Fellowship Hall gasped as they watched the mayhem on the massive flat screen unfold.

Virgil stood erect and ran, stumbling up the center aisle of the balcony. The shadow of a man running out of the dark balcony was the only thing that could be seen from the choir stand. He charged down the stairs, partially covering his face with a denim jacket, and pushed aside two small boys at the base. The foyer was still empty as he crossed to the exit of the church.

Virgil tripped on the cement steps and rolled to the ground. After regaining his footing he ran to Hezekiah Cleaveland Avenue and vanished among the houses and cars on a quiet side street.

Samantha broke free from Dino, who was trying to protect her body from danger. She ran up the steps to her husband. Some members of the choir had dashed from the stand, while others crouched and wept behind seats.

The organist sat frozen in fear on the bench as several people ran, overwhelmed and screaming, out the double doors.

Samantha dropped and cradled Hezekiah's head on the arm of her suit. Her bracelet sparkled from the light in the church's stained glass. She screamed hysterically. "Hezekiah, baby. Hezekiah, don't die! I need you." She lovingly placed her head on his chest which caused blood to smear on the collar she had so carefully selected. "Hezekiah! Please, God, don't take him from me!"

After a respectable moment Willie Mitchell and Reverend Percy Pryce gently separated Samantha from Hezekiah's body and briskly escorted her, crying and thrashing, out the side door. Hezekiah's lifeless body lay at the top of the steps, clutching the microphone, while Dino tried unsuccessfully to resuscitate him.

Jasmine had not attended church that morning. Samantha had instructed Etta to let her sleep in. She did not want Jasmine to witness her father's assassination.

By two o'clock the church grounds were teeming with police cars and news vans. Satellite dishes pointed to the heavens, and high heels stumbled over electrical cords crisscrossing the parking lot. The police had emptied the sanctuary of parishioners, and the double doors were cordoned off with yellow tape. Members were now milling in the halls and outside the church, giving and receiving comfort. The final word had already spread that the pastor was dead.

Cynthia Pryce retreated to a far corner of the parking lot. Her hands shook as she dialed Phillip Thornton's number.

"Hello, this is Phillip. I'm not available right now. Please leave your name, number, and the reason for your call, and I'll call you back as soon as I can." Then came the beep.

"Phillip, this is Cynthia," she whispered through tears.

"Call me as soon as you get this message. Hezekiah is dead. Someone shot him this morning. I want you to stop the story. Do you understand? Do not print that story. If you print it, I'll deny I ever talked to you."

Several reporters for the local and national news networks, with microphones and cameras in tow, cornered members for their reaction to the tragedy. Television programming around the country had been interrupted to report on the assassination of Pastor Hezekiah T. Cleaveland.

The hats, fresh haircuts, and pain of New Testament Cathedral were beamed live to televisions throughout the country.

The television monitors in Fellowship Hall had been turned off by the time the police had arrived. Folding chairs were clustered in small groups to accommodate mourners around the room. By then, most of the tears had turned to sobs of disbelief and an occasional outburst of anguish.

Scarlet Shackelford took the news of the pastor's death especially hard. The hat she wore that morning was now bouncing on the table she pounded with an open palm as she cried inconsolably. The paramedics were summoned from the parking lot and gave her a sedative to relieve the shock. Her thoughts were of her daughter, who never knew the identity of her father, and the father, who never knew his child. That morning the astonishing realization that she actually still loved him took her fragile world by surprise.

Hattie sat nearby as the paramedics checked Scarlet's blood pressure. "That's all right, Scarlet. Let it out. It's going to be all right," she said, rubbing her back. Hattie was unable to block the emotions of the crying woman in her arms. After a while she stopped trying. The pain Scarlet Shackelford felt now was very appropriate.

The covered body of Hezekiah was quickly removed from the church. Cameramen scrambled to get a shot of the gurney being lifted into the rear of the van. Women crying, with children clinging to their thighs, provided a dramatic backdrop for the parting shots of the vehicle.

On the sofa inside Hezekiah's office, Samantha sobbed into a crumpled tissue. The suit jacket Hezekiah had worn that morning was draped over her lap, and blood from his head had dried on her sleeve. Reverend Pryce and Cynthia sat on either side of her. Somewhere in the corridor between the sanctuary and the office, Samantha's tears had become real. Yes, she wanted him dead, but they had shared many years together, and he was the father of her daughter.

Samantha had called home shortly after being taken to the church office.

"Jasmine, honey," she said. "This is Mommy. Something terrible has happened."

At that moment Jasmine looked out her bedroom window and saw three police cars, with red and blue lights flashing, roll up the long driveway toward the house.

She jumped from the bed and cried into the phone, "Mommy, the police are here! What's going on? I'm afraid."

"There's nothing to be afraid of, darling. Everything is going to be all right," Samantha said gently.

"Where's Daddy? I want to talk to my daddy."

Samantha paused before responding. For the first time she questioned her decision. "You can't talk to Daddy right now, honey."

Jasmine's voice began to tremble. "Why not? Something has happened. Why won't you tell me what is happening?"

"I'll be home as soon as I can, honey, and I'll tell you everything."

"Tell me now. Is Daddy all right? Tell Daddy I need him to come home to me now."

Samantha took a deep breath before she spoke. "Daddy has been shot, Jasmine. He's dead."

Jasmine dropped the phone and fell to the floor, screaming. Etta heard her from downstairs and immediately ran to her room. Samantha then broke the news to Etta and instructed her not to turn on any television in the house. "I'll be home as soon as possible. Don't leave Jasmine alone."

A police officer was stationed at the door leading to Hezekiah's office with instructions not to let anyone in, especially the media. Willie Mitchell, Reverend Pryce, and Cynthia remained in the room the entire time. The full weight of what had just occurred kept Reverend Mitchell pacing the floor. Samantha had requested that he stay with her. She wanted to keep a watchful eye on him. She didn't want him to panic and speak to the ravenous reporters around the scene. He tried to remain calm, but all could see that he was rapidly losing control. Samantha told him to sit down and drink a glass of water.

Reverend Pryce did not speak while in the office. His thoughts flashed to the words of his wife, Cynthia. This could not be a coincidence. He lamented the plight of the beautiful woman on the couch. Percy periodically gave Samantha a tissue, then retreated to the opposite side of the room. With what he knew, he could not look her in the eye.

Danny St. John watched the news coverage on the television in his living room. He stared blankly at the footage of Hezekiah's body being placed in the van. Danny was empty. His soul had left his body and hovered above the room to protect him from the horror of the images on the screen. He understood why sleep had evaded him for so many days.

Nina Simone was playing on the CD: "Someday I know he's coming to call me. He's going to handle me and hold me. So, it's going to be like dying, Porgy, when he calls me. But when he comes, I know I'll have to go."

Danny wanted to cry, but he couldn't. He could not find the tears. He could not feel his soul. All he could feel was a familiar emptiness that had been a part of his life for as long as he could remember. It was a void he had not felt for the last year.

***

Reverend Pryce and Cynthia had offered to go home with Samantha, but she graciously refused their company.

"I'll be all right. Etta is there, and I have to spend time alone with Jasmine."

Samantha rode home in the rear of a police car. When they arrived in front of the house, she saw the three police cars. Two officers stood ready at the entrance.

A strong-looking female officer walked Samantha to her front door and asked, "Mrs. Cleaveland, would you like me to come in with you for a while? I can stay as long as you need me."

Samantha still held Hezekiah's jacket. "No, thank you. My housekeeper is here. I need to be alone with my daughter."

"Ma'am, I am very sorry about what happened. Two officers will be stationed here as long as you think it necessary. Please call me if you have any problems or questions about the investigation."

"Thank you, Officer. You've been very kind. Good night."

Etta ran down the foyer stairs, clutching a tissue, when Samantha entered the house. "Oh Lord, Mrs. Cleaveland. This is terrible. Just terrible. Are you all right?"

"No, Etta, I'm not all right. How are you?" The two women hugged. "Is Jasmine in her room?"

"Yes, ma'am. There wasn't much I could do for her. She's been hysterical since you called."

When Samantha entered her room, Jasmine was sitting on the floor beside her bed. A blanket was wrapped around her shoulders. She didn't look up. Samantha sat down on the floor and put her arms around her crying daughter. "It's okay, honey. Mommy's here."

"I should have been there. Why didn't you wake me this morning? I could have helped him."

"No, honey, there was nothing anyone could have done. It all happened too fast. He didn't feel any pain."

"Why? I can't understand. Everybody loved Daddy. What kind of monster would do something like this?"

"I don't know, baby, but I'm sure the police will find whoever did this."

They stayed together for most of the night, until Jasmine cried herself to sleep. Samantha pulled the covers over her chest and kissed her forehead. When she went downstairs, Etta was reading a Bible at the kitchen table.

"Thank you for staying tonight, Etta. You should get some rest. Jasmine is asleep now, and I'm going to my room."

Etta was silent for a moment; then she looked suspiciously at Samantha. "Mrs. Cleaveland, who could have hated the pastor so much that they wanted him dead? I can't understand that kind of hate. Whoever did this must've come straight from hell."

"Try to get some rest. I'll see you in the morning."

Samantha didn't trouble herself with the ramblings of the housekeeper. At the moment hell was the least of her concerns. She undressed, neatly placing the bloodstained dress on the hanger. She sat at the vanity mirror and began to remove her makeup. A smile emerged from under the mask she had worn all day. She took a deep breath and thought, It's over. *I'm finally free. No one can get in my way now.*

It was 11:00 p.m. The streets of downtown were empty, except for encampments of homeless people under cardboard boxes. Willie Mitchell was driving to the Los Angeles Community Center, where he saw the figure of Virgil Jackson pacing in front of the building. Virgil opened the door of the car and jumped in before Willie could stop completely.

"Where the fuck have you been? I've been waiting here for five hours," Virgil said before closing the door.

"I had to lock up the church. You did a good job, boy. I'm proud of you."

"Fuck that. Where's my money? I'm getting out of here tonight. It seems like the fucking police are everywhere I look."

"It's in the trunk. I'll get it when I drop you near the bus station. Relax, boy. It's over. No one will ever find you. Give me the gun so I can get rid of it."

Virgil anxiously removed the gun from his waist and handed it to the reverend. "Here. I never want to see the fucking thing again."

Willie parked the car two blocks from the bus station.

"Why are we stopping here?" Virgil asked, looking over his shoulder.

"I don't want to be seen with you in front of the depot. You can walk from here."

Both men exited the car. Reverend Mitchell opened the trunk and handed Virgil a brown paper bag. As Virgil opened it to inspect the contents, the reverend quickly removed the gun from his coat pocket and shot him in the chest. His body lay half in the street, and half on the sidewalk, holding a bag filled with folded pages of the Sunday paper.

25

Once again, Samantha stood before five outfits hanging in her closet. It was the night before Hezekiah's funeral.

She searched her collection for the perfect black dress, shoes, and accessories. *No need to buy anything new for this,* she thought. *I'll only be able to wear it once.*

She took special care in selecting each piece. *After all,* she thought, *this is a special occasion. Hezekiah would want me to look my best.* Samantha was a firm believer that women never looked more beautiful than on their wedding days and on the days they lowered their husbands into the ground. Samantha wanted to look stunning for the many mourners who would see her in person and on television. She felt she owed it to the memory of Hezekiah.

She needed an outfit that prompted such observations as "Even on the most difficult day of her life, Mrs. Cleaveland looked radiant" and "The brave widow of the slain minister, Hezekiah T. Cleaveland, looked more glamorous than ever." Even more important, "So young, beautiful, and dignified. Samantha Cleaveland should be the next pastor of New Testament Cathedral."

No acrobatics would be required on this occasion. She simply needed to convey dignity, class, and strength. Samantha selected three outfits from the section of black dresses in her closet and hung them in a row. The first was a simple black linen suit with a tuxedo-cut jacket. Next to it hung a silk dress, with an intricately laced gold collar. The third was a black dress with a halter neckline accented by a band of crystal beads.

Samantha modeled each of the outfits in front of her floor-to-ceiling mirrors. She ultimately selected the black suit and a pair of black Italian leather pumps. She felt it was elegant, yet dignified. Samantha viewed her selection from every angle. She sat in a chair and crossed her ankles and placed her gloved hands gently into her lap and struck a pose. She leaned over a table in the center of the room to emulate the move she would make when leaning in to kiss Hezekiah's cheek. *Perfect,* she thought. *There's just enough leg to give the cameras something to look at.*

Hezekiah T. Cleaveland Avenue was lined with a row of six black Rolls-Royce limousines, filled with family members and friends, in front of New Testament Cathedral.

Streets were cordoned off within a two-block radius of the church due to the massive crowd attending the funeral. At the foot of the church steps was a black hearse containing Hezekiah's body.

An army of television and newspaper reporters provided blow-by-blow coverage of the events that were unfolding in front of the church. News vans sent live footage from satellite dishes to stations around the world, and six helicopters buzzed overhead waiting for the perfect shot of Samantha walking behind the casket into the church.

Dino exited the driver's seat from the limousine that sat directly behind the hearse. The gun was tucked discreetly in a shoulder holster under his jacket. Six additional armed bodyguards stood around the limo as Dino opened the rear door.

Samantha extended her sleek black-leather-clad foot to the sidewalk and paused for a brief moment. Dino took her arm as she exited the car. The helicopters zoomed in, causing her silky hair to blow gently in the breeze. She brushed the stray strands away from her dark-tinted sunglasses.

Jasmine Cleaveland emerged next from the rear seat.

She wore a black suit that mirrored her mother's. Jasmine chose to wear a hat to cover her puffy eyes and tearstained cheeks.

Everyone in the room stood as Samantha and Jasmine walked in, hand in hand, behind the mahogany casket, down the center aisle, and to the front row of the sanctuary.

Their movement was accompanied by a hymn played by the orchestra. Samantha clutched a handkerchief in her left hand and placed her right arm around the shoulders of her sobbing daughter.

Cynthia Pryce sat quietly in the second row. The brim on the black hat she wore was so wide that it blocked the views of two mourners in the seats behind her. It cast a shadow over her eyes and nose. Only the red of her lips could be seen, except on the rare occasions that she lifted her head. She stood when Cynthia, Jasmine, and Hezekiah's coffin entered the sanctuary. Leave it to Samantha to wear something that flashy to her husband's funeral.

Cynthia reached out and embraced Samantha when she reached the front row, whispering, "I'm so sorry, Samantha. He was such a good man."

"Yes, he was," Samantha responded. "Thank you, Cynthia."

"You know Percy and I are here for you," Cynthia continued.

Samantha pulled away when she heard the last words. She looked Cynthia directly in the eyes and whispered, "I know you are, dear. Just make sure that you keep out of my way."

Cynthia flinched at the words and clutched her handbag tightly under her arm and breast. She looked up and saw Percy peering down from the stage at her. He looked intently at the exchange and then quickly averted his eyes away from her glance.

Percy's heart pounded in his chest as the coffin was positioned at the foot of the steps. Waves of guilt caused his shoulders to tense. He felt like he was going to pass out.

I'm going to leave her, he thought while the women embraced. *I'm going to leave her penniless.*

He looked down again in Cynthia's direction and saw her red lips peeking from beneath the brim of the hat.

They were full, and the gloss seemed to shimmer like a drop of dew on the petal of a lily. *God, she's beautiful*, he thought as his mind wandered. *I'm sure she loves me. I know she thought she was doing the right thing. Maybe . . .*

The sweet and pungent smell of the flowers on Hezekiah's coffin summoned him painfully back to the somber occasion, which was unfolding at his feet. The tension in his shoulders returned.

Victoria and her husband, Reverend Sylvester Johnson, sat in the seats behind Samantha. Beads of perspiration formed puddles under Sylvester's toupee. The off-kilter hairpiece sat atop his scalp and shifted with every turn of his head.

Victoria's head was floating from a mix of gin and the little white pills she had consumed during the car ride to the church. "Don't tell me what to do," she had chided her husband. "There's no way I can get through this funeral without something to calm my nerves."

Victoria leaned forward and placed her gloved hand on Samantha's shoulder and whispered, "Don't worry, Sammy. We're going to get that bitch. She'll wish she were in that coffin when we get finished with her."

Samantha placed her hand on Victoria's and said, "Thanks, honey. You are such a dear friend."

A slight smile appeared on Samantha's face as she thought, *Thank God she remembered. I knew I could count on Victoria.*

The funeral attendants removed a heavy spray of yellow, white, and red roses from the coffin and lifted the lid to reveal Hezekiah's serene body lying in state.

Hattie Williams sat in her usual seat on the center aisle, third row. She wore the dress that she had worn to her husband's funeral years earlier. She did not stand when Samantha walked passed her, but she could feel Samantha approaching from behind. She's more concerned about which direction the cameras are pointing than about her dead husband, or Jasmine.

A string of dignitaries paraded across the stage and expressed their sorrow over the loss of such a great man.

Sandra Kelly blended into the crowd. On the surface she was just another somber face. Another black suit and one more handkerchief poised to catch a tear. But beneath the grieving facade, her dark heart distinguished her from most others in the room.

I wish I had been the one who pulled the trigger, she thought as she dabbed her eye to wipe away the tear that wasn't there. Now it's Samantha's turn, and I'm going to make sure she gets everything she deserves.

Renowned gospel artists serenaded the body and the distraught family. The Jumbotron flashed images of Hezekiah in various incarnations of his life. Then the crowd heard, "Ladies and gentlemen, the president of the United States."

The somber face of the commander in chief appeared on the twenty-foot screen and said, "Hezekiah was not only a great man, a shepherd to millions of people around the world, and the pastor of New Testament Cathedral, but also he was my friend and confidant. He will be missed by all of us. To Samantha and Jasmine, please know that you can call on Megan and me anytime for support, and if you just need a friend to talk to. We love you. You will always be in our hearts and prayers."

Samantha pressed her gloved fingers to her lips and directed a heartfelt kiss toward the twenty-foot head on the screen.

For the mourners in the back row of the sanctuary, Hezekiah's coffin on the floor below looked like a postage stamp with a red dot in the center. They were so close to the ceiling of the building, they could feel the heat from the bright lights. Danny St. John sat quietly in the most extreme corner seat of the last row. He felt dead inside. *It might as well be me in the coffin*, he thought as the president spoke. *She's done it.* A single tear broke free from a dark place in his heart and fell to his shoulder. It was over. Hezekiah was at peace, and he was alone again.

"I never thought I would live to see this day," Reverend Davis said. "I think the pastor must have known something was going to happen to him."

Cynthia, Percy, and Reverend Davis walked slowly away from the grave site. Hezekiah had been laid to rest on a quiet hill in Inglewood Park Cemetery, overlooking the city.

Cynthia waited for what she considered to be a respectable amount of time; then she said to Reverend Davis, "It is a sad day. I guess we have to start thinking about who is going to take over as pastor. I don't want to appear insensitive, but I assume we have your support for the nomination of Percy as Pastor Cleaveland's successor. I think he already has the support of most of the members of the board of trustees."

"Cynthia, please," Percy said, looking her directly in the eyes and squeezing her hand tightly.

She flinched from his grip.

"Show some respect for the man. His body isn't even in the grave yet."

"That's okay, Percy. Cynthia is right. We do have to start talking about this. I've been thinking about it, since the pastor raised the subject. I have decided to recommend you to the trustees." He lowered his head in shame as he spoke the painful words.

Cynthia clutched Percy's arm and said, "That is wonderful, Reverend Davis. You won't regret it. Percy will make a great pastor."

26

If only her life could have been as neat and tidy as her kitchen. She had arrived in Los Angeles as a young girl from the South. Her mother wanted a better life for her, so she sent her to live with relatives in California. She was smart and beautiful her entire life, but she never really knew it. Her shyness was often mistaken for conceit. Boys found the shy, attractive Southern girl captivating. Her naïveté and soft voice garnered proposals of marriage long before she turned eighteen.

At nineteen, she became secretary for Hezekiah Cleaveland. Scarlet was smart and efficient, and Hezekiah was immediately attracted to the young beauty. He pursued her from the start. She was flattered by the attention from the handsome minister, but she flatly refused his constant advances. She often cried after work, and wondered what she had done to elicit such carnal responses from the man she admired.

After a year Scarlet could resist no longer. She gave in to the pastor and began a two-month affair. Hezekiah was the first man she had ever been with. He was gentle and attentive, and never made her feel cheap. Scarlet soon learned she was pregnant. Hezekiah offered to put her up in an apartment until the baby was born. After that, he told her, she would have to put the child up for adoption.

She was devastated. Not because she was pregnant, but because the man she had fallen in love with did not share her joy. Samantha had soon learned of Scarlet's condition and immediately fired her. Scarlet then married a man who had pursued her since she was fifteen. It wasn't easy, but she convinced her new husband that the baby she was carrying was his.

For five years the couple lived a turbulent life filled with physical abuse and mistrust. Her new husband never believed the cute little girl named Natalie was really his.

In a violent argument he threw Scarlet and Natalie out on the street. Scarlet never loved her husband, so the divorce came as a relief, but the pain of her secret lingered. She still held it close to her chest like an unwanted family heirloom that she had been entrusted to protect.

The death of Pastor Cleaveland only served to reopen the wounds that had taken her years to heal. Her feelings for Hezekiah flooded back, as if she were nineteen again.

Over the years she never stopped hating Samantha. The woman who had treated her so cruelly. The woman she had once admired.

Scarlet rejoined New Testament after her marriage ended and soon became a trusted and valuable member of the church. Hezekiah, who never lost his deep feelings for her, eventually appointed her to the board of trustees.

She had harbored loathing for Samantha Cleaveland for years, and now that intensified. She always suspected that Samantha would want to take over the church if Hezekiah ever died, and Scarlet vowed to do all within her power to prevent it if she ever tried.

As the tea kettle on her stove simmered, the telephone rang.

It was Willie Mitchell. "How are you, Scarlet?"

"I'm fine." Like everyone else, Scarlet knew that when Willie called, he wanted something.

"I'm calling about the trustee meeting this week. We've got to decide who is going to replace Pastor Cleaveland, God rest his soul. I wanted to know who you were going to support."

"What do you mean, who? There is only one obvious choice—Reverend Pryce."

"Scarlet, you know I never like to disagree with you, but how about Samantha? She is much more qualified, and I think Pastor would have wanted her to replace him."

Scarlet leaned against the counter and laughed.

"Samantha Cleaveland? Why would we do that? I never have, and never will, consider her for the position. Also, we need someone right now. The woman must still be in shock. Her husband's body isn't even cold yet, and she already wants to be pastor."

"You know Samantha better than that, Scarlet. She's a fighter."

"I know that. But she's not a pastor. I've never trusted her to have the best interest of New Testament." Scarlet grew impatient. "You've caught me at a bad time. We can talk about this at the trustee meeting."

"All right, Scarlet. Just think about it, would you?"

"I've already thought about it. Good-bye."

Scarlet sat down at her kitchen table and wondered why Reverend Mitchell was so intent on Samantha becoming pastor. Had she bribed him? Her concern grew. Typically, if Reverend Mitchell wanted something from the board, he usually got it. She would have to work twice as hard to convince them not to select Samantha Cleaveland.

27

Willie Mitchell slammed the conference table and jumped to his feet. "Everyone, please, please be quiet. If this room does not come to order, I'm going to end the meeting right now."

It was the Thursday after Hezekiah's funeral. The five members of the board of trustees exhibited their frustrations by throwing pens onto the table, slamming notebooks, and rolling eyes in disgust. They had gathered to decide who would replace Hezekiah. Reverend Davis, Scarlet Shackelford, and Hattie Williams each spoke adamantly in favor of appointing Reverend Pryce. Reverend Mitchell and Reverend Larry Sullivan supported the appointment of Samantha Cleaveland as pastor.

Percy Pryce and Samantha did not attend the meeting.

Samantha had already given Willie instructions not to adjourn the meeting until they appointed her as pastor. "Do whatever it takes, Willie. I'm counting on you."

Willie wiped the sweat from his lip and went on. "Now, I'll be the first one to agree that Percy has served this church well over the years, but, no disrespect to Reverend Percy, he is no leader. He never did anything around here without asking permission first. We need someone who can inspire us through this difficult time. We need someone who can take charge and show the world that New Testament Cathedral is here to stay. We need Reverend Samantha Cleaveland to stand in the pulpit as pastor and tell the world that New Testament is going to be all right."

Scarlet Shackelford responded, "Samantha Cleaveland is in mourning. We need someone right now. There's already talk of some people leaving. We can't wait for Samantha to pull herself together. It takes time for a woman to get over the loss of a husband—"

"I spoke to Samantha before this meeting," Willie interrupted, "and she said, if appointed, she would be prepared to assume the position immediately. You know she's a strong woman."

Reverend Davis jumped in. "Yes, but how will members react when they hear we've appointed a woman as pastor? Sorry, Sisters, but you know it's the truth."

"Come on, Reverend Davis," said Larry Sullivan. "There are women pastors all over the country. And remember this isn't just any woman. Samantha Cleaveland helped Hezekiah build this ministry. I think we owe it to Pastor's memory to at least appoint her as interim pastor, and give her a chance."

"Reverend Sullivan makes a good point." The room fell silent as Hattie Williams spoke. "I admit I have concerns about Samantha Cleaveland, but this isn't about her. It's about the survival of New Testament. It's about keeping people coming in those doors every Sunday. The church needs to regain some stability. And if that means putting another Cleaveland in the pulpit, then, I guess, I'm in favor of it."

There was silence. Willie's stomach muscles relaxed.

He knew no one could resist the wisdom of Hattie Williams. Now that she was on his side, his battle was almost won.

Scarlet felt betrayed. She never imagined that Hattie would side with Samantha Cleaveland. She had seen the way the old woman looked at Samantha every time she saw her.

Willie broke the silence. "Scarlet, are you at least willing to support Samantha as interim pastor? We'll all keep a close eye on her, and if it doesn't work out, we'll find someone else."

Scarlet did not speak.

Willie went on, "How about you, Reverend Davis? Are you willing to give her a chance? Remember, it's for the church."

Reverend Davis avoided looking into the red eyes of Reverend Mitchell. They had been there for almost four hours, and he was exhausted. He closed his folder and said, "I'll agree only as interim pastor, and only if we review her performance every month."

Willie slammed the table and said, "Good. I knew you'd do the right thing. Come on, Scarlet. You're the last vote. This has to be unanimous."

Scarlet searched the eyes of her fellow trustees. They all avoided her glance, except for Hattie.

Scarlet finally spoke. "All right. I'll agree on one condition— that you appoint me as head of the committee in charge of her monthly evaluation, and finding her replacement."

"Wait a minute, Scarlet. You're getting ahead of the process. Let's take this one step at a time—"

"No, she isn't, Willie," Hattie broke in. "Somebody has to do it, and I trust Scarlet. Appoint her the chair of the Evaluation and Search Committee and you have my vote."

Signs of agreement were seen around the table. Relieved heads nodded yes and eye contact was made, again. Willie had no choice. "All right, then. It's unanimous. Reverend Samantha Cleaveland is now interim pastor, and Scarlet Shackelford will head the Evaluation and Search Committee to find a permanent pastor if we, as a board, determine that Samantha is not suited to serve as permanent pastor. Meeting adjourned."

He hit the table with his fist. Samantha would not be pleased, but he had done his best.

Samantha received the call just after nine o'clock that night. She'd been clutching her phone and chain-smoking cigarettes in her study.

"Samantha, you're in, baby. It was unanimous. You're the new interim pastor of New Testament Cathedral."

After the word "interim" registered, Samantha spoke. "What do you mean, interim?"

Willie's stomach churned. "It was the only way I could get Scarlet Shackelford and Hattie Williams to agree. They almost ruined it."

"I knew you would screw it up." Blood began rushing to her head. "Why did you let them get away with that?"

Willie's voice began to shake. "It's not as bad as it sounds. We can drag this out for years. Pretty soon they'll forget it's a temporary position."

It was now time for Samantha to perform her final chore. Willie had been a bundle of nerves since the murder.

She hoped now to give him the final push over the edge. She steadied herself and said, "Willie, I've been thinking. You're the only person who can connect me to Hezekiah's death, and that makes me nervous."

"What are you talking about? I'm in this shit as deep as you are. Who the hell am I going to tell?"

"No, Willie, you don't understand. I'm not involved in this 'shit' at all. As a matter of fact, I might make a call tomorrow to my friend Jack, the chief of police. I'm thinking of telling him I remembered an argument between you and Hezekiah in which you threatened to have him killed. After they start snooping around, it won't take the police long to figure out that you murdered Virgil Jackson too."

"Why are you saying this? You know I love you. I'll never say anything to anyone." Pain in his gut caused beads of sweat to form on his brow. The walls in his living room began to move closer around him. He gasped for breath, and managed to choke out, "You fucking bitch, I'll kill you if . . ."

Samantha laughed. "Thank you, Willie. Now I can honestly tell Jack you threatened me too."

"I'll tell them everything," Willie sputtered. "I'll tell them you paid Virgil to kill him . . . that the whole thing was your idea."

"You are as dumb as I thought. You forget, I never paid anyone anything. Besides, who would believe a fat, sweaty, good old country boy like you over me?"

Willie dropped the telephone and jolted to his feet. He kicked over the coffee table in a rage and began ransacking his living room. He then retrieved the phone from the floor and cursed aloud. "You fucking whore, how could you? I did all this for you and you threaten to fuck me over like this."

Samantha listened calmly for a moment and said, "Willie, you sound upset. It's late and I just lost my husband, so I'm going to bed. Good luck with your trial."

Willie heard the dial tone and threw the phone across the room. His stomach convulsed as he continued the rampage. Pictures were knocked off walls, the television was tipped over, and lamps pulled from sockets and thrown to the floor. He violently lifted the sofa from the floor and saw the gun he had hidden there. He grabbed it and randomly fired a bullet into a mirror. The sound of the gun caused the room to spin around him. The pain in his gut made him drop to his knees. He tried to focus, but the walls only twirled faster.

The pain felt as though he had been kicked by a wild horse. He placed the gun between his sweating lips. The last bullet in the chamber went through the roof of his mouth and out the top of his head. It lodged in a wall, and the room suddenly stopped spinning.

28

The white gloves swung open the double doors once again. The faithful stood to their feet. The choir marched down the center aisle and sang: "We are on our way. We're on our journey home. We are on our way. We're on our journey home."

Reverend Pryce stood firm in a black suit behind the podium as he spoke. "Brothers and Sisters, this is a sad time for New Testament Cathedral. We have lost two of our leaders, and our friends. The tragic death of Reverend Willie Mitchell is a sad reminder for us all never to let go of God's hand. No matter how heavy the load gets, we need to hold on to his hand. Hold on to Jesus, and He will never let us fall."

Through muffled tears the congregation responded, "Amen, Preacher. Amen."

"God also saw fit to call home our beloved pastor. Now, it's not our job to question why."

"Tell it, Reverend," echoed from the rear of the sanctuary.

"It's our job to look to God and say, 'Whatever my lot.'"

"Yes, Lord," came the reply.

"Thou hast taught me to say, 'It is well. It is well with my soul.'"

Cries of agreement erupted throughout the room.

Reverend Pryce went on. "As hard as it may seem, we've got to go on. We've got to let the gentle hands of God heal our hearts and get on with the work of the church. Our beloved first lady, Sister Samantha Cleaveland, has suffered a great loss. Sister, we know your heart is heavy right now. But know that God is going to see you through. Just hold on, Sister. Hold on."

Samantha sat in the seat of honor on the pulpit. The gold braiding on her white robe glistened in the light.

There was a hush in the room as Reverend Pryce continued.

"She's a strong woman. She's a godly woman, and the Lord is going to bless her greatly. In spite of her grief, and in spite of her sorrow, Sister Cleaveland has agreed to do what is best for New Testament Cathedral. Ladies and gentlemen, Brothers and Sisters, it is with great pleasure I present to you our new interim pastor, the Dr. Reverend Samantha S. Cleaveland."

Samantha approached the podium, and the faithful jumped to their feet. Applause burst from the back of the sanctuary and rode like a wave to the front and up through the choir stand.

The crowd chanted, "Thank you, Jesus. Yes, Lord. Yes, Lord."

Scarlet Shackelford's hand reached past the mints and hand lotion in her purse for a tissue. *How could this have happened?* she thought. *How could this woman who has tormented so many now be standing in this sacred place of honor?*

The congregation continued to show their approval for the next moments as Pastor Samantha Cleaveland basked in the glow of the stained-glass windows and bright lights.

She stretched out her arms and the long robe unfurled to its full and radiant splendor. Her eyes looked upward, then back to the adoring adulation of the faithful.

Samantha interrupted the praise and spoke her first words as pastor. "Good morning, New Testament Cathedral! Does anybody here know that God is still a good God?"

In response to her question the congregants jumped once again to their feet and released a thunderous round of applause.

The silk flowers in Cynthia Pryce's hat trembled as she struggled to contain her rage. She searched the room for a sympathetic face but found none. She loathed the grace with which her husband relinquished the podium to Samantha, and she wished she had married a man more like Hezekiah Cleaveland.

Samantha interrupted the clamoring mass a second time. "I am a living witness that God is in the business of healing. I wouldn't be here this morning if it were not for Him."

Jasmine held the bottle of sleeping pills in her hand. Her bedroom was dark. She had succumbed to the grief of losing the man who loved her so much. The man who held her hand when she was a little girl and protected her, as best he could, from the dangers of the world. *How can I go on without Daddy?* she silently questioned.

She had always believed that only her father would notice if she were no longer on earth, and now that he was gone, there was no reason to remain. She could either die in the dignity of her own room or in a crack house in South Central. Thoughts of her mother did not enter her mind as she swallowed the handful of blue tablets. Her fears were soon replaced by the warmth and comforting embrace of sleep.

Samantha adjusted the microphone and said, "Yes, my heart is heavy, but I'm going to praise God anyhow. I'm going to continue the work of my late husband, Hezekiah T. Cleaveland. We are going to finish the construction of our beautiful new cathedral and then continue to spread the gospel of Jesus Christ through this country and throughout the world."

Hattie Williams sat quietly while those around her danced and shouted praises in the sanctuary. Her eyes were closed, but her heart was open. Light from the windows touched her hands as she looked up and prayed silently, *God, have mercy on New Testament Cathedral this Sunday morning.*

30

The white lace curtains in Hattie Williams's open bedroom window rustled gently in the evening breeze, barely shielding the dark room from the glow of a full moon. The room smelled of talcum powder mixed with the sweet fragrance from a bouquet of roses picked from her garden that day.

The sheets on the bed were the crispest of white, a true white achieved only from the addition of bluing poured by an experienced hand. Pillowcases printed with yellow and pink flowers and a patchwork quilt, sewn so many years ago by her mother, were tangled and strewn across the disheveled bed. Beads of perspiration gathered on Hattie's lip as she tossed restlessly in a fitful sleep. It was two o'clock in the morning.

"No. No, not the pastor. Not Pastor Cleaveland," Hattie sputtered as her gray hair thrashed from side to side.

The image of a man wearing a tailored black suit fills her dream. His eyes are wide open and staring straight at her, but there is no life, no sparkle, just an empty shell. He is lying in a pool of glistening blood. She can hear screams in the background, but no one is there except the lifeless body of her pastor, Hezekiah T. Cleaveland.

Her body convulses as she tries in vain to revive the lifeless man in her dream. And then it happens: she feels the distinct presence of two people just beyond her reach. One is familiar, but the other she does not know. Hattie can feel waves of hate and anger weighing down on her as she kneels over Hezekiah. Gradually, the source of the feelings moves closer and closer. The pain is almost unbearable. Hattie knows the source of this energy. It is one she has felt on so many Sunday mornings.

The second, unrecognizable force vies for her attention. There is warmth, but she can't see the source. The person hovers timidly in the background, afraid to move in closer, afraid to come into view. Hattie can clearly discern the emotions. There is an overwhelming sorrow, but permeating through it all, there is love.

She feels a cold hand on her shoulder. The touch sends a shudder through her body. She fights the urge to look over her shoulder, but she has no choice. The woman smiles down on her as Hattie looks up. The bright glow from her white teeth covers Hattie's and Hezekiah's bodies in light.

Hattie bolted upright in her bed and screamed out loud, "Oh Lord! Why, Samantha? Why?" Her body was drenched in perspiration as her eyes fixed on her trembling reflection in the vanity mirror across the room. Her silver hair was tangled and tossed. Her hands shook as she cried out, "Hezekiah loved you so much, Samantha." Hattie prayed that it wasn't true. She hoped that this would be the one time her empathic gift had failed her.

Samantha Cleaveland stood in the floor-to-ceiling window of her office at the Cleaveland estate, wrapped in an aqua silk robe that caressed the curves of her long, graceful body. A strand of velvety black hair tumbled over her chiseled cheek as she reached for a burning cigarette in an ashtray on the glass desk. With perfectly manicured fingers, she moved the stray lock from her view and took a long, deep puff from the cigarette. At thirty-nine years of age, she looked more the part of a glittering Hollywood starlet than the grieving widow of Pastor Hezekiah T. Cleaveland.

Her thoughts ebbed and flowed with each rhythmic wave of the ocean. Feelings of accomplishment over her recent appointment as interim pastor of New Testament Cathedral washed through her with every gentle beat of her heart. As the waters receded from the shore, memories of her late husband, Hezekiah, replaced her jubilation with loathing. She pondered the question of how she had come to hate the man she had once loved so deeply, and chastised herself for waiting so long to take fate into her own hands.

I should have killed him years ago, she thought as she took another puff from the cigarette. *He got exactly what he deserved for making a mockery of our marriage with a man and jeopardizing the entire ministry. He brought it on himself. God would have wanted it this way.*

"He gave me no other choice," Samantha reasoned, looking out over the horizon. "It was either him or New Testament Cathedral. I know God would have wanted it this way."

A gentle tap on the office door drew Samantha back from the hypnotic spell of the sea.

"Come in," she said without turning from the window.

Etta entered the room, carrying a tray with coffee, a freshly baked scone, and the morning paper. She wore a simple black dress and sensible shoes. The lower half of her body was covered by a white apron. "Good morning, Mrs. Cleaveland," Etta said as she walked toward the desk. "I thought you might like a cup of coffee and a bite to eat."

"Put it on the desk," Samantha said to Etta as she extinguished the cigarette butt in the ashtray. "Is my driver out front yet?"

"No, Mrs. Cleaveland."

Samantha's body tensed when she heard the response. She looked up at the woman pouring the cup of coffee and asked, "Etta, how did you address my husband when he was alive?"

Etta's hand shook when she heard the question. The tremble was so slight, it was apparent only in a ripple in the cup of coffee. "I'm not sure what you mean, Mrs. Cleaveland," she replied softly.

"It's a very simple question, Etta. What did you call my husband when he was alive?"

"I believe I called him Pastor Cleaveland."

"That is correct. You always said, 'Good morning, Pastor Cleaveland,' or 'Can I get you anything else, Pastor Cleaveland?' Now that I am the pastor of New Testament Cathedral," Samantha said as she casually picked up the cup of freshly poured coffee, "I think it only appropriate that you address me as Pastor Cleaveland from now on. Is that understood?"

Etta looked stunned. She averted her eyes from Samantha's gaze. *You are not my pastor,* she fumed silently.

Etta's hand trembled again, but she gripped the tray firmly to hide any sign of fear from Samantha. She knew her life at the Cleaveland estate would never be the same now that the man she had admired and respected so deeply was gone. Hezekiah had, over the years, acted as a buffer between her and Samantha.

He had comforted Etta when Samantha's wrath, which always simmered just below the surface, was directed at her. "Don't take it personally, Etta," Hezekiah had said on many occasions. "Samantha is under a lot of pressure. You know she didn't really mean what she said."

Hezekiah would also remind the impatient Samantha, "Everyone makes mistakes," on the rare occasions that Etta had not served a meal in the exact way she had requested, or if the spotlight that pointed to the Picasso hanging in the foyer had not been turned on at exactly six o'clock each evening. Who would protect her now?

"Is that understood?" Samantha repeated in a sterner tone.

The wave of fear was followed quickly by revulsion. As Etta raised the tray, she straightened her back, looked Samantha directly in the eye and with a slight nod of her head replied, "Yes, I understand . . . Pastor Cleaveland."

Etta turned on her heel and walked to the door.

"Oh, and, Etta," Samantha called out to the retreating woman, "tell Dino to pull the car around now. I have a meeting at church this morning."

Etta stopped in her tracks without turning around and said, "Yes, Pastor Cleaveland," and then quickly exited the room.

The *Los Angeles Chronicle* lay where Etta had placed it on the desk. It had been three weeks since Hezekiah's murder, and every day the front page of the paper carried the latest update on the investigation and the state of affairs at New Testament Cathedral. PASTOR'S MURDER BAFFLES POLICE. GRIEVING WIDOW TAKES HELM OF THE SIXTH LARGEST CHURCH IN THE COUNTRY read the headline.

Samantha glanced down at the paper. A somber color photograph of the widow occupied a fourth of the page. Her grim expression gave curious readers no hint of what lay beneath the perfect skin, chocolate eyes, and sparkling white teeth. *Of all the pictures they have of me on file at that rag, they chose that one,* she thought. *I look like a goddamn nun.*

Samantha sat at the desk and unfolded the newspaper.

It has been three weeks since the brutal assassination of Reverend Hezekiah T. Cleaveland in his mega church, in front of fifteen thousand stunned parishioners and television cameras. The police still have no suspects or leads as to who was responsible for the murder, which sent shock waves through the American faith community. On Sunday, July 18, Pastor Cleaveland was shot in the head and chest by an unknown gunman, who fled on foot from the downtown Los Angeles mega church.

California State Bureau of Investigation spokeswoman Mandy Tidwell told CNN's Gideon Truman that Cleaveland had trauma to his head and body, but declined to elaborate. "We don't have any leads," she told the Chronicle *on Sunday.*

Officials have spoken with trustees and members of New Testament Cathedral, where Cleaveland had served as pastor for the past eleven years. "Pastor Cleaveland was loved by everyone who met him," said a longtime member who preferred not to give her name. "He was a loving father, husband, and pastor who . . ."

Samantha stopped reading and quickly scanned the rest of the article in search of her name.

Cleaveland is survived by his daughter, Jasmine Cleaveland, and wife, the Reverend Samantha Cleaveland. Shortly after his death, Reverend Samantha Cleaveland was installed as the interim pastor of the multimillion-dollar church and television ministry. Mrs. Cleaveland has yet to speak to the press about the circumstances surrounding her husband's death. It has been rumored, however, that she will give an exclusive interview to Gideon Truman in the coming weeks.

The article went on to tell of her courage, strength, and commitment to her husband's dream of completing the construction of the church's new 25,000-seat, glittering crystal cathedral in downtown Los Angeles.

Samantha had been hounded by the press since her husband's death. Local, national, and international news networks, talk shows, and newspapers from around the world had been covering the investigation from day one, but she had skillfully avoided any contact with the media. Her silence had served only to increase her fame. This was just as she had planned.

Samantha closed the paper and walked back to the window. She looked out at a flock of salty white seagulls skimming the ocean surface in the distance, trees dancing in the wind and clouds drifting by.

Gideon Truman, she thought silently. *I wonder if it's true what they say about him. If it is, I'm sure Hezekiah would have liked him.*

Cynthia Pryce paced the living room floor in the twenty-third-floor penthouse. The blue sky dotted with clouds and the sun rising over rolling green hills in the distance were overshadowed in her presence. The glow of her morning skin rivaled the splendor of the panorama outside her window. Luxurious strands of burnt-caramel hair responded obediently to every tilt of her head. A creamy peach satin robe swirled around the calves of her long legs as she made a series of sharp turns in front of the windows. The face of Samantha Cleaveland on the front page of the *Los Angeles Chronicle* taunted her from the coffee table.

"Interim pastor," she muttered softly as she continued her march. "This isn't over, Samantha. Don't get too comfortable."

She felt a sharp snap of jealousy as she silently recalled the events of the last three weeks. *If only those idiots, Hezekiah and Lance Savage, hadn't gotten themselves killed, Percy would be the pastor of New Testament Cathedral today.*

She pushed the image of Samantha standing at the center of the pulpit before the entire congregation and all the cameras from her mind. A rage that she could hardly contain swelled in her stomach. *Pull yourself together, girl,* she thought. *This isn't over. You almost destroyed Hezekiah. You can do the same to Samantha.*

The slight glimmer of hope that her husband could still one day become pastor made the sight of Samantha's smug face on the front page of the newspaper hurt a little less. She reached down and, without looking at the paper, turned it over on the coffee table.

Just as she stood up, her husband, the Reverend Percy Pryce, entered the room. His tall frame was dressed in a smoky gray suit, a butter-yellow shirt, and a tie that picked up the hues in the suit, the shirt, and his rich almond skin.

"Is the paper here yet?" he asked coldly, without greeting her.

"It's on the coffee table. Of course, she's on the front page again."

"Why does that upset you so much?" he snapped.

Cynthia turned sharply toward him and said, "It upsets me because you should have been appointed pastor, not her."

"The trustee vote was unanimous. It's over, Cynthia. Samantha is the pastor. We just have to live with it."

"Wrong. They voted unanimously to appoint her as interim pastor. If everyone was so convinced that she was the best successor for Hezekiah, they would have made her permanent pastor. So it's not over. There's still a chance for us . . . for you to prove to them that you are the best person for the job. Hezekiah would have wanted it that way, and you know it."

"It doesn't matter what Hezekiah wanted at this point. If God wanted me to be pastor, he would have made me pastor. We have to live with the decision."

"Why are you so naive? It was Samantha's scheming that got her the position. God didn't have anything to do with it. The only thing we have to do is expose her for the conniving, greedy woman she is. If you would only do what I tell you and let me—"

Percy walked rapidly toward her at the window and cut her off. "You've done enough already. Lance Savage is dead because of you," he said.

"What are you talking about? I didn't have anything to do with his death."

The image of the *Los Angeles Chronicle* reporter Lance Savage lying dead on the floor of his home on the canals in Venice flashed in Percy's mind. "If you hadn't leaked the story about Hezekiah being gay to Lance, he would still be alive," he replied, barely containing his anger.

"The police don't know who killed Lance, and they haven't said anything about his death being linked to the story he was writing. Besides, who would kill him because of that?"

Percy looked away when he heard the question. Cynthia continued, "Look at me, Percy. You have to be a man and fight for what is rightfully yours." Cynthia walked to him and put her soft hand on his cheek. "Darling," she whispered, "you were born to be pastor of New Testament Cathedral. We can make that happen. You just have to listen to me."

Percy bowed his head and tried to look away, but the soft touch of her hand caused him gradually, and unwillingly, to succumb to her breathless commands.

Cynthia was relentless. She raised his head and looked directly into his eyes. "I have it all figured out, baby. You have to trust me. Do as I tell you and everything will work out in our favor."

She drew him closer and placed his head on her shoulder. He could feel the warmth of her sweet breath on his ear. She expertly kissed his neck and lips. The intoxicating smell of her body replaced the fear and guilt with longing.

"I love you, Percy," she whispered. "Make love to me, baby. I need you inside me."

As she pulled him closer, she could feel the rigid evidence of his desire. His hands grudgingly tugged at the cord of her robe. He slowly removed it from her bare shoulders and let it drop to the floor, exposing her naked body for all to see in the floor to ceiling window. Percy caressed every inch of her creamy skin and felt her moistness as they panted in unison and pressed their lips together.

With nimble fingers she unzipped his pants and released his throbbing member. Cynthia raised her leg and rested it on the leather belt above his hip. With one hand she guided him into her and released a gasp when he thrust deep inside her.

"Just do as I say, baby," she repeated over and over as he made love to her in the window of the penthouse apartment. "Just do as I say."

Mondays were the hardest for Danny St. John. For him, the day marked the beginning of another week without Hezekiah. Another week he would not hear his voice whisper, "I love you, Danny." Another week he wouldn't feel his arms around his waist or taste the sweetness of his kiss.

Danny had rarely left his apartment in the three weeks since Hezekiah's murder. The air was stale and musty. All the shades were drawn, and the windows were closed tight. At times, he found himself stumbling through the house, wearing only baggy shorts, to the refrigerator for orange juice, or to the cupboard for saltine crackers and canned soup. He had no appetite for anything more substantial.

Parker never let Danny out of his sight. The scruffy gray cat followed his master from room to room. He sat on Danny's lap on the couch and curled next to him when he lay crying in bed.

The television in his bedroom had been on for three weeks. It was always either tuned to the local news, CNN, or the Home Shopping Network. Whenever he heard Hezekiah's name mentioned, he turned up the volume. The CNN reporter Gideon Truman offered the most comprehensive coverage of the killing. Although much of the information he reported was inaccurate, Danny found it difficult not to listen to the handsome journalist's account of the life and death of the man he had loved so deeply.

Newspapers were piled in heaps on the floor next to the couch in his small apartment. Each day the articles served to remind him that he would never see Hezekiah again. The headline on the Monday after the murder blazed: PROMINENT LOS ANGELES PASTOR GUNNED DOWN IN FRONT OF HORRIFIED CONGREGATION. Wednesday's announced: WORLD MOURNS THE DEATH OF PASTOR HEZEKIAH T. CLEAVELAND. The tragic headlines continued on Friday: SLAIN PASTOR TO BE LAID TO REST. MILLIONS EXPECTED TO VIEW TELEVISED SERVICE.

The stories never seemed to end, and they all landed with a thud on Danny's doorstep each day, courtesy of the *Los Angeles Chronicle*. The telephone on the nightstand next to his bed rang several times a day, but he never answered. The most frequent calls came from his friend Kay Braisden. "Danny, it's Kay again," her messages would say. "Honey, I know how you must be feeling right now. Please pick up the phone." When there was no response, she would continue. "Danny, I know I hurt you the last time we spoke. I'm sorry. I am so sorry. Please forgive me. I was just so surprised when you told me you were involved in a relationship with Hezekiah Cleaveland. I didn't know how to handle it. I was wrong."

On another day the message was, "You are my best friend, Danny. I should have been there for you, and for that I apologize. But I want to be there for you now. Please call me. I'm going to keep calling for as long as it takes for you to forgive me. I love you, Danny, and I'm praying for you."

Danny's eyes filled with tears each time he heard a message from Kay. He wanted to speak with her, but the right time had not yet come.

31

Scarlett Shackelford's eyes were red and puffy from all the tears she had shed since Hezekiah's death. She now had the face of an angel touched by sorrow. Three weeks had gone by, but she had found only fleeting moments of relief from the agonizing grief she felt over the loss. This morning she sat at the dinette table in the kitchen window of the modest stucco tract home she shared with her second husband, David, and her daughter, Natalie.

The morning sun reflected off every surface in the bright and cheery kitchen. A tea kettle simmered on the stove. White-glazed tile countertops held stainless-steel appliances, a neatly lined row of cookbooks, and a ceramic rooster cookie jar that required beheading before it would yield its sugary treats.

The fact that Samantha Cleaveland was now the pastor of New Testament Cathedral only added to her misery. This was the same woman who had treated her so cruelly as a young girl; the woman who had fired her as Hezekiah's secretary after learning she was pregnant with his child; and the woman who she, in some remote corner of her heart, believed was involved in the death of the father of her daughter.

Only three people on earth knew Natalie was Hezekiah's daughter: Samantha Cleaveland, Hezekiah, and herself. Now only two were left to guard the secret. The responsibility of keeping such a secret was a heavy burden that she managed as best she could under the circumstances. She had told her husband, David, that Natalie was the product of her first failed marriage. Another tear escaped as she sat in the window. The kettle on the stove began to boil, but Scarlett's thoughts were on matters more important than the whistling water.

"Scarlett, turn off the kettle," came a booming voice from another room.

She did not respond.

"Scarlett, are you in the kitchen? Would you please turn that thing off?"

Still there was no reply.

Finally, David Shackelford huffed into the room, wearing only a robe and carrying the front section of the morning paper. The rich timbre of his voice matched perfectly his handsome face and muscular, six-foot-four frame. The robe he wore was stretched to the limit to conceal his well-contoured chest, and long runner's legs peeked through the front flap with every step he took.

"Honey, don't you hear the kettle? Why didn't you turn it off?"

Scarlett was startled when she heard his voice. "What?" she asked, looking blankly up at him.

"The kettle, it's been whistling for five minutes."

"I'm sorry. I didn't hear it," she said as she stood from the table. "My mind was somewhere else. Would you like a cup of tea?"

"Scarlett, what is wrong with you?"

She turned her back to him and mechanically began preparations for the tea. "Nothing is wrong. I just didn't hear it."

David walked behind her and sat the newspaper on the countertop. Samantha Cleaveland's face on the front page looked up at Scarlett. He took her by the shoulders and turned her around to face him.

"Scarlett, this has got to stop. This is unnatural. I know you cared for Pastor Cleaveland. It was tragic, but you have to be strong and accept the fact that he's gone. I know you're worried about the church, but Samantha will be fine as the new pastor. Everything will work out in time."

Scarlett jerked away from him and shouted, "Everything will not work out. You don't know what you're talking about. You don't know her. She'll ruin everything that is good about New Testament Cathedral. You don't know that woman like I do."

Scarlett began to cry and tried to walk around him, but he blocked her path. "Wait, honey, we have to talk about this. You can't go on like this. It's ruining our marriage. You're neglecting Natalie and—"

When she heard her daughter's name, she began to cry harder and fell into his arms. David stroked her head and tried unsuccessfully to calm her. "Honey, it's going to be all right. Hezekiah is in a better place, and there's nothing we can do about it. You've got to come back to us. Natalie and I need you."

"You don't understand, David," she said through her sobs. "Everything is so complicated."

"Then help me understand. I love you. We can work through whatever it is together."

"I can't . . . I can't tell you. You'll hate me if I do."

"I could never hate you, Scarlett. Now, tell me what is upsetting you this much."

Scarlett slowly pulled away from his chest, walked back to the dinette table, and sat down again in the window with her back to him. David did not move. She pulled a white paper napkin from a holder at the center of the table and dabbed her wet cheeks. The tears continued to flow, but the sobbing slowly subsided.

David waited to allow her to compose herself and then reiterated, "I love you, Scarlett, but you have to let me know what's upsetting you before I can help."

Scarlett looked out the window at a large blooming magnolia tree in her front yard. Their Japanese gardener raked leaves into a neat pile and waved to her, but she didn't wave back. David walked behind her and placed his hand on her shoulder. "Talk to me, Scarlett."

She clutched the soaked napkin in her fist and held it to her mouth. "I lied to you, David."

David planted his slipper-clad feet firmly on the yellow linoleum floor but did not speak. His hand remained on her trembling shoulder.

Scarlett placed her clasped fists on the table and took a deep breath. "My first husband is not Natalie's father."

David removed his hand from her shoulder and said, "Michael is not her father? Then who is?" He knew the answer before he said the last word.

There was a long silence before she spoke again.

"I was young, pregnant, afraid, and had no job. The only choice I saw at the time was to marry Michael and persuade him that Natalie was his. I didn't know what else to do. I didn't want to give her up. She's my baby. She is my world. I wouldn't give her up for anyone. I paid dearly for that mistake. Four years of hell. You know the story already. When Michael wasn't drinking, he was abusive."

David took a step backward but did not take his eyes off the back of her head. The wall around her well-kept secret crumbled with every word she spoke. There was no turning back now.

"Samantha tried to force me to give her up for adoption, but I refused. She didn't care about me or my baby. She only cared about her reputation. She only cared about how it would look for her husband to be the father of a child that was not hers. She only cared about how much money they would lose if anyone found out that Hezekiah was the father of my child."

David barely heard her last words. His heart pounded in his chest. It took all of his strength to remain standing in the middle of the kitchen.

"I'm so sorry, David. Once the lies started, I couldn't stop them. But you have to believe I did it all to protect Natalie, not to hurt anyone, especially not you. I've tried a thousand times before to get up the nerve to tell you, but I couldn't." The sobbing began again. Scarlett placed her head on the table and cried into her arm.

David stood frozen in the middle of the room. He wanted to speak, but the words would not come.

Dino Goodlaw, Samantha's driver and security guard, pulled the black Cadillac Escalade with tinted windows in front of the Cleaveland estate at exactly 10:00 A.M., just as he had been instructed.

Dino served as the loyal bodyguard, driver, and keeper of all things secret for Samantha and Hezekiah. His muscular frame and uncanny ability to disappear into the background made him perfectly suited to stand between the Cleavelands and dangers seen and unseen. But in the silence of his world, he also blamed himself for Hezekiah's murder.

"If only I had been closer to the pulpit, I would have been able to get Hezekiah to the floor before the second shot to his head," he had told the police hours after the murder. "Hezekiah would still be alive if I had just been a few feet closer."

From that moment on, he had vowed that he would die before any harm came to Samantha. "Any bullet aimed at Samantha will have to go through me first," he would say to his reflection in the mirror each morning while shaving.

A steel-gray handgun in his shoulder holster was visible for a brief moment as Dino exited the vehicle. He quickly buttoned his black suit coat to conceal the weapon before Samantha opened the front door.

The air was clear and smelled of ocean mist. Palm trees lining the winding driveway leading to the stately home stood like sentries guarding a king's palace. The neo-Baroque covered porch with cream-colored wrought-stone columns and twelve-foot double doors served as the perfect stage for the statuesque woman.

Dino stood near the rear car door at the foot of the stairs. He checked his watch nervously and resisted the urge to pace the granite cobblestoned surface. When the front door finally opened, Samantha emerged, carrying a brown leather case. Strands of hair flowed like molten lava around her face as she walked down the stairs. She wore dark sunglasses and a mint-green pantsuit over a simple cream silk shell that only hinted of the perfect form that was beneath.

"Good morning, Pastor Cleaveland," Dino said as she descended. "Another beautiful day today."

"Good morning, Dino," she responded with a smile normally reserved for cameras, full arenas, and six-figure donors. However, Samantha and Dino shared a unique bond. They were the last people to touch Hezekiah when he was alive, and the first to touch his body when he lay dead on the pulpit floor. "How are you today, Dino? I hope you're sleeping better. I worry about you."

"That is very kind of you, Pastor Cleaveland, but it's my job to worry about you. Please don't give it another thought. I know you have enough on your mind these days."

Dino opened the rear door of the Escalade when Samantha reached the bottom step. She handed him the brown case and entered the plush automobile. When she settled in the rear, he passed the case back to her and firmly closed the door.

"I do have a lot on my mind, Dino," she said from the rear as the car drove down the rolling driveway, "but you were very brave on that day, and you've been kind to me through this entire ordeal. Just knowing that Hezekiah's killer is still out there somewhere makes it difficult some days for me to even leave the house. I'm still afraid, but knowing you're here makes me feel much safer."

Dino tensed when he heard the words. "With all due respect, Pastor, I may have been brave, but it wasn't enough. I failed you and Hezekiah," he said, approaching the wrought-iron gate at the end of the winding driveway.

"That is not true. You did everything possible to save him. No one would have guessed in a million years that someone would shoot him in front of the entire congregation. It took an astonishingly bold person to do something that brazen, and no one, not even you, could have stopped it." A faint smile crossed her lips as she spoke the words. "It was God's will, Dino. We have to learn to accept it and get on with the business of living."

Samantha soon grew weary of comforting the hulking Dino. He recognized the impatient look in her eye when he glanced at her in the rearview mirror, and simply replied, "Yes, Pastor Cleaveland. Thank you."

The estate's wrought-iron gate glided open at the sight of the car. Dino waved good morning to a uniformed security guard who was posted in the gatehouse. The man waived at Samantha as well. The tinted windows of the car shielded the guard from the look of disdain she gave in return to his greeting.

Dino merged cautiously into a trickle of Mercedes, red Ferraris, SUVs, and the stray Rolls Royce. As the two drove in silence, Samantha's cellular telephone rang. "This is Pastor Cleaveland," she answered in a tone befitting a recent widow.

"Good morning, Pastor Cleaveland," replied the apologetic voice on the telephone. It was Samantha's assistant, Veronica Cotton. "I'm sorry to disturb you."

"I'll be there in fifteen minutes. Is this something that can wait?" Samantha snapped.

"I have Gideon Truman on the line, Pastor Cleaveland. He insisted you would want to speak with him."

"Did I ever tell you I wanted to speak with him?" Samantha snapped again. "I don't want to speak with him, and tell him that I requested he stop spreading rumors that I've agreed to give him an exclusive interview."

With that, Samantha ended the call and rode in silence. The Monday morning Los Angeles rush hour traffic had subsided. Cars on the freeway moved at a decent clip. Dino was determined to get Samantha to New Testament Cathedral in the fifteen minutes she had anticipated.

The car turned onto Hezekiah T. Cleaveland Avenue. I wish someone would knock down those street signs, she thought silently. I'm going to erase every memory of him from the face of the earth. In a year the world will forget he ever existed.

To her left, Samantha saw the two-block-long and five-story-high New Testament Cathedral.

Groundskeepers in green uniforms scurried about, mowing grass, pruning trees, and coddling roses, as the limousine drove by. On Samantha's right Hezekiah's legacy was slowly rising from the earth. Construction of the new 25,000-seat crystal cathedral had continued at Samantha's insistence. Cement trucks churned along dirt roads. Scaffolding hung precariously along the side of the steel skeleton, and workers pounded, bolted, and soldered at all levels of the structure.

The car pulled into the reserved space near the administrative wing of the building. Dino scanned the parking lot before exiting the vehicle. He stood and did a 360-degree rotation to ensure no one was near the car before he opened the rear door.

Samantha extended her elegant Prada-clad foot from the vehicle. When she stood from the car, the morning light appeared like a pool at her feet and hovered around her head. The fiber of her mint pantsuit seemed to glow as she walked toward the building. Dino closed the car door and followed closely behind. He took a double step ahead of her and opened the door as she moved forward without altering her stride and stepped aside.

Samantha entered the office, which was filled with staff members. Young men in dress shirts and ties and women who looked like knockoff versions of Samantha studied glowing computer screens. Ringing telephones were greeted with "Thank you for calling New Testament Cathedral. God loves you, and so do we. How may I help you?" No one looked up as Samantha crossed the room, heading toward her office. They each had been instructed on the day they were hired, "Do not make eye contact with or address Samantha Cleaveland unless she speaks to you directly."

Samantha entered the outer office of the suite that had three weeks earlier been occupied by her husband. Her assistant, Veronica, sat upright at her desk when she entered. She wore a neatly tailored navy blue suit over a perfectly pressed white blouse and a floral scarf was draped over her shoulders.

"Good morning, Pastor Cleaveland," the attractive young woman said. "I'm sorry to have disturbed you earlier, but he was very insistent."

Samantha ignored the woman's contrition and instead said, "I want my entire staff in the conference room in ten minutes. Make it happen."

"Yes, ma'am."

Samantha looked coldly at the woman and said, "I've asked you not to call me ma'am. You're not in Mississippi anymore, and I'm not your mother. You will refer to me as Pastor Cleaveland. If ma'am slips from your lips again, consider yourself fired. Is that understood?"

Veronica looked down at the neat desk and responded, "I understand, Pastor Cleaveland."

"Good. Now, make sure everyone is in the conference room. Let them know that whoever is not present can pick up their last paycheck in accounting." The door to Hezekiah's office shut behind Samantha on the last syllable.

The large office, with antiques from around the world, overlooked the grounds of New Testament Cathedral from the fifth floor. The construction site across the street was partially visible in the corner of the window. Lush burgundy carpeting muffled the sounds of traffic below, and an oil painting of the Cleavelands hung over a fireplace encased in an ornately carved oak mantelpiece.

The message indicator on the telephone on the desk blinked as Samantha removed the dark sunglasses and sat in the high-back leather chair. She pressed a button and heard, "Hello, Reverend Cleaveland. This is Gideon Truman. May I offer my deepest sympathies for your loss. Pastor Cleaveland was a wonderful man. I never had the opportunity to meet him but heard good things about his work over the years, and everyone I've spoken to who knew Hezekiah speaks very highly of him. I understand this must be a very difficult time for you, but I would like to invite you to appear on my television program for an interview. You are a beloved American icon, and of course, the public is very interested in hearing from you and learning how you are handling the unfortunate death of—"

Samantha erased the message and prompted the next. "Hello, Reverend Cleaveland. This is Gideon Truman again. Your assistant just informed me that you believe I am spreading rumors about an exclusive interview. I can assure you that is not true. I have the highest respect for you and would never play such a manipulative game. I'm not sure how that got out there, but please believe that neither I nor anyone on my staff is involved. I would, however, be honored if you would allow me a few moments of your time to talk about a possible appearance on my program. Your assistant has my info. I hope to hear from you."

Samantha leaned back in the chair and spun toward the window. She could see a crane hoisting a steel beam up the side of the new cathedral. You can wait a little longer, pretty boy, she thought. I'll let you talk to me when the time is right.

The intercom buzzed, slicing through the silence. Samantha slapped the button and barked, "Yes? What is it?"

"I'm sorry, Pastor Cleaveland, but Catherine Birdsong is here. She would like a brief moment with you before the staff meeting."

"Tell her she can see me in three minutes, along with everyone else in the conference room."

"Yes, Pastor Cleaveland," was the timid reply.

Catherine Birdsong, the New Testament Cathedral Chief Operations Officer, stood at Veronica's desk in shock as she heard the line disconnect on the speaker. The wool, steel-gray suit she wore stood stiff like a suit of armor. Only her hand shook as she spoke. "Who in the hell does she think she is?" she mumbled to the air as she turned and marched out of the room.

32

It was ten-thirty on Monday morning at New Testament Cathedral. The entire administrative staff had gathered rapidly in the building's main conference room, just as Samantha had ordered only ten minutes earlier. Everyone scrambled for the seats that were positioned farthest from the front and center of the room.

Men in suits, with neckties waving behind them, sprinted toward the conference room past panting, well-dressed middle-aged women, who, as they entered the room, searched frantically for any open seat. This was to be the first meeting Samantha had convened with the full staff since the untimely death of her husband.

Nervous chatter filled the room. "Do you know what this is about?" was heard from a table near the center of the room.

"Here we go. I don't think this is going to be pretty," said a man as he straightened his tie. "I just hope she doesn't fire me in front of the whole room."

Associate Pastor Kenneth Davis sat at a table in the front. The others at his table noticed the nervousness behind the thin veneer of composure. Reverend Percy Pryce shared a table with Catherine Birdsong and Naomi Preston, the director of public relations. Naomi sat with her eyes fixed on the front of the room. Her stiff, shoulder-length hair turned like a hat on the odd occasions she looked to see who entered through the rear door.

The room fell silent as a door in the front opened and Samantha appeared. She stood in the threshold for a moment and scanned the room. A smattering of applause began at the back of the room and slowly rolled to the front, until Samantha held up her hand, motioning them to stop immediately.

She walked to the front of the crowd and stood firmly. "Good morning, New Testament Cathedral family."

A jumbled chorus of "Good morning, Reverend Cleaveland," "Good morning, Mrs. Cleaveland," and "Good morning, Pastor Cleaveland" followed from the crowd.

Samantha threw the room a disappointed glare and said, "I see some of you are still not sure what to call me. Well, let me help you out. As of last week's board of trustees meeting, I am the pastor of New Testament Cathedral. Therefore, it is appropriate for you to address me as Pastor Cleaveland."

A collective look of bewilderment swept across the faces of everyone present.

Samantha continued, "Now that that is out of the way, let's get down to business. I want to first assure you that the death of my husband will in no way interfere with the operations of New Testament Cathedral. We will continue with all scheduled television broadcasts. Our elementary, middle schools, high schools, and college will continue to provide quality education to the future generations of doctors, lawyers, teachers, and missionaries. Our monthly magazine will continue to be published, and most importantly, construction of the new crystal cathedral will go on as scheduled."

Again, the room applauded, this time uninterrupted by Samantha. She flashed a short-lived smile and continued. "What that means for you is you will have to work harder and longer than you ever have before. I expect full and complete loyalty from everyone who works in this ministry. My husband and I have very different styles of management, and if you are given the opportunity to continue working here, you will soon understand what I mean by that."

Samantha took commanding and well-timed steps toward the center of the room as she spoke. "That brings me to my next point. No one in this room should feel secure in their job. Over the next few months you each will have to prove to me that you have what it takes to be a part of the New Testament Cathedral family."

She turned as she spoke until a full circle had been completed and eye contact had been made with virtually everyone in the room. "You will have to prove your loyalty to this ministry. You will have to demonstrate that you are willing to do whatever God asks you to do to spread his message to every living being on this earth. You will have to show me that you are able to raise more money than this church has ever raised in the past."

She paused to observe the looks of terror and fear on their faces and took mental note of those on which fear was not apparent. *You'll have to go, you and you,* she thought. "The last thing I want to discuss with you is a few structural changes. As of today I will be functioning not only as pastor but also as chief operations officer."

Subdued gasps were heard from every corner of the room, the loudest of which came from Catherine Birdsong. Samantha ignored them and continued. "Until further notice, all questions, payment requisitions, and personnel issues that were previously directed to Catherine will now come to me."

Catherine looked directly at Samantha with a questioning expression. She resisted the urge to stand and walk out of the room.

Samantha returned her gaze but spoke to everyone present. "Are there any questions?"

All eyes were focused on Catherine in anticipation of a heated exchange between the two most powerful people in the room. Catherine instead broke the eye contact with Samantha and cast her gaze down at the table.

"Good. I want every department head to contact my assistant to set up an appointment with me. Be prepared to give me a detailed report on the state of your division, the role of each of your employees, and to explain to me why I should allow you to keep your job."

Everyone in the room sat frozen in their seats. Some exchanged wounded glances, while others avoided eye contact with their tablemates.

"Now," she went on, looking menacingly across the crowd, "unless anyone else has something to add, I think we should all get back to work. Have a blessed day, everyone."

No one moved or exhaled until Samantha exited the room through the same door she had entered. When the door closed behind her, some slumped in their chairs, some stood dazed and bewildered, while others quickly exited the room.

Kenneth Davis's long legs quickly carried him across the room. He was the first to approach Catherine as she moved away toward the rear door. "Catherine, I'm so sorry. Did you know about this? Why didn't you tell me?"

Catherine did not turn around as she marched through the crowded room. Staff members stepped aside to clear her path. "I didn't tell you because this is the first I've heard of it," she said with her back to him.

The two were the first to exit the room. Kenneth struggled to keep up with her rapid pace as they walked side by side down the hall. "You mean she never talked to you in private?"

"That's exactly what I mean. The bitch fired me in front of seventy people."

"I didn't hear her say you were fired."

"Neither did I, but how else am I to interpret that performance? She now runs everything and everyone. She's always wanted me out of here, and now she has the power to make it happen." The two rounded the final corner in unison and stopped in front of Catherine's office.

"You need to talk to her and find out what her plans are. Don't assume she wants you out. If she did, I think she would have said it long before this morning."

"I'm so upset right now, I don't trust what I would do or say if I were alone with her. She had no right to humiliate me in front of everyone. She's evil, Kenneth. What possible motivation could she have to treat me like that? I've been loyal all these years to them both and to New Testament Cathedral. She's always been a power-hungry woman who doesn't care whom she hurts as long as she gets what she wants, and now that Hezekiah is gone, there's no one who can stop her."

"That might be true, but you still need this job. Where are you going to go? You love New Testament Cathedral," Kenneth said, escorting her into her office.

"I'm not so sure about that anymore. Hezekiah would have never treated anyone so cruelly. It's different now, and I'm not sure that I want to be a part of it."

"Just remember she is only the interim pastor. The trustees will see how wrong she is for the position and vote her out. You have to be patient and let her hang herself."

Catherine laughed out loud. "If the trustees were naive enough to put her in the position, they'll never vote her out. She'll manipulate them the same way she manipulated Hezekiah and everyone else she wants to control."

"All I'm saying, Catherine, is that you should speak with her first. Let her know that you aren't a threat. That you only want what's best for New Testament Cathedral."

Catherine sat at her desk and rested her head on the back of the cushioned leather chair, willing herself not to cry as Kenneth hovered above her. She took a deep breath and let out an exhausted sigh. "I'll think about it, Kenneth. But I'm not optimistic."

A fountain poured threads of water into a gently gurgling stream that wound through the center of the room. The only hint that it was a Japanese restaurant was the army of attractive and young Asian waiters moving silently from table to table, attending to the whims of diners. Gideon Truman checked his watch as the waiter poured more water into his glass. The trendy restaurant was dimly lit by modern lanterns hanging from the ceiling. The surfaces throughout the dining room were a mix of gleaming polished steel, cold gray cement, and highly glossed teak.

"Are you ready to order, sir?" inquired the waiter, who was wearing the regulation white shirt, black bowtie, and black pants.

"No," Gideon replied politely. "I'm waiting for someone. Looks like they're running late."

"I'll check back in a few minutes," the waiter said as he bowed his head.

Patrons of the restaurant discreetly craned their necks to sneak a glimpse at the handsome news reporter. Sushi chefs peeked at Gideon through the glass shield on the counter to ensure their illustrious lunch guest was comfortable and receiving the best service as they expertly sliced rich red strips of fresh tuna and molded fists of jasmine rice.

Gideon was used to the attention. At forty-five he was the host of a top-rated investigative news program on CNN. His talent for unearthing sensational facts that eluded his competition, coupled with a handsome yet boyish face, made him one of the most popular reporters in the country.

Every evening Gideon's face could be seen in the living rooms, bedrooms, and boardrooms of millions of American viewers. B-list celebrities clamored for the opportunity to appear on his program and be questioned to the point of tears as they confessed to being molested by their uncle when they were children, or to deny being the father of a silicone-injected stripper's love child. On the other hand, A-list celebrities, politicians, corporate CEOs, and heads of state did their best to avoid being caught under the glare of his bright light for fear of involuntarily revealing the one secret that would send their careers plummeting into the depths of public humiliation and obscurity.

His perfectly brown skin provided the ideal contrast for teeth that matched the luster of the finest Australian pearl. The warmth of his deep caramel eyes could seduce, comfort, and then, if he chose, dissect the powerful with surgical-like precision.

Gideon had not fully understood the impact of his striking looks until his first television job at a small station in Philadelphia. It was there he learned that most people were far more interested in what he looked like and with whom he slept than the stories he reported, a fact that never pleased him. There was always a subtle hint of embarrassment in his tone whenever he spoke to the cameras. It was as if he were saying, "I'm sorry if I am distracting you from this important story." This modesty provided viewers with yet another indescribable something that made him even more desirable.

Rumors of his questionable sexuality were frequently the topic of conversation at beauty salons, smart dinner parties, and on the cover of tabloids. No one knew definitively, but the gay community assumed he was "family," while ever-hopeful females defended his heterosexuality as if he were their husband-to-be or favorite son.

As Gideon reached for a full water glass, Cynthia Pryce approached the table. "Good afternoon, Mr. Truman," she said, extending her hand. Gideon bumped the table when he stood and gently took her hand. He appeared slightly rattled.

"I'm sorry. Did I startle you?" she said with a curious expression on her face.

"No. No, not at all. I must, however, confess that I wasn't expecting you to be so . . . Please sit down."

Cynthia smiled. "Thank you. To be so what?"

"Well, so attractive," he replied, uncharacteristically embarrassed.

Cynthia smiled and said, "Really? What exactly were you expecting?"

Gideon quickly regained his composure. "I'm not sure. Maybe a more matronly church-lady type, wearing lots of lace around her neck and a big hat with silk flowers."

They laughed gently. Both revealed pearly smiles that demanded the attention of diners from other tables.

After being directed by the chef, the waiter returned promptly to the table. "Good afternoon, ma'am. May I offer you something from the bar?" he asked Cynthia.

"I'll have a glass of dry white wine," she said without looking up.

"And you, sir?"

Gideon looked up with a smile and replied, "I'll have the same. Thank you."

When the waiter was out of earshot, Gideon spoke softly. "I must say, Mrs. Pryce, I was surprised when you contacted me. I've been trying to reach members of the board of trustees and senior ministers from New Testament Cathedral for three weeks now, but no one has been willing to speak with me. It seems a veil of silence has dropped over the entire church. It's almost as if you all have something to hide."

Cynthia smiled but did not speak. The waiter returned with the two glasses of wine and took their orders.

"Mr. Truman—"

Gideon interrupted, "Please, call me Gideon."

"All right then, Gideon, you mentioned secrets. How much do you know about Hezekiah Cleaveland's personal life?"

"At this point not very much," Gideon replied. "Only what's written about him on the church's Web site. As I said, no one has been willing to talk with me. That is, no one until now."

"Are you familiar with a *Los Angeles Chronicle* reporter by the name of Lance Savage?"

"Isn't he the reporter who was found dead in his home a few weeks ago?"

"That's correct," she said with a pleased expression. "Do you know anything about the story he was working on when he was murdered?"

"I don't. Did it have something to do with Pastor Cleaveland?"

Cynthia's response was interrupted by the waiter arriving with a small platter of intricately displayed sushi. When he bowed and left, she continued, "I'm not going to play games with you, Gideon. I happen to know the content of the story Lance Savage was working on."

"And how do you know that?"

"Because I was the source of his information," she said with a tinge of pride.

"Go on," he said, his words punctuated by a slight gesture of his hand.

"Before I say more, I'll need some assurances from you. What I tell you can never be attributed to me. I must remain anonymous. It will be up to you to prove or disprove what I say."

Gideon silently calculated the cunning of his prey and concluded that, if the information was as titillating as she seemed to believe, it was worth agreeing to her terms.

"That sounds reasonable. However, I must tell you that if what you say is in any way fabricated, I will be very displeased that you have wasted my time, and believe me, Mrs. Pryce, you don't want to lie to someone like me."

She smiled and said, "I can assure you that everything I'm about to tell you is absolutely true. And please, Gideon, call me Cynthia." Cynthia picked up her leather purse from the floor. From it she retrieved a folder containing a stack of papers and handed it to Gideon. "These are copies of e-mails I printed from Hezekiah's computer six months before he was killed. They are correspondences between him and his lover."

"When you say 'lover,' I assume you are referring to his wife, Samantha?" Gideon asked innocently.

"I'm afraid not. Hezekiah's lover was a man. A young man named Danny St. John."

Gideon took the folder, leaned forward, and asked suspiciously, "Are you saying Pastor Hezekiah Cleaveland was gay? Who else knows about this?"

"I'm not exactly sure. The only people I am aware of are Lance Savage, Phillip Thornton from the *Los Angeles Chronicle,* and my husband, Percy."

"How about his wife? Does she know about this?"

"That I don't know."

"Are you suggesting this has something to do with his murder?"

"I suspect it does. I don't know that for a fact, but think about it. In the week before the story was scheduled to run in the *Los Angeles Chronicle,* there were three deaths. All of them were people associated with Samantha Cleaveland. Lance Savage, the Reverend Willie Mitchell, and Hezekiah Cleaveland. It all strikes me as very suspicious."

"Who is Willie Mitchell?"

"Reverend Mitchell was a senior minister at New Testament Cathedral. He was also one of the largest individual donors to the new cathedral construction project and a man who would do anything Samantha told him to do. It was an open secret that he was in love with her, and she used that to control him."

"How did he die?"

"Poor man shot himself in the head on the night Hezekiah was killed," Cynthia answered with as much sympathy as she could muster. "It was such a tragedy."

"Do the police think there's a link between Hezekiah's murder and Mitchell's suicide?"

"No."

"So what makes you think there is?"

"Reverend Mitchell was madly in love with Samantha. So why would he kill himself after the man he believed stood between him and Samantha was now out of the way? It doesn't make sense."

Gideon still had not opened the folder that lay on the table. "Is Danny St. John a member of New Testament Cathedral?"

"No. He's a social worker who works with the homeless at an agency in downtown Los Angeles. I've never seen him before, but Lance told me he is quite beautiful. You should pay him a visit. You might like him."

Gideon ignored the poorly veiled reference to his orientation and opened the folder. The first e-mail was dated February twelfth two years earlier. It was sent from Hezekiah's New Testament Cathedral e-mail address to a Google address for Danny St. John.

> Hello, Danny
> I'm between meetings and wanted to tell you how much I love you. I think about you so much, sometimes it's hard for me to concentrate. I was just counseling a couple whose marriage is falling apart, and all I could think about was holding you in my arms and kissing your body from head to toe. I love the way you taste, the way you smell, and the way you make me feel. I can't wait to see you tomorrow night.
> Love you,
> Hez

Gideon continued reading randomly through the stack of e-mails. They ranged in tone from completely innocuous to sexually graphic. Some were innocent communications, while others spoke to the undeniable emotional and physical bond between one of the nation's most powerful religious leaders and a young, naive social worker. After a while Gideon looked up from the papers at Cynthia, who had been studying him the entire time he read. There was silence at the table as they each planned their next move.

Gideon went first. "So, what do you want out of this? Our network has a firm policy that we don't pay for stories."

Cynthia had anticipated that these would be the salivating journalist's next words and reverted to her best minister's wife impression.

"I'm not seeking any type of financial remuneration," she responded indignantly. "I don't want anything but for God's will to be done. My heart goes out to Samantha. Who knows what diseases he may have given her? Also, what if this Danny St. John killed Hezekiah in a jealous rage? She needs to know for her own safety."

"Why didn't the *Los Angeles Chronicle* run the story?"

"It was scheduled to be their lead story on the Monday after the Sunday Hezekiah was killed. Obviously, Hezekiah being killed was a much bigger story than him liking to suck dick. And, afterward,

I'm sure they realized there would be a significant backlash if they were thought to be maligning the dead." From the expression on Gideon's face, Cynthia realized her choice of words didn't fit with the preacher's wife image. "I'm sorry if I offended you."

"Not offended. Just a little surprised." Gideon took a mental note of the multifaceted woman and continued. "If this is true, it has the potential to be one of the most sensational stories of the year. Have you spoken to anyone else in the media?"

"No, I haven't. I wanted to speak with you first."

"Why me?"

"Because I believe you will handle the story in a way that will do the least amount of harm to New Testament Cathedral. You strike me as ethical, sophisticated, and talented enough to make the story about the man and not the ministry. Good people sometimes do stupid things. Hezekiah's behavior was certainly stupid, but the ministry he built is not. Millions of people around the world rely on New Testament Cathedral for hope, direction, and comfort. I think you can understand how important that is and will report the story in a way that will allow those of us who remain to continue to share the love of God throughout the world."

"That's a nice speech, Cynthia, but isn't your husband the next in line to become pastor if Samantha doesn't work out?"

Cynthia pulled her most offended expression from the depths of her gut and responded, "Yes, but that has nothing to do with this. I only want what's right for New Testament."

"Save the pious bullshit for your television audience. You seem to forget I'm a reporter. I knew everything about you and your husband ten minutes after you called me. I'm assuming your husband, Percy, isn't quite as ambitious as you are. What really happened, Cynthia? He didn't have the balls to throw Samantha under the bus and take over New Testament Cathedral after Hezekiah died? You had done all the dirty work by leaking the story." Then, to test her sensibilities even further, he added, "I wouldn't be surprised if you also had to fuck a few guys, or even girls, at the *Chronicle* to keep this story on track."

Cynthia leaned back in her chair unfazed as Gideon continued. "You would be the first lady of New Testament Cathedral today if

Hezekiah hadn't gotten himself shot in the head the day before the story was scheduled to run. But you don't give up easily, because here you are, trying your damnedest to convince me to pin Hezekiah's death on his widow or his lover."

Cynthia looked him directly in the eyes as she reached for the folder between them. "I'll take those if you're not interested," she said with a wicked smile. "I'm sure I won't have a problem finding someone who is. Maybe Anderson Cooper," she said wryly.

Gideon quickly placed his hand firmly on the folder. "Hold on. I didn't say I wasn't interested. I'm going to investigate the story, but on my terms. No one, including you and your husband, are off-limits. If I find out that your role in this was anything other than what you've said, it will be my decision whether or not to include it in my story."

Cynthia smiled slightly. "You don't frighten me, Gideon Truman," she said mockingly. "The role I played is exactly as I've described it. Just remember, if you call on me to corroborate any of this, you're out of luck. Based on your obviously brilliant skills of deduction, it shouldn't be too difficult for you to figure out why. I'll deny we ever met and sue you personally for libel if you ever try to drag me into this."

"It seems to me you've already dragged yourself into it, Cynthia. Can you get me an interview with Samantha? She won't take my calls."

"Don't worry about that. She knows you want to interview her, and she'll contact you when she feels the time is perfect for her to milk Hezekiah's death for her own benefit. By the way, when you do meet with her, don't forget to ask about his other extramarital affairs."

"What do you mean, other? Have there been more?"

"Of course there have been others, but none like this one. Who cares how many choir girls he's fucked over the years? That will all be eclipsed by the lovely Danny St. John."

33

Reverend Percy Pryce's office was the third largest in the New Testament Cathedral administrative suite.

Percy could smell the sweet fragrance of Cynthia's perfume still on his hands as he removed his coat and sat behind his large black lacquered desk. The fog that ecstasy brought slowly began to fade as the realization of his deeds came to the forefront of his mind. Once again the unsuccessful attempt he and Kenneth Davis had made to pay Lance Savage $175,000 in exchange for not running the incendiary story about Hezekiah played like a recording in his brain. The violent struggle with Lance Savage, which had left the living room of the little bungalow in shambles. The image of the reporter's crumpled body lying dead on the floor among the litter of one-hundred-dollar bills was ever looming.

His hands trembled slightly as he relived the scene. His palms felt moist and his mouth dry when the intercom buzzer sliced through the silence. "Excuse me, Reverend Pryce," exclaimed the disembodied voice. "Reverend Davis is here to see you. Should I send him in? He said it will only take a moment."

Percy took a deep breath and rubbed his dewy hands together. "Thank you, Carol. Send him in."

Kenneth entered like a whirlwind, closing the door behind him. "She's out of control. We have to do something."

Percy looked up and calmly replied, "We only have ourselves to blame for this. We all knew who Samantha was long before Hezekiah was killed. We voted her in as pastor, and now we have to live with the decision."

"How can you be so calm about this? That woman is going to destroy this ministry with her ego." Kenneth walked anxiously toward the desk and continued. "This morning she announced that she is going to be functioning as the COO. She certainly knew how to run Hezekiah, but she doesn't know anything about running New Testament Cathedral."

Percy remained calm. "I think you're wrong. Samantha is a smart woman. The public loves her, and she raises more money than all of us put together. Some people think she's been running the church from day one and Hezekiah was only the front man."

"That may be true, but what about the spiritual needs of our members? You know as well as I do that if they can't write a check for ten thousand dollars or more, she won't want any part of them."

Percy paused and turned toward the window. He looked out over the grounds of New Testament Cathedral and replied mournfully, "I must admit that I worry about that too, Reverend Davis."

Kenneth sat down on the couch and, along with Percy, looked out the window. "And so you should. She's going to run this place like a coldhearted corporation. It will be all about money and her fame, not about saving souls."

The two men sat quietly, each searching the horizon for answers. Percy finally broke the silence. "Have you heard anything from the police about Lance Savage? Every time someone knocks on my door, I jump, thinking it's them coming to arrest me."

Kenneth moved anxiously to the edge of the couch. "I've told you to forget about that, Percy. There is no link between us and his death. As far as the police are concerned, Lance walked in on a burglar robbing his home and was killed."

"I just can't stop thinking about him lying there," Percy said nervously. "He's dead because of us, Kenneth. I don't know if God can forgive us for that. I don't know if I can forgive myself."

"It was an accident. You know it. I know it, and so does God. You didn't intend to kill him."

"Cynthia knows when something is bothering me."

Kenneth stood and walked behind Percy's desk. He spun the chair toward him, kneeled down in front of Percy, and placed his hand on his knee. "Have you said anything to her about this?"

Percy looked startled. "No," he replied emphatically. "I could never tell her I did something like this."

"Good. Let's keep it that way. As time passes, you'll learn to manage your feelings better, but for now don't say a word to anyone. Trust me, it will get easier. If you need to talk about it, call me. Understand?"

Percy nodded his head in affirmation, then turned away.

Kenneth continued, "The only thing we need to worry about now is Samantha and New Testament. We have to figure out a way to prevent her from being appointed as permanent pastor. Everyone knows you should be pastor, Percy."

"You sound like Cynthia. That's all she's been talking about since Hezekiah's death."

Kenneth stood up, sat on the desk and said, "You should listen to her. She's right."

"She might be, but there doesn't seem to be anything that can be done about it now. It's unlikely the trustees are going to reverse their decision. Once she starts bringing in money, they won't have any choice but to make it permanent. They're no match for her. No one is."

"You underestimate yourself, Percy. Cynthia believes in you. I believe in you, and so do thousands of other members of this congregation. You just have to have faith."

"I think I'll need more than faith to go up against Samantha. Right now I'm more concerned about Catherine. She's talking about leaving."

"Like I said earlier, Samantha is not stupid. She'll learn quickly that she can't run this place without Catherine. I'll try to talk some sense into her later this week."

"I don't think she'll listen, but it's worth a try."

"I think you, Catherine, Naomi, and I should meet. Let's put our heads together and see if there's anything we can do about this," Kenneth said.

Percy looked sharply at him and said, "You seem to have forgotten what happened the last time the four of us put our heads together to solve a problem." He stood up and walked away from the desk. "It was bribing Lance not to run the story. What were we thinking? It only made matters worse. Now the man's dead, for Christ sake."

"It was a good plan, Percy. He just got greedy and wanted more. It would have worked if you hadn't gotten so angry. We could have offered him more money."

"We should have never offered him any money at all," Percy said bitterly.

"You know we had no other choice," Kenneth rebuked. "A scandal like that would have brought this entire ministry down. At least that crisis was averted."

"Yes, it was averted, but at what cost? Two men are dead, Kenneth. Was it worth it?"

"How could you ask that? Of course it was worth it. You forget how many millions of people this ministry touches. You forget about all the people whom we've led to Christ. Was it worth it?" Kenneth repeated as his voice escalated. "Hell, yes, it was worth it, and deep down I believe you agree."

"Today my guest is the new pastor of the mega church New Testament Cathedral in Los Angeles and one of my dearest friends, the fabulous Reverend Dr. Samantha Cleaveland."

The audience of the nationally syndicated *Renee Adasen Show* was filled with well-dressed, smiling middle-class women who had collectively waited years for tickets to the talk show. The cantilevered seats held a sea of peach, blue, yellow, and spring pastels. Everyone stood to their feet and applauded when they heard Samantha's name.

Renee raised her voice over the applause and swung her arms in a sweeping motion. "Please help me welcome Pastor, Reverend Dr. Samantha Cleaveland."

The claps became louder and were accompanied by hoots of approval and gasps of admiration when Samantha walked onto the platform from behind a series of backlit blue panels and screens.

"So, you're so . . . gosh," the host said enthusiastically. "You're such an amazing woman. For those of you who don't know—I can't imagine who that would be—Samantha . . . I can call her Samantha because we're friends." The comment was greeted with laughs from the audience and a broad smile and a touch of Renee's hand by Samantha.

Renee continued in a more somber tone. "Anyway, there has been no modern-day tragedy since the King and Kennedy assassinations, at least not one that I can think of, that has moved the country like your story, Samantha. For those in our audience who don't know this, Samantha's husband, the Reverend

Dr. Hezekiah T. Cleaveland, was brutally assassinated. I don't know any other way to put it, but he was assassinated in front of you and the entire congregation of New Testament Cathedral in Los Angeles. I mean you literally held him in your arms as he was dying."

The cameras panned the audience. Women clutched their chests and dabbed tears from their eyes. A closeup of a woman shaking her head, with her hand covering her mouth, filled the screen for a brief moment. The camera cut back to the two beautiful women sitting in modern, comfortable chairs covered in butterscotch-toned leather.

Samantha wore a simply cut black two-piece suit and a white blouse with an oversize collar that revealed only enough cleavage to remind everyone that she was a voluptuous woman. Renee wore an apple red knit dress with a round neckline that dipped slightly to the left, similarly revealing enough flesh to remind viewers that she, too, was a desirable woman.

The women faced each other at a slight angle. Their perfect legs crossed at the knee, with one spiked heel of their handmade Italian shoes planted in the carpet, causing the tip to point graciously toward the audience.

"I know everyone would like to know. . . . I know I would. What was going through your mind at that moment?" the host asked unapologetically. "When you first heard the gunshots? I can only imagine how terrifying that must have been for you."

Samantha's expression, on cue, faded from that of a radiant television personality to grieving widow within seconds. "Renee, let me first tell you how much your support has meant to me through this very difficult time," she said sincerely.

Renee reached out, held her hand, and said, "That's what friends are for. I know you would have done the same for me."

The audience responded with loud yet respectful applause.

"So tell us, Samantha, what was going through you mind that day?"

"Renee, much of it is still a blur. It was a beautiful Sunday morning. Hezekiah and I were always our most happiest on Sundays. I was with him in his office before the service started, and like I always did, I straightened his tie, kissed him, and told him how much I loved him before he went out to the pulpit. I took my seat on the front row, and I remember thinking how lucky I was to be married to such a wonderful man—"

Renee interrupted, "Did you sense anything was wrong or that something bad was about to happen?"

"I had no idea. Everything seemed perfect. Hezekiah was about halfway through his sermon when I heard the first shot. I thought one of the overhead lights had burst." Samantha put the tip of her freshly manicured finger to her lips and paused before she continued. "Then I saw him lean forward and put his hand on his chest. That's when we all heard the second shot. There were screams coming from everywhere. It was horrible," she said with an air of introspection. "Just horrible. I honestly don't remember anything after that."

Renee dabbed a tear from her eye. She again reached across and took Samantha's hand and asked, "Do the police have any clue as to who may have done this?"

Samantha looked even more mournful and said, "So far they don't have any suspects. They think it might have been someone who had been stalking him for at least a year, but they're not sure. The Los Angeles Police Department has been wonderful. I have every faith that they will find the person or persons responsible for my husband's death."

Renee paused before continuing. "Yeah," she said, "I mean, for many people Hezekiah was an icon, but for you he was more than that. He was your husband, your partner, your lover. It must be surreal for you. . . . Is it disbelief? It's hard to believe still? It's still hard to believe he's gone?"

Samantha shifted uncomfortably in the chair and said, "It is, Renee. Some nights I turn over in bed and reach for him, only to find that he's not there. Anyone who's lost a loved one knows the grief is almost unbearable. It's as if you've lost a part of your own soul. I miss him more than you can imagine."

Renee pressed on. "Now, the entire thing was caught on tape?"

"Well, yes. It was Sunday morning service. There were cameras everywhere."

"Unfortunately, the tapes were leaked to the media and have been played . . . seems like nonstop since it happened. How does it feel when you see it now?"

"I haven't seen it. I haven't turned on a television or radio since it happened. I'm too afraid of hearing his name on the news or accidently seeing the footage."

"Well, unfortunately, I have seen it. I suspect most everyone in the country has seen it," Renee replied. "And like I said, it's surreal. I don't know how you've gotten through this with such grace."

"I can honestly say that I don't have any hate for the person who did this. My heart goes out to him, and every night I say a prayer for him. Its times like these that your faith is tested, Renee. This has, of course, tested my faith, but I know that God has a plan, and this has only increased my faith in him."

The last words triggered a round of applause from the audience.

Renee acknowledged the audience with an affirming smile and continued. "Now, this only happened a month ago, right?"

Samantha nodded yes. "It's been just over a month, and the amount of love I have received has been amazing. Thank you, America, for all the love and kindness you've shown me," Samantha said, smiling warmly past the camera to the audience. "Your love and the love of God are the only things that keep me going."

More applause erupted from the now entranced audience. Samantha was everything they had dreamt a friend of Renee's would be.

The host waited for the applause to die down and then continued. "Maybe you're not in this space yet—it's been a month since his death—but when you are able to go to the space where you're able to remember the warmest place and thoughts about your husband, what do you think those thoughts will be?"

Samantha contemplated for a moment and said, "I think what I will remember the most is his kindness. Not only to me, but to everyone he met. When people talked to Hezekiah, he had this uncanny ability to make them feel they were the center of his world. That whatever they were thinking or feeling at the time was important to him, and that he really cared. I loved him deeply, and I believe he also loved me just as much. I'll miss the feeling of security you get when someone cares so deeply for you and would do anything in the world to make you happy."

Renee followed another introspective pause with, "Do you remember the last thing you said to him or the last thing he said to you?"

"I love you."

Renee smiled and said, "I love you. . . . Isn't that a good thing? I understand that you've been selected to replace Hezekiah as the pastor of New Testament Cathedral."

Samantha feigned shock and quickly replied, "I could never replace Hezekiah. No one could replace him. He was a great man. He was my life. He was my soul mate, my rock, and most importantly, he was my friend. Sometimes I'm not sure if I can go on without him, but inevitably, at those lowest moments someone will say to me, 'Don't give up, Samantha. We need you,' or 'You can do it, Samantha. Do it for Hezekiah.' And, Renee, when I hear encouragement like that, I just . . . I get energized. They inspire me to work harder, to move a little faster, and to go on with the work my husband and I began together."

"You are amazing, girl. Isn't she amazing?" Renee asked over her shoulder of the audience.

Their unanimous response was given in thunderous applause.

"So what's next for you, Samantha?" Renee asked.

"I'm glad you asked," replied Samantha with a playful smile. "New Testament Cathedral is going to be bigger and better than ever."

The audience responded as if that was just what they wanted to hear.

"We are about to complete the construction of our new campus and twenty-five-thousand-seat cathedral. The television ministry is expanding now to South Africa, Thailand, and Australia. So we want the world to know New Testament Cathedral is very much alive and growing."

Renee stood up and said, "Wow." Samantha stood with her, and the two women embraced. The audience stood and clapped, as if to solidify the obvious bond between the two women.

Renee raised Samantha's hand as if she were a victorious prizefighter and said above the applause, "I said it once and I'll say it again. You're an amazing woman." She then faced the audience, still holding Samantha's hand in the air, and said,

"Pastor Samantha Cleaveland, everyone. Thank you so much for being here with us today and sharing your courageous story. You are an inspiration and a role model to me and to women everywhere."

Samantha's and Renee's skin looked radiant, magnified on the sixty-two-inch flat-screen television that hung on the wall in Cynthia Pryce's den. Cynthia sat with her feet curled under her in one of two overstuffed black leather chairs that had been positioned at viewing distance in front of the television. A pair of Fendi black suede pumps lay strewn on the floor, and the black jacket of the Dolce & Gabbana pantsuit she wore that day had been tossed casually on the back of the chair.

The curtains were fully drawn and the room was dark except for the piercing glow from the two women on the screen. The room was filled with sleek Scandinavian chairs and a well-cushioned brown leather sofa. The dark stained teak floor offered no assistance in absorbing the crystal clear voices booming from the surround-sound speakers.

The clarity made it impossible for Cynthia to miss any syllable the two women spoke. Her silky hair shifted with every disapproving tilt of her head. As their words reverberated through the room, when they shared a knowing glance, and when the audience gushed, an invisible knife was driven deeper and deeper into Cynthia's heart.

Cynthia pointed the remote as if it were a gun and pressed the trigger when the credits mercifully began to scroll across the screen. The television went black, and Cynthia was left in silence to contemplate the spectacle she had just witnessed.

Is the American public so gullible that they can't tell when someone is acting? she questioned silently. *How could they not see her for the horrible, conniving bitch she is?* she thought, staring at her reflection in the screen.

It had been two days since Scarlett confessed to her husband that Hezekiah was the father of her daughter, Natalie. Two days of David avoiding eye contact when they passed each other in the hall. Two days of sleeping in separate bedrooms, and two days of wondering whether he would leave her life as quickly as he had come. Scarlett loved her husband, but her grief over Hezekiah's death made it difficult for her to worry about her domestic troubles.

Her sleep had been fitful, and there was no appetite. The little strength she had was used to comb Natalie's hair before school each morning and to greet her with a smile and a kiss every day after school. There were stretches of time during the two-day period that she didn't even know if David was in the house. Her thoughts rarely strayed from memories of the brief time she had loved and made love to Hezekiah, or the hurt she had endured at the hand of Samantha after she had learned that Scarlett was pregnant with his child.

David felt betrayed when he learned of the years of deception and lies. The pain was compounded by knowing Hezekiah Cleaveland had shared the secret with the woman he loved. His stomach churned when he thought of all the times he had shaken Hezekiah's hand after church with Scarlett standing by his side and Natalie in his arms.

"You outdid yourself with that sermon, Pastor," he had said to Hezekiah on several Sunday mornings. "You've made me want to be a better husband to my wife and a better father to our daughter."

The hurt festered in the silent home. Every time he saw Scarlett standing in the bathroom mirror or sitting and looking out the living room window, he would imagine Hezekiah groping her delicate body or making love to her in some cheap motel room. He could almost hear her gentle moans of ecstasy when he thought of Hezekiah pounding away at the woman he loved.

He wanted Hezekiah to feel the hurt he felt. *How do you hurt a dead man?* he had thought more than once. *If he wasn't already dead, I think I would kill him.*

Scarlett stepped from the marble and glass enclosure after a long hot shower. Beads of warm water rolled from her dripping hair, over the curves of her breasts, around her hips, and onto the carpeted floor. The water glimmered on her naked body as she wrapped herself in a plush pink towel. The room was filled with steam, leaving only a ghostly reflection in a wall of mirrors that stood before her.

The bathroom door opened, and David stood in the threshold as she dried her hair. "Does Samantha know about this?" he asked coldly.

Scarlett jerked her head in his direction. "You startled me. Why didn't you knock?"

"Now you want me to knock when I enter my own bathroom," he replied with a hint of irony.

"Yes, considering you haven't said a word to me in two days."

"Correction, Scarlett. We haven't spoken to each other in two days. You haven't answered my question. Does Samantha know about Natalie?"

Scarlett wrapped her damp hair in a towel as she spoke. "I told you she did. David, don't torture yourself over this. It doesn't concern you. This is my problem. I've handled it alone up until now, and I will continue to do so."

"What do you mean, it's your problem? You're my wife, and Natalie has been like a daughter to me."

"I appreciate that, David, but now that you know the truth, you don't have to worry about us anymore."

David looked confused. "How can you be so cold to me? I love you, and I love Natalie. Do you expect me just to turn off my feelings?"

"I don't expect you to do anything. I apologize if I've hurt you, but you need to understand that I did everything for Natalie, and for that I won't apologize. If you want to leave, that's up to you. I love you and I want you to stay, but I will understand if you choose not to."

"What does Samantha have to say about it?"

Scarlett did not respond. She turned her back to David and sat on the edge of the bathtub. The pain that had simmered just beneath her thin veil of confidence began to seep to the surface. She took a deep breath before she spoke. "I've already told you how she felt. She tried to force me to have an abortion. She threatened to publicly humiliate me and to say that I had seduced Hezekiah. At the time I was his assistant. She fired me and forbid Hezekiah to have anything to do with the baby."

"So why did you stay? Why didn't you leave the church?"

Scarlett stood abruptly and walked to him. She put her hand on his cheek and pleaded, "David, please don't dig this up again. Why are you torturing yourself? This happened years ago. Hezekiah is dead, and we have each other. Why does any of this matter anymore?"

Scarlett reached for his hand, but David grabbed her wrist roughly and pushed her hand away. "It matters because you lied to me. It matters because Natalie will eventually need to know who her real father is. It matters because the Cleavelands need to pay for how they walked away from her."

"Pay?" she asked. "I've never asked them for anything, and I never will. I've made it on my own for this long, and I will continue to do so with or without you."

"Why do you insist on making me the bad guy in this? I'm not the one who's been lying to you all these years. I'm not the one who's been lying to everyone that ever gave a dime to New Testament Cathedral, like Hezekiah and Samantha have been doing. Remember, I'm the guy who's been made a fool of while the three of you exchanged knowing glances behind my back. I'm the one whose wife has been in love with someone else for years. You've been acting like the grieving widow all this time, and now I understand why."

"You're not being fair, David. I love you."

"Don't give me that bullshit," he snapped. "You've hardly known I was in the house since he died. It was probably a relief that I didn't speak to you for the last two days."

"Is this about money? Because if it is, I told you I survived before I met you and I'll survive after you've gone."

"It's not about money!" he yelled with indignation.

She matched him tone for tone. "Then what is it? Is it about your ego? Are you afraid that he might have been a better lover than you? Are you concerned that his dick might have been bigger than yours? What is this all about?"

David froze in the middle of the bathroom floor. Her shocking words mingled with the thick shower steam and invaded his lungs. He didn't recognize the woman who stood before him. Although her face was distorted by the fog, he could still see her puffy eyes and sneering lips. The woman glaring at him through the mist was not the Scarlett he loved. She was not the woman whose gentle touch alone could make him forget all his troubles.

David had served as Scarlett's attorney when she divorced her first husband. The first day he saw her in his office, he knew professional boundaries were in jeopardy of being crossed. She had looked so fragile sitting across from him at the large mahogany conference table. From the moment the beautiful woman began to recount the physical and emotional abuse she had endured at the hand of her first husband, he was overwhelmed by a need to protect her and to destroy anyone that would do her harm.

And destroy he did. The eventual divorce settlement David won left Scarlett's first husband almost destitute. David was merciless and, by some standards, unscrupulous in winning her the million-dollar home in Brentwood, a vacation home on Lake Tahoe, full custody of the child he thought was his, alimony and child support so high that it forced her ex-husband to rent a studio in the less than affluent Leimert Park section of the city.

"It's about trust, Scarlett. It's about you not trusting me enough to tell me the truth about Natalie. It's about Hezekiah not taking responsibility for his daughter. If I had known, I would have made him pay."

"I know you would have. And that's another reason I never told you. I've never wanted anything from Hezekiah or Samantha. I saw how you destroyed my first husband, and I didn't want you to do that to Hezekiah."

"Why not? If Natalie is his child, he had a legal and moral responsibility to care for her," David said with a mix of lawyerly wisdom and wounded rage.

"I know what you're capable of, David. This would have consumed you. It would have been less about you looking out for Natalie's well-being and more about you wanting to destroy someone you felt had hurt me."

"Is that so wrong?" he asked, walking closer to her. His voice became calm as he cupped her bare shoulders with each hand. "I love you, and I love Natalie. I would do anything to protect you."

"That's just it, David. I didn't need you to protect me from . . ." Her voice trailed off as she held back tears.

There was no need for Scarlett to complete the sentence. The veil of sorrow that shrouded her face confirmed for David what he already believed.

"It's because you were . . ." David removed his hands from her moist shoulders and stepped back. "Because you *are* still in love with him."

Scarlett avoided his glare. "That's not true, David."

"Throughout our entire marriage you've been in love with Hezekiah."

"No, David," she pleaded.

"That's why you never left New Testament Cathedral."

"Don't do this, David."

"You wanted to be near Hezekiah Cleaveland."

Scarlett's knees went limp, causing her to wilt onto the edge of the bathtub. "David, please stop. It isn't true," she pleaded. "I love you."

"You don't love me. How could you?" David stood menacingly above her.

"Everything you've done since you met me has been to keep you close to Hezekiah. Pressuring me to join New Testament Cathedral, you accepting the appointment to the board of trustees, insisting that Hezekiah officiate at our wedding. Were you still sleeping with him? How could I have been so stupid? It's always been about Hezekiah Cleaveland."

"It's not true, David," Scarlett cried. "I swear to you, none of that is true."

34

The morning traffic had given way to cautious older drivers on their way to the local market or the post office, and the odd public bus making another round of the city. Danny stood alone in the window of his small apartment looking over Adams Boulevard.

His apartment was his only refuge.

Danny's bohemian taste was reflected in the eclectic mix of flea market and garage sale finds that filled every room. His toes curled on the worn threads of an Asian rug he had found left on a curb in front of a home in Santa Monica. He took another sip from a steaming cup of tea pressed to his lips.

The endless parade of Joan Rivers jewelry, clothes for the plus-sized woman, and revolutionary new cleaning products that promised to permanently rid his home of life's residue had kept his mind from lingering too long on the memory of Hezekiah. Danny hadn't slept the night before. His room glowed from the television, which was tuned to the Home Shopping Network.

Danny had spent his late teens and much of his twenties searching for the one person who would be willing to look into his eyes and, without reservation, tell him truly what he saw. Was there a hideous monster lurking behind his liquid brown eyes, waiting for just the right moment to pounce and devour his prey, or was an angel there only to serve and guard the weak and frail? Until Hezekiah there had been no one.

Hezekiah had shown him, through his gentle touch and tender kiss, that he was neither a monster nor an angel, neither good nor evil. He had shown Danny that he was more than a cliché, and too beautiful to label, that his love and his hate were one and the same, and that his fear and courage were of the same substance.

Among the jumble of his fears, the thought of forgetting all that Hezekiah had taught him about life, love, and about himself often emerged as the one whose weight seemed most unbearable. What if he forgot how to love?

The telephone in Danny's apartment rang intermittently the entire night. Each time the caller ID flashed the name Kay Braisden.

Danny stared at the glowing name on the telephone as it rang for the last time. The beep was followed by, "Danny, it's Kay again. If you're there, please pick up the phone." Then there was a moment of silence, but she did not disconnect. "Danny, I don't know what else I can say to—"

Danny's hand, of its own volition, reached for the telephone. "Hello, Kay."

"Danny, is that you?"

"Yes."

Kay began to cry. "Why haven't you returned my calls? No, don't answer that. I know why. I behaved like an idiot when you told me about Hezekiah."

"Yes, you did," Danny agreed flatly.

There was an awkward chuckle between her sobs. "I deserved that. Honey, I am so sorry. I've missed you so much. And then when I heard about . . ." Kay stopped midsentence. "How are you holding up through all this? When I saw it on the news, I almost fainted. All I could think about was the pain you must have been in."

"I wish I had died along with him," Danny said softly. "You weren't there for me. No one has been here for me. You were the only person I ever told about Hezekiah. You really disappointed me, Kay, and I don't know if I can forgive you."

"I deserve that, Danny. I feel horrible that I haven't been there for you. But I'm here now if you need me."

Danny was silent. He did need her now more than he had ever needed anyone. He needed someone to know the depth of his pain and loss. He needed someone who could remind him of the person he was before he met Hezekiah, because he had forgotten. He couldn't recall what his face looked like when he smiled. He didn't remember what his laugh sounded like or what his life was before the cloud of grief had descended and enveloped his entire world.

Kay interrupted the silence. "Are you still there, Danny?"

Danny began to cry. Kay was the first person to hear Danny's sorrow since Hezekiah's death. He had isolated himself and didn't allow anyone close enough to hear him cry. At work he behaved as if everyone else's problems were much greater than his own. No one knew of his loss. No one knew of his pain.

"It's okay, Danny. Let it out. I'm here for you, baby. I'm here," Kay said through her own tears.

Their combined sobs served as words for the next five minutes. Danny curled into a tight ball on his couch and cried with the phone clutched to his ear. His chest heaved as he gasped for air between deep wails. He needed someone to hear him cry, to acknowledge his pain, and to recognize his sorrow. Until that moment his loss didn't seem real. It was as if he were suspended in a dream.

If a man cries alone, does he make a sound? he had written in his journal one evening, while lamenting alone. *He does not,* the scribe continued. *In the absence of sound, pain runs deeper. When there is no shoulder to cry on, the chill of sorrow is colder. The weight of grief more unbearable. If no one is there to share your loss. The pain must live with you and you alone.*

As their weeping gradually faded into sputtering breaths, Kay spoke. "Danny, I don't want you to be there alone. I'm coming home on the earliest flight I can get tomorrow."

"That's not necessary, Kay. I'll be all right."

"I know you'll be all right. That's not the point. We need our friends with us at times like this, and I am your friend."

Danny needed her desperately, but he continued, "You're busy, Kay. My mother is only ten minutes away. I can call her if I need to."

"Does your mother know about Hezekiah?"

Danny paused before answering. "No."

"Do you plan on telling her?" Kay asked in the tone of a woman who knew.

"No. She would never understand. I know my mother loves me, but I couldn't risk her abandoning me the way you—"

"I didn't abandon you, Danny."

"Bullshit, Kay," Danny said bitterly. "You didn't call me for months. You made me feel like our friendship all these years was a lie. That there were rules and limits you never bothered to tell me about. I don't want to take that chance with my mother."

"Your mother loves you so much, Danny. I don't think there's anything you could do or say that would change that."

"I'm not sure if that's true. She has her own preconceived idea of who I am. Anything that deviates from that and she's not interested." Danny sighed into the receiver. "Look at what happened when I thought you would never leave me. Our friendship was the one thing I thought I could count on, no matter what. But I was wrong."

"I deserve every horrible thing you have to say to me. There is no excuse for the way I reacted. All I can say is, I hope you can forgive me. You mean the world to me, and it hurts me to see you suffer alone like this."

Danny wanted to withhold his forgiveness, but it was impossible. He needed Kay in his life. "Our friendship is very important to me too."

"Does that mean you forgive me?"

Danny could hear a slight smile in her voice. He paused, not to decide if he could forgive Kay but rather to keep her in suspense for a moment longer. "Of course I forgive you," he finally responded. "Now, how soon can you get here?"

Kay laughed while wiping her tear-streaked cheek. "I'll be on the earliest flight I can get tomorrow."

White noise from sprays of water from a fountain in the middle of the cavernous glass room muffled the frenzied clamor of tourism. Gideon Truman sat in the lobby of the Bonaventure Hotel, intently studying his glowing BlackBerry. Faces from all corners of the world whizzed by, toting rolling suitcases, children, and cameras. Giddy bodies glided up and down the walls of the hotel in glass elevators along the perimeter of the lobby. Every surface glittered from natural and unnatural light. Concrete pillars dotted with pinpoint lights jutted from the marble floor up through the atrium's thirty-five stories to the rooftop revolving cocktail lounge and supported spiraling ramps that led guests upward through the lobby's core.

A tall, pale German man wearing white, yellow, and red plaid khaki shorts, leather sandals, white socks, and a Mickey Mouse cap complete with trademark stiff black ears, with his similarly dressed wife and three small blond children at his heels, stopped in his tracks when he saw Gideon, through an elaborate arrangement of tropical flowers, sitting alone in an overstuffed gray chair in the center of the room. His wife bumped into him, and the three little children collided into her.

Spoils of a day of foraging through the gift shops and concession stands at Disneyland hung from their bodies. Stuffed animals with price tags still connected were Gideon sat in a comfortable seat and contemplated his next move. Cynthia Pryce had handed him the explosive twist of Danny St. John. He was now faced with the question of whether he should pursue the alleged homosexual affair, and inevitably sully the name and reputation of a much-cherished icon, or simply do what he had originally set out to do, report on the investigation into Hezekiah's murder.

He now held a piece of information that, if true, had the potential of toppling one of the most influential dynasties in the country and tarnishing the memory of one of the most renowned ministers of the twenty-first century.

Gideon was already famous, so the pursuit of acclaim would not factor heavily into his decision. He was potentially the only living reporter in the country that knew of Danny St. John. If he broke the story, it would serve to silence his many critics that claimed he was merely eye candy and not a serious journalist. Whenever he read the cutting critiques of his work, a chill would race up his spine. He had worked harder than his contemporaries but was never taken as seriously because his smile and dashing good looks always landed him on the cover and in the bowels of tabloid magazines. The question was, "Who is Gideon Truman dating now?" rather than "How did he find the nerve to ask the secretary of state that question?" The media coverage of his work usually read, "Gideon Truman looked devilishly handsome in a black Armani tuxedo at the inauguration ball," instead of "Gideon Truman asked the new president hard-hitting questions that were undoubtedly on the minds of every American."

A story this big would surely establish him as a serious journalist, worthy of the respect he so desperately desired. But at what cost would this be? New Testament Cathedral would likely be destroyed. Thousands, maybe millions, of people around the world would question their faith. One more high-profile black man would be subjected to a modern-day lynching and, in this case, would be unable to defend himself.

But the public has a right to know, Gideon thought. Hezekiah Cleaveland had set himself up as an icon. It was his decision to espouse a pious lifestyle that, if this is true, even he couldn't live up to. It was his choice to cheat on his wife and his choice to have an affair with a man.

It wouldn't hurt to talk to St. John, he thought, continuing along this line of reasoning. *I can't believe there's anything to this, anyway. I can decide whether or not to pursue it after I've spoken to him.*

Finding Danny's telephone number was an easy task. A visit to the Los Angeles mission where Danny worked, flashing a smile at the receptionist, and signing an autograph on the back of the mission's brochure yielded not only his cell phone number but also his home phone number, home address, and e-mail address, which he already had.

Danny St. John's name and telephone number appeared on the screen of the BlackBerry. After a brief hesitation he pressed TALK. The phone rang three times and then, "Hello. This is Danny. I can't take your call right now so . . . Well, you know the routine. *Ciao.*"

Gideon smiled when he heard the message. He also felt a warm flow rise from his belly as he listened to the deep, gentle timbre of the voice, which caused him to pause again.

"Hello, Mr. St. John. My name is Gideon Truman. I work for CNN. I'm covering the investigation into the death of Hezekiah Cleaveland. I was told that you may have known him. I was wondering if I might be able to speak with you briefly about this. I won't take much of your time, and I really would appreciate it. When you get this message, please give me a call on my cell at 310-555-4455."

***

Hattie bent over in her garden to pluck another red tomato from a vine that slumped under the weight of a season's bounty. She stood on the rich soil between perfectly carved rows of greens, yellows, whites, and reds. The collard greens stood tall in the gentle breeze. They always reminded her of baby elephant ears when they flapped in the wind. Bushes of yellow zucchini shielded their precious fruits from the sun, and climbing green beans twisted and tangled themselves on elaborately constructed trellises made of wire and wood and set in a row.

The garden was her pride and refuge. It occupied the entire width of her backyard and one half of the length. A meticulous six-foot pink brick fence that her husband had built when the children were young served as the backdrop to the summer harvest. After each season, as soon as the last vegetable was plucked, Hattie would begin preparing the soil for the next round of crops. There was always something delicious growing in Hattie's backyard: carrots, onions, bell peppers, mustard greens and collard greens, broccoli, and cabbages. Always something to share with her neighbors, children, and friends.

The lower half of her body was covered by a faded yellow apron, tied securely around her waist, with oversized deep pockets that bulged from all the tomatoes she had picked. Moist dirt encased the soles of her sturdy black rubber shoes, and the wide-brimmed straw hat she wore caused a grid of light and shadows to form on her forehead.

Even with the warmth of the sun on her shoulders and the mud squishing under her feet, Hattie could not escape the memory of the dream she had had two nights earlier. Who was the other person, the one she could not see in the dream? Why didn't they show themselves to her? Why were they hiding from her? Was it a man or a woman? Whoever it was, they clearly loved Pastor Cleaveland very deeply. Certainly more than Samantha had loved him.

Hattie shoed away a bee that buzzed near her ear, and another ripe tomato found its way into the apron's deep pocket. One of the many red and black dotted ladybugs in the yard landed on her shoulder. She did not brush it away. "Lord knows I can always use some good luck," she said, looking down at the ladybug.

Throughout her life, Hattie had always known what was going to happen to people around her long before it happened. She had cradled each of her four grandchildren in her dreams and had stroked their curly locks years before they were born. The vision of her mother's death at the hands of "sugar" had startled her from sleep many nights as early as seven years before the old woman succumbed to diabetes. The premonition of the man with the surprisingly dark skin sitting behind the desk in the Oval Office, just staring out the window, had come to her late one night two years before it actually became a reality.

She had learned to live with these foresights, whether they were good or bad. "Only you can change the course of a man's life," she often reaffirmed in her prayers to God and to herself. "And I ain't you, Lord, so let your will be done on earth just as it is in heaven." Hattie lived by these words. *Don't interfere with the paths men have chosen for themselves. It just ain't my place. If they want to change it, that's between them and their God.*

But today even her firm conviction left her wondering if she had done the right thing by keeping silent. She had seen Hezekiah falling in the sanctuary days before he was killed that horrible Sunday morning. She had known well in advance that someone close to him was trying to destroy him. Should she have warned him?

"Pastor Cleaveland, you know I ain't one to meddle in other people's business, but I feel I just got to tell you. Something just ain't right around here," the conversation would have gone. "Now, I know you love your wife, and so you should. But that woman is just pure evil. She don't mean you no good, Pastor. One day that woman's gonna do something terrible to somebody. Maybe even you. I know she is. I can feel it in my spirit."

Of course, Pastor Cleaveland would have looked at her as the kindly old lady that she in fact was, reached for her weathered hand, and responded something along the lines of, "Now, Mother Williams, I know your premonitions have always been accurate in the past, but this time I think you may have gotten your spiritual wires crossed. Samantha loves me. You know that. She would never do anything to hurt me."

It was not until the most recent dream that Hattie learned who was behind the assassination of her pastor. The horror of the revelation had made sleep almost impossible the last few nights. Every time she thought about the coldness that passed from Samantha when she touched her shoulder in the dream, the same chill crept up her spine again. The light pouring from the evil woman's smile that enveloped her caused her vision to blur momentarily. Hezekiah gazing up from the pool of blood with that vacant look in his eyes made her stomach ache from pains of sorrow.

The figure she could not see still haunted her. "Who was it?" she questioned as she stood transfixed in the garden. "I hope that poor soul is not next."

35

Gideon Truman drove the rented silver SUV to the entrance of the Cleaveland estate. He had finally been summoned by Samantha Cleaveland.

The call had come to his cell the day before. "Good afternoon. May I speak with Mr. Gideon Truman please?" the polite voice had asked with a slow, deliberate, and somewhat artificially sweet tone that hinted of Southern roots.

"This is Gideon Truman. How can I help you?"

"My name is Chantal Maxwell, Mr. Truman. I am Pastor Samantha Cleaveland's scheduling secretary. How are you today, sir?"

"Well, well. Finally, someone from New Testament Cathedral calls me back. I was beginning to take the snubs personally."

"Oh, no, sir. Please don't take it personally, and thank you for your patience. I must deeply apologize for the delay in returning your calls, but as I'm sure you must understand, this has been a very difficult time for everyone at New Testament Cathedral, and especially for Pastor Cleaveland. You are not the only reporter we've had to put on hold over the last three weeks, but you should know you are one of the first we have contacted."

"I'm honored," Gideon said, barely concealing the excited tone in his voice.

"Mr. Truman, Pastor Cleaveland would like to invite you for lunch at the Cleaveland estate in Bel Air tomorrow at one o'clock. Would that be convenient for you, sir?"

"I'll be there," he replied quickly, forgetting to keep his excitement in check.

"Wonderful, sir. Would you like me to send a car for you?" The more she talked, the thicker her accent became and the slower the pace.

"That won't be necessary."

"Do you have any dietary constraints that you would like the chef to be made aware of?"

Gideon was surprised that no attempt was being made to conceal the conspicuous wealth of the Cleavelands: drivers, private chefs, Bel Air estate. *I guess the days of being embarrassed for getting rich in the name of the Lord ended with Jim Baker,* he thought.

"Thank you for asking, but I'll eat anything."

"Very well then, Mr. Truman. Also, Pastor Cleaveland has asked, will there be a film crew accompanying you? And if so, will they require any special accommodations? The estate is equipped with a state-of-the-art studio and media center."

Gideon paused, almost dumbfounded. "What was your name again, darling?"

"Chantal, Mr. Truman, Chantal Maxwell."

"Chantal, please tell Pastor Cleaveland that I'm hoping this will be the first of many conversations between her and myself. So, no, I won't be bringing a film crew with me this time."

"Yes, Mr. Truman, I will pass that message on to Pastor Cleaveland. I look forward to meeting you tomorrow. I've taken the liberty of texting you a confirmation, the address and directions."

As she spoke the familiar beep on his BlackBerry sounded and the Cleaveland estate address and a Google Maps link appeared on the screen.

Chantal continued, "Now, if there is anything else I can do for you prior to your visit, please do not hesitate to contact me. May you have a blessed day, and remember, God loves you and so do we."

The telephone disconnected before his quick mind could form a snappy reply.

The next day Gideon found himself parked in front of the estate. "Good afternoon, Mr. Truman," a deep male voice said from the gatehouse. "Welcome to the Cleaveland estate. Pastor Cleaveland is expecting you. Please drive in and follow the road to the main house."

The grounds were surrounded by an eight-foot white stucco wall that extended so far up the street beyond the entrance that he was not able to see where it ended. The electronic iron gates, emblazoned with the initials *HC*, glided open. As he drove through, he saw a camera pointed directly at him. It followed him as he passed through the gates.

Within the confines of the stucco wall the temperature seemed to drop ten degrees. A thick canopy of trees and lush greenery gave the grounds an almost enchanted feel. The road was lined with palm trees standing at attention, as if they were guarding a castle. Movement to his left demanded his attention. Gideon did a double take. Three large peacocks on the shimmering green lawn flared their iridescent turquoise tail feathers as he drove by. In the background he could hear the muffled roar of the Pacific Ocean.

"If I start to hear harps playing, I'm leaving," he mumbled. The grounds were immaculate. He could see men in green uniforms riding in what appeared to be a golf cart filled with gardening equipment on a path to his right. A tennis court with striking white lines was followed by a gazebo that looked out over the ocean. Then he saw what he assumed was a guesthouse tucked behind a grove of even more trees.

Finally, he could see the main house looming ahead. As he drove closer, the dense cover of trees unfurled like curtains on a stage. The house was drenched in sunlight, which seemed to appear just as he approached.

It was a magnificent glowing white Mediterranean villa flanked on each side by spectacular views of Los Angeles and the Pacific Ocean, and above by a strikingly blue sky dotted with fluffy white clouds. Gideon never remembered seeing the sky such an amazing shade of azure before. Two massive stone double stairways curved around a fifteen-foot stone fountain pouring water into a pond filled with night-blooming water lilies and black, gold, and white koi fish, led up to a covered porch. The landing held four twenty-foot-high carved pillars, two to the left and two to the right of what were the largest and most intricately carved wooden doors he had ever seen.

Before he could completely stop the car, a gentle tap on the side window startled him. A tall, well-built man who appeared to be of

Italian decent, wearing a black suit and dark sunglasses, opened Gideon's car door.

"Good afternoon, Mr. Truman. Welcome to the Cleaveland estate. Please leave your keys in the car. I assure you it will be well taken care of."

Gideon noticed a brown leather strap under his coat as the man gestured for him to exit the car. *Armed security?* Gideon thought. *She must be terrified with the killer still on the loose.*

"Security's pretty tight around here," Gideon said, exiting the car.

"Yes, sir. We do take every necessary precaution. You will be very safe during your time with Pastor Cleaveland. Enjoy your lunch, Mr. Truman."

With that, the armed man climbed into the SUV and drove around the side of the house.

Gideon stood for a moment alone at the foot of the stairway. In every direction he looked, he could not see the perimeter of the property. The only sounds he could hear were the occasional high-pitched calls of the peacocks and the splash of the fountain.

In his career Gideon had interviewed two presidents, a host of A-list celebrities, war heroes, and the Pope, but he had never been as nervous as he felt at that moment. *Must be the peacocks,* he thought as he began the ascent up the stairs. He checked his breast pocket to make sure he had his recorder, a pen, a pad, and his BlackBerry. As soon as he set a foot on the porch, the double doors swung open.

A woman appeared in the center of the doorway. The first thing he noticed was that her skin was as smooth as alabaster. Her features were fine and worthy of her pale complexion. Shoulder-length hair, the most perfect shade of deep dark red, flowed in slow motion, as if blown by an unseen wind, as she walked toward him with an extended hand.

I see Samantha Cleaveland likes to surround herself with lovely things, both animate and inanimate, he thought as he walked to the beautiful young woman.

"Welcome to the Cleaveland estate, Mr. Truman," the woman said, exposing a smile too perfect even for her flawless face. "I'm Chantal Maxwell. We spoke on the telephone yesterday."

"Thank you, Chantal. I've been looking forward to my visit."

"Please come in. Pastor Cleaveland will be down shortly," Chantal said, directing Gideon over the threshold and closing the doors behind him.

The foyer surpassed the splendor of the exterior of the home. The oval-shaped room was bathed in warm golden light. Gideon couldn't tell if it was natural or artificial. Double doors on the left and on the right led to the living and dining rooms. A round marble table stood in the center of the room, balancing the most elaborate floral arrangement he had ever seen.

Two stairways on the left and right, with black wrought-iron banisters contoured to the shape of the curved walls, led up to a second-floor landing that overlooked the foyer.

Gideon's eye went directly to the painting that hung on the wall opposite the main entrance. He pointed at the picture and stammered, "Is that . . ."

"Yes, it is, Mr. Truman. Pastor Hezekiah Cleaveland gave it to Mrs. Cleaveland on their thirteenth wedding anniversary."

It was the first of two Picassos in the Cleaveland home. The deconstructed portrait of a woman whose dreamy expression had mesmerized the world for decades, ignored the two standing in front of her. Painted hands formed the triangle in her lap through which all life must pass. Her slanted head and blissfully closed eyes hinted of the erotic dreams that caused her pouting red lips to smile.

Gideon resisted the urge to blurt out, "Holy shit!" and instead said to Chantal, "He must have really loved her."

"Yes, he did, Mr. Truman. This way please."

Gideon followed the young woman and her smoldering red hair into the living room. Antique furniture and classic French, Italian, and Flemish masterpieces were arranged throughout the cavernous room. The placement of each object was so precise that Gideon correctly surmised that the blueprint was the work of one of the world's renowned interior designers. Finely woven Persian rugs served as the canvas upon which the well-thought-out ensemble of wingback chairs, marble-topped tea tables, and satin couches were displayed. A massive crystal chandelier hung in the center of the room, and Lalique vases glittered throughout. A cold black

Steinway baby grand piano rested in front of a wall of glass that overlooked the grounds.

Gideon's eyes soon found their way to the second Picasso, which hung over a gaping fireplace. The five women of *Les Demoiselles d'Avignon* looked unimpressed as they surveyed the room. Their faces were primitive, and the jagged edges of their pink flesh formed sharp angles that jutted out in every direction.

An eight-by-six-foot oil painting of Hezekiah and Samantha hung on the wall opposite the Picasso. Their two smiling faces served as the perfect aesthetic counterbalance to the seductive five women across the room. But as lovely and masterfully executed as the two paintings were, their beauty was eclipsed when Samantha Cleaveland entered the room.

"Good afternoon, Mr. Truman."

Gideon tore his gaze away from the paintings and turned to see Samantha standing in the threshold, enveloped in a pool of light from the foyer. She wore a powdery pink pantsuit that had obviously been sewn in strict obedience to every curve of her statuesque form. A pair of flat Ferragamo shoes, the exact color of her suit, barely touched the carpet as she glided toward him.

Gideon could not move. His feet felt like they each weighed a hundred pounds. She was, he thought, one of the most beautiful women he had ever laid eyes on.

Gideon had forgotten that Chantal was in the room until he heard her voice. "Mr. Truman, this is Pastor Samantha Cleaveland," she said, as if introducing a guest on a late-night talk show. As she spoke, she took a step back to clear the path between Samantha and Gideon.

"It is so nice of you to come on such short notice. I hope you didn't have any trouble finding the house," Samantha said.

As she spoke, she extended her hand. Gideon was distracted once again, this time by the glitter from a diamond bracelet on her wrist, which seemed to catch every particle of light in the room.

"Thank y—you for inviting me," he stuttered. "Finding the home was a challenge."

"It's a bit hidden, but when my late husband first saw it, he insisted on having it."

"It's a beautiful home."

"Thank you. It was built by a steel magnate. He lived here for less than a year. I originally was not very fond of it, because it's so large, but now it's filled with so many of our memories, I could never dream of moving."

As the two spoke, Chantal exited the room, unnoticed. The only evidence that she was ever in the room came in the form of a click as she closed the double doors behind her.

"I hope you're hungry, Mr. Truman. My chef has prepared a special meal for us. He apparently is a fan of yours."

Gideon's years of experience as an investigative reporter slowly began to emerge through the fog of awe. He silently chastised himself for the momentary paralysis caused by the extravagance of the estate and the stunning beauty of the woman now standing before him. *Pull yourself together, man. You've interviewed royalty, for God's sake.*

"I'm afraid I won't be able to stay for lunch, Pastor Cleaveland. I simply wanted to meet you to get a feel for who you are as a person and to discuss your appearance on my television program."

Samantha looked slightly disappointed. "I'm sorry to hear that. My chef will be disappointed. Can I at least offer you something to drink?"

"Water would be fine. Thank you."

"Chantal, please have Etta bring water for Mr. Truman and coffee for me," Samantha said into an intercom sitting on a tea table next to the sofa.

"Yes, Pastor Clea—" came Chantal's disembodied reply as Samantha disconnected the line.

"Please sit down, Mr. Truman."

For the first time since she had entered the room, Gideon was able to move his feet. Samantha sat on the sofa in front of the fireplace topped by *Les Demoiselles d' Avignon*, and Gideon sat in a plush chair opposite.

Samantha spoke first. "Let me say, first of all, that I have not agreed to appear on your television program. I, too, first wanted to meet you and get a feeling for who you are. As you can imagine, I am cautious about speaking to the media. They have not always been kind to my husband and I."

"I completely understand." Gideon removed the recorder from his pocket. "Would it be okay with you if I record our conversation?"

Samantha did not blink and simply replied, "Of course."

Gideon placed the recorder on the coffee table between them and began. "Pastor Cleaveland, let me start by extending my deepest sympathies on the loss of your husband. I never met him, but by all accounts he was a great man."

Samantha's face turned somber. "Thank you. It was a tragic loss, not only for me and my daughter, but for all the members of our congregation."

"How are you doing now?"

"Right now I'm living my life one day at a time, and every day is a challenge. The only thing that keeps me going is my knowing that it was God's will that he be taken from me. I don't know why, and may never know, but I do find comfort in knowing that all things work together for good for those that love the Lord. Are you a religious man, Mr. Truman?"

"Somewhat. I imagine that you must miss him terribly. Can you talk a little about your relationship? What he meant to you and how his death affected you?"

There was a gentle tap at the door before it opened. Etta appeared, carrying a silver tray holding a crystal decanter filled with water, a goblet, and a cup of steaming coffee, and moved toward Samantha. She placed the tray on the coffee table and poured the water. "Will there be anything else, Pastor Cleaveland?" she inquired coldly. Her tone didn't go unnoticed by Gideon.

Samantha looked lovingly up at Etta and replied, "Thank you, Etta dear. That will be all for now."

As Etta moved toward the door, she could hear Samantha say, "That is my housekeeper, Etta. She's been with us for years. She's like a family member. I don't know what I would have done without her. Now, where were we?"

"You were about to tell me about your relationship."

"Hezekiah meant the world to me. Not only were we partners in building the ministry, but he was—please excuse the cliché—he was my soul mate. When I was growing up, I never imagined I could love someone as much as I loved him, or be loved by someone as much as he loved me. Over the years, we went through so many trials and tribulations and fought so many battles together, but each one only served to strengthen our union. We were a team, partners, lovers, and he was my best friend."

"How has his death affected you personally?"

"I'll be honest with you, Mr. Truman. There are some days that I think I can't go on without him. But then I remember how much he loved me. I also think about how much he loved the ministry we built together, and I know that he would want me to continue building the vision that we shared."

"And what is that vision?"

"It is a simple one, to share the message of God's love with every living being on earth."

"And you are well on your way to achieving that, a global ministry, the sixth wealthiest congregation in the United States, a multimillion-dollar cathedral, university, and multimedia complex currently under construction. Some have speculated that without Hezekiah, the ministry might not be able to continue growing at the incredible rate that it has over the last ten years."

Samantha's face tensed for a fraction of a second, then returned to that of the lovely grieving widow. The brief and almost undetectable change would have easily gone unnoticed by a television camera or a sanctuary filled with adoring worshippers, but to Gideon's experienced eye the faint facial contortion hinted that he had touched on a sensitive topic.

"What some people fail to realize, Mr. Truman, is that Hezekiah and I were equal partners. We built the ministry together. So it's not as if I'm trying to fill shoes that I haven't been wearing up until now."

Gideon decided not to pursue the line of questioning, but rather to save it for when the cameras were rolling. Instead he replied, "Pastor Cleaveland, you strike me as a woman who is capable of doing just about anything."

Samantha smiled. "I'll assume you meant that as a compliment. But I have no doubt that the ministry will continue to grow. Not because of who I am, but because of God. This is his ministry and I am his servant and I truly believe this is God's will."

"If I may change the subject, do you have any idea who might have done this to your husband? Was it an enemy from the past, a deranged viewer, an ex-lover possibly?"

Again, her brief facial tic registered. "I have no idea who killed my husband, Mr. Truman, and I assure you that Hezekiah was completely faithful to me, if that is what you're implying."

"I'm sorry. I didn't mean to offend you."

"I'm not offended, but I do want to be assured that if I were to appear on your television program, infidelity will not be one of the topics you broach. There would be no point, because Hezekiah was completely and utterly devoted to me and would never have broken the vows of our marriage. I know because he was that kind of man."

"I assure you, Pastor Cleaveland, that I will not touch on any topic that is not substantiated by fact. Have the police given you any indication that they are any closer to finding out who killed your husband?"

"The Los Angeles Police Department has been absolutely amazing throughout this entire ordeal, but I'm afraid they are at a loss as to who assassinated my husband."

"How does it make you feel knowing that this person is still out there? Are you at all concerned about your own safety and that of your daughter?"

"I, of course, am concerned, but more so for my daughter. As I'm sure you experienced when entering the property today, security on the estate is very tight. I never travel alone and am always surrounded by a number of highly trained security guards, seen and unseen. I must admit that sometimes it terrifies me that his killer has not been caught. I am afraid for my life, but I will not allow fear to control me. There is work to be done, souls to be saved, and a message to be preached. I've made the promise to God, to the members of my congregation, to Hezekiah, and to myself that I would go forward, and I will not allow anything or anyone to stop me."

A chill traveled up Gideon's spine as the woman spoke. Beneath the beautiful veneer, he detected the soul of a woman who would stop at nothing in her quest for power, wealth, and fame.

"Do you have any questions for me, Mrs., excuse me, Pastor Cleaveland?" he asked and once again noticed her stiffening cheek muscle. "I do hope that you will agree to appear on my show. I know my viewers would love to hear from you."

"Only one. Why?"

"Why what?"

"Why do you want me to appear on your show? And, please, be truthful. I detest dishonesty."

Gideon calculated at lightning speed his response. He knew her consent hinged on his answer. "Because millions of viewers would tune in if they knew a woman as beautiful and powerful as you was sitting across from me."

"If you had said anything other than exactly that, I would have known you were lying. Have your people call my office to make the arrangements."

"Wonderful," Gideon said, barely containing his pleasure.

"The head of my security team will need access to your studio at least one day prior," Samantha said, standing to her feet to indicate the meeting was to end.

"My studio?"

"Yes. Isn't that where you plan on conducting the interview?"

Gideon stood obediently, following her cue. "I appreciate your willingness to come to me for the interview, but I was hoping we would be able to conduct it here in your home, in this room, as a matter of fact."

Samantha looked at him intently. "Here?" she questioned. "I don't think I'm comfortable with that idea."

"Oh . . . I had assumed you would be more comfortable if we did it in your home. I also wanted to show my viewers a different, more intimate side of you, Pastor Samantha Cleaveland at home. Something I believe the American public has never seen before."

The opulence that even took me by surprise when I arrived at the estate, Gideon thought as Samantha pondered the possibility. *The peacocks, the burly security guards, the lush rolling grounds, the fountains, and Picassos. If it weren't done so tastefully, it would be considered vulgar. No surprise she doesn't want the public to see this.* He refused to let the opportunity pass to interview Samantha Cleaveland in her home.

"You are correct, Gideon. We have never had cameras in our home. You see, my late husband and I always viewed this as our sanctuary. The one place we could go for peace and privacy."

"I assure you, Pastor Cleaveland, no hint of this location will be given, and we'll only show areas of the home that you preapprove and are comfortable with."

There was a silence that seemed like an eternity to Gideon. Samantha scanned the room and made a mental note of the more expensive pieces that would have to be removed before filming. The pricier pieces of art were at the top of the list.

"All right, Mr. Truman," she finally said. "You can do the interview here. However, I don't want any exterior shots of the house."

"Agreed," he quickly replied. A small concession for the opportunity to film the bounty contained within the walls of the Cleaveland estate.

After exchanging pleasantries and gracious good-byes, Gideon was met in the foyer by Chantal.

"Hello again, Mr. Truman," she said, matching his stride as he walked to the door. "I trust your visit with Pastor Cleaveland was a pleasant one."

"Yes, it was. Thank you. She is a remarkable woman."

Chantal did not respond.

"What's it like working for someone as powerful as Pastor Cleaveland? I would imagine she can be very demanding."

"I feel very blessed that I am able to serve such an anointed messenger of God."

"I'm sure you do, but what is she really like?"

As the two reached the threshold, Chantal opened one of the double doors. "Thank you for coming, Mr. Truman. Your car is waiting at the bottom of the stairs. Have a blessed day."

Before Gideon could respond, Chantal gently closed the massive oak door. Once again, he stood looking out over the grounds. Again, he could hear the call of the peacocks in the distance and the gentle whoosh of the fountain. The sun seemed brighter than it had been when he entered the house. Every flower petal seemed to have a ray of light dedicated to its beauty. Drops of water in the fountain shimmered like crystals falling into a lake of diamonds. This was an enchanted place, and now it was even more so after being in the presence of Samantha Cleaveland.

As promised, his car was waiting at the bottom of the stairs, accompanied by yet another security guard wearing the regulation black suit and dark sunglasses. Again, Gideon noticed the revolver-shaped bulge in his coat. As Gideon descended the stairs, the man opened the driver's side door. "Thank you for visiting the Cleaveland estate, Mr. Truman," he said in a rich baritone. "Will you be able to find your way back down to the city all right?"

"Yes, thank you," Gideon said as he entered the car.

"Very well then, sir. Have a nice day," the man said as he gently closed the car door.

Gideon drove the car to the main road. To his left he could see a mother deer and her fawn nibbling in a dense patch of brush. A flock of Canadian geese flew overhead in a V formation, honking as they landed on an open stretch of lawn to his right. He instantly regretted agreeing to not show the exterior of the estate. "America would never believe this," he said out loud. "How many old ladies' pensions does it take to pay for all this?"

The wrought-iron gates glided silently open as he approached. He could see the poorly camouflaged lens of a camera on the gatehouse follow him as he exited onto the road. At the bottom of the long, winding hill the smog of the real world slowly became visible again. In the rarefied heights of the Cleaveland estate, smog was apparently not permitted. The preening peacocks were replaced by dusty gray pigeons, and instead of the soothing purr of the flowing fountain, he heard blaring horns and sirens from ambulances whizzing by.

Gideon felt disoriented. Samantha Cleaveland had left a distinct impression on him, but he could not figure out what it was. Yes, he was repulsed by the lavish exhibit of wealth: the shameless disregard for the sacrifices made by members of her church to maintain a lifestyle that would make most Hollywood celebrities jealous.

Yet Samantha Cleaveland was undeniably one of the most beautiful women he had ever been in the presence of. The way she carried her body through space, the sensuous, almost breathy tone of her voice, which seemed to echo in his head, when she spoke. Only a woman like that could eclipse the timeless splendor of Picasso. Only Samantha Cleaveland could make you look away from the breathtaking city and ocean views when she walked into the room.

An intoxicating vapor seeped from her pores. Her seductive brown eyes invited those under her gaze to let down their defenses and trust the pearls that dripped from her red lips. However, Gideon couldn't help but sense that there was something sinister lurking just beneath the well-polished veneer, something simmering behind the sparkle in her eyes. A thing that was capable of destroying anything, and anyone, in her path to protect and maintain what she had made.

That was the Samantha Cleaveland that he now knew he must expose. He wanted his viewers to see the real Pastor Samantha Cleaveland. More importantly, he wanted to see her for himself.

I wonder if she knew about her husband's alleged affair with a man, Gideon thought. *She doesn't strike me as the type that would look the other way. She's got too much to lose. I think it's time for me to meet this Mr. Danny St. John.*

36

Danny had managed to shave, shower, and dress himself that morning. His boss had called the day before and told him he had missed too many days in the last month and he either had to get a doctor's note or come in to work the next day.

"I can't keep covering for you, Danny," he'd said in a sympathetic yet firm tone. "I'm worried about you. Are you doing any better? You haven't told me what's wrong with you, and you don't have to tell me if you don't want to but . . ."

"I understand Gregg, and I appreciate you not pressuring me. I'm sorry I've missed so many days, but I'm doing much better now. I'll be in tomorrow."

The large room in the homeless drop-in center in the skid row section of downtown was filled with haggard and weather-beaten men and women who had survived another night on the streets of Los Angeles. Some were watching television on a big screen, while others sat quietly, sipping tepid coffee from paper cups. Old women surrounded by plastic shopping bags and bundled in tattered coats huddled against walls, trying to be invisible. Young children clutched their mother's thighs as they spoke to attentive social workers in cubicles piled with boxes of clothing donations.

A group of six men sat on folding chairs in a corner and exchanged stories they had accumulated from the night before. "The cops showed up at three o'clock in the fucking morning and made us pack up all our shit and move out of the park," a little man with sunburnt skin and a missing front tooth said to the captivated group. "Bastards took my shopping cart and everything I couldn't carry away in my arms."

"Some strung-out crackhead tried to rob me last night over on Sixth Street," another began. "Son of a bitch pulled a knife on me." The man then lifted his shirt and showed the group a gash that ran from his left nipple to his belly button. "Cut me here, took my last fucking beer and all the money I panhandled yesterday."

Some attempted to wash away the city's dirt in the facility's shower area, while others slept in heaps on the floor, trying to recover from a night of aimless wandering.

Danny sat in his cubicle. There were eighty-seven e-mails waiting for his attention, and the red blinking light on his telephone indicated there were twenty-eight messages waiting to be heard.

The cubicle was only large enough to fit two chairs in front of his desk. The five-foot-high gray carpet–covered partitions offered little privacy for the exchange of often personal details between client and social worker. A picture of Parker, Danny's cat, was pinned to one of the cubical walls and surrounded by flyers announcing the latest shelter opening, food basket giveaway programs, free clinics, and dozens of other services available to his clients.

A weathered old man sat across his desk. Danny could smell the stale remnants of Night Train and cigarettes on his breath. His grizzled hair and mustache were stained yellow, and his face and hands were covered in dried blood and scabs. The heavy jacket he wore was covered in dirt from every corner of the city, and his left big toe stuck out from the tip of his worn over shoes.

"I haven't eaten in two days," the old man sputtered. "Somebody stole my County debit card last week. I need that card, man. I ain't been able to get my medical marijuana in over a week now."

Even though Danny had heard the sad story a thousand times before, his eyes were filled with a compassion that comforted the weary homeless man more than any words he could have spoken. Danny would listen intently to every tragic story he was told as if it were the first time he had ever heard it. He made a point of looking directly into the eyes of each person who sat at his desk and, as often as possible, shook their hand regardless of how grimy they looked. When appropriate, he would gently touch the shoulder of those beaten down by life. No person he encountered was unworthy of his time, compassion, and expertise.

The noise in the drop-in center made it difficult for Danny to speak to the man. Wobbly shopping cart wheels clanked against the cement floor, multiple conversations meshed into an indecipherable hum, and children cried in their mother's arms.

"I'm sorry to hear about your card being stolen," Danny said to the man. "I'll contact your eligibility worker and request that another be sent to you here as soon as possible. When we're done here, you should go to the dining area and get something to eat."

The man did not respond, but Danny could see the sense of relief in his face. As the two men continued their conversation, Danny noticed the noise level in the center had dropped to a whisper. The only sounds he heard were the occasional sniffle, cough of a small child, and Judge Judy on the big-screen television.

What's going on out there now? he thought to himself. Then, suddenly, the center's receptionist appeared at the opening of his cubicle. "Danny," said the young Asian woman wearing faded denim jeans and a baggy white sweatshirt, with a sense of excitement in her voice, "there's someone here to see you. He said it's very important."

Danny looked annoyed by the interruption. "Have they signed up on my list? I've already got nine people in the lobby waiting to see me."

The receptionist's excitement level increased slightly. "No, he's not on your list, Danny," she replied discreetly. "He's not a client, Danny, and I think you should see him as soon as possible."

Danny could see the disappointment on the old man's face. "He's going to have to wait. This is not a good time," he said to the anxious receptionist.

To his surprise a broad smile appeared on her face. She walked closer to the desk. With her back to the old man, she looked Danny directly in the eye and said through her smile, "Trust me, Danny, you don't want to make this guy wait."

Danny looked puzzled but agreed. "Okay," he said grudgingly. "As soon as I'm done with Mr. Wycliffe, you can send him in."

The oddly delighted receptionist hurriedly exited the cubicle. Danny returned his attention to the man. "I'm sorry about that interruption, Mr. Wycliffe. Where were we?"

Danny spent another fifteen minutes with the man, filling out documents, making telephone calls on his behalf, and loading him up with clean socks, vitamins, and a bar of soap. The old man slowly stuffed the items into his coat pocket and staggered from the cubicle. Before Danny could place the document he had completed into a file, the receptionist appeared again at the entrance to his cubicle.

"Danny," she said in a now professional tone, "Mr. Gideon Truman is here to see you."

Danny froze in place. The documents he held were suspended above the manila file folder. A look of surprise and curiosity came across his face as Gideon Truman appeared in the entrance to his cubicle.

When Gideon saw Danny sitting behind the wooden desk in the cluttered cubicle, he saw a world of sharply conflicting contrasts. Danny's rich brown skin seemed to flicker in the dingy cubicle like a firefly trapped in a jar. His eyes were so clear, they seemed almost transparent. The purity in his eyes forced Gideon to avert his gaze for the briefest of seconds. His perfectly carved shoulders and chiseled swimmer's frame were surrounded by rickety metal bookshelves stacked with worn binders and tattered books containing the once latest treatments for alcoholism, borderline personality disorders, and chronic substance abuse.

Gideon was paralyzed at the sight of the beautiful young man. For a brief moment he was oblivious to the smell and sound of the human misery within the walls of the homeless drop-in center. The man that sat before him had overwhelmed his senses. His thoughts went immediately to Hezekiah Cleaveland. *He must have been a hell of a man to attract two such uncommonly beautiful people.*

Danny looked suspiciously up at Gideon and waited for him to speak.

Gideon willed himself back to the task at hand. "Hello, Mr. St. John," he sputtered, regaining control. "I'm sorry to disturb you at work, but I was very anxious to speak with you."

Danny placed the papers in the file, stood up, and cautiously shook Gideon's warm hand.

"My name is Gideon Truman."

"I know who you are," Danny replied.

"Is there somewhere we can speak privately? I promise I won't take up too much of your time."

"You can use the conference room, Danny," the receptionist interjected. "There's no one in there now."

Danny again looked irritated at the eager receptionist. "Thank you," he said, motioning for her to leave. He turned to Gideon. "I'm not authorized to speak to the media on behalf of this agency. You'll have to speak with my boss. I believe he's in his office. You can wait here and I'll get . . ."

Gideon looked intently at Danny as he spoke. He couldn't help but notice the long eyelashes that seemed to flutter in slow motion as his lids opened and closed. To Gideon's eye, Danny was enveloped in a warm and inviting mist that seemed to emanate from his core. The air around him was somehow immune to the stench that filled the rest of the drop-in center.

Gideon hadn't expected to meet such a beautiful man in the bowels of skid row. Danny's voice echoed in Gideon's head in the same way Samantha's had. His voice was hypnotic. In this encounter it became plausible that this man was Hezekiah Cleaveland's lover. He understood clearly how a powerful man could fall in love with Danny St. John. It would be harder to believe that he could resist.

"Danny, may I call you Danny? This isn't about the homeless. I'd like to speak with you about Pastor Hezekiah Cleaveland."

Again Danny froze in place. Struggling to regain his composure, he said slowly, "Hezekiah Cleaveland? Isn't he the pastor who was killed recently?"

"Yes, he is, Danny. Did you know him?"

Danny feigned surprise and forced a laugh. "Why would I have known Hezekiah Cleaveland?"

The two men locked eyes for what seemed forever. Then Gideon looked over the five-foot-high cubicle partition and saw that every eye in the cavernous waiting area was looking in his direction. The eager receptionist had returned to her counter but watched his every move. The group of men who had been exchanging war stories in the corner was silent. Pairs of beady eyes peered from beneath piles of sooty clothes on the floor. All activity in the room had stopped. Gideon was comfortable with the attention, but he felt the need to protect Danny, for reasons he could not understand at the moment.

"Danny I would really prefer it if we had this conversation in private."

Danny also saw the effect Gideon's presence had on the facility. He walked from behind his desk and simply said, "Follow me."

Gideon followed Danny through a maze of cubicles; eyes were peeping out at every turn. Gideon smiled as someone greeted him. "Hey, aren't you Gideon Truman?"

"Yes, I am," he replied politely.

"Danny, you in some kind of trouble?" came from another cubicle.

The two entered a dark room together. Danny turned on a light, which flickered and sputtered before it fully lit the room, revealing dingy white walls. Four small folding tables were arranged in the center of the room to form one larger conference table, which dominated the stark space. It was surrounded by a hodgepodge of twelve tattered plastic, worn fabric, and faded leather chairs. Posters of wide-eyed children pleading for compassion and homeless men looking longingly into the camera hung on the walls. A large, round white-faced clock with bold black numbers ticked loudly as the second hand propelled the two men forward in time.

Gideon closed the door. "Would you like to sit down?"

"I'd rather stand," Danny responded curtly. "I don't have much time. There are nine clients waiting for me . . ."

"I understand. I'll get straight to the point. I'm doing a story on the life and death of Pastor Hezekiah Cleaveland. Your name came up during an interview with someone who worked very closely with him. So I'll ask you again. Did you know Pastor Cleaveland?"

"I've already told you I didn't know him."

Gideon reached into the breast pocket of his coat, removed a sheet of neatly folded white paper, and handed it to Danny.

"Do you recognize this e-mail, Danny?"

Danny unfolded the paper and read silently.

From: Danny St. John
Sent: Wednesday, December 16, 2010 9:37 a.m.
To: Hezekiah Cleaveland

Subject: Re: Lunch

Okay. See you then. I love you too.
D.

Danny St. John
Social Worker
Los Angeles Homeless Drop-In Center

From: Hezekiah Cleaveland
Sent: Wednesday, December 16, 2010 9:36 a.m.
To: Danny St. John
Subject: Lunch

I miss you, Danny. Are you free for lunch today at two
o'clock? I'll pick you up at work.
Love you,
Hez

Pastor Hezekiah Cleaveland
New Testament Cathedral
Los Angeles, California
Remember, God loves you and so do we.

Danny remembered the e-mail as if he had just received it that
morning. His hand began to tremble slightly as he reached for a
chair at the table and sat down. "Where did you get this?" he asked
without looking at Gideon.

"I can't tell you that, Danny. But I can tell you I've seen dozens
of other e-mails between you and Hezekiah."

Danny sat motionless, staring at the white paper.

Without thinking, Gideon walked next to him, placed his hand
on his shoulder, and gently said, "I'm very sorry for your loss. I
can tell from the e-mails that he loved you very much."

The gentle touch of Gideon's hand and his kind words released
a single tear from Danny's welling eyes. He could almost smell
Hezekiah in the room. The weight of Gideon's hand on his shoulder
made him remember Hezekiah's touch; and the salty tear, the
taste of his lips.

Gideon sat down in the chair next to him and covered the hand that held the white paper with his own. "How long were you together?"

Danny had no wall to hide behind. There was no hedge to duck under. His emotions had again bubbled to the surface for all to see. "One year," he replied softly.

"You must feel very alone now that he is gone," Gideon said instinctively. There was no hint of guile, no clue of an ulterior motive or tone of deception in his voice. He could feel Danny's pain as if it were his own. Although his eyes were dry, he still felt the moisture of Danny's tears on his own cheeks, as if they each had fallen from his own eyes. Gideon had never felt the pain that accompanied the loss of someone so loved, but today he felt the pain that was the companion of sorrow.

Gideon released Danny's hand and put his arm around his shoulders. Danny rested his head on the nape of his neck and wilted into his comforting embrace. Gideon was helpless as the pain melded them into one. He couldn't tell if the gentle sobbing was coming from his lips or from the man in his arms. Loneliness enveloped the two like a damp blanket and made their bodies quiver from the cold.

"It's okay, Danny," he whispered. "I know Hezekiah loved you."

When Danny heard the words, his cries deepened.

"I know that you loved him too," Gideon continued.

"I did," Danny said through his tears. "I loved him, and he loved me."

The raw confession of love released the first tear from Gideon's closed eyes. He didn't question the source of the tear, because it seemed natural and right. In that moment he wasn't the hard-hitting investigative reporter. He wasn't the award-winning newscaster or the host of a syndicated television show viewed by millions. He was simply a man who held in his arms someone he felt he had loved forever.

37

Samantha sat behind the desk back in her old office. The room and all its contents were completely white except for an arrangement of thirty-six long-stemmed, blood red roses. The flowers sprayed from a large etched-crystal vase sitting in the center of a liquid glass, round conference table that was surrounded by ten white high-back leather chairs. The plush snowy white carpet showed no hint of footprints or remnants from treading shoes. There was not a speck, twig, or fleck on any inch of the entire room. There were eight massive mirrors, each framed in carved white lacquered wood. No light fixtures were visible anywhere in the room, yet each surface was illuminated from sources unknown. The room was a stark, yet elegant canvas that served only to display Pastor Samantha Cleaveland.

Samantha's glass desk held only a white telephone and a white computer screen. There were no papers or mementos, family pictures or holders of things normally associated with a workstation. The glass was so clear that the telephone and computer screen seemed to float in the air.

The sound of the intercom pierced the stark white silence. "Excuse me, Pastor Cleaveland," interrupted the voice. "Catherine Birdsong would like to see you. Shall I send her in?"

Samantha did not hesitate. "Yes, send her in."

Samantha spun her white leather chair to face the office door and waited, steely-eyed, for the door to open.

Catherine entered, fueled by anger and hate. She didn't pause at the threshold but instead walked purposefully toward the desk at the opposite end of the long room.

"What can I do for you, Catherine?" Samantha asked matter-of-factly.

Catherine found no need for decorum. "You can start by telling me what I've done to deserve being treated with such disregard."

"I'm not sure I know what you're talking about."

"You know exactly what I mean. You humiliated me in front of my entire staff. You demoted me without having the common decency of first explaining to me why."

Samantha remained seated and said, "First, let me remind you who you're speaking to, Ms. Birdsong. I'm not Hezekiah, and I don't have an overwhelming need to be nice or polite to the hired help. Secondly, I feel no need to show you the respect that you have never shown me, and I don't have to explain my actions to anyone."

Samantha rose from the chair, walked around the desk, stood squarely in front of Catherine, and continued. "I haven't fired you yet, Catherine. I'm giving you the opportunity to prove that you can be loyal to me and meet my expectations. I'm not Hezekiah. My standards are higher."

"Everyone here knows you're not Hezekiah, Samantha."

"Do not call me Samantha," she snapped. "If you are to remain in my employ, you will address me as Pastor Cleaveland."

Samantha took a step closer and continued. "God in His wisdom saw fit to take my husband from me. I don't know why, but I have learned to accept it as his will. God has also seen fit to place me at the helm of this ministry, and I will do everything in my power to make sure it grows even larger than Hezekiah could have ever imagined. In order for this to happen, I need to surround myself with people who share my vision. And to be honest with you, Catherine, I've never felt you ever really understood what I'm capable of."

"I think I understand perfectly what you are capable of."

"No, I don't think you do. You see, Hezekiah underestimated me, too, and you see what happened to him."

Catherine looked at her curiously. Samantha's words slowly registered. Catherine felt a chill envelop her body as Samantha stared coldly into her eyes. There was fear like none she had ever experienced, a fear that could be caused only by the presence of pure evil. Catherine took a step backward and looked away from Samantha's frozen glare.

"I . . . I understand, Pastor Cleaveland," Catherine stammered and physically demurred. "I don't ever want to be perceived as an impediment to achieving your vision for the ministry."

"No, you don't," Samantha chimed firmly.

"I hope you know that was never my intent."

Samantha did not respond but held her gaze.

"I apologize if I ever made you feel unsupported. I think you are an amazing woman . . . Pastor Cleaveland."

Samantha gestured with her head for her to say more.

"I think it would be best for all parties involved if I submitted my resignation, effective immediately."

Samantha broke her gaze and slightly relaxed her posture. She turned away from the wilting woman and returned to her seat. "I think that would be best, Catherine."

Catherine looked bewildered and dazed. She attempted to speak, but Samantha interrupted.

"I will have security meet you in your office while you clear your things."

Catherine looked at her one last time and said, "Thank you, Pastor."

She began the long walk to the door over the harsh white terrain. Her pointed shoes left no indentations in the woolen snow. As she reached for the door handle, she heard Samantha call out and turned abruptly.

"Catherine," Samantha said.

"Yes, Pastor?" she asked hopefully.

"Please don't speak to anyone on your way out," Samantha said with a smile usually reserved for television cameras. "I'll inform your staff you decided to leave us for unexpected personal reasons."

Samantha's personal security guard, Dino, opened the rear door of the black Escalade at the construction site of the new sanctuary. Samantha extended the tip of her brown alligator pump from the rear of the car. Her four-inch spiked heels landed firmly in the soft dirt.

"Shall I wait at the car, Pastor Cleaveland?"

"No, come with me," she instructed Dino as she walked toward the shell of the building. "This may be a difficult conversation."

Dino unsnapped the leather holster under his left arm, then buttoned his jacket. Construction of the new sanctuary had not stopped after Hezekiah's death. Samantha had received a call on the Monday after the assassination from the site foreman, asking if they should stop working for a day of mourning.

"No," Samantha had answered abruptly. Then she'd remembered she was in mourning. "No. Please have your crew report for work as planned," she'd said with an added dose of grief. "I know Hezekiah would want the work to continue."

"Hello, Pastor Cleaveland," said a round, ruddy-cheeked man wearing a plaid shirt and faded denim overalls.

Benny Winters was the general contractor for the cathedral construction project.

Samantha did not extend her hand but instead continued her stroll into the building. "This is the first time I've been on-site since my husband's death, and I want to make sure you and I are on the same page."

Dino followed a short distance behind the two.

"First, let me say how sorry I am about what happened to Pastor Cleaveland," Benny said, removing his fluorescent yellow hard hat in respect. "He was an amazing man."

"Thank you, Benny. We all miss him very much. My first question is, are we on schedule?"

Benny looked surprised. "Yes, ma'am, we are on schedule. Building inspectors from the city were out just last week and gave a green light to the HVAC system. The satellite tower is en route on a barge from Beijing as we speak and will be in place by the end of next month. The subcontractors handling the stained-glass windows have been here every day this week, preparing for installation next month."

Samantha, Benny, and Dino continued the tour through the interior of the building. Workers balanced on ladders connecting webs of electrical wiring. Sturdy men and women in hard hats drilled, hammered, sawed, and screwed as the three walked past. The smell of cut lumber and burning solder filled the building.

The three entered through the main doors of the new sanctuary. The cavernous room spilled down in cantilevers in front of them. The pulpit seemed like it was a mile away. The ten-story-high, slanted, and jutting cathedral walls were constructed of five hundred thousand rectangular panes of glass. They were woven together by threads of glistening steel, forming a patchwork quilt of light and blue sky.

"We've got three new Jumbotron screens waiting to be installed. There's going to be one there, there, and there," Benny said, pointing to the front and both sides of the sanctuary.

Samantha looked out at the massive effort laid at her feet with mild amusement. "Where will the waterfalls be placed?"

Benny looked bewildered. "Waterfalls?" he asked cautiously. "There are no waterfalls in the plans."

Samantha looked perturbed. "I told Hezekiah I wanted waterfalls."

"I'm sorry, ma'am, but he never discussed that with me. I'm afraid we're too far along in construction to make major changes like that."

"Nonsense," she snapped. "I want one on either side of the pulpit. Each constructed with boulders that lead to pools of water on the pulpit. Don't worry. I'll oversee the design personally."

"But, ma'am, that's just not possible. Something like that could add at least a million onto the cost and . . ."

Samantha looked Benny in the eye, and Dino stepped closer. "You seem to misunderstand me, Mr. Winters. I'm not asking your permission. I'm telling you what I want. This is not a debate."

Benny's bulbous head became flushed. He noticed the imposing Dino staring coldly at him over Samantha's shoulder.

"Is that understood?" she asked after a brief silence.

"I suppose we can move the two side Jumbotrons a little farther from the front and place the fountains there, but . . ."

"Please, no buts, Mr. Winters. If you are unable to make this happen, please let me know now so that I can have you replaced."

"Replaced?" he barked loudly. "What do you mean? We're in the final stages of . . ." He saw Dino move in closer. "I haven't made a move on this project without Pastor Cleaveland's approval. You can't—"

"You are not in a position to tell me what I can or can't do, Mr. Winters. My husband is dead, and I am now the pastor of this church. I am paying for this cathedral. I am signing your check, and I am going to be the one standing on that pulpit every Sunday. So what I say goes. Is that clear?" she asked, with her tone escalating at each syllable.

Dino slowly unbuttoned his jacket without taking his eye off Benny. Benny could see the leather strap leading to the bulge under his armpit.

He looked over his shoulder into the structure that had been his life for the last two years. Sweat began to form in crevices all over his little round body. He then looked again at Samantha, took a deep breath, swallowed, and replied, "Yes. I understand, Pastor Cleaveland."

"Good," she answered in a slightly softer tone.

Dino rebuttoned his jacket.

"Now, tell me more about the pipe organ. I'm not sure it's going to be big enough. Where is the baptismal pool going to be placed? I want to see swatches of all the carpets Hezekiah selected and samples of the tiles. Our tastes were very different. I want the pastor's suite of offices to be in a different location than the one Hezekiah selected. Follow me. I'll show you where I want them."

The conversation continued for the next three hours, with Samantha changing much of what Hezekiah had approved and Benny repeatedly responding, "Yes, Pastor Cleaveland," as Dino closely monitored the exchange.

After the lengthy talk with Benny at the construction site, Samantha went back to her office. She had made a point of changing as much of the building design as possible, especially elements that she knew her husband had been the most excited about: the color of the carpet, the marble in the baptismal pool, the custom light fixtures that Hezekiah had designed himself, the tile in the hallways and, especially, the design of the podium. She changed the solid mahogany podium to a glass one so the cameras would always have a full and complete view of every curve of her figure. Give the men a reason to send in checks and the women a reason for envy.

"Excuse me, Pastor Cleaveland. You have a call from Brother David Shackelford. He would like to speak with you for a moment. He said it's important."

"What does he want?"

"He wouldn't say what it was regarding. Only that it was very important that he speak with you."

"Why do you put these people through to me without screening the call? Tell him I'm busy and to make . . ." Samantha paused mid rebuke. She remembered that she was only the interim pastor and would possibly require Scarlett's vote to make her position permanent.

Samantha despised Scarlett for the affair she had had with Hezekiah when she was his secretary, and hated her even more when she learned she was carrying his child. When Hezekiah appointed her to the board of trustees, Samantha knew it was only to keep her from leaving the church. Samantha had forbidden him to have any contact with the child. But she could see the way he looked so lovingly at her some Sunday mornings from the pulpit. She could see that he loved the little girl that Scarlett held in her arms as much as he loved Jasmine.

"Never mind. Put him through." She paused a moment, then said, "Brother Shackelford, so nice of you to call. How is Scarlett? I know she took Hezekiah's death very hard."

"I would imagine that you more that anyone knows just how hard she took his death," he replied ominously.

David sat in his car, looking out over the Pacific Ocean from a parking lot at the Santa Monica Pier.

He had been parked in the same spot for two hours. The car smelled of cigarettes and alcohol. He had driven around the city until he ended up at the end of the earth in Santa Monica after the shocking revelation from his wife. He hadn't realized that he was in the parking lot until the pimply-faced parking attendant said, "Sir, sir, that'll be ten dollars."

Samantha sat upright in her chair. She deliberately placed the solid gold pen she had been using to sign thank-you letters on the desk. "Yes, I know how much she cared for Hezekiah," she said, proceeding cautiously.

"I would imagine they were very close when Scarlett was his secretary. What do you think, Pastor Cleaveland?"

Samantha did not respond.

"Samantha? May I call you Samantha? Are you still there?" he asked coldly.

"Yes, I'm still here. Brother Shackelford, I appreciate you calling with condolences, but I was just about to—"

"Oh, this isn't a condolence call, Samantha. By the way, why don't you call me David? After all, we're almost related."

"I'm not sure what this is about, but I really must be going."

"I think you'll want to hear what I have to say, Samantha."

"Then, please, say it. I'm very busy."

"I'm afraid you are not in a position to rush me, Samantha." David's tone turned aggressive. "Wouldn't you like to know how Natalie is holding up, or are you that cold of a bitch?"

Samantha did not speak.

"You can imagine how difficult it must be for a child to lose a parent."

"I don't know what you're talking about," were the only words Samantha could think of to stall for time to plan her next move. "Have you been drinking?"

"As a matter of fact, I have. I've got a half-empty bottle of Jack Daniel's sitting between my legs like a hard dick. Oops, I hope I didn't offend you, Pastor. I get like that after a few drinks."

Samantha knew there was no need to pretend. "What do you want?"

David laughed loud and hard, so hard that it quickly turned into a bone-rattling cough. He tossed a smoldering cigarette butt out the car window and onto the pavement. "I don't know what I want," he finally replied.

"Is this about money?"

"Don't insult me," he shouted.

Samantha removed the telephone from her ear. "Calm down, David," she said softly. "I didn't mean to insult you."

David dropped the cell phone into his lap and took a deep breath. He could feel the familiar racing of his heart. His eyes blurred, and the sound of the rhythmic beating of ocean waves seemed to throb in his head. He knew from experience that a panic attack was sure to follow. He began gasping for air. Beads of perspiration formed on his forehead.

The attacks had, years earlier, forced David to abandon a full partnership in one of the city's most prestigious law firms. While standing before judges and packed courtrooms, he would suddenly experience an overwhelming and all-consuming fear. White-collar clients who he knew were guilty of fraud, embezzlement, and other gentlemanly crimes sat on the edge of their seat. Jurors would stare blankly at the frozen lawyer. Bailiffs would stand at attention, fearing the statue that he had become mid-sentence would reanimate in a violent rage. After the third incident, the other partners in the firm decided his work should include only cases that didn't require court proceedings. His cases now consisted of advising rich old ladies of the best way to disperse their worldly possessions after their deaths.

"Hello . . . David. Are you there?" came Samantha's voice from his lap.

The pier and the sun-drenched tourists began to spin in time with the Ferris wheel. David shut his eyes tight and took three deep breaths, as his therapist had recommended. As the panic slowly subsided, he retrieved the telephone from his lap.

"Samantha, are you still there?" he finally asked breathlessly.

"Yes, I'm here. Are you all right?" Samantha asked.

"I'm fine."

"Are you sure?"

"I said I'm all right!" he shouted. "I don't need your sympathy. I don't need anything from you but the truth. Was Hezekiah Natalie's father?"

"I'm not comfortable having this conversation over the telephone. Why don't you go home and sober up? Come to my home later this evening, and we can talk about this there."

After the telephone conversation with Samantha, David went home. Scarlet was in the kitchen when he arrived.

"David, where have you been? I've been calling your cell. Are you all right?"

David didn't look at her or respond. He walked past her, placed his keys calmly on the white tiled countertop, and exited the room.

Scarlett followed him through the narrow hallway. "David, I know you're hurt," she called out to his back. "Honey, we have to talk about this." She matched his stride and touched his broad shoulder. "David," she cried. "Please, stop and look at me." The tears began to fall again.

David stopped abruptly but did not turn around. He could hear the gentle sobs in her voice.

There was silence as she caressed his shoulders with both her hands.

Then he spoke. "Are those tears for me or for your pastor?" he asked coldly.

Scarlett dropped her hands from his shoulders. They each stood frozen in front of their bedroom door, in silence.

David waited for a reply, but there was none.

"That's what I thought," he said, reaching for the door. He paused again while gripping the handle, hoping for a response. His gesture was greeted by a chilling silence, which answered even more questions than the one he had asked.

David entered the bedroom and gently closed the door behind him. She felt the guilt and shame associated with breaking a man's heart. She did not shun the embarrassment that came with lying to the world for so long. But intermingled with these painful feelings was a faint hint of relief. *At least now he finally knows the truth,* she thought as she walked through the long hall back to the safety of her sunny kitchen.

38

The Cleavelands' mansion felt like a crypt to David as he squirmed from side to side in the stiff chair. David sat alone in the living room of the Cleaveland estate. There was a dead, still quiet. He could faintly hear the waves outside the French doors surrounding a baby grand piano, which he dared not approach.

David had been in the home only once before. Hezekiah had requested his legal advice on a generous bequest by a wealthy church member. The deceased family had contested a will that left two million dollars to New Testament Cathedral and nothing to three children and four grandchildren. David was successful in proving the validity of the will. He charged New Testament Cathedral nothing for his services. "This is the least I can do for you. Scarlett has told me how kind you were to her when she worked for you," he had told Hezekiah as they exchanged a bonding handshake.

What an idiot, he thought. *If I'd known, I would have kicked the fucking bastard in the nuts.*

He didn't hear the door open as Samantha walked into the room. David was startled when she spoke. "Hello, David," she said as she approached. "Thank you for coming. I hope you're feeling better."

When he heard her voice, David jumped to his feet and stumbled slightly. His awkward move did not go unnoticed by Samantha.

"Please sit down. You still seem a bit tense. Would you like a drink? I usually have a sherry in the evening. My housekeeper, Etta, is out, but I'd be happy to get it for you."

Like most men, David was mesmerized by the woman that stood before him. Her casual demeanor was countered by a beauty that caught most off guard. He couldn't take his eyes off her silky black hair. It looked like every strand had been attended to separately, then combined to form ribbons of shimmering black water pouring from a fountain. The room seemed to come to life now that she was present. Was there music playing softly in the background now? Did the chairs seem more inviting? Was that the call of a peacock he heard in the distance?

"Yes, I'll join you. I wouldn't want to interfere with your evening routine," he said in an attempt to appear at ease.

Samantha poured them each a glass of sherry from a decanter on a console behind one of the couches. "Let's sit down," she said, handing him the cut glass.

Samantha sat down in an equally stiff chair directly in front of David. They were separated by a cream-colored, six-foot distressed wood coffee table with claw feet. The table held an alabaster bust of a Greek goddess, a spray of exotic flowers, and three crystal bowls. There was a large black Bible with gold embossing in the middle of the table.

David stared blankly at the ancient leather-bound book.

"It's beautiful, isn't it?" Samantha said, sipping from her glass. "It's a sixteen-eleven King James, first edition pulpit Bible, very rare. There are less than two hundred of them in the world. It was a gift to us from Pope John Paul the Second."

David looked up in amazement.

Samantha immediately stared directly in his eyes. "Now, what was that nonsense you were talking about this afternoon? You sounded a bit disoriented. I was concerned about you."

David took a sip of sherry. "I wasn't disoriented, and you know exactly what I was talking about, don't you?"

"Unfortunately I do. I take it Scarlett has told you our little secret."

"The *secret* is not so little anymore. Natalie is five years old."

"I'm aware of that. I see her occasionally at church. She's a lovely little girl," Samantha said with a warm smile.

The patronizing tone of the woman sent a chill up David's spine. His head quickly became clear and lawyerly. "Don't patronize me, Samantha. You and Hezekiah abandoned her. Scarlett made a mistake, but it wasn't only her fault. Hezekiah was just as guilty. But you kicked her to the curb without any regard for the child. What kind of heartless, hypocritical monsters are you?"

Samantha listened quietly until he finished. "That's not entirely true, David. Did Scarlett also tell you that I offered her a substantial amount of money?"

David looked surprised. He tried to read her face for a trace of deception, but there was none apparent.

"I also offered to relocate her to another state," Samantha continued, "but she turned it all down."

"I don't believe you. She said you tried to convince her to have an abortion."

"I don't deny that. At the time it seemed like the right thing to do."

"The right thing for you!"

"Yes, for me, but also for New Testament Cathedral and for Scarlett. She was young, alone, and stupid enough to get pregnant by my husband. Hezekiah wasn't going to leave me for her, so what other options did she have? I presented her with good choices, and she foolishly turned them all down."

David was repulsed by the casual way she spoke of the life-altering events.

"Ask her, David. Ask her how much money I offered her to leave the state." Samantha's tone grew harder. "You're a big boy, David. You know how much was at stake. There was no way I was going to let some young, silly girl destroy all that I had built because she couldn't keep Hezekiah from getting into her pants."

David flinched at the harshness of her words.

"I'm curious, David. Why did she tell you this now? Hezekiah has been dead less than a month. Does she want to cash in on this death?" Samantha stood from the chair and walked around the dazed man to a writing desk behind him. She removed a checkbook and pen from a drawer. "Now that Hezekiah is dead, she realizes she'll never have him," she said with a slight laugh. "So how much does she want? One million, two? I hope she's going to be reasonable about this."

David leapt to his feet. He could take no more of the callous woman. He rushed to the desk and snatched the checkbook from under Samantha's moving pen. David threw the checkbook across the room. He grabbed Samantha's wrists, forcing her to stand directly in front of him. Her hair glided across her face with the abrupt turn.

"You disgust me," David said in her face. She could smell the sweet sherry on his breath. "Scarlett doesn't even know I'm talking to you. She has no interest in your fucking money, and neither do I."

Samantha tried to twist from his powerful grip, but he held her tight.

"Then what do you want?"

"I want you to pay for what you did to Scarlett. I want you to know how it feels to lose everything. I want you to suffer, and I wish your husband was alive so that he could suffer with you. I'm going to the press. I want everyone in the world to know what hypocrites you are."

Samantha stopped struggling to free herself from his grip. "Haven't we all suffered enough, David? If you go public with this, you'll ruin Natalie's life and everyone will know your wife for the whore that she is."

David quickly released Samantha's hand and slapped her hard on the cheek. Her head jerked from the blow. He grabbed her wrist again and pulled her back to his face. "I'm willing to take that risk as long as you are brought down in the process. You'll be preaching to bums on skid row after I get through with you."

A wicked smile crept across Samantha's face as a drop of blood fell from her lips. She tossed her hair from her eyes. The strands brushed against his cheeks, and she said, "There must be something I can do to make this right for you, David. You're a reasonable man, and I'm a reasonable woman. We can work out some arrangement that we both can benefit from."

Samantha moved closer, until their bodies were pressed together. David could smell a hint of lilac in her hair. He could feel the warmth of her breath. Her breast pressed against his heaving chest.

"I'm so lonely, David. Please don't do this to me," she pleaded breathlessly. "I need someone like you in my life right now." Samantha leaned forward and kissed him on the lips. "I don't want to be alone," she whispered, pressing her lips to his. "I need you near me."

He could taste the sweetness of her blood on her lips as she gently kissed him. A momentary confusion and fear overtook him. The image of Scarlett crying at the kitchen table flashed in his mind. *What is happening?* he thought. *What am I doing? This is Pastor Samantha Cleaveland.*

Then he saw Hezekiah shaking his hand while he held Natalie in his arms. *Nice sermon this morning, Pastor,* David heard himself say as Hezekiah touched the little girl's head.

She is such a beautiful little angel. You are a lucky man, David.

Yes, I am, Pastor.

Fear and confusion were replaced with betrayal and rage after seeing the image. David held Samantha at arm's length and looked in her eyes.

"Don't push me away, David," she pleaded.

David saw Hezekiah's face again, but this time it was pressed against Scarlett's lips. With that thought he slapped Samantha again hard on the cheek. Her hair twirled from the impact of the blow.

"I don't care if you hurt me," Samantha whimpered. "Do whatever you want to me. Beat me, hurt me, but don't leave me."

David grabbed her shoulders and yanked her head to his and kissed her deeply. The flow of blood increased from the roughness of his kiss. His large hands groped the fullness of her body through the silk dress.

"Make love to me, David," she panted.

Samantha could feel David's erection pressing against her stomach. She knew now he was hers to possess. In a frenzied motion Samantha ripped open his shirt. Little white buttons popped free from his fresh white shirt and scattered to the carpet. His chest heaved as she caressed him and undid his belt buckle.

"Do whatever you want to me, David. Hurt me, slap me, but please make love. I'm yours."

David unfastened the lobster clasp from her neck. The weight of the gunmetal yoke dragged the dress over her breasts, around her hips, to form a pool of silk at her feet.

David could feel her hand guide his erect member as he caressed her exposed breast and kissed her moist lips.

In unison they fell to the carpet. Samantha pulled his full weight to her, and he landed on her with a thud, with his shirt draped from his shoulders and his pants around his ankles. As they writhed on the floor, he entered her with one violent thrust.

Her hair formed a velvet fan on the carpet as she threw her head back and cried out in ecstasy. "Hurt me, David," she panted. "Harder. That's it. As hard as you want to."

With her commands his thrusts intensified. Each one delivered harder than the one before. "You bitch," he moaned in time with each blow. "You fucking bitch."

As he pounded into her flesh, she moaned in agony and pleasure. With each plunge her cries became louder and his breath more shallow.

"I'm going to cum you, bitch," he moaned. "You fucking whore, you're going to make me . . ."

Before he could finish his last assault, his entire body stiffened, and he let out a gut-wrenching cry.

Samantha matched his tone. "That's it, David. I want all of you inside me," she demanded.

For moments afterward they lay tangled and twisted in each other's arms, until the room slowly stopped spinning.

Samantha stroked his temples and nuzzled under his cheek. He belonged to her now to do with as she pleased.

Hattie Williams hummed along with the hymn on her crackling radio: *Walk in the light, beautiful light. Come where the dewdrops of mercy shine bright. Oh, shine all around us by day and by night. Jesus is the light of the world.*

A large mixing bowl filled with snapped green beans rested in her lap. A straw basket filled with the vegetables from her garden was at her feet. She reached into the basket for another handful of fresh beans. One at a time she nimbly snapped off the tips of each bean and peeled away the stringy strip along the side. She then snapped each bean into three equal parts and dropped the pieces into the bowl.

The next hymn on the radio began, and this time Hattie sang along. "I am on the battlefield for my Lord, and I promised him that I would serve him till I die. I am on the battlefield for my Lord."

Hattie sat in her favorite chair in the kitchen window, looking out over the garden. As she reached for another handful of beans, she heard the doorbell ring. Hattie looked at the rooster clock that hung above the window over her sink. It was 3:27.

"Lord, now who could that be?" she said, placing the bowl on the table. Hattie opened the front door without hesitation to reveal a solid metal screen and security-bar door. She could see only the silhouette of a man standing on her porch.

"Good afternoon, ma'am," came the greeting from the shadow. "My name is Gideon Truman. I'm looking for Mrs. Hattie Williams."

"I'm Hattie Williams," she replied cautiously. "How can I help you?"

"It's very nice to finally meet you, Mrs. Williams. I've been trying to find you for a week now. I'm a reporter with CNN, and I'm doing a story on the life of your pastor, Hezekiah Cleaveland. May I trouble you for a few minutes of your time?"

Hattie hesitated for a moment, but her Texas roots prevented her from not inviting the man into her home.

She unlatched the security-bar door and said, "I don't know how I can help you, but come on in." Hattie directed Gideon to the living room. "It's hot out today. Can I offer you some lemonade or ice water?"

Gideon accepted graciously. "Yes, ma'am. That is very kind of you. Lemonade would be very nice, but only if it's not too much trouble."

While she was in the kitchen, Gideon looked around the small but comfortable room. *I'll bet she hasn't moved any of this furniture in fifty years,* he thought. Gideon felt oddly at ease in the home. *Amazing how everyone's home from her generation always feels and looks the same.*

Gideon felt like he was in his grandmother's living room in Texarkana, Arkansas.

After a brief moment Hattie returned to the living room with a tall, clear glass with embossed flowers, which she placed on a coaster on the coffee table. She sat down and with a huff said, "Arthur is really acting up today."

"I'm sorry, ma'am. Who's Arthur?"

Hattie laughed. "You're too young to know anything about Arthur. But keep living. You'll meet him soon enough." She could see the look of confusion on his face and said, "Arthritis, boy. I'm talking 'bout arthritis. My knee is aching badly today."

"I'm very sorry to hear that. Is there anything I can do?"

"Nothing nobody can do. Just got to keep moving, or else you lay down and die, and I ain't ready to die just yet." Hattie rubbed her swollen knee and continued, "So you said you were writing a story about Pastor Cleaveland. What kind of story, exactly?"

Gideon proceeded with caution. He knew it was common for someone of Hattie's age to hold her secrets close to her chest. "First, let me extend my condolences on the loss of your pastor. I know that must have been difficult for you."

"It's so sad. So, so sad. But you got to believe everything happens for a reason. God don't make mistakes."

Despite the expensive clothes and the transparent smile, Hattie felt a warmth surrounding the handsome man. *He's got an old soul*, she thought. *I bet his people are from Texas.*

"I agree with you, ma'am. God does not make mistakes. I'm investigating his death, and I'd like to talk to the people who were the closest to him. I know you are one of the founding members of New Testament Cathedral and a trustee, so I just wanted to ask you a few questions."

I wonder, does his mama know about the homosexual thing? Shame. He's such a good-looking boy. Sho'll would make some pretty babies, she thought.

"New Testament Cathedral is one of the largest churches in the country, and Pastor Cleaveland touched so many people, I wanted to do a kind of tribute to him on my show."

Gideon's words said one thing, but Hattie heard another. *So you trying to find out who killed him,* she thought. "I think that would be very nice. He was a great man and deserves some kind of tribute," she said.

Hattie felt a power around Gideon that she usually only felt around politicians or corporate executives. *Sure is a powerful man to be so young and not be a politician,* she thought.

"What newspaper did you say you write for?"

"I'm sorry, Mrs. Williams. You misunderstood me. I don't write for a newspaper. I'm a television reporter. I have a program on CNN."

That explains it, she said to herself and nodded.

Hattie trusted Gideon. The slick, well-mannered, smiling reporter didn't impress her. What lay beneath the surface was what mattered to her. *His heart is in the right place,* she thought. He'd been hurt as a child. He looked to God for healing and found it. *I hope he finds a good man soon,* she thought. *Too nice of a young man to be alone in this world.*

"You're not drinking your lemonade. Is it too sweet for you?" she asked.

"No, ma'am. It's perfect."

Gideon saw a familiar glimmer in Hattie's kind eyes. It was the same twinkle he would see every time he looked in his grandmother's eyes. At that moment he missed her very much. *I really should go and see her soon,* he thought.

"God's given you a gift, boy," his grandmother would say every time Gideon went to visit her in the little shotgun house in Texarkana. "Don't waste it."

"How's your grandmother doing? Is she still with us?"

Gideon froze as he lifted the glass of lemonade to his lips. He didn't remember saying anything about his grandmother out loud.

"Don't look so surprised, boy," Hattie said casually. "You got a good spirit, and somebody's praying hard for you. I assumed it must be your grandmother."

Gideon sat the glass on the coaster and blotted his moist hands on his trousers. He was quiet for a moment. He did not question the old woman's wisdom. He knew from a lifetime of experience with his grandmother that there were some people in the world who saw and knew things that most others did not.

He smiled at Hattie and said, "You are correct, Mrs. Williams. I was raised by my grandmother, and yes, she is still alive. Her name is Virginia."

"That's good, 'cause she still has a lot more she can teach you. You need to get home and see her soon. She misses you."

"Yes, ma'am, I was just thinking the same thing."

"Now, young man, I can't sit here, talkin' all afternoon. I got a basket full of green beans that need snappin'. What did you want to ask me?"

Gideon had interviewed some of the most powerful, notorious, and famous people in the world, but he found himself unprepared for Hattie.

He reached into the breast pocket of his coat and took out a small recorder. "Do you mind if I record our conversation? It's easier than taking notes."

Hattie did not reply but simply nodded her head in approval. Gideon pressed a red button on the little box and placed it on the coffee table between them.

"How long had you known Hezekiah Cleaveland?"

"I've known both Hezekiah and Samantha since they first started New Testament Cathedral fifteen years ago. Their first church was just a block from here. My husband and I, rest his soul, and my grandkids used to walk there every Sunday morning. Couldn't been more than ten members back then. But I knew he was somethin' special."

"How do you mean special?"

"Are you a religious man?"

"Yes, ma'am. I was raised in the church."

"Then you'll understand what I'm about to tell you. God loves everybody, but He put some people on this earth to do great things. I knew Hezekiah was one of those people the moment I laid my eyes on him. Deep calling unto deep. He was covered in light the first time I saw him, and it stayed around him until the day he died. The Bible says sometimes those gifts are a vexation. It's a heavy burden to carry. That's why I stayed with him all these years."

"To intercede on his behalf?" Gideon said as if a light had just turned on in his head.

A pleased smile came across Hattie's face. "You are a religious man. Not a day went by that I didn't pray for Hezekiah."

"Did he know that?"

"He would sometimes call me at three or four in the morning and simply say in the phone, 'Mother, would you pray for me?' and hang up."

Gideon saw a single tear fall from Hattie's brown eyes. She reached for a crumpled handkerchief from the pocket of the floral-print apron tied at her waist and dabbed her cheek.

"When I saw him lying on the floor, covered in his own blood, that Sunday morning," Hattie continued, unprompted by Gideon, "I couldn't help but feel I had let him down."

"It certainly wasn't your fault. There was nothing anyone could have done to prevent it from happening."

"I knew. I knew something terrible was gonna happen," she said, looking out the window.

Gideon leaned forward in the chair. "How did you know?" Gideon asked gently.

Hattie looked him in the eye, smiled, and said, "Old people just know some things, boy."

Gideon knew Hattie would say nothing more on the subject and decided to move on. "Can you tell me about your new pastor, Samantha Cleaveland?" he asked.

Hattie looked back to the window, sighed, and dabbed her cheek again. "What would you like to know?" she asked while clearing the thoughts of Hezekiah from her mind.

"Just give your general impressions of her. How do you think his death has affected her? Do you think she will make a good pastor? Things like that."

"Whether or not she'll make a good pastor is in the hands of the Lord."

"Then I assume you don't see the same light around Samantha Cleaveland as you saw around Hezekiah." Gideon sensed Hattie was holding back. "This can be off the record if you'd prefer. Would you like me to turn off the recorder?"

"No need," Hattie scoffed. "There's no light around Samantha Cleaveland."

"But it's my understanding that you and the other members of the board of trustees voted unanimously to make her interim pastor. If you didn't see any light around her, why did you vote for her?"

Hattie didn't hesitate in her response. "Because I love New Testament Cathedral. I believed that she's the only person right now that can keep the ministry together. She will keep people coming in the doors and turning on the TV every Sunday morning. You've seen her. She's beautiful, and people around the world love her, but there ain't no anointing there. New Testament needs her until God sends us the right shepherd. People need that church, and I didn't want to see it fail. That's why I voted the way I did."

Gideon was honored by her candor. "Thank you for being so open with me, Mrs. Williams. I assure you I will not use any of this in my story."

"I know you won't," she said calmly. "Because that's not why you came here."

"Then, why do you think I'm here, ma'am?" he asked, somehow knowing that she actually knew the answer.

"Because you want to know who killed Hezekiah."

Gideon tried to conceal his discomfort. He felt vulnerable and exposed sitting in the chair, facing the old woman. It was as if she could see parts of him that he himself didn't know existed.

Gideon felt weak. There was no point in denying the truth. "So who do you think killed Hezekiah Cleaveland?" he asked, not as the acclaimed reporter, but as the vulnerable little boy sitting on his grandmother's couch.

Hattie gave a wry smile. "I know a lot of things, son. For example, I know you're about to meet somebody you've been looking for your whole life. And they've been looking for you too. I know you're scared to death that one day people will find out about that secret you've been hiding for so long. But don't worry 'bout that, boy. People are gon'na love you no matter what."

Hattie paused to allow the handsome young man to digest all that she had said. Gideon struggled to maintain his composure. Then she continued, "I know there's a dark cloud near you, and you seem to be walking right into it. Do you know what that means?"

Gideon could hardly speak. He managed to choke out, "No, ma'am."

"It means you might be gettin' in over your head with this one. Be careful, boy. You're heading toward someone who's more dangerous than you could ever imagine."

Kay Braisden exited the green and white cab in front of Danny's apartment. She tipped the driver five dollars.

"Thank you," said the scruffy, woolen-capped driver. "Hope you enjoy you stay in L.A."

Kay rolled her single black canvas suitcase to the door. The wheels made a clanking sound on the pavement, which Danny could hear from his apartment. Kay and Danny were the same age, but she looked older and wiser. She wore comfortable traveling clothes that hid the fact that she had gained weight since the last time they saw each other, three years earlier. Her hair was in a tight bun knotted on the back. Kay never wore makeup, and today was no exception. By Los Angeles standards, she was a plain girl who most people would forget a few minutes after they met her. Their friendship had survived the distance. They would talk two and three times a week before Danny told her about Hezekiah. In between telephone calls were text messages and e-mails.

Have you seen bouncy Beyoncé's latest video? one such benign text message from Kay had read. Wish I had legs like those.

Danny's responses were typically. LOL . . . last time i saw u did have legs like hers just shorter ;).

LOL . . . , came Kay's rapidly texted reply.

But after Danny told her about Hezekiah, all communication had stopped for months.

Before she could lift her hand, the door opened. Danny stood in the threshold, and they looked in each other's eyes. She could see he had been crying. Kay extended her arms, and Danny gladly stepped into her embrace.

"I told you I would pick you up at the airport," he said, still in her arms. "Why didn't you call?"

"It was just as easy for me to take a cab," she said, squeezing him tighter. "I've missed you so much, Danny St. John."

"I've missed you, too, Kay Braisden. I'm so glad you're here."

Danny placed her suitcase in the little entry hall and made them each a cup of tea. The two sat on the couch, Danny's legs curled under him and Kay sitting sideways, looking Danny in the eye.

"How are you holding up?" she asked, already knowing the answer.

"It's been weeks, but every day it feels like it just happened. When is it ever going to stop hurting?" Before Kay could respond Danny answered his own question. "I don't think it ever will."

Kay took his hand and said, "I can't tell you how sorry I am for not being there for you when you needed me."

Danny did not respond.

"It all just took me by surprise. You never mentioned anything about him to me in the entire year you were seeing him. Why didn't you tell me?"

"Because I was afraid you would react the way you did. I knew you wouldn't approve, and I was already feeling guilty enough without you adding to it."

Kay looked embarrassed. "And of course, I, like an idiot, acted true to form."

Danny paused and then said with a smile, "Yes, you did."

Kay smiled with him. "I don't know why I reacted the way I did. I'm not as old-fashioned as you may think."

"Then what happened? Why did this have such a negative impact on you personally?"

Kay had decided before she boarded the plane in Washington, D.C., that she would—no matter how painful it would be—tell Danny the truth about how she felt about him. From the first day they met in college, she had been in love with him. She'd followed him everywhere he went for their entire undergraduate years. She would join the same clubs on campus. She arranged her class schedule so she could take as many classes with him as possible. He never touched her in a way that was sexual. She had longed to kiss him on so many occasions but never got the nerve. To her painful dismay, he would always introduce her as "my best buddy, Kay," to his friends and family. But she'd wanted so much more.

"Danny, I reacted the way I did because I wanted so much more for you. It's not because you're gay," her self betrayal began. "It hurt me so deeply that you didn't tell me about Hezekiah sooner. We've always shared our secrets with each other, and I was angry that you didn't trust me enough to tell me the biggest secret of your life." Kay sat her now tepid cup of tea on the coffee table. "It's selfish, I know, but that's the embarrassing truth. I felt left out of your life."

A tear dropped to her cheek as she spoke. It fell from the pain of not being able to summon the courage to tell the truth to the man she had loved for so many years.

Danny lifted his hand and gently brushed the tear from her cheek. She grabbed it before he could remove it. Her heart fluttered as she held his soft hand. "I'm so sorry, Danny," she said through mounting tears. "Can you ever forgive me?"

"I forgive you, Kay," Danny said gently. "Now, come here and hug me. I need a hug."

Kay could feel the warmth of his breath on her shoulder as they embraced. She could smell the familiar scent of his favorite sandalwood soap on his skin. His strong arms held her tight as she cried more tears of unrequited love.

"Do you want to talk about it?" Danny asked, still holding her close.

Kay froze, and the tears abruptly stopped. *Has he seen through that clumsy attempt at hiding my real feelings?* she thought. *Could he possibly feel the same way about me?* For a brief moment she felt a glint of hope. "Talk about what?" she asked without breathing.

"About my relationship with Hezekiah," Danny said curiously.

The hope that had made her heart miss a beat at the thought he could possibly love her in the same way left as quickly as it had come. "Of course, of course," she said, embarrassed, wiping tears from her cheek with the back of her hand. "I want to hear all about it. But only if you feel up to it."

Danny was eager to tell someone he knew about Hezekiah. In the year of their relationship he had never spoken his name to anyone.

Danny leaned back on the couch. He cradled the cup of tea in his lap as he spoke.

"I met him purely by accident on the street. I was helping a homeless person downtown, and he pulled up next to me. He said there was a homeless woman near his church and asked if I would speak to her. After I helped her, he asked if he could do outreach to the homeless with me one afternoon. Kay, I swear it all was so innocent at first. I had no idea he was gay, and it never crossed my mind that he was attracted to me. But when we were alone in my apartment—"

"Alone in your apartment?" Kay interrupted. "How did that happen?"

"He came with me one afternoon to do outreach. You know, handing out socks, vitamins, condoms to people on skid row.

When we finished, his driver was late picking him up, so he asked if he could hang out with me until he came." Danny paused and looked at Kay. "Are you sure you're all right hearing this? You seem tense."

Kay suddenly became conscious of the fact that her fist was clenched in her lap and her jaw was tight. She took a deep breath and replied, "I'm fine, Danny. It's important that you talk about it. It's part of the healing process. Go ahead. I'm listening."

"Well, anyway," Danny continued, "we went back to my apartment, and everything seemed perfectly innocent. We sat right here on the couch, just like you and I are right now, and just talked. He was nothing like the man I'd seen on television. He was funny, vulnerable, and relaxed and, I guess, just a normal guy. He wasn't that bigger-than-life, one-dimensional cutout."

"A normal guy who just happened to be one of the most famous people in the country and married," Kay said.

"Are you judging me? Because if you are, I don't need it," Danny said defensively. "Believe me, I've already judged myself. If you are, we can stop this conversation right now."

"I didn't mean it that way. I'm sorry. Go ahead."

Danny proceeded with caution. "I was walking him to the door, and we stopped right over there," he said, pointing to the arched threshold leading from the living room to the entry hall. "We stood directly in front of each other, looking into each other's eyes and not saying a word. Then it was like a magnet pulled us together. We made love the first time that afternoon right here on the living room floor."

Kay felt her stomach tighten. She tried to push the image of their two male bodies writhing on the floor out of her mind.

"Kay, he was an amazing person. Not because he was so special or unique, but because he loved me like no one has ever loved me before. He once told me he knew every inch of my body and remembered everything I'd ever said to him. I can't tell you how much that meant to me. That someone knew everything about me. I was so lonely at the time I met him. You had moved away. I rarely went out. I was working seven days a week just not to be at home alone. And, more than that, I was also afraid."

"Afraid of what?" Kay asked with a level of compassion that even surprised her.

Danny thought for a moment. "Afraid that I would never find someone to love me."

A tear fell from Danny's eye as he spoke.

"I had been alone up until that point. I was afraid I would never find someone that wanted to know who I really was. Not just a body or a paycheck, but a person who loves, who has fears, who makes mistakes. Someone who was interested and cared enough to know that I like my coffee with two sugars and a drop of cream. That I love to watch Woody Allen movies on Sunday afternoons, curled up on the couch. Someone who cared that I have panic attacks. That Picasso is my favorite artist or that I've never been to Las Vegas. And after learning all the insignificant and silly and even the horrible things about me, he loved me even more in spite of what he'd learned. Hezekiah was that person. He took the time to discover things about me that I didn't even know myself. And with all he knew, he still loved me."

Danny tried to stop talking, but he couldn't. He needed someone to understand. More importantly, he needed Kay to understand.

"He was the head of a multimillion-dollar ministry, and I never set foot in his church until the day of his funeral. I wasn't a part of that part of his world, and when he was with me, neither was he. He wasn't Pastor Hezekiah T. Cleaveland with me. He was simply Hez. That's what I used to call him."

"Did you ever meet his wife?"

Danny shifted slightly on the couch. "No, and I never wanted to meet her. I, of course, knew about her, and toward the end he told her about me, but I begged him to never tell her who I was."

"Why?"

Danny looked mournfully out the window at the traffic below. "To be honest with you, Kay, I was afraid of what she might do."

Kay looked surprised and said, "Afraid she might hurt you?"

There was silence. Danny shifted again. His body tensed, and the hand holding the cup of tea trembled slightly.

"Danny," Kay said into the silence. "What do you mean? Did she threaten you in any way?"

Danny looked her in the eye and said, "I wasn't afraid for myself. I was afraid of what she might do to him, and I think I was . . ."

Kay sat upright on the couch. She placed the now cool cup of tea on the table. "Danny, you're not saying you think she had something to do with his death?" she asked in disbelief.

Danny did not respond.

"Danny, that's crazy. You're talking about Samantha Cleaveland. She's . . . she's Samantha Cleaveland, for Christ's sake. How could you think that? The woman is a saint, a beautiful and strong God-fearing woman. Look how well she's managed with such grace and dignity after his death. People love her."

Danny shook his head gently. "You don't know what she's capable of. Hezekiah would tell me things about her that even frightened him."

"Danny, this can't be true. I watch her every Sunday morning. She's like a role model to me. I love Samantha Cleaveland. Everybody loves Samantha Cleaveland."

"I know, Kay. But beneath that exterior there's an evil woman who would do anything to maintain and further her position in life. She built New Testament into what it is today, not Hezekiah. He admitted that to me. She pushed him into television. She persuaded him to build the new cathedral. He didn't want it. She forced him to buy that mansion in Bel Air and hire the drivers and security guards. He didn't want any of that stuff. He told me he hated that house."

"I don't believe any of this. You must be mistaken," Kay said defensively. She looked at Danny and saw the disappointment on his face. She could see the hurt her last statement had caused.

"I didn't mean it that way, honey," she said, reaching for his hand. "I simply meant maybe Hezekiah stretched the truth to ease his own conscience. This whole affair—I mean relationship—must have been very difficult for him."

"It was," Danny said. "On the day he was killed, he had planned to announce that he was stepping down as pastor."

Kay gasped and clutched her hand to her gaping mouth. "No," she said in disbelief.

"Yes, and Samantha was the only person, other than me, who knew. I never believed she would ever let that happen. If he'd stepped down because of a homosexual affair, she would have lost everything. The credibility of the Cleaveland dynasty would have been in shambles, and everything she'd built would have crumbled around her two-thousand-dollar Gucci shoes. Even the great Samantha Cleaveland wouldn't have been able to salvage it."

Kay sat in disbelief. She couldn't stop her left leg from shaking. Her foot bounced nervously on the faded throw rug in front of the couch. "This is incredible," she said, her voice trembling. "I can't believe what you're telling me. You actually believe she killed him."

"Of course she didn't pull the trigger, but I believe she was behind his murder. Have you seen the footage of the service that Sunday morning?"

"Everyone in the country has seen it. Gideon Truman played it almost nonstop on CNN for two weeks."

"Didn't anything about it look strange to you?" Danny asked.

"The whole scene looked strange. Who would have ever imagined that he would have been killed on live television on a Sunday morning in front of his entire church?"

"More than that, what about the obvious outrageousness of the entire melee? I mean her performance after he was shot. When she rushed to the pulpit and cradled his head to her chest. It all looked rehearsed to me. Every move she made appeared choreographed. I could swear she was trying not to get his blood on her white suit."

"Danny, you're being cruel. She doesn't deserve that. The woman had to witness the man she loved being shot in the head."

"All I'm saying is she knew she was about to be humiliated in front of the entire world and, more importantly, she was about to lose everything. That is the perfect motive for murder. The police haven't been able to find any suspects. They can't find anyone with a motive. They're not looking at her, because she's too smart for them. She's fooled the police, just like she's fooled everyone else in the world. She doesn't fool me. Even though I have never met her, I feel like I know her better than anyone. Hezekiah told me everything."

"Have you talked to anyone else about this?"

"No. You're the first person I've spoken to." Danny paused for a moment. He suddenly remembered the conversation he had had with Gideon Truman. "I take that back," he said, as if a light had been turned on in his head. "I forgot that I've spoken to Gideon Truman."

Another gasp escaped from Kay's lips. "*The* Gideon Truman? From CNN? You talked to Gideon Truman?"

"He came to my job and asked a bunch of questions. Someone gave him copies of e-mails between Hezekiah and me." Danny shuddered as the words escaped.

"That means someone out there knows you exist," Kay said.

"I never thought of that."

"Maybe you should talk to the police."

"And tell them what? That I was Hezekiah's lover and I believe his wife had him assassinated? They would believe I killed him before they believed she did it."

"Oh my God, Danny, this is horrible. I'm afraid for you. Your life may be in danger. You suspect someone killed Hezekiah because he was about to come out of the closet. Who's to say the killer doesn't know about you too? You've got to talk to someone. Maybe you should speak to Gideon Truman."

Danny remembered how kind Gideon had been to him in the grungy little conference room at his job. He remembered how gentle Gideon was when he wept on his shoulder and the comforting words he'd whispered. *I know Hezekiah loved you.*

"What good would that do? He can't protect me."

"He can help the police find the killer. He's been investigating Hezekiah's murder from the beginning," Kay said urgently. "He's dedicated more time to the story than any other network. You have information that might help him find the killer. If you are in danger, then that clearly helps you."

Danny considered her words. He hadn't feared for his life before, and he still didn't. The thought of the killer, possibly Samantha, knowing his identity did not frighten him. His world had been so empty without Hezekiah in the past few weeks, he couldn't think of many reasons to cling to life, anyway.

Kay could sense his hesitation and said, "If your safety is not motivation enough to talk to Gideon, then think about Hezekiah. Don't you want the killer to be caught? And if it is as you suspect, then the world needs to know the real Samantha Cleaveland."

39

The grounds of New Testament Cathedral glistened in the afternoon sun. Plush grass flowed like a tranquil river over the ten-acre compound. Gurgling fountains and the coo of pigeons provided a soothing soundtrack for a tense conversation between the four coconspirators.

Cynthia Pryce walked between Reverend Kenneth Davis and Catherine Birdsong; her husband, Percy, kept pace in the rear. The four walked along the cobblestone paths, pausing intermittently to say "Hello" or "Welcome to New Testament Cathedral" to groups of passing tourists.

They had assembled at the request of Kenneth. Meeting out in the open seemed like the safest way to talk without being overheard.

"We've got to do something," Kenneth said as he waved to a couple in the distance. "She's not suited to be pastor. Her heart isn't in the right place. Samantha is going to destroy this ministry if we don't replace her."

"I agree," Cynthia said, looking straight ahead.

"First, she humiliated Catherine in front of the entire staff, and then forced her to resign," Kenneth continued. "Benny Winters called me in a panic this morning, saying she's demanding changes to the new cathedral design that could run into the millions. I'm afraid to think of what she'll do next. Replace me? Force you and Percy out of the church?"

"There's nothing that can be done, Kenneth," Catherine said. "Everyone loves her. Our television ratings have almost doubled since she took over. Contributions have been pouring in like never before. Did you see how much we took in last week? It was more than we usually get in a month."

"This isn't about money, Catherine," Cynthia interjected. "It's about God's will, and I agree with Kenneth. Her heart is not in the right place. I don't believe for a minute that she's interested in bringing souls to Christ. She's about the almighty dollar, and I'm not afraid to say it."

"Cynthia, please," Percy said from behind.

"Well, someone had to say it, Percy, and you all know it's true. The only thing that's important to her is maintaining her embarrassingly lavish lifestyle. I can't believe that any of you think that it's God's will or that you would sit idly by and allow her to fleece all the saints that support this ministry. The thought of all those lovely people sending in their hard-earned money to buy her another piece of art just breaks my heart. Every night since she's been pastor, I've prayed that God will forgive us for being negligent stewards over the blessings he has given this ministry."

Percy walked behind with his head held down. He'd never seen Cynthia pray in the fifteen years they had been married.

"But what can be done?" Kenneth asked.

Cynthia spoke before anyone could respond. "There are five votes on the board of trustees. Yours, Kenneth, and Percy's, Scarlett's, Hattie Williams's, and Samantha's. I know Scarlett can be persuaded to vote her out. I'm not sure about Hattie. But even without her, that's three to two."

"It's not a question of votes, Cynthia," Percy finally said. "It's a matter of how a move like that would be received by the congregation. If she's replaced, we run the risk of a mass exodus of members and supporters. We could be left with half the congregation."

Cynthia stopped dead in her tracks and turned swiftly to face her husband. Percy froze in his steps, and everyone stopped with her. The four formed a circle in the middle of the pathway.

"I don't think that is true, darling," she said icily, looking her husband directly in the eye. "You are mistakenly assuming this is a personality-driven ministry. I don't believe it is. I have faith in God and in our members that they will be loyal to the message and not the messenger, and so should you," she said pointedly.

Percy did not respond but instead met her gaze with equal contempt.

"You're all forgetting one important piece of this," Catherine said, breaking the petrifying silence. "Who could replace her?"

Again there was quiet, until Kenneth said, "Well, I think that is obvious. Percy, you were always the heir apparent."

Percy looked down at the pavement and faintly said, "I don't think . . ."

"Slow down, Kenneth," Cynthia interjected before Percy could finish his response. "I think it's premature to have that conversation. Percy and I have never thought in those terms. It would mean a significant adjustment in our lives. We would need to pray about it before he could even consider becoming pastor. What's important at this stage is that we all agree that Samantha cannot be made permanent pastor of New Testament Cathedral."

"I think we've established that we agree she should be removed," Kenneth said. "But it seems like a moot point since we don't know where Scarlett and Hattie stand on this. Someone should speak with them. It's obviously a very sensitive subject, so it has to be handled with the utmost tact."

"I agree," Cynthia said. "It obviously can't be Percy. Catherine, you are technically an employee of the board of trustees, so I think it would be inappropriate for you to have that conversation with them."

"That's fine with me," Catherine said, relieved.

"So, Kenneth, that leaves either you or me," Cynthia said, dismissing the others in the little circle. "What do you think?"

Kenneth looked off into the distance. "Because Samantha is a woman, it might be interpreted as chauvinistic if I was the one suggesting to them that she be replaced."

"I never thought of it in those terms," Cynthia said believably. "Then I'll speak with them."

From the window of her fifth-floor office, Samantha looked down on the assembled group. *So they finally got up the courage to meet,* she thought. *How dare they do it on my property and out in the open?* She could see that Cynthia was at the center of the conversation. *I suppose she thinks that spineless husband of hers is man enough to replace me.*

Samantha walked back to her desk and calmly sat down. *Poor, silly woman,* she thought. *She really doesn't know what I'm capable of.*

***

Hattie Williams pulled the damp white sheet from the bulging wicker laundry basket at her feet. She wore her favorite short-sleeve sundress covered with yellow sunflowers and a white apron with a red trim border that she had stitched on by hand. She stood in her backyard, under the clothesline that was suspended between two metal poles. It was the same clothesline that her husband had installed at her insistence fifty years ago.

"We don't need a clothesline," her husband, Howard, had said. "I just bought you that brand new Maytag washer and dryer."

"Don't argue with me, Howard. Ever since I've been using that dryer, my sheets and pillowcases ain't been nearly as white as I like them. The washing machine is fine, but I ain't got no use for that dryer. The sun makes clothes white, and it kills germs. The sun was good enough for my grandmama and my mama, and it's good enough for me. So go downtown to Mr. Kroger's hardware store and get the rope and some poles. I want my clothesline."

Howard knew even back then that once Hattie had made her mind up about something, there was nothing he could do to change it.

"And don't get no cheap rope," she said as Howard gathered his keys and headed to the door. "I want that line to last, so get some good sturdy rope."

Last it had. The ropes that extended from the now rusting poles had not been changed in the fifty years since Howard strung them up on that Saturday morning in 1961. Hattie found the edges of the sheet and extended it above her head. She fastened the first corner to the cord with a wooden clothespin. Arms still raised above her head, she applied the next pin to the center of the sheet and finally the third at the end. The sheet billowed gently in the breeze. Hattie took a step back and looked at the white fabric with pride. *Good enough for my mama,* she thought.

It was a perfect day for drying laundry. The sun had reached its high point. The air was still, except for the occasional breeze that danced between the pillowcases and towels. As Hattie reached down into the basket for the next sheet, she felt a familiar twinge in her stomach. The twinge that heralded the coming of understanding. The feeling foretold of images to come. Hattie stood upright and waited patiently for the vision to begin. She stared blankly into the white sheet that she had just hung as the images slowly began to appear.

The sun had descended from the heavens and rested in the upper right corner of the sheet. The golden rays flowed down onto what she immediately recognized as the sanctuary of New Testament Cathedral. The room was full of saints. She could see rows and rows of colorful felt, straw, and satin Sunday hats. The crowd seemed to be energized by the rays of the sun.

She could hear chords of heavenly music coming from the pipe organ. Everyone was singing in unison, "Walk in the light. Beautiful light. Come where the dewdrops of mercy shine bright. Oh, shine all around us by day and by night. Jesus is, Jesus is the light of the world."

Hattie found comfort in the beautiful refrain. She had sung it herself on many Sunday mornings. There was joy in the hearts of all those present. She could feel the love and contentment emanating from every row, aisle, and corner of the sanctuary. Then, suddenly, legions of people began to pour down the center aisle toward the pulpit. She could see tears of joy in their eyes.

Thank you, Jesus, Hattie thought as she saw the new converts make their way to the pulpit. So many souls coming to you, Lord. It was by far more people than Hattie had ever seen accept the invitation to the church. Their arms were waving in the air as they walked briskly to the pulpit. She could hear them shouting and crying out, "I've been gone for so long. I've made so many mistakes," and "I'm so tired of running. I'm ready to come home." The chorus of pleas from the repentant filled the room.

Hattie was overwhelmed with joy at the sight of so many souls turning their lives over to God. She felt her own eyes fill with tears as she witnessed the scene that unfolded on the white canvas of her freshly washed sheet.

With her eyes wide open, she followed the crowd as they made their way to the front of the church. Hattie suddenly began to feel the temperature around her drop as the throngs of people formed a crowd at the foot of the pulpit. Even though she could still see the sun in the corner of the sheet, the rays were no longer sufficient to warm her exposed arms or sooth her arthritic knee. The room slowly dimmed, but to her surprise, the praises from the crowd continued to grow louder and more insistent.

As quickly as it had come, the joy she felt suddenly turned to dread. She feared how the scene would finally play out. Hattie braced her spirit and said a silent prayer: Lord, give me strength.

Then she saw her. Samantha stood at the edge of the pulpit. Her arms outstretched, welcoming the euphoric masses. She was radiant. Like a queen. The elaborate gold-jewel-festooned robe she wore glowed so brightly that it eclipsed the now waning sun. Samantha did not speak. She looked lovingly over the masses as a shepherd would over a flock of sheep.

Hattie resisted the sight of so many people being persuaded by Samantha to come to the pulpit. Her heart was both joyous and crestfallen. Although she tried, Hattie wasn't able to blot from her mind the images of the thousands of transformed people standing at Samantha's feet. She stood as the helpless witness to the future of New Testament Cathedral.

The emotional scene ran its course and forced Hattie to view every tear, every conversion, and the transformation of the multitude of lost souls. Her emotions ranged from despondence to delight and from pleasure to pain. Her feet were planted firmly in the perfectly mown sod, unable to move. She folded her arms in an attempt to shield her exposed flesh from the cold. Hattie eventually gave in to the scene. She grew too weary to resist.

The images soon faded from the sheet. The whiteness was now even more apparent than when she first hung it. Time had stood still during the vision. She had no idea how long she had been staring at the sheet. It could have been minutes. It could have been hours. The pain she felt in her knees gave a hint to the length of time she had been standing. She reached out and touched the sheet. It was almost completely dry. The sun was no longer directly above her head. She looked down at the ground and saw her shadow extended across the green grass.

Hattie bent down and retrieved the last towel from the basket. It, too, was almost dry. After hanging it on the line, Hattie made her way to the back steps of her house. She paused on each step, dragging the basket behind her. When she reached the door, she walked inside. "Thy will be done, Lord, on earth just as it is in heaven," she whispered as she closed the door behind her.

***

It had been two days since Gideon first met Danny St. John. In that time he couldn't get the gentle young man out of his mind. Danny was in his thoughts when he drove through the crowded Los Angeles streets. Images of Danny sat across the table from him when he had his morning coffee and muffins.

How could a sweet guy like that get himself involved in a horrible situation like this? he thought as he transcribed notes from his recorded interview with Hattie Williams. Gideon could still smell the distinct scent of sandalwood he had recognized the day Danny cried on his shoulder in the dingy little conference room.

It was nine thirty at night. Gideon sat alone in the office of his home in the Hollywood Hills. The room was a soothing shade of beige, with a white contoured ceiling. There was a sitting area with a couch, two comfortable chairs, and a coffee table, which held a stack of books he had read. His housekeeper had left the room in pristine condition after she had cleaned that morning. A wet bar in the far corner of the room had gone untouched since the day he moved into the house three years earlier.

While sitting at the desk, in front of his laptop computer, Gideon continually stopped and started the recording of Hattie Williams. Half the screen was filled with the haunting words she had spoken.

"There's no light around Samantha Cleaveland," came Hattie's muted voice from the recorder. Gideon rewound the tape and played it again. "There's no light around Samantha Cleaveland." And again, "There's no light around Samantha Cleaveland."

Gideon thought again about Danny as he typed the words on his laptop. *I wish there was something I could do to help him.*

Gideon abruptly stood up from the desk and walked to the window. Laid out before him was the twinkling Los Angeles skyline. The jagged jumble of tall obelisk high-rises were each dotted with lighted windows on every floor. Neon signs blinked over the canvas in an attempt to lure customers in to buy Nikes, big-screen televisions, cigarettes, and malt liquor.

You've got to stay objective, man, Gideon silently admonished himself as he stood at the window. *For all you know, Danny could have killed Hezekiah himself.*

Even in the face of all he had learned as a reporter, Gideon could not stop thinking of how wonderful Danny had felt in his arms. He wanted to protect him.

Protect him from what? he thought. *Protect him from Hezekiah and Samantha. Maybe protect him from himself.*

Gideon had never been in love in his entire forty-five years. He purposefully hadn't allowed himself to get close enough to anyone and had never allowed anyone to get close to him. Every ounce of psychic energy had been reserved for his career. He had known he wanted to be a reporter since he was in the fifth grade at the little Union Elementary School in Texarkana.

His third grade teacher, Mrs. Perry, had recognized Gideon's natural curiosity and desire for finding the "answers behind the answers." She assigned him the task of writing a short article for the school newsletter on the upcoming school election. Gideon had instinctively interviewed all the young candidates, the teachers overseeing the election, and even the school principal. The directness of his questions had surprised some of the adults even then. The attention he garnered from that article was the beginning of his goal to be a news reporter.

He considered emotions like love and fear a distraction. There was no room for distractions in his world. This was complicated by the fact that all his life he had been primarily attracted to men. In the 1980s there was little room for a black journalist at the major newspapers and television stations and even less room for a black gay journalist. It was hard enough to get an entry-level job. He saw his sexuality as an unnecessary distraction for the white editor or news producer sitting across the desk from him during his many interviews after college.

Until he met Danny, the emotions of love and desire had seemed irrelevant. Over the years he had rarely acted on his desires for fear of being publicly exposed as a homosexual. The occasional nameless encounters with ciphers from the Internet were far less frequent than the numerous proclamations of love, proposals for marriage, and other more temporal propositions he received almost daily from admiring fans, men and women on the street, other celebrities, and the occasional network executive.

But somehow the sight of Danny St. John two days earlier in the crowded homeless drop-in center had reminded him that he was not exempt from the need to love and be loved just like every other human in the world.

Gideon tried to resist his feelings for Danny, but the more he looked into the death of Hezekiah Cleaveland, the more he found himself looking into the eyes of Danny St. John. The more he transcribed notes from church members, the more he remembered Danny. Whenever he thought of Samantha Cleaveland, his thoughts would inevitably rush to the fragile young man who had needed him so deeply for those brief moments after he had confronted him with the e-mails from Hezekiah.

Gideon felt himself teetering on the edge of an ethical precipice. *A reporter reports the news.* The words of his Journalism Ethics and Standards professor echoed in his head. *Always remain objective, and most importantly, never, ever become part of the story.*

Danny called to him from across the ethical divide. The canons of journalism had served as his bible throughout his career. The words *Professional integrity is the cornerstone of a journalist's credibility* greeted him each day when he turned on his computer and scrolled across the screen each time the computer fell asleep.

Gideon longed to touch Danny's soft skin again. He wanted to feel his body again in his arms. He resisted the urge to pick up his cell phone and dial Danny. "Get a hold of yourself, man," he said out loud. "He's not worth jeopardizing your entire career."

But Gideon's heart said otherwise. *He's so beautiful. He's the most beautiful man I've ever met.* This time the words went unspoken. Gideon walked away from the window and returned to his desk. The white computer screen stared back at him. Of all the words on the screen, the only ones he could see were Danny St. John.

How do you fall in love with someone you've only met once? he silently questioned. "It's not possible. Maybe this happens to people who watch too many soap operas," he said aloud. *You're better than that, Gideon Truman. You're stronger than that.*

40

Hattie Williams sat in the conference room at New Testament Cathedral. A stack of checks that needed her signature were on the table in front of her. Given that she was one of the founding members, a board trustee, and a longtime confidant to Hezekiah Cleaveland, Hattie's was the second signature required on all checks issued by the church. Like clockwork on each Friday afternoon at three o'clock a black Escalade pulled in front of her modest home. The driver would politely tap on her iron-bar door and say, "Good afternoon, Mother Williams. I'm here to take you to church to sign checks." The driver would then slowly escort her down the front steps and into the rear of the waiting SUV.

"She's too old for this. She doesn't know enough about church business to be a signatory," Samantha had often said to Hezekiah. "Why in God's name don't you make me the second signer? You don't trust me?"

"Of course I trust you, darling," Hezekiah would lovingly reply. "I've told you a thousand times, you and I both can't be signers. We don't want to appear that we are a dynasty. It's just not appropriate."

"But we are a dynasty, and you need to stop pretending we're not. We are the Cleavelands. We're worth millions of dollars. We run one of the largest ministries in the country, yet you still want to run it like some jackleg preacher in a storefront with all his brothers, sisters, aunts, uncles, and cousins as the only members. Grow up, Hezekiah. Whether you want to accept it or not, this is a business, and you need to start running it like a business."

Hezekiah's patience always grew thin at this point in the conversation. "That's where you and I differ. This isn't a business. It's a church. It's a ministry whose sole purpose is to bring souls to Christ. Not to make millions of dollars. And don't you ever forget that."

"I realize that," Samantha would snap back. "And please do not admonish me. You are not in any position to take the moral high road. I am your wife, and I know all your little secrets. You spend their tithes on expensive clothes and your little toys just like I do."

"I don't want to argue about this again, Samantha," Hezekiah would say impatiently. "Hattie is the signatory, and that's how it's going to stay until either she or I leaves this world."

Each Friday Hattie would be greeted in the air-conditioned conference room by an attractive young assistant. "Good afternoon, Mother Williams. How are you today?" she would politely inquire.

"I'm fine, baby. God is good."

As usual there was a stack of checks, a gold pen, a pitcher of ice water, and one glass neatly arranged on the table.

"If you need anything, Mother, just buzz me on the intercom."

"I'll be fine, dear." In the years Hattie had been signing the checks, she had never used the intercom.

Hattie leaned her cane against the large table and settled into the comfortable leather chair at the head of the table. She placed her patent leather purse on the floor, near the heel of her sensible shoe. Utility bills, payroll checks, payments to the many vendors necessary to maintain the mega church, the weekly $3,055.00 check to the florist, each year millions of dollars would pass under her signature. Hattie had only one rule. She would never approve personal expenses for Samantha Cleaveland. The checks to Samantha's dressmaker always went unsigned, until one day they stopped appearing in the weekly stack. Payments to her personal hairdresser, manicurist, and any other person who contributed to her beauty were routinely placed in a separate stack and left unsigned. Those, too, were eventually left out of the pile. No one ever dared ask why she refused to sign them, because everyone already knew.

As Hattie worked her way through the checks, which now displayed Samantha Cleaveland's calligraphic signature, there was a gentle tap on the door. Before she could respond, the door opened.

"Excuse me, Mother Williams," Cynthia Pryce said, peering in. "I know you're busy, but may I have a word with you?"

Hattie looked up from the papers at Cynthia and said, "Come in, baby. I'm about done with these. What can I do for you?"

Cynthia closed the door and sat at the table. "Mother Williams, I wanted to talk to you about Samantha."

Hattie sat the gold pen down and took a sip of cold water.

"May I be direct with you?" Cynthia said, leaning in closer.

Hattie treated it as a rhetorical question.

"Some of the members have been talking, and well . . . we're very concerned about Samantha."

"How so?" Hattie asked calmly.

"It's only been a month since Hezekiah's death, God rest his soul. We are concerned that she may not be giving herself enough time to grieve. She was back in the pulpit only a week after he died, and now she's taken on being the interim pastor. Some of us think we, I mean the board of trustees, may have overestimated how strong she really is. As you well know, it takes time for a woman to get over the loss of a husband. How long did it take for you to get over the death of your husband?"

Again Hattie did not respond.

Cynthia stumbled briefly in the silence but quickly regained her purpose and continued. "I think . . . I mean some of us think, that in the shock of Hezekiah's murder, the trustees may have put too much on Samantha too soon. She needs time to heal, wouldn't you agree, Mother Williams?"

Hattie studied her intently. She could see her glow of intensity. *Too cool of a customer to sweat, but not too cool to hide her true heart.*

Hattie heard the words Cynthia spoke, but even more clearly she heard her heart. She acknowledged there was some truth in the trustees acting too hastily in appointing Samantha as interim pastor. There was also truth in a widow needing time to grieve. But Hattie knew Samantha was not grieving. However, the truth was overshadowed by the vision of Samantha leading the masses of lost souls to God. The poorly veiled entreaty by Cynthia to make her husband, Percy, pastor once again forced Hattie to decide what was most important. Leading souls to Christ or seeing to it that Samantha got all that she deserved.

"Sister Pryce, who do you think should be pastor?"

"I think it's obvious, don't you? Reverend Pryce and I have prayed about this ever since Hezekiah was killed, and with God's help, and your prayers, we are willing to take the position, for the good of the church and for Samantha Cleaveland."

Hattie grew weary of the insults to her intelligence and said calmly, "You mean for the good of Cynthia Pryce, don't you?"

Cynthia's charming and pious facade quickly melted to reveal her heart. Her face grew hard, her jaw clenched, and her eyes tightened. "No, not for me, Mother Williams," she said curtly. "This would be an enormous sacrifice on my part." Cynthia could barely contain the contempt she felt for the old woman who held so much power in her arthritic hands.

A side of Hattie that few rarely had the opportunity to see emerged in full force. "You've been chomping at the bit for years, and now that Hezekiah is gone, you see it as the opportunity to get what you've always wanted—to be the first lady of New Testament Cathedral."

In the face of such candor Cynthia found it impossible to continue the charade. "Okay, Mother Williams," she said coolly. "There doesn't seem to be any point in denying that to you. Yes, I want to be first lady, and I think I'd make a damned good one. But that's not the point. New Testament Cathedral needs someone at the helm who can lead us all through this grieving process. Someone who can give their all to this ministry, and there's no way Samantha can do that now. The woman just buried her husband. She can't focus on saving souls. You'd be doing her a favor by making Percy the pastor."

"I think you underestimate Samantha Cleaveland."

"No, Mother, I don't think I have in this case."

"So, what are you asking me to do?"

"Reverend Davis is going to call a special session of the board of trustees. At that meeting Percy will be nominated for the position of pastor. I'm asking you to support Percy as the permanent pastor of New Testament Cathedral."

Danny sat alone in a window seat at the coffee shop a short walk from his apartment in the West Adams District. The room was comfortable, with clusters of cushioned chairs, worn wooden tables, and racks of throwaway neighborhood newspapers and magazines scattered on surfaces. The space was so comfortable, it felt contrived to Danny. The tables, floors, and walls were all made from distressed wood that could not have been as old as some of the magazines scattered around the room.

Must have taken a lot of planning by some West Hollywood queen to make it look this lived in, he thought.

There were only two other customers. An attractive young woman was sitting on a comfy couch in the center of the room.

The only other customer in the shop was a man who on occasion discreetly tried to make eye contact with Danny. He looked to be in his mid- to late forties. In an odd way he reminded Danny of Hezekiah. But that was not unusual. The mailman, bus drivers rolling by, and even Lester Holt from the *Today Show* reminded Danny of Hezekiah.

The room smelled of freshly roasted coffee beans being brewed by the lone barista. The mournful voice of Nina Simone whispered gently from places unknown: *I want my whole life to be/Lived with you/Lived with you.*

Danny wished the song would end. It seemed the music was playing so cruelly just for him, a sad soundtrack to his life.

You don't know/What it's like/Baby, you don't know.

As Danny looked out the window at the steady stream of cars whizzing by on the boulevard, he heard a gentle tap on the wooden table.

Danny looked up sharply and saw the warm smile of Gideon Truman, who was standing above him.

"I'm sorry if I startled you," Gideon said. "I said your name, but you didn't hear me."

Gideon looked very casual wearing a navy blue jogging jacket over a white T-shirt, denim jeans, and white running shoes.

"I was listening to the music," Danny said without standing. "Such a sad song. It reminds me of my life. Have a seat."

"Let me order you another coffee. What are you having?"

"I've barely touched this one," Danny said, noticing his drink for the first time in the last ten minutes. "You go ahead. Maybe I'll get another one later."

When Gideon returned, he sat at the table, directly opposite Danny. "Thanks for agreeing to meet with me again," he said, casually placing a freshly brewed cup of coffee and a napkin on the table. The vapor from the cup formed an aromatic partition between the two men. "I wasn't sure if you'd want to see me again after our last encounter."

"What do you mean? You were very kind to me. I have to apologize for getting so emotional. You caught me off guard with those e-mails."

"I should be the one apologizing. It was very insensitive of me to confront you like that. I've been a reporter for so long, I guess I sometimes forget people have feelings."

"Thank you. I realize you're just doing your job."

"That's no excuse. I should have been more aware of how this all must have impacted you."

Danny looked Gideon directly in the eyes and asked, "Have you ever lost someone you loved?"

"I have not. I can only imagine what you're going through, Danny. It must be very difficult for you."

The world seemed to go on carelessly, oblivious to Danny's pain.

"Some days I don't think I can get out of bed, it hurts so much," Danny finally responded. "It's as if it was me who was shot that morning. Sometimes I wish it had been me. Then at least I wouldn't have to live with this pain."

Gideon resisted the urge to reach out and touch Danny's hand. Instead, he motioned to the barista behind the counter to bring another glass of iced coffee for Danny.

"I know it feels like your life has ended, but it's true that time heals wounds. Give yourself permission to mourn. It's all part of the healing process."

Danny looked again at Gideon but did not respond. In the midst of the silence, the barista arrived with a tall glass of cold coffee. The ice cubes clinked against the sides of the glass as he placed it in front of Danny.

"Thank you," Danny said to the young man, seeing the tattoo of a snake wrapped around his arm.

"Do you have anyone in your life you can talk to about how you're feeling?"

"Hezekiah was my confidant. I've only told one person about him. I was too afraid he would get hurt if someone knew about us. He had always warned me if anyone found out about us, it would destroy him. Ironic, isn't it? Before he died, he told me about a reporter who had found out about us. The reporter who was found dead in his home two days after Hezekiah was killed."

"Do you think their deaths are related?"

"I didn't think that until you showed me the e-mails. Now it feels out of control. I don't know how many people out there know about me. Are you going to tell me who gave you the e-mails?"

"I'm sorry, Danny. I can't."

It hurt Gideon to hold back the information from Danny. He wanted to tell him everything, everything he knew about Hezekiah, but more importantly, everything he knew—and those things he didn't know—about himself. When he looked in Danny's eyes, he sensed Danny could tell him things about himself that he didn't know. It was the exact sense of vulnerability he had felt in the presence of Hattie Williams. He felt Danny could see into his soul and tell him secrets he had kept from himself.

Gideon felt exposed and in dire need of a diversion. "Who do you think killed Hezekiah?"

Danny did not hesitate in his response. "I know who killed him. She may not have pulled the trigger, but I know she had something to do with it."

Gideon looked surprised. "*She?* Who are you talking about?"

"His wife, Samantha Cleaveland." When Danny said her name, he felt a sense of relief. By saying it to Gideon, the knowledge was no longer his burden to bear alone. He didn't know why, but he trusted Gideon. Not to keep a secret, but to be sensitive enough to know which facts were important enough to share and those that were best kept private because they might harm someone unnecessarily.

"Did she know about you too?"

"Hezekiah told her a few weeks before he died. On the morning he was killed, he had planned to announce that he was stepping down as pastor."

"How do you know that?"

Danny had a puzzled look on his face. "He was my lover for a year. We talked to each other about everything. We didn't have secrets from each other. I didn't want him to give up everything for me, and I tried to talk him out of it. But his mind was made up. It wasn't only me he was leaving the church for. He was leaving it for himself too. He felt his life had been a lie up until that point. He felt he . . ." Danny stopped mid sentence. "I don't know why I'm telling you all this. Are you going to report this on your show? I guess it would make you an even bigger reporter than you already are."

Gideon had forgotten he was a reporter until Danny reminded him. He felt more like a man helping someone he loved through a difficult time. At that moment Gideon was embarrassed he was a reporter, and wanted to apologize for the profession he had chosen.

"Danny, I want you to know I would never do anything to hurt you. If you tell me something that you would prefer be kept between you and me, then you have my word it will go no further than us."

Danny looked into Gideon's eyes and said, "For some reason I believe you. Maybe it's because I *need* to believe you."

"I wouldn't lie to you, Danny. I respect and like you too much to lie to you."

"Why not? You're a reporter. I thought you guys would do or say anything to get a story."

Gideon was embarrassed again. His face was flushed beneath the sun-bronzed skin. He needed to convince Danny that he could be trusted. "I won't deny I've said and done some things in my career to get a story that I'm not proud of, but for some reason I want you to trust me. For some reason I feel the need to earn your trust."

"Why is that?"

"I don't really know. Maybe because deep down I'm the one who really needs someone to trust."

"I understand that. Hezekiah and I came to the same conclusion. He once told me he loved me so deeply and gave his love unconditionally because he needed me to love him. He felt I was the only person who could truly love him. I felt the same way about him. The more I loved him, the more he seemed to love me in return."

Gideon resisted the urge to touch Danny's face. He understood how Hezekiah could fall so deeply in love with this gentle soul that sat across the table from him.

"So, what makes you think Samantha had something to do with his death?" Gideon asked, again needing a distraction from his raw emotions.

"Have you met her?"

"Yes, only once."

"I suspect once is enough if you're able to look beyond that thin veneer of piety. She's an evil woman. I know that sounds dramatic, but I also know it's true."

"But she loved him?" Gideon asked with genuine naïveté.

"Samantha Cleaveland only loves herself. It's obvious. If the world had found out Hezekiah was gay, she would have lost everything. The church, the television ministry, the house and, most importantly, the power. She ran New Testament Cathedral when Hezekiah was alive, and now that he's out of the way, she doesn't have to stand behind him anymore. With him dead, she gets to play the brave grieving widow and keep everything. She's the only person that benefits from his death. I warned Hezekiah she would do anything to stop him from leaving her, and she did. He didn't believe me."

Gideon sat in disbelief. "Can you prove any of this?"

"I can't prove anything. I don't care what happens to Samantha Cleaveland. I just want to move away from this city and put this behind me. I feel like that's the only way I'll ever survive this."

"But you can't just let her get away with it. If what you're saying is true, don't you think she should be held accountable?"

"She will be," Danny replied calmly.

Danny looked again to the window. He could see Hezekiah's reflection looking back at him in the glass. The man he had loved so deeply was now reduced to a faded image in a window plastered with flyers for the next local spoken-word competition, workers' comp attorneys, and car-detailing discounts.

Gideon continued, "Have you considered, Danny, that you might be in danger? If she killed once, who's to say she wouldn't do it again?"

"Of course I've considered it. I'm awake half the night thinking about it," Danny said sharply. Hearing Gideon speak the words made the threat more real and frightening. "If you were able to find me, I'm sure she's already done so by now."

"All the more reason for you to come forward about your affair," Gideon said, leaning over the table that separated them. "If no one knows about the connection between you and Hezekiah other than Samantha and possibly the person who killed him, then if something happens to you, she would have no fear of it being linked to Hezekiah's murder."

Gideon's voice grew louder as he spoke. Danny scanned the room for prying ears. The man in the suit had left. The attractive young woman was engrossed in her book, but now with the addition of earbuds. The tattooed barista was distracted by the grind of roasted Sumatra coffee beans.

"Don't you see?" Gideon continued, lowering his voice to a whisper. "If you spoke publicly about it, I don't think she'd be stupid enough to touch you, for fear of both trails leading back to her. The longer you hide, the longer you're in danger."

"And, more importantly, you would get another salacious story to add to your already impressive credits," Danny said sarcastically.

Gideon flinched from the directness of the comment. The fragile young man had somehow made him forget again that he was a reporter. There was no denying the outing of Pastor Hezekiah T. Cleaveland would launch his already enviable career into the stratosphere. But while he was sitting in the little coffee shop with Danny, the thought had never entered his mind. Instead, he had become consumed with figuring out how he could come to Danny's rescue.

"I can understand how you could think that," Gideon said after recovering from the blow. "But that was not my motivation for suggesting you come forward."

"Then what is your motivation, Mr. Truman?" Danny asked suspiciously.

Faced with the blunt question, Gideon was reminded of how he felt whenever he was confronted by one of his many obsessed fans: the marriage proposals from women who believed their union was destined by God; the neatly wrapped packages of homemade cookies, which were immediately tossed into the garbage; the woman who had professed her eternal love for him every morning and every evening at the studio gate, forcing him to file a restraining order against her. *If he knew how I felt about him after only meeting twice, he would file a restraining order against me too,* Gideon thought.

"I'm suggesting it because I don't want to see another person hurt," Gideon finally said. "You may think I'm an opportunistic talking head, and I can understand how you could come to that conclusion, but I'm not. I don't like to see bad things happen to good people, and if I were in your position, I would hope someone would care enough about me to give me the same advice."

"Well, you're not in my position, are you?" Danny said coldly. "And I don't believe for a second that you're not interested in exploiting me to benefit your own career. It's because of people like you that Hezekiah and I had to look over our shoulders for a year. You're no better than the reporter who found out about us. He was willing to destroy anyone and anything in his path to get a headline, and I have no reason to believe you would not do the same."

Danny stood up abruptly. His chair scraped the wood floor, sending a screeching reverberation through the room.

Without looking at Gideon, he calmly said, "You don't seem to understand that if I came forward, I'd be placing myself in even more danger than if I stayed silent. At least this way I won't have to deal with the wrath of the whole country for defiling their beloved pastor Cleaveland. It would be like putting a target on my back. This meeting is over, Mr. Truman. I'm sorry I agreed to meet with you and that I wasted your time."

Danny moved swiftly toward the door.

Gideon stood and shouted, "Danny, wait!" But it was too late. The front door had already closed behind Danny. Gideon could see him walking past the window and jaywalking across the street.

The young woman, still reading love poems on the couch, resisted the urge to look in his direction. *Hope they work it out,* she thought. *They make a cute couple.*

"And we're on in five . . . four . . . three . . . two and . . . "

"Good evening, America. I'm Gideon Truman, and welcome to *Truman Live.*"

Four cameras were pointing at Gideon from different vantage points in the television studio. Each capturing a side more attractive than the one before. He was framed by an electric blue backdrop that made him resemble a living Andy Warhol painting hanging in a Manhattan gallery. He was bathed in blistering studio light. Crew members pushed buttons, moved hefty electrical cords, and focused lenses as Gideon read from the scrolling teleprompter just below the camera in front of him.

"We are continuing our coverage this evening of the brutal murder of Reverend Hezekiah T. Cleaveland, pastor of New Testament Cathedral and head of the worldwide television network."

The key to Gideon's popularity was his ability to make each viewer believe he was talking only to him or her. The viewers felt that they were having a quiet chat with an old friend in their living room or bedroom. A fact he himself didn't even realize.

"Less than a month ago, Reverend Hezekiah T. Cleaveland, the pastor of New Testament Cathedral in Los Angeles, was brutally gunned down during a Sunday morning service in his fifteen-thousand-seat mega church."

As Gideon spoke, images of the mayhem that followed Hezekiah's death that Sunday morning flashed on the screen. Camera crews had captured the reactions of members of the congregation who witnessed the assassination. A woman in a pink suit with an equally pink hat wept in her husband's arms. Children clung to their mothers' waists, and police scurried about, looking brave for the evening news.

"My guests this evening are well-known ministers in their own right," Gideon continued. "First, we have Pastor Maurice Millier joining us via satellite from his mega church, Good Shepherd Ministries, in Atlanta, Georgia."

The screen split, and suddenly Gideon was joined by a smiling man with a receding hairline, wearing a black-and-white pin-striped suit. He didn't have the benefit of Gideon's gifted and devoted makeup artist. Instead, his forehead glowed like a fallen halo.

"Welcome, Pastor Millier. Also joining us is Dr. Joyce Goodhart. Dr. Goodhart is a professor of theology at Fuller Seminary in Southern California. Thank you for being with us this evening."

Dr. Goodhart had a sour, yet somber expression. Her pageboy haircut, which she had worn since high school, gave hint to her precise and logical mind.

"And, finally, a very dear friend of Pastor Cleaveland," Gideon continued. "Reverend Richard Johnson, pastor of First Bethany Church of Los Angeles. I want to thank you all for being here this evening."

The screen now contained their four images. Gideon, as the host, dominated the upper screen. The three guests shared the lower third. Snippets of the daily news stories scrolled beneath their stern faces. Viewers were once again given their nightly free front row seat to the *Truman Live Show*. Gideon wore a sleek black suit with a bold plaid red and white shirt. His tie was white with yellow and red stripes that seemed to twirl like a barber's pole every time you blinked your eyes.

"Why don't we start with you, Reverend Johnson? You and your wife, Victoria, were very close friends with the Cleavelands. How is Pastor Samantha Cleaveland doing since her husband was so brutally slain?"

"Thank you for having me, Gideon," Reverend Johnson blustered. An expensive toupee was perched precariously on his head. His necktie formed a puddle on top of his round belly and then made a dramatic slope to this belly button. "Let me first say to your viewers that my church, First Bethany Church of Los Angeles, is celebrating our twenty-fifth anniversary this Sunday, and everybody is welcome to come out and celebrate with us. To find out more information, just go to our Web site at www.newbethany—"

Gideon looked confused and cut in tactfully. "Congratulations, Pastor, on twenty-five years, but our viewers would be interested to hear how Pastor Samantha Cleaveland is doing after her husband's murder."

"Well, Gideon, as you said, my lovely wife and I have known the Cleavelands for years now," Reverend Johnson said reverently. "Our daughters went to school together. My wife and Samantha often meet for lunch and to pray together. This tragedy has rocked the very core of religiosity in our country." Reverend Johnson leaned in toward the camera and then pointed at it. "America needs to repent. When something like this happens to one of our great black leaders, it's a sign that we as a country have lost our way. The government doesn't want people like Hezekiah Cleaveland to have that much power. Especially if he is a black man. Martin Luther King, Jr., and now Hezekiah Cleaveland. This is a sign of the end times, America. Come to Jesus while there's still time."

Gideon diplomatically tried one last time. "Have you talked to Samantha Cleaveland since this happened?"

"I did briefly, but the poor woman was so grief stricken, she hung up on me. I can tell you, though, that Samantha is devastated by this tragedy."

"Let's hear from our other guests," Gideon said, moving on quickly. "Dr. Goodhart, what do you think about what Pastor Johnson just said? Is this a sign of our country's moral decline?"

Dr. Goodhart gave a slight but sarcastic smile for the camera. Her face became the sole image on the screen. "Though this is without question an almost unimaginable tragedy, I think it might be a slight overgeneralization to say it is indicative of some larger moral descent in our country. Let's remember this was the act of one deranged person."

The screen then split, and now Reverend Johnson shared half the spotlight. "That's what they said about Martin Luther King, Jr., but we all know the truth about that," Reverend Johnson smirked.

"Martin Luther King was assassinated by James Earl Ray, not the government," Dr. Goodhart blurted out.

"All I'm saying is that when a black man in this country gets too powerful, he somehow gets conveniently eliminated," Reverend Johnson said, leaning back in his chair with his hands clasped, forming a steeple at the top of his belly. "Millions of people around the world were devoted followers of Pastor Cleaveland, and I think people in high places felt threatened by that," he said with an air of wisdom and insight, parting his hands and then returning them to the steeple formation when he concluded.

Dr. Goodhart's stone face smirked at the last comment.

"What do you say about all this, Pastor Millier?" Gideon asked. "Is Hezekiah Cleaveland's death a symptom of something more sinister happening in our country?"

Pastor Millier was an elegant man with a hint of gray at his temples. His glasses framed penetrating, yet gentle eyes, which had seen more than most. He'd survived only by closing them and looking inward.

"With all due respect to my colleague, Pastor Johnson, I absolutely don't think this tragedy is a sign of the end of the world or that it's linked to any government conspiracy."

The camera showed the slightly betrayed look on Reverend Johnson's face.

"I must agree with Dr. Goodhart," Pastor Millier continued. This is a tragic but, nonetheless, isolated incident perpetrated by a very sick individual. It's our job as Christians to hold up the members of New Testament Cathedral in our prayers and for us as pastors to show our love and support to Samantha Cleaveland."

"Well, that brings me to my next question," Gideon said. "Samantha Cleaveland was recently selected by the church's board of trustees to replace Hezekiah as pastor. What do you think of that? Is it too soon, considering she just lost her husband? Should they have selected someone from the outside, and do you think she is the best person to get the ministry through this crisis? Dr. Goodhart?"

"I've never met Samantha Cleaveland, but—"

"Well, I have met her," Reverend Johnson interrupted, "and I feel that if anyone can lead New Testament Cathedral, Samantha can. Now to the question, is this too soon? I have to be honest, I was surprised when I heard she was taking over. Now, don't get me wrong. I have all the love and respect in the world for Sister Samantha, but I'm not convinced that that was the best decision on the part of the trustees."

"What do you think they should have done?" Gideon asked provocatively.

Reverend Johnson responded with gusto. "Well, I think they should have possibly considered combining their church with another, similar church."

"Similar in what way?" Gideon goaded.

"Similar in size and teachings . . ."

"You mean like your church."

"Well, my church, First Bethany Church of Los Angeles," Reverend Johnson said, looking directly into the lens of the camera, "is only half the size of New Testament Cathedral, but I think that would have been the logical and responsible thing to do. It would keep their church members together but also give poor Samantha some time to grieve and to decide if being the pastor is really what she wants to do."

"What do you think, Pastor Millier? Was it a mistake to place her in the leadership role so soon after her husband's death?"

"From what I've seen of Samantha Cleaveland, I believe their board of trustees had no other choice but to name her as pastor."

"What do you mean?" Gideon asked probingly.

"I mean that she is a dynamic leader, a gifted teacher, and has always been the backbone of their ministry. She, more than anyone else, is best suited to lead New Testament Cathedral through this crisis and to continue the good work and teachings of her late husband."

Again, the look of betrayal was hard for Reverend Johnson to conceal, and Dr. Goodhart slowly faded into the background.

"Let me direct my next question to you, Pastor Johnson. Often when a well-known person dies, skeletons from their past seem to surface. You knew Pastor Cleaveland better than most people. Should we be bracing ourselves for a mistress or maybe an illegitimate child or some other scandal to surface involving Pastor Cleaveland?"

Reverend Johnson leaned forward confidently and said with all the Sunday morning religious fervor he could summon, "I've known Hezekiah for years. I was his confidant, and he was mine. I can assure you that he loved his wife more than anything in the world. He would never have cheated on her, and I know for a fact that he never did. Sure, like any other man, he was tempted occasionally by a beautiful woman, but he never gave in to temptation. If anybody comes forward with a lie like that, you can believe it's for only one thing—money."

Samantha sat comfortably in the rear of the Escalade as it glided through the streets of Los Angeles. She was scheduled to meet her friend, Victoria Johnson, the wife of Pastor Richard Johnson, for dinner. The two had not seen each other since

Hezekiah's funeral. The sun was setting over the city, and the streetlights slowly flickered on, unnoticed by pedestrians and drivers. Dino guided the vehicle with trained precision through the remains of the city's rush-hour obstacle course.

Samantha checked her watch. It was 6:40 p.m. She was already late for dinner. Samantha lowered the tinted-glass partition she had had installed between the front and rear of the car to shield her from the prying eyes and ears of drivers and security personnel. "How much longer, Dino? I'm already late," she inquired with a hint of irritation.

"Ten minutes," Dino replied over his shoulder as the partition glided closed.

As the car hurtled along, Samantha's cell phone rang. She retrieved it from her purse. The telephone screen read NO CALLER ID. Only five people had the number to her private cell: her personal assistant, Dino Goodlaw, Etta Washington, Hezekiah, and her daughter. If anyone wanted to speak to her on that phone, they would have to go through one of those five people. It wasn't Dino. She knew neither Etta nor her assistant would dare call her from a phone other than the one at the house or the church, and she doubted Hezekiah would be calling from the grave. That left Jasmine. *God, please don't let her be in jail again,* she thought. *Or even worse, the hospital got my number from her phone to call about another overdose like the one she had just after Hezekiah was killed. Poor little thing almost died that time.*

After the third and final ring Samantha pressed the TALK button. "Hello," she said curtly.

No one responded.

"Hello," she said again.

She could now hear someone breathing on the line. "Who is this?" she said cautiously.

The breathing continued. Not heavy like the precursor to an obscene call, but natural breaths.

"Jasmine, is that you? Where are you?" she said, growing irritated.

After a moment's silence she heard, "Is this Samantha Cleaveland?"

"Who is this? How did you get this number?" Samantha asked, furious at the idea of having to change her private number again.

"I'll ask the questions," came the breathy response. "Is this Samantha Cleaveland?"

Samantha removed the phone from her ear and pressed the DISCONNECT button. The phone rang again before she could return it to her purse.

NO CALLER ID, glowed from the screen again. Samantha dropped the phone in her purse. After the third ring there was a pause, and then it started again.

The Escalade pulled into the artificially lit circular drive of the restaurant. Yellow lights positioned on the ground shone up on palm trees and dense shrubs encircled by the driveway. Women in sleek summer dresses and glittering jewelry stood near the edge of the driveway with their black-suited escorts, waiting for red-vested valets to retrieve Bentleys, Maseratis, and Ferraris.

The phone rang again as Dino slowly rolled toward the drop-off point. Samantha snatched the phone from her purse and asked, "Who is this?"

"Hang up on me again and you'll regret it," came the breathy reply. "Now answer my question. Is this Samantha Cleaveland?"

"Yes, it is," she said calmly. "What do you want?"

Samantha heard a tap on the window. She didn't unlock the door. Dino knew not to disturb her if she did not respond to his tap. Instead, he stood at the ready by her door, in front of the main walkway to the restaurant entrance. Other patrons looked discreetly from the corners of their eyes to see who would emerge from the car guarded by the hulking man. Was it a rapper perhaps, or maybe a movie star?

"I know about Danny," the voice said, waiting for a reaction.

"Who is Danny?" she asked impatiently.

"I think you mean, who was sleeping with Danny? And we both know what the answer is. Pastor Cleaveland."

"Look, whoever you are, I don't have time for this bullshit. Either get to the point or I'm hanging up and calling the police," she said.

"Such a filthy mouth for a pastor," the caller said sarcastically. "Did you suck your husband's holy dick with that mouth? I know Danny did with his."

"I'm hanging up. Don't call me again, or I will call the police."

"If you hang up this phone," the voice said urgently, "I'll be forced to turn over evidence to the press that shows before your loving husband died, he was in love with a very handsome young man."

Samantha leaned forward in the seat. "What evidence?" she said. "You're crazy. My husband wasn't gay."

"To start, I've got a stack of e-mails full of language so graphic, it would make even you blush. There's some in there that even prove you knew about it."

"You're lying."

"Don't call me a liar again, bitch, or this time next week you and your dead husband will be on the cover of every tabloid in the country," the voice said angrily.

"How dare you threaten me? I just buried my husband. What kind of monster are you?"

"You can save the grieving widow routine for your Sunday morning sermon. I know you were glad to get rid of him. His dick almost cost you millions. I wouldn't be surprised if you had something to do with his death yourself."

Samantha froze after hearing the last words. With lightning speed and cold logic, she weighed the cost of either revelation surfacing in public and decided she could not risk even the rumors being discussed.

"What do you want from me?"

"Now, that's what I like, a woman who knows when she's been screwed."

"There's no need to be vulgar," Samantha said coolly.

"You're not in a position to preach to me. In this relationship I'm the preacher. You do what I say. Got it?"

Samantha was silent. During the conversation the well-heeled patrons in front of the restaurant came and went, many without benefit of seeing who occupied the black Escalade. Dino stood firmly at the rear door, unfazed by the irritated valets, who were forced to maneuver around the car in the narrow drive.

"I want one million dollars, cash. You have seventy-two hours to make it happen. That gives you until Saturday night to come up with the money."

"A million dollars, you're out of your mind," she said.

"Maybe I am. Then I guess I should hang up and let Gideon Truman decide if I'm crazy."

"No, wait," Samantha said quickly. "Don't hang up. I don't have that kind of money."

"Bullshit," the caller said loudly. "You collect three times that much every Sunday morning. Why don't you take up a special offering this Sunday? Tell them it's for your favorite charity."

"There is no way I can come up with that much cash on such short notice."

"Every time you lie to me, the price goes up five hundred thousand. It's now one-point-five million."

"You can't prove any of this. My husband was not gay," Samantha said emphatically.

"Two million," the voice said calmly.

Samantha paused to regain her composure. "What will you give me in return?" she finally asked.

"My word that you will never hear from me again," the voice said sincerely.

Samantha scoffed. "The word of a blackmailer . . ."

"I prefer to think of myself as a keeper of secrets."

"I'll need more time," Samantha said hesitantly.

"You don't have more time. I will call you in two days with instructions. If you contact the police, I will immediately send copies of every e-mail in my possession to all the major news outlets in the country. I know this all sounds like such a cliché, but trust me, Samantha, this is real life," the voice said with a slight chuckle and disconnected the line.

Samantha sat momentarily dazed. She could see Dino through the darkly tinted window. The cell phone was still warm in her hand.

Two million dollars, she thought. *I'll kill the son of a bitch before I give him two million dollars.*

Samantha released the lock, and on cue Dino opened the door. Her slender calf emerged from the rear of the vehicle. The curiosity of the onlookers waiting for their cars to be brought around was fully satisfied as the beautiful woman emerged from the rear of the vehicle.

Even for those few in the crowd who didn't know exactly who she was, her carriage, her stunning beauty, the exquisite liquid dress, and the sparkling diamonds that encircled her wrist immediately elevated her in their eyes to the status of celebrity. Samantha hated making eye contact with empty faces in a crowd, and tonight was no exception. She ignored the awestruck gasps and such whispers as "That's Samantha Cleaveland," from envy-stricken women and such replies as "My God, she's stunning," from their ogling male companions.

She was greeted by the tuxedo-wearing owner of the restaurant, who eagerly swung the doors open to welcome her. "Good evening, Pastor Cleaveland. We're so pleased you decided to dine with us this evening. I am so sorry for your loss. He was a very good man."

Samantha extended her down-turned hand, which the well-dressed man lifted and kissed gently. "Your dinner companion is waiting for you at our best table in the house. Please follow me," he said with his most impressive French accent.

Samantha, however, was not impressed. The words *two million dollars* continued to ring in her four-carat-diamond-studded ears. As she made her way through the restaurant behind the owner, other diners craned to see her entrance. Samantha raised the bar in the restaurant, which catered to the city's wealthiest and most beautiful citizens. Conversations paused as she walked by. The nibbling of escargot, foie gras, and Almas caviar stopped mid chew when her presence was felt seconds before she was seen. Everyone felt someone important had entered the building. If she had been the wind, the room's temperature would have dropped twenty degrees, tables would have been toppled, and freshly coiffed hair would have been left in ruins.

Victoria stood as Samantha approached. She wore a tight-fitting cream pantsuit. Her signature diamond broach shaped like a butterfly twinkled on her lapel. One hand was still gloved in sleek buttery-cream-colored leather.

The owner stepped to one side and, with a sweep of his hand, presented to Samantha a perfectly appointed table filled with crystal, silver, and white linens. A single candle flicked in the center. He waited patiently behind a chair he positioned for Samantha as the two women exchanged air kisses.

"*Bon appétit*, ladies," said the owner, who was honored to be dismissed by Samantha.

Before the women could settle into their comfortable chairs, a tall man with a chiseled face and wavy black locks tucked behind his ears approached. "Good evening, ladies. I am Rancor, your sommelier."

"I don't care who you are, handsome," Victoria snapped. "I've been sitting at this damn table for the last ten minutes with nothing to drink. Bring us a bottle of nineteen-sixty-six Dom Pérignon."

"I thought you were trying to cut back," Samantha said.

"I am, dear. I'm only having one bottle tonight," Victoria replied, removing the last glove. "Don't start lecturing me again, girl. I'm a grown-ass woman."

"I know you are. I wasn't lecturing, just asking."

The sommelier vanished, unnoticed by the women. Word slowly spread through the gold-lit dining room as to who the two beautiful women were.

"Who is the woman dining with Pastor Samantha Cleaveland?" a man in a party of six at a nearby table asked his waiter.

The waiter bent down. "That is Victoria Johnson," he whispered. "Her husband is the pastor of another mega church."

"I must find out who Samantha's designer is," a stylishly dressed French woman at another table said to her tanned and toned husband. "That dress is fabulous."

"Oh, shit, I'm sorry, honey. I forgot about Hezekiah," Victoria said loudly, causing even more heads to turn. "I haven't seen you since the funeral. So you finally went ahead and did it?" she said, laughing.

Samantha leaned in and looked at her hard. "Keep your voice down. What do you mean, did it?"

"Killed that prick. I didn't think you had it in you, girl. I told you to break his legs, not kill him." Victoria laughed out loud again. "Where is that gay-ass waiter with my champagne?" she said, craning her neck, which caused the diamond butterfly on her lapel to flicker in the candlelight. "At least you know he won't be fucking around on you anymore."

Samantha's hand trembled slightly. "That isn't very funny, Victoria. You know I didn't kill him," she said angrily.

"Calm down, girl. I was only joking," Victoria said, reaching across the table to touch Samantha's trembling hand. "Sammy, what is wrong with you? You're shaking. Are you all right?"

At that moment the sommelier arrived, placing a pedestaled ice bucket next to the table. Victoria reached for the crystal flute before he could fill it completely.

"That's enough, thank you," she said curtly. "What do you think I am? A drunk?"

"No, ma'am. I'm sorry. Your waiter will be with you shortly. Enjoy your meal."

Victoria took a long sip and continued. "Now, what is going on with you? I know this isn't about Hezekiah. Shit, I wish some crackhead would kill Richard. Hell, I'd pay him myself."

Samantha was silent and took a sip of champagne.

"Come on, girl. I don't like seeing you like this. Did I upset you with my big mouth?" Victoria said softly. "You know better than to take me too seriously."

"No, no, it's not that. I just got a frightening telephone call on the way here."

"From whom?"

"I don't know," Samantha said.

"What was it about?"

Samantha took another sip of champagne and said, "Blackmail."

Victoria choked on her drink when she heard the word and coughed loudly, again drawing attention to the table. "Blackmail?" she blurted. "What do they want?"

"Please keep your voice down," Samantha said firmly. "A ridiculous amount, two million dollars."

Another choking cough escaped from Victoria's red lips. "Oh, shit," she said, this time in a whisper. "What the fuck for?"

"Hezekiah, of course," Samantha said scornfully.

Samantha surveyed the room to ensure their conversation could not be overheard. She hesitated, but Victoria prompted her to say more with a swipe of her hand.

"I never told you this, Victoria. I guess the indignity of it was much too embarrassing for me, but Hezekiah was having an affair with . . . with a man before he was killed."

Victoria's jaw fell open. She cupped her mouth to prevent a gasp from escaping. There was silence at the table while the two women looked desperately into each other's eyes.

"Oh . . . my . . . fucking . . . God," Victoria finally said, pausing after each word. She reached for the bottle of champagne, filled her glass to the rim, and took two long gulps. "Sammy. Honey, this is un-fucking-believable. Sleeping with every whore he could stick his dick into wasn't enough. The bastard had to have dick too. Un-fucking-believable."

"I don't know what I'm going to do," Samantha said softly.

At that moment the waiter appeared mysteriously at the table. "Good evening, ladies. Welcome to Le Cheval. My name is—"

Victoria immediately held up her hand. "I don't need to know your name," she said without looking in the shocked man's direction. "Could you please give us a moment?" she said sharply. "We'll let you know when we're ready."

The stunned waiter vanished without another word.

"Honey, you need to call the police."

"I can't do that, and you know it," Samantha said. "If this gets out, I'll be a laughingstock. I could lose everything."

"What are you talking about? People won't blame you if your husband was a faggot. If anything, they'll feel sorry for you."

"That's exactly the point. I don't want people feeling sorry for me over some dumb bullshit like this," Samantha said angrily. "It's bad enough I have to hear, 'I'm so sorry for your loss,' from every asshole I talk to. And the timing could not be any worse. I've got the board of trustees and that bitch Cynthia Pryce watching my every move. They're just looking for a reason to not make me permanent pastor. A public scandal like this would be just enough for them to kick my ass to the curb."

As she said the words, a couple appeared at the table. The woman was close to six feet tall and wore a slinky yellow silk dress. Her hair was ribbons of golden locks that cascaded around a model's face. Her companion seemed almost half her height. A Rolex watch weighted his arm down to his pudgy side.

"Pastor Cleaveland," he said, extending his hand. "We don't mean to disturb you, but we wanted to extend our condolences for your loss. I met your husband a few times, and he was a great man."

Victoria let out an irritated huff in response to the interruption.

Samantha lit up as if she were on television. Her back straightened, and she flashed her signature smile. "That is very kind of you," she said. "May I introduce you to my friend Victoria Johnson?"

Victoria grimaced in the couple's direction but said nothing.

"Again, we're sorry to bother you. We just wanted—"

"We got it. You're sorry. Condolences, blah, blah, blah," the champagne said on Victoria's behalf. "Now, could you please leave us alone?"

"Victoria," Samantha said sharply. "You'll have to excuse my friend. She just got a bit of bad news. Thank you very much for your kind words."

The wounded couple slipped away silently.

"That was unnecessary, Victoria."

"I don't care about them. I'm more worried about you right now. What are you going to do?"

Samantha leaned back in her chair and placed a napkin in her lap. "I don't think I have a choice. I can't let even a rumor like that get out. I've got to pay him."

"Do you have that kind of money?"

"Of course I do."

"How the hell are you going to explain that to your accountants?"

"I won't have to. I have offshore accounts that not even Hezekiah knew about," Samantha said dismissively. "It's not a question of the money. I'm just so mad at this son of a bitch. I don't like to be manipulated like this," she added, clenching the champagne flute almost to the point of breaking it. "If I ever find out who he is, I swear I'll . . ." Samantha stopped mid sentence.

"I told you, girl, I know people who specialize in shit like this. They can make this whole thing disappear if you want. It'll be expensive, but nowhere near two million dollars," Victoria said wickedly.

"Thanks, girl. I knew I could count on you," Samantha said, shaking off the fear that had gripped her since the telephone call, "but I think I can handle this on my own."

"Are you sure, girl? This could be some psycho. How do you know it's not the same nutcase that killed Hezekiah?"

"I don't know that," Samantha said, avoiding eye contact. "It did cross my mind when I was speaking to him."

"Are you sure you don't want me to make a call for you? Believe me, these boys will root out the motherfucker in a day, and that will be the last anyone will ever hear from him."

"If I can't handle it, you'll be the first person I'll call."

"All right, honey. But you better be fucking careful," Victoria said, reaching across the table to take Samantha's hand. "I don't want to go to any more Cleaveland funerals this year."

Gideon knocked on the heavy wire-mesh security door at Danny's apartment. His button-down downy white shirt, perfectly pleated khakis, and brown Gucci loafers seemed out of place in the respectable yet edgy neighborhood. The pounding made a familiar tinny rattle that was often heard in neighborhoods where barred doors and windows were required for relatively intruder-free living. He pounded harder the second time.

Gideon saw a cat lounging on the windowsill in Danny's apartment. The scraggly gray cat seemed oblivious to the pounding on the door. Then, suddenly, the preoccupied cat casually lifted his head and looked over his shoulder into the apartment. Gideon saw the drape move slightly, and Danny appeared in the window.

Gideon waved and held up a small box tied with a red ribbon. Danny looked blankly at Gideon and was clearly deciding whether to open the door to the uninvited guest or simply to ignore him.

Danny disappeared from the window, and the lazy cat rested his head on the sill again. Gideon then heard the deadbolt locks on the wooden door behind the security screen turn, and the door opened. He could see only the silhouette of Danny through the security screen.

"What do you want?" Danny asked coldly.

"Hello, Danny," Gideon said. "I wanted to apologize for the other day. I didn't mean to offend you."

"Apology accepted. Is there anything else?"

Gideon held up the box. "This is for you."

"I don't want any gifts from you."

"It's not a gift exactly," Gideon said sheepishly. "It's more a peace offering. I felt bad that I had hurt you. You don't need any more hurt in your life, and I was devastated to think that I had caused you any additional distress." Gideon extended the box toward the door and said, "Please. I don't expect anything in return, other than assurance that you accept my apology."

Danny stood with his feet planted firmly on the hardwood floor in the entry hall. Gideon couldn't see the suspicious expression on his face through the black screen; then suddenly he heard the metallic churning of another lock, and the prison door swung open. Danny stood shirtless in the threshold. Gideon immediately noticed his well-defined torso. He had a swimmer's build. His skin was like brown whipped butter spread over a perfectly flat stomach, moderately muscular shoulders and chest. He wore a pair of baggy, faded blue jeans that sagged just below the waist, exposing the red elastic band of his boxer shorts.

"You can come in only on one condition," Danny said flatly.

"What's that?" Gideon asked, slightly raising his eyebrow.

"You have to swear you won't involve me in any way in your investigation. It's too dangerous, and I don't want to live the rest of my life looking over my shoulder for that horrible woman."

Gideon, without hesitation, raised his right hand and said, "I don't want you to live in fear, either. I promise."

Danny looked him in the eye, as if attempting to discern the sincerity of his promise. Without saying a word, he slowly stepped aside and allowed Gideon to enter. Gideon followed Danny into the living room.

"How did you find out my address?" Danny asked in a softer tone.

Gideon smiled and said, "You forget I'm a reporter. We have our ways."

"That's the problem. I can't forget you're a reporter. Sometimes I think you wish I would. You want a cup of coffee or tea?"

"Sometimes I wish I could forget myself," Gideon said as he instinctively surveyed the room. "Coffee would be nice, if it's not too much trouble."

"I just made a pot. Hope decaf is okay. Have a seat," Danny said, disappearing down the hall toward the kitchen.

"That's fine," Gideon called out to his well-defined back.

Gideon sat on the edge of the couch under the bay window and placed the box on the coffee table. The cat purred and licked his paw on the sill, unfazed by his presence. His reporter instincts immediately kicked in, and the deductions quickly mounted.

Not many pictures on the walls, he thought. *He's not comfortable here. This isn't home to him. Only a couch, and no chairs. Doesn't get, or want, many visitors. Stack of newspapers all folded to stories about Hezekiah. He's still looking for answers. The plants are wilting. Hasn't, as of yet, gotten back into a routine since Hezekiah's death.*

"Do you take sugar and cream?" Danny called from kitchen.

"Two sugars," he responded

The apartment is neat, but a faint layer of dust is evident on the coffee table. Gideon's observant mind continued without his consent. *He can manage some chores, but that's limited to those that make his life bearable. Less pressing ones are dismissed.*

He looked for signs that Hezekiah had been in the room, a Bible perhaps, or an expensive piece of art out of place amid the neat but thrift-store decor. But there was nothing: no photographs of the handsome pastor, no coat that looked too large for Danny hanging on the coatrack, no gold pen on the desk, no hint of a wealthy ecclesiastical presence ever having been in the room.

Danny returned with two steaming mugs and placed them on the coffee table. While away, he had put on a white T-shirt that did little to conceal his chiseled frame. Danny sat at the opposite end of the couch.

"Thank you," Gideon said, reaching for the mug. "What's his name?"

"What's whose name?" Danny asked suspiciously.

Gideon pointed over his shoulder and said, "The cat."

"Oh . . . that's Parker."

Gideon reached over his shoulder and scratched Parker behind his ear. The cat purred even louder. After several rubs he stood, stretched, and climbed down the back of the couch and found a place on Gideon's lap.

"Parker, get down," Danny commanded.

"No, he's fine. I like cats."

The cat ignored the human exchange, curled, and twisted until it found just the right position.

"You haven't opened the present," Gideon said. "I hope you like it."

"You don't have to give me anything. I believe you. I believe you're not trying to use me to get your story."

"Thank you," Gideon said with obvious relief. "But I'd feel even better if you accepted it." Gideon reached for the box, being careful to not disturb Parker, and handed it to Danny. "Please take it. It's really nothing."

Danny reached across the space between them and took the box. "What is it?"

"The best way to find out is to open it."

Danny pulled the ribbon on the small black box and lifted the hinged lid to reveal a Slate Serti Rolex watch. It was two toned, with a circle of cobalt blue around a champagne-gold face. The shiny metal band was silver with a gold strip running down the center. The second hand ticked proudly, as if it knew exactly how much the little time machine cost.

Danny immediately shut the box lid. "I can't accept this," he said, handing the extravagant gift back to Gideon. "Gideon, you don't give expensive gifts like this to someone you just met," he added in a firm but sympathetic voice.

He had read the rumors about Gideon like everyone else in the country. *TMZ* had speculated endlessly about his sexual orientation. The tabloids contained weekly pictures of the handsome Gideon Truman in restaurants or walking to his car, with titillating headlines such as: IS HE OR ISN'T HE? and GAY'DEON TRUMAN?

Danny could sense the handsome man's dejection and embarrassment.

"I've done it again. Danny. I'm so sorry. I didn't mean to offend you. It's just . . ."

Danny laughed softly and said, "You didn't offend me. It's just, well, a little inappropriate, don't you think?"

"I've never been any good at this. I inevitably say or do the wrong thing," Gideon said, resting his head on the back of the couch.

"Good at what?"

Without lifting his head, Gideon turned toward Danny at the opposite end of the couch and said shyly, "Letting someone very special know that I care about them."

"So, it's true," Danny said softly.

"Yes. Most of what you've read or heard is true."

"So, I'm assuming you don't get much practice at this," Danny said with a gentle smile.

"Nope," he replied, rolling his head from side to side on the back of the couch. "Actually, I get none at all."

"That is very sad. I'm sorry."

"No, don't be. I was actually fine until I met you," Gideon said, looking at the circa 1970 light fixture dangling from the ceiling. "I understand why Hezekiah loved you. You are the gentlest, most centered person I've ever met. I feel grounded when I'm around you, and I would give anything for you to feel safe with me."

Danny sat back on the couch, his position matching Gideon's. The two men gazed up at the light fixture, and Parker continued to purr on Gideon's lap. Gideon continued to rub Parker's soft head with his right hand. Without looking in Danny's direction, Gideon laid his left hand, palm up, halfway between them on the center cushion. Except for Parker's little revving motor, the room was silent.

Danny longed to feel safe with someone again. His world had become so dark and lonely. A stark and devastating contrast to the year he had spent with Hezekiah. There was never a lonely moment when they were in the world together. Even during the times when they weren't in each other's presence, they each knew the other was very near. They called each other two, sometimes three, times a day and e-mailed or texted even more frequently. They each seemed to instinctively know when the other needed to hear their voice. In moments of impending despair, fear, or fatigue, the telephone would ring at just the right time.

"I was thinking of you," either of them would say, "and wanted to tell you how much I love you." The looming despair, fear, or fatigue would dissipate. Or, Are u all right? the text would read. Just got a funny feeling that u needed 2 hear from me. The reply would inevitably be, I did need 2 hear from u. Much better now. Will call ASAP. XOXO.

Then one day the telephone calls suddenly stopped. The e-mails didn't come. The text alert that had provided a year of sweet music to his ears didn't chime. That was the hardest part for Danny. His world had gone silent in the time it took the bullet to leave the gun, cross the expanse of the sanctuary and enter Hezekiah. Now the quiet seemed to taunt him. Danny had instinctively checked his iPhone for messages from Hezekiah for weeks after his death, even when he knew there would be none. Somehow the act of sliding the screen awake and tapping the message icon provided him a bit of comfort, and he welcomed the comfort, no matter how small, wherever he could find it.

Gideon's hand remained extended between them on the sofa cushion. He hadn't realized how empty his life had become until he met Danny St. John. Parties in Manhattan with six-foot Nubian goddesses on his arm; holding court at the finest restaurants in Los Angeles, San Francisco, London, and Paris, with A-list celebrities, politicians, and corporate moguls competing for the pearls that fell from his lips, all felt empty. Each evening, when the parties were over and all the autographs had been signed and the models had been sent home in cabs, Gideon was alone. The void had never been apparent, because there was always another party the next night. The frantic motion of his life served as the lush green camouflage that covered the pit that ambition, fame, and wealth had dug.

Somehow Danny had removed the brush and exposed the gaping hole in his soul. It was so dark and deep that he couldn't see the bottom. When he spoke, his words echoed against the walls of loneliness. When he cried, his tears fell and never touched the floor of the bottomless pit. Today, sitting on the couch with the cat purring in his lap, he needed someone to catch his tears. He needed someone to hear his words in the pit to make them real. He needed to love someone other than himself and nourish something other than his career.

Just as Gideon was preparing to accept rejection and pull his hand away, he felt the warmth of Danny's gentle touch on his palm. The touch sent a vibration through his entire body. He felt like a tuning fork that had been tapped with a delicate silver mallet. The two men remained hand in hand at opposite ends of the couch, still and silent, for the next half hour.

41

"I'm leaving you, Scarlett. I want a divorce."

"David, why are you doing this?"

"Our entire marriage has been a lie. It's over."

David stood firmly in the doorway to the kitchen. The house smelled of freshly brewed coffee. He was fully dressed for the day in a chocolate-brown suit that molded perfectly to his frame, a banana-yellow silk necktie, and a powder-blue shirt. He clutched a briefcase in one hand and car keys in the other.

The two had not spoken in days. Neither of them had made an attempt to reach out to the other. They each had their own reasons. In between shedding tears for Hezekiah, Scarlett had only enough energy left to care for Natalie. Combing her hair in the morning and preparing her lunch for school left her exhausted. She didn't have the strength to worry about David and hated herself for not caring.

David was still reeling from the passionate love he and Samantha Cleaveland had made on her living room floor. He could still smell the sweetness of her perfume. The thought of her touch only made him long for more. She had possessed him and now owned his soul, which he willingly gave.

"Can't we talk about this? I've told you I wasn't in love with Hezekiah. I love you. Why can't you just accept that and allow us to move on?"

"This isn't about you for once, Scarlett."

"I told you I lied to you for Natalie, not for myself."

"I don't believe that, and on some level, I don't think you believe it, either," David said coldly. "You lied because you wanted to cover your tracks and preserve the ridiculous victim routine that you've used your entire life. You slept with Hezekiah because you wanted to. He didn't rape you. You were an adult. I don't buy for a minute your 'young and naive' excuse. You knew exactly what you were doing. You wanted him, and Samantha called your bluff and put you back in your place."

"How dare you? I was the victim. I walked away on my own because I didn't want anything from them," Scarlett replied indignantly.

"Correction, darling, you walked away because you knew you couldn't get the one thing you wanted—Hezekiah. Then the wounded little girl nonsense was the perfect cover for your being slapped back into reality by Samantha. It didn't matter that I or anyone else didn't know about Natalie. The important thing was that you knew and you could feel like the victim back in your safe little cocoon of self-pity, and since then you've been alone."

Scarlett raised her hand and slapped David hard on the cheek. His head turned from the blow, but his body remained firmly planted.

"I suppose now I'm supposed to slap you back. Is this a page from your battered wife script?" he said, rubbing his stinging cheek. "I'm afraid you'll have to remind me what my next line is. I don't seem to remember this scene."

Scarlett was unprepared for his lack of emotion and his painfully pointed words. His cold demeanor was completely unexpected and left her at a loss. His words swirled in her head, almost making her dizzy. Was she the perfect victim? Did the world, in fact, revolve around her and not Natalie? Was there some twisted desire to be abandoned and left alone with her scars and wounds? Was this the monster she'd created?

She slapped him again and waited for a response. But she was greeted only with a questioning stare.

"I hate you," she finally said in almost a whisper.

"You don't hate me. Scarlett. You hate the truth about yourself."

Scarlett looked puzzled. The words stung. Her entire life she felt she had sacrificed her happiness for others. But in the face of such a damning statement, she slowly began to realize that in fact she had made all the sacrifices for herself. She needed to be the victim. It was all she knew. It was familiar and was where she felt safe and, ironically, in control.

"You're a coward to leave me for this," she said, turning her back to him and walking to the sink. "I thought you were a better man than that."

"That's where you're wrong again," he said with a hint of irony. "I'm not leaving you because you're a liar. I'm not even leaving you because you're delusional."

Scarlett turned from the sink to face David. He had not moved from the threshold. Now the span of the room divided them. Steam from the coffeemaker on the marble island formed a mist between them. "Then why?" she asked, her question tinged with a dare.

"I'm leaving you for Samantha Cleaveland."

"Pastor Cleaveland," came the voice from the intercom in Samantha's office. "I'm sorry to disturb you, but you have a call from someone who says he's a business acquaintance. He's very insistent on speaking with you."

"Who is it?" Samantha asked, placing her reading glasses on the desk.

"He refused to give his name. He said it is urgent that he speak with you now. He said to tell you it's about Danny boy."

Samantha immediately snatched the telephone from its cradle and snapped, "Put him through."

"Good morning, Samantha," the calm voice said. "It's a beautiful day, isn't it?"

Samantha cringed when she heard her name in the receiver. She resisted the urge to insist she be called Pastor Cleaveland and said, "Why are you calling me here? You have my cell number."

"It was a little test. I wanted to see if you would take my call at church. And look at this. You did. You must really like me," the voice said sarcastically.

"No, I don't like you," she said without emotion. "I pity you."

"And why is that, Samantha?"

"I pity any man who would blackmail a widow. Your mother must have fucked you up pretty bad."

"Holy shit," came the amused reply. "Do you pray for your flock with that filthy mouth?"

"Look, asshole, I have the money. Where do you want me to leave it?"

"Now, that's a good girl. Who else have you told about this?"

"Who am I going to tell? You asked for the money. I got it. Now, stop wasting my time and let's get this over with. Where do you want to meet me?"

"Griffith Park. Tomorrow, Saturday night. At midnight. At the entrance on Western Avenue drive up the road to the first parking lot. Park, turn your lights off, and wait for me."

"How will I know you?"

"I'll be the man you hand the money to. And remember, come alone. No driver and no police. If I see anything or anyone that looks suspicious, I'll leave and go straight to Gideon Truman. You know Gideon, don't you, Samantha?"

"Yes, I know him."

"I think he'd be very interested in who your late husband was sleeping with, don't you?"

"I'll be alone, but let me warn you, my friend. I'm holding up my end of this, and I expect you to hold up yours. I don't want to hear from you ever again, and you'll forget about Danny St. John. If you don't you will be very sorry you ever fucked with me," she whispered. "I won't mind losing everything I have to hunt you down like the animal you are and kill you myself."

"Don't worry. After this is over, you'll never hear from me again. Until tomorrow, then, Pastor."

Samantha heard the dial tone. The office was still. Sun poured through the windows, offering a bright and cheery contrast to the blackness she felt in her soul. A leather-bound Bible on her desk was opened to 1 Chronicles 16:22.

Saying, Touch not mine anointed, and do my prophets no harm.

It was the text she had chosen for the Sunday morning sermon. Samantha reached under her desk and retrieved a black leather duffel bag. She walked across the room to a glass console that held a crystal decanter filled with water, a set of six etched Waterford glasses on a silver tray, and a spray of exotic purple, pink, and red flowers. The 450-year-old painting of Madonna and child, *A Sacra Conversazione,* hung above the table. Samantha had bought the painting at Sotheby's only months before Hezekiah was killed.

The three darkly clothed figures in the massive oil masterpiece fawned over a squirming cherubic infant as Samantha reached behind the gold-leaf frame and released a latch. The painting slowly glided up the wall toward the twenty-foot-high glass and steel-beamed ceiling, exposing a small, cold gray vault embedded in the wall.

Samantha unzipped the duffel bag and placed it on the console, rattling the delicate glass arrangement and causing the flowers to shudder. With perfectly manicured fingers she gently manipulated the tumbler. At forty-three the dial emitted a gentle click. The second click came at thirty-nine. When she spun the dial to fifty-four, the heavy metal door gave a double click and obediently succumbed to the expert touch of the only person on earth who knew the sequence to its heart. It was simple for those who knew. The numbers were the first two digits of her, Hezekiah's, and Jasmine's cell phone numbers.

The metal box was filled with only a fraction of the Cleaveland fortune, one of several fractions that Hezekiah had known nothing of. A single-strand pearl necklace once owned by Marie Antoinette was nestled in a purple velvet box. A flawless 6.04-carat black diamond from South Africa sat uncased on a stack of stocks, bonds, and deeds to commercial properties in Milan, Santa Monica, and New York, to a villa in Saint-Jean-Cap-Ferrat, a Brazilian horse ranch, and a penthouse in Hong Kong. Her prize possession, however, sat in the front of the metal cave. It was a simple silver cross and chain that she had removed from her husband's neck as she cradled his dead body in her arms in the pulpit on the day he was murdered.

Samantha picked up the cross and ran the smooth, cold chain between her fingers. It served as evidence that she alone was the master of her fate.

In the rear of the vault were stacks of hundred-dollar bills. Each stack contained fifty thousand dollars, held together by a single white paper strip. Samantha retrieved forty of the stacks and tossed them indiscriminately into the duffel bag. The cross swung from the chain in her hand each time she threw another bundle into the bag. Their absence left only a small dent in the remaining piles of money.

The final item she pulled from the vault was a small matte black Smith & Wesson Centennial 442 snub-nosed revolver. She held the gun in the same hand as the cross and looked at it as one would an old friend or trusted ally. She expertly spun the cylinder to ensure all five cartridge chambers were filled and ready. Samantha gently placed the gun on top of the disheveled bundles of money and zipped the bag.

Samantha returned the cross to the front of the vault and closed the door. With a click of the switch on the wall, Madonna and child descended from the heavens and covered the evidence of Samantha's true heart. The cash, jewels, stocks, deeds, and bonds no longer existed. There was only the most virtuous of mothers cradling the squirming infant in her loving arms.

Samantha walked to her desk with the duffel bag swinging at her side. The extra weight caused her heels to dig deep into the plush white carpet. The door to her office flung open, and David Shackelford stormed in with a frantic assistant at his heels as Samantha returned the bag to its place under her desk and sat down.

"Pastor Cleaveland, I'm so sorry, but he just barged past me. I couldn't stop him," the nervous woman said.

"I told you it's all right," David said, blocking the woman. He moved quickly toward Samantha. "She will want to see me. Samantha, I need to talk to you now."

"Pastor Cleaveland, would you like for me to call security?" the woman called out over David's shoulders.

Samantha stood from her desk and said, "No, Amber. This is Brother Shackelford. He's a friend of the church. You can leave us alone. Thank you."

"Are you sure, ma'am? I can—"

"I said leave us alone," Samantha snapped.

The young woman walked backward with the two in her sights until the door was closed.

"What do you want, David? This is not a good time for me. I was on my way out."

David walked behind her desk, placed his hands on each of her shoulders, pulled her close, and pressed his lips to hers.

Samantha pushed him away and said, "What the hell are you doing? Are you crazy? Someone could walk in."

David kissed her hard again and said, "I don't care if someone comes in," as he nuzzled her neck.

Samantha struggled to break free. "Let me go, David. This is not the place for this."

"I love you, Samantha," David panted breathlessly. "You're all I've been able to think about. Make love to me now. Right now!"

"David, honey, stop. Stop, baby," she said, pushing him away. "There'll be plenty of time for that later. But not now, damn it. I've got a major problem I have to deal with."

David tried again to remove the distance between them, but Samantha held up her hand.

"If you have a problem, let me help. I'm here for you now, full-time."

"What do you mean, full-time?" Samantha asked suspiciously.

"I mean I've left Scarlett."

"You did what?" Samantha asked coldly. "Why on earth did you do that?"

"Because I'm in love with you, Samantha Cleaveland. I want to be with you."

"Don't be ridiculous, David. Go back to your wife. I don't want you. I don't want anyone right now. For Christ's sake, I just buried my husband."

"That's all the more reason for you to be with me. You need me. A woman like you needs a man in her life. What is the problem you're dealing with? Tell me about it. Let me help."

Samantha looked David in the eye. She could see the desperation and longing. She could also see the tent in his expensively tailored slacks.

"I don't think you can help me, David. I don't think anyone can," she said and walked to the desk and sat down.

"Try me, baby. I'm here for you." David walked to her and placed his hand on her shoulder. "Tell me. What's going on? Do you need a lawyer?"

"No, no, I don't need a lawyer. I've already got lawyers coming out my ass."

"Then what is it? Tell me."

Samantha sighed, as if exhausted. She looked toward the window and said, "All right, David, I'll tell you. I'm being blackmailed."

"Blackmailed?" David shouted. "By whom? For what?"

"I don't know who it is. It's about Hezekiah." Samantha pulled a silk handkerchief from her purse and dabbed a nonexistent tear from her eye. "It's horrible, David. Hezekiah was . . ." Samantha paused. "Hezekiah was involved with a man for a year before he died."

"What do you mean, involved?"

"Sexually. Someone found out about it. They can prove it."

"How much do they want?"

"The first payment is two million dollars. He said he'd keep coming back for more every year. There's no end to how much he'll demand."

"Oh my God. Have you called the police?"

"I can't get the police involved. I'd be ruined. The church would be ruined. New Testament could never survive a scandal like this. If it came out, that would be the end of the entire ministry, and there's more."

"More? What else?"

"He's threatened to kill me if I don't pay."

David kneeled down in front of her. "Kill you? What did he say?"

"He said if I didn't pay him every time, he would contact the media and then hunt me down like an animal and kill me."

"Baby, this is horrible," David said, squeezing her hand. "What are you going to do?"

"I don't have a choice. I have to pay him, and I'll have to keep paying him every time he asks. David, I'm so afraid."

"Maybe I should talk to him."

"And say what? 'Please don't do this anymore'? It won't work, David. There's nothing you or anyone can do. I'm going to meet him tomorrow night and give him the money." Samantha reached under the desk and slid out the duffel bag. "Here it is," she said, unzipping the bag to reveal the piles of cash and the revolver.

"What is that for?" David asked, looking at the gun.

"I told you he said he'd kill me. I want to be able to at least protect myself if necessary."

"Samantha, you can't go out there alone. It's too dangerous. You don't know what kind of psychopath this guy is. I'm going to come with you."

"No," Samantha said, standing and walking to the window. "He said I had to come alone."

"Then I'll follow you from a distance. Give me the gun. If it gets out of hand, I'll be right there."

Samantha smiled. "You are such a sweet man. I don't want to get you involved in this."

David walked behind her and placed his hands on her shoulders. "I'm in love with you, so that automatically gets me involved."

Samantha leaned back into his arms. "Have you ever shot a gun before, David?" she asked, staring out over the construction site of the new cathedral. "Do you think you could actually kill a man?"

She could feel David's heart pounding in his chest. He did not respond. Samantha leaned farther back and pressed her waist against the mound that was growing in his pants. She twisted slightly from side to side and whispered again, "Do you think you could kill a man?"

David could smell the sweet aroma of her perfume. Her warm breath sent an intoxicating bouquet to his nostrils. Before he could think, he heard the words slip from his lips into her ear. "For you I would kill a man."

Scarlett clumsily rummaged through the mirrored medicine cabinet in her bathroom. She pushed hairbrushes, bottles of lotion, and shaving creams aside, causing a container of dental floss to tumble to the counter, with minty string trailing behind. Her hands shook as she searched frantically for her Zoloft prescription. She finally found it behind two plastic bottles of peroxide. She shook the bottle, but she had taken so many after Hezekiah's death, it was empty. Next to it, however, was her prescription for Xanax, and behind that a full bottle of Prozac.

Over the years her therapist had prescribed a variety of anti-anxiety potions and notions to deal with the stresses that had defined her life. Zoloft was her favorite, but today she would settle for a Xanax. Scarlett swallowed the pill without water. Her knees wobbled as she made her way into the living room. Her head had not stopped spinning since the startling announcement from her husband earlier that day.

It's happening again, she thought as she stumbled to the sofa in the center of the room, blanketed in pink, green, and purple pillows. A pristine brick-framed fireplace, which had never known fire, served as the focal point of the room. Most notably there were no photographs on the mantelpiece, or anywhere else in the room, of Natalie, David, or herself. Large potted plants flanked a sliding glass window that opened to a paved patio and a modest backyard. In the center of the window was a small lemon tree, whose fruit no one in the home had ever tasted.

Scarlett ran her trembling fingers through her disheveled silky hair. She had long since given up on trying to stop the tide of tears that had been flowing since David left the house.

She's doing it again, she thought as she looked at the tree sagging from bulbous lemons on the verge of bursting and falling to the ground to rot. *Why does she have to destroy everything I love?*

The telephone on a table next to the sofa rang as she pondered the mysteries of her life. She didn't answer. On the third ring she heard, "Hello, Scarlett. This is Cynthia Pryce. When you have a moment, could you please call me? I need to talk to you about Samantha Cleaveland. My number is seven-six-one—"

Scarlett lunged across the sofa and grabbed the receiver. "Cynthia," she said with no hint of sorrow. "Hello. I was in the garden, picking lemons from my tree, and didn't hear the phone. How are you?"

"I'm doing well. Do you have a few moments to talk about a church matter?"

"I do, but could you hold on for just a moment? I need to put these lemons in the sink."

Scarlett put the telephone on mute, wiped her wet cheeks with the sleeve of her blouse, and took three deep breaths. The little pill had begun to work its magic. Her hands had stopped shaking, and the pain from the thought of her husband leaving her was reduced to only a dull, throbbing ache. She longed for her Zoloft. One pill and she would have been completely numb by now.

"Cynthia, I'm back. I'm making lemonade for David and Natalie. Now, how can I help you? You said something about Samantha Cleaveland."

"Yes. Scarlett, this is kind of a sensitive topic. I hope I can count on your discretion."

"Of course. Now, what is this about?"

"Percy and I were approached by some of the other trustees. Now, understand if it were only one, we wouldn't have paid much attention to it. But we've been approached by a number of them."

"About what?" Scarlett asked impatiently.

"About Samantha Cleaveland. You see, dear, some of the trustees feel they may have acted in haste by naming her as interim pastor so soon after Hezekiah's death, God rest his soul. We were all terribly devastated by Hezekiah's death, and obviously not thinking clearly. They feel we put the needs of the church before her needs. As I'm sure you will agree, the pain a woman feels after the loss of a spouse is second only to the loss of a child. The poor woman has just lived through one of the most traumatic things a woman can experience, and here we are, thinking about ourselves and the church. It's terrible, just terrible, and some of the trustees feel they've made a mistake by acting so quickly."

Scarlett listened intently to the woman's rambling. She easily detected the tinge of deceit in her voice. Cynthia had never been able to fully conceal her contempt whenever she spoke of Samantha Cleaveland, no matter how hard she tried.

"Hello . . . ? Scarlett, are you still there?" Cynthia asked into the silence.

"I'm here. Go on," Scarlett said.

"Well, as I was saying, people feel we really must act quickly to correct this lapse in our judgment . . . for Samantha's sake."

"What trustees said this to you?"

Cynthia answered quickly, "I really can't say, dear. They've all spoken to me, us, in the strictest of confidence. But trust me, it's more than a majority of the trustees."

"So why are you telling me this?"

"Well, dear, as a member of the board of trustees, and as a woman, don't you think you have some responsibility to Samantha, as well? Surely you must see that action must be taken to protect her and give her time to heal, don't you?" Cynthia asked.

"So what are you proposing?"

"I'm not proposing anything, dear," Cynthia said innocently. "Rather your fellow trustees are proposing that Samantha be relieved of the awesome burden of pastor, at least for the time being, and be allowed to properly mourn the loss of her husband."

"And who do the *trustees* propose to replace her with?" Scarlett asked, already knowing the answer.

"Isn't it obvious? Percy," Cynthia said, barely concealing her arrogance. "It will completely turn our lives upside down, but Percy has convinced me that it is the right thing to do for Samantha and for New Testament. Believe me, dear, it is the last thing I want for my life right now, but I do feel some responsibility to my sister Samantha and to the memory of Hezekiah. I've spent many nights praying about this, and the Lord told me that my husband is right."

Scarlett wasn't offended by the woman's transparent attempt to deceive her. Neither was she insulted at being considered so naive as to believe she wouldn't recognize a blatant power grab. Instead, she was pleased that someone else had taken it upon themselves to challenge Samantha Cleaveland's absolute and unbridled power over New Testament Cathedral and, more importantly, her life.

"You know, *dear*," Scarlett finally said, "I've never really thought of it in those terms. I'm not sure what we were thinking. I guess it was as you said. We must have all been so traumatized after Hezekiah's death, God rest his soul, that we never considered how this would affect Samantha. The poor woman must be going through hell right now, and all we could do was think of our own needs. I feel just terrible about this."

"We all do, dear. We all do. I'm so glad you agree."

"So how are the *trustees* proposing we reverse the vote?"

"There will be a special meeting of the board of trustees where Percy will be nominated to serve as the pastor. Can I . . . I mean can New Testament and Samantha count on your vote?"

Scarlett did not hesitate with her response. "Definitely, Cynthia. I have always felt Percy would make an excellent pastor. I'm sure Samantha will be relieved. You, I mean New Testament Cathedral and Samantha, can count on my vote."

***

Samantha sat directly in front of Gideon Truman in a seventeenth-century Gothic throne-like chair in the living room of her estate. The top edge of the ornately carved back of the dark walnut seat hovered just above the top of her satin hair. A wall of French doors served as the backdrop, revealing the perfectly maintained grounds of the estate. Light poured into the room, enveloping Samantha in a warm glow. On occasion a pair of preening peacocks could be seen through the window, strolling across the freshly mown lawn.

The idyllic scene was, however, upstaged by Samantha Cleaveland's presence. Her skin took on the rosy hue of the spray of flowers in an etched Lalique crystal vase placed on a glass table next to her. She wore a peach floral silk blouse that revealed only enough cleavage to hint at her perfect, full breasts.

Two cameramen positioned themselves at angles to Samantha to capture her left and right, and two others pointed theirs to Gideon. He wore a black suit and his trademark plaid shirt with a blue and red striped necktie. Bright lights mounted on tripods were directed at them just beyond the cameras' view. The first thing he had noted when he entered the home was that both Picassos had been replaced by nondescript pieces of abstract art.

The other person in the room was Gideon's producer, Megan, a fresh-faced brunette who was the daughter of a faceless network executive. Megan handed Gideon large index cards containing the questions America had for Samantha Cleaveland, and provided final directions and assuring comments to Samantha.

"Pastor Cleaveland, just be natural. If you make a mistake or get confused, don't worry about it. We can edit it out later." Megan turned to Samantha when she spoke and slightly brushed against the table holding the vase and flower arrangement.

"I don't get confused or make mistakes," Samantha said coldly. "Would you please be more careful? That vase probably cost more than your house. Are we ready to start yet? I'd like to get this over with."

"Yes, ma'am," Megan said with a stammer. "We are ready whenever you are."

"I was ready when you invaded my home two hours ago," Samantha responded with an irritated gesture of her hand and a raised eyebrow.

Megan retreated sheepishly to her place behind a monitor just beyond the eyes of the cameras and said, "Okay, everyone, we're rolling in five . . . four . . . three . . . two . . . and . . ."

"Good evening. I'm Gideon Truman, and welcome to *Truman Live*." Gideon's face filled the monitor. His eyes sparkled, and he flashed the smile that made people all over the world welcome him into their homes.

"Tonight we are honored to have a woman who until recently was one half of a power couple who for years has captivated the hearts of people around the world. Her recent tragedy made national and international headlines and rocked the religious world to its core. Please welcome Pastor Samantha Cleaveland of New Testament Cathedral in Los Angeles. Good evening, Pastor Cleaveland, and thank you for inviting us into your lovely home."

Samantha came to life when the camera was rolling. Her skin captured the light around her and sent it back to the world brighter than it had come.

"Thank you, Gideon. It's my pleasure."

"I'm sure I speak for millions of people when I say how sorry I am for the tragic loss of your husband, Pastor Hezekiah Cleaveland."

"Thank you," she said with a gracious nod of her head.

"Let me start by asking, are the police any closer to finding out who assassinated Pastor Cleaveland?"

"The Los Angeles Police Department has been amazing throughout this entire ordeal," she said as if by rote, "but unfortunately they are no closer today to finding his killer than they were the day it happened. A part of me feels we may never know who killed Hezekiah. The important thing, however, is that this person will have to answer to God either in this life or the next."

"You are a woman with strong religious beliefs. Are you in any way able to forgive the man or woman who did this to you, your family, and all the people who love you?"

"I'm so glad you asked me that question." Samantha looked Gideon directly in the eye and continued, "I have already forgiven him. This has caused me and my daughter immense pain and anguish. There were days when I didn't think I could go on without him. But you know, Gideon, God promised us all that he would never give us more burdens than we could bear. And with that knowledge I was able to get up one morning a few weeks after it happened, put on my makeup, and face another day. Don't get me wrong, though. I still cry every day, and I miss him more than you can imagine, but life must go on, and every day I grow a little stronger."

"You mentioned your daughter, Jasmine. How is she handling the loss of her father?"

"Jasmine took her father's death very hard. They were very close. She was daddy's little girl," Samantha said with a smile. "They were inseparable from the day she was born until the day he died. She couldn't bear to be in the house after he was killed, so she's staying temporarily with very dear friends of our family in Malibu. I speak with her every day, and we pray together on the telephone every evening, before she goes to bed. God and time heals all wounds, and every day she becomes stronger. As painful as this has all been, I know that someday she will come to understand that this is all part of God's master plan."

"Can you think of any reason anyone would want to kill your husband?"

Megan looked away from the monitor and scanned her copy of the questions they had developed together. Gideon's last question was not on the list.

Samantha's suddenly dilated pupils were the only visible reaction to the unexpected question. "I've thought a lot about this and have had multiple conversations with detectives, who wanted to know the same thing. Everyone loved Hezekiah. He was the kind of person that would give you his last dollar if you needed it. I've never known him to make an enemy. I can't think of anyone who would have wanted him dead."

"New Testament Cathedral is the sixth largest church in the country. Your television ministry generates millions each year. Do you think jealousy may have played into this?"

"I would hate to think jealousy was a factor, but anything is possible," Samantha said languidly. "There are many troubled people in the world. We may never know what motivated this person to do what he did."

"Do you think you may have factored into his death in any way?"

Megan swiftly removed her glasses, stood up, and took a step toward Gideon. Samantha saw her from the corner of her eye and held up her hand, issuing the universal sign for "stop."

"I'm not sure what you mean," Samantha said. Her eyes were a centimeter tighter than before.

Gideon saw the almost imperceptible shift in her demeanor. He pressed on, unfazed by the icy glare from his guest or the rustling of the producer behind his shoulder. "What I mean is, could you have done something to contribute to the murder of your husband, inadvertently, of course?"

Megan clutched her mouth to prevent a gasp from escaping. The four cameramen looked nervously at each other, then zoomed in on Samantha's stone face.

"Anything is possible, of course. I'm sure I've made decisions in the ministry that may have possibly upset some people, but I honestly don't think I've done anything to anyone that would elicit such an extreme response as this. What your viewers need to understand is that for the most part the world is filled with people who have no desire to hurt anyone.

"I've traveled all over the world and met so many people from different cultures, and I'm always amazed to find people just like you and me, all believing in the same God, but maybe calling him by a different name, who simply want to live their lives without doing harm. There are, however, a small minority of people out there who don't have God in their lives, and unfortunately, they sometimes make misguided decisions that hurt other people."

Gideon pushed a little harder. "I find it difficult to fathom that a man as powerful as Hezekiah Cleaveland, one of the most high-profile and wealthiest ministers in the country, didn't have any enemies. So do you think this was a random shooting?"

"My husband was human like everyone else. He made mistakes, and like us all, he did things that, if he were alive, I'm sure he wouldn't be proud of. But I'll say it again. I don't think he ever did anything that would warrant him being killed. If that were the case, we all would have to walk down the street looking over our shoulders."

"Let's talk about New Testament Cathedral," Gideon said, flipping the index cards. "Shortly after Hezekiah's death you were installed as pastor. How has the transition from first lady to pastor been for you?"

"I believe it was a blessing for me. The appointment was totally unexpected. I didn't even know I was being considered for the position until I received a call from the president of our board of trustees," Samantha said, batting her mink eyelashes.

She went on. "I, of course, was honored and a little concerned about whether it was too soon after losing my husband. However, the trustees had faith in me and were insistent that it was the best thing for New Testament Cathedral. Initially, I said no because I felt I needed more time to mourn my loss. But my daughter said something that changed my mind."

"What did she say?" Gideon asked.

"Something very simple. She looked me in the eye and said, 'Mommy, Daddy would have wanted it that way.' So I prayed through my tears and through my grief and God . . ." Samantha paused and gingerly dabbed the corner of her eye with the tip of her finger. "God spoke to my heart late one night and said, 'Samantha, this is my will. With me you can do all things.' After I heard that, I knew I had to either live what I've been preaching all these years or just walk away. I decided I would stand by God's word."

Gideon looked down at the index cards so the camera could not catch the smirk on his face. An image of Danny flashed in his head as he pondered his next question. He resisted the urge to ask, "Were you aware that your husband was involved in a homosexual affair for a year with a man named Danny St. John?" Or, "How do you think the millions of people who send you their hard-earned money every year would feel if they knew about it?" And his knockout punch, "If the public found out that one of the most loved ministers in the country was gay, it would have cost you millions. What did you do to Hezekiah when you learned of the affair?"

Suddenly Gideon's hand felt warm from the memory of Danny's touch. He remembered the fear in his voice and the worry in his eyes.

Megan braced herself for the next unscripted question, and the cameramen stood in anticipation, with the lenses zoomed in on the hunter and his prey.

"Pastor Cleaveland," Gideon said, looking up again. "I think your board of trustees made an excellent decision."

An audible sigh of relief could be heard from Megan in the background.

For the remainder of the one-hour interview Gideon stuck to the script, asking one softball question after another, each skillfully spun by Samantha to solidify her image as the brave grieving widow who set aside her own needs for the good of the church.

"Pastor Cleaveland, it has been a pleasure speaking with you today. I now see why America has fallen in love with you. I wish you, Jasmine, and New Testament Cathedral the best."

"It's been my pleasure."

The cameramen stood up straight and deeply exhaled. Megan dashed from behind the monitor to Samantha and said, "Pastor Cleaveland, that was brilliant. You looked beautiful on the screen and . . ."

Samantha stood up, removed the mike from her blouse, and walked past Megan before she could finish the sentence and said, "I want you all out of my house and off the property in ten minutes."

Gideon, Megan, and the cameramen stood frozen as Samantha left the room.

"What the fuck were you doing, Gideon?" Megan finally said. "You practically accused her of killing her husband. Why didn't you stick to the questions we agreed on?"

"They were softball, bullshit questions," Gideon said defensively. "Trust me, I had tougher ones I could have asked, but I restrained myself. The whole fucking interview was like a Samantha Cleaveland infomercial. I feel like a goddamned idiot."

"So you think that's why she stormed out of here in a puff of smoke like Endora?" Megan asked sarcastically.

The cameramen wasted no time in packing the equipment, rolling up cords, and returning the room to the perfect state it was in when they arrived.

Gideon and Megan continued their discussion while the four men worked frantically to meet the ten minute deadline.

"Gideon, do you know something you're not telling me? What is this about?"

"I don't know anything. I just don't like that phony bitch."

"So you accuse one of the most popular women in the country of being involved in her husband's death just because you think she's a bitch? Have you forgotten about professional detachment?"

Gideon could not deny that his emotions had caused him to straddle the fine line between the television ratings game and good journalism. But for the love of Danny, he had stayed in the shallow waters of compliments, sympathy, and scripture-laced sound bites.

"How do you think viewers are going to react when they see you insinuate that Samantha Cleaveland caused her husband's death?" Megan continued. "You're going to look like an asshole."

"I don't care what I look like. I've got more important things on my mind."

Cynthia Pryce abruptly turned off the big-screen television in her bedroom. Gideon's interview with Samantha had just aired for the third time since the taping.

"The coward, the fucking coward," she said out loud, throwing the remote control across the bed. "He didn't even mention any of Hezekiah's affairs."

Cynthia reached for her cell phone and dialed Gideon's number.

"Hello. This is Gideon Truman."

"What the fuck was that all about?"

"I beg your pardon. Who is this?" he said, immediately evoking the image of another crazed fan.

"This is Cynthia Pryce. We had a deal. I gave you the information, and you were supposed to report it. Was that so difficult?"

Gideon was driving up Hollywood Boulevard when he received the call. Traffic was bumper to bumper. Tourists wearing the latest strip-mall fashions walked in droves along the star-embedded street. Gideon pulled his car into a bus zone and continued. "We did not have any such deal," he said firmly. "I told you I would check out your story, but I never promised to report it."

"She got to you, didn't she?" Cynthia said coldly. "What did she do? Threaten you? Fuck you? Oh, wait a minute. I forgot. That wouldn't work on you."

Gideon took the phone away from his ear and looked at it in surprise. "I'm not sure who you think you're talking about, Mrs. Pryce. But I assure you no one 'got to me'. I simply chose not to pursue the story."

"Then why? This is the biggest story of your career. Don't you journalists have to take some kind of oath that says you have to report on stories that affect the public?"

"There is no such oath. Journalists have complete discretion as to what they report. I exercised my discretion," he said, attempting to manage his indignation.

"No, what you did was cover up a story. And the only reason I can think of is that somehow Samantha Cleaveland got to you. Did she pay you? God knows she's got plenty of my money and everyone else's to do it with."

"I resent you accusing me of accepting bribes," Gideon said, raising his voice. Cars continued to creep by as he spoke.

A tour bus filled with camera-toting tourists stopped next to his car. Someone on the bus yelled out, "Hey, look. It's Gideon Truman." Everyone on the bus immediately rushed to the windows and began shouting, "Oh my God. It is him," and "Hey, Gideon. Look over here," as they snapped pictures and waved in his direction.

Gideon ignored the gawking fans and continued, "If you must know, I considered the story to be in poor taste in light of the circumstances. The man was murdered, for Christ's sake. Why do you need to crucify him even further? You're a smart woman. I'm sure you can figure out a way to sleep your way to the top."

"I'm sure I can, too, Mr. Truman," Cynthia said sharply. "But as I've already told you, this is not about me. It's about doing what's right."

A Metro RTD bus wormed its way through the traffic and stopped inches from Gideon's bumper. The bus driver blasted his horn at Gideon, causing a chorus of more car horns from behind the bus.

"I don't have time for this bullshit," he finally said. "If you want to be the first lady of New Testament, you're going to have to find some other asshole to do your dirty work."

With that Gideon hung up the phone and dashed back into traffic, giving a wave of apology to the bus driver.

"Fucking bitch," Gideon said, slamming the steering wheel. "How dare she?"

Gideon honked his horn impatiently at cars he felt were moving too slowly as he wound up Hollywood Boulevard. Cynthia had touched a nerve. Was he now, in fact, participating in a cover-up? Had his attraction to Danny caused him to cross the line between reporter and story? Was he a part of the story? The prospect frightened him. Had he compromised everything he believed in for the remote possibility that Danny could ever feel the same way he did?

"Faggot," Cynthia cursed, tossing the phone on the bed. "Never send a gay boy to do a woman's job."

Cynthia grudgingly conceded one truth Gideon had spoken. She in fact was unashamedly willing to sleep her way to the top. She thought of the pounding she had endured from.

It would have worked if the little bastard hadn't gotten himself killed, she thought. *His dick was so small, it wasn't really like fucking at all,* she recalled. *It was more like masturbation.*

42

The sun slowly dipped behind the hills in the distance as streaks of clouds filtered the remains of the day in the orange Arizona sky. Cactus dotted the horizon like pitchforks retired for the day by exhausted ranch hands. The desert was still except for lizards darting between rocks as the sun ended its scorching assault on the barren landscape. It was eight o'clock and time for the evening group at the Desert Springs Drug Rehabilitation Center in Phoenix.

Desert Springs was the rehab facility the rich, the famous, and the notorious chose when they needed to send their alcohol-guzzling, pill-popping, and needle-poking children for treatment away from the prying eyes of paparazzi, police, and custody attorneys.

The group facilitator, Dr. Ron, appeared to be an adolescent himself, but he was not. His doctorate in addiction psychology, his seven published books on the treatment of every addiction know to modern man, and his numerous appearances on *Oprah, Dr. Phil,* and *The Dr. Oz Show* gave the parents of his wealthy young patients solace when they handed him their forty-thousand-dollar check for twenty-eight days of treatment.

"It's eight o'clock, everyone," Dr. Ron said in a voice that echoed his pubescent face. "Let's get started."

The last of the youths slumped into their seats. Tattoos, pierced noses and lips, spiked hair, and lit cigarettes were the accessories of choice for most in the group. Several, however, wore diamond tennis bracelets, Manolo sandals, and Rolex watches. The one thing they all had in common was they each looked at least ten years older than their fifteen, sixteen, and seventeen years.

"We're now two weeks into your four-week stay at Desert Springs," Dr. Ron said. "I think tonight is a good time to talk about our families. I want each of you to share what it's like in your home.

Your parents, siblings, staff, pets, or anything else you'd like to share with the group. Who wants to start?"

"Why the fuck do you want to know that?" came the first response from the boy wearing the Rolex watch and sporting a two-hundred-dollar haircut. "You plan on selling our stories to *People* magazine? Forty thousand dollars for a month times twenty isn't enough for you?"

The comment elicited a smattering of uneasy snickers from the group and also from Dr. Ron.

"Forty thousand dollars a month is plenty for me," he said dismissively. "You all know that anything you say in this room will never leave this room. We've all signed confidentiality agreements. This is a safe place. Probably one of the safest places some of you have ever been in your lives. Now, again, who wants to go first?"

"I'll go," was the earnest response from a girl with a loop ring in her nose and a burning cigarette on her fingertips. "I'll do anything to get this over with. Okay," she said, folding her legs beneath her. "I have a little brother and sister. A dog named Sammy Davis Jr., three nannies—two of them are fucking dear old dad—and God knows who all those other people are who are in our house twenty-four hours a day. My mother has her first vodka and tonic at ten in the morning, and I'm usually too fucked up at night to know when she's had her last one. The only time I see my father is when I pay ten bucks like every other asshole to see one of his crappy movies. Is that enough? Can I go home now? I think you cured me. Dr. Ron, you're a genius."

Some in the group laughed, while others stared blankly out the window, writhed in their seats, or struggled to keep their hands from shaking.

Dr. Ron smiled and said, "No, I'm not a genius. No, I don't think you're cured, and no, you can't go home yet."

"Oh, please, Dr. Ron. I'll give you another forty-K," the girl said with smoke billowing from her mouth.

"That won't be necessary," he said patiently.

"How about a blow job? Everyone says I'm pretty good at it."

"I'll let you go home if you give me a blow job," said one of the twitching boys.

"I'm sure you're great at it, Rory," Dr. Ron interrupted, "but what I'd rather have from you is a little less sarcasm and a lot more honesty. Why don't you take a minute to think about what you'd like to get out of this session, and we'll come back to you? Ian, let's hear from you. Tell us about your family."

Ian was slightly overweight. His face was covered with freckles, and his flip-flop sandals clapped the terra-cotta tiles nervously when he spoke. "Me, uh," he stammered. "There's not much to tell. Uh, we live in D.C. My mom and dad are pretty cool. I'm home a lot by myself when my parents travel or when Congress is in session."

"Is that when you drink?" Dr. Ron asked.

"Yeah," the chubby adolescent said. "I, um, get bored alone in the house and, well, the place is full of liquor and, um . . ."

"How long have you been drinking?" asked Dr. Ron.

"Since I was about ten, I guess. I don't drink that much, though."

"Looked like you had a lot to drink when the paramedics rolled you out of your penthouse last month," said one of the other youths. "You looked like shit in that oxygen mask on the news, by the way."

"I saw that too," blurted another member. "Your father must have shit bricks when he saw the news. Guess he won't be running for president anytime soon."

There was more laughter from the group.

"How did your father react, Ian?" Dr. Ron asked.

"He, well, he was cool about it. . . . I mean, he was upset and everything. My mom freaked out, though. She said if I didn't come here, she was going to send me to military school."

Seven of the eight in the group told similar stories. Privilege, unlimited access to credit cards, minimal adult supervision, heroin overdoses, multiple sex partners, and numerous encounters with the law, all of which were neatly brushed under the rug by brooms made of money and power.

Dr. Ron looked in the direction of the one person in the room who had not spoken, and said, "I guess you're the last one, Jasmine. Why don't you tell us about your family?"

All the members looked sympathetically in her direction. Jasmine did not speak.

"I know it's difficult for you, Jasmine, but the only way you're going to make any progress is if you talk about it," Dr. Ron said gently. "Remember, you're among friends here. Everyone has a similar story to yours."

Jasmine looked in his direction. Her eyes were still puffy from weeks of crying. "Is that right?" she said coldly. "Who else in this group had their father killed in front of millions of people? Who else tried to commit suicide, only to have some son of a bitch doctor pump their stomach and bring them back to this place?"

The room was silent. The hands stopped shaking, sandals stopped clapping the tile, and bodies stopped squirming in the seats.

"We all realize that part of your story is unique, Jasmine," Dr. Ron said softly. "But the process of healing is the same for all of us, regardless of what we've been through."

"He's right, Jasmine," said the ringed-nosed Rory. "I know I sound like a bitch sometimes, but I have to admit it does help to talk about it. It's nice to get the shit out in the open so other people can smell it, too, and sometimes they can tell you it doesn't smell as bad as you thought it did."

All eyes were still on Jasmine. She looked to the floor at the checkerboard tile, then to the skull hanging over the fireplace. After silent moments she said in a whisper, "My mother hasn't called me since I've been here. She's too busy saving the fucking world. She didn't love my father. As a matter of fact, I think she hated him. The only time they weren't arguing was when the cameras were on."

"How was your relationship with her?" Dr. Ron asked.

Jasmine released a pained chuckle and replied, "I don't have a relationship with my mother. The only time she paid any attention to me was when she trotted me out in front of the church or the cameras. I'm a stage prop. Most of the time she doesn't even know or care if I'm in the house. I was raised by nannies, housekeepers, and security guards."

"How about your dad? What was that relationship like?" Dr. Ron asked, pressing on.

"I loved my father, and I know he loved me. But he was always so busy too. I remember when I was a kid, he used to take me with him everywhere. But . . ." Jasmine paused to clear her throat and stifle a tear and then continued. "But the church kept getting bigger and bigger. Then the television thing took off. After a while

I just got left behind. There would be weeks when I would only see him on Sunday morning in church."

"Jasmine," said the boy with the Rolex watch. "Your mom must care about you. She sent you here, didn't she?"

Again Jasmine chuckled. "She sent me here because she didn't want anyone to find out I tried to commit suicide. She didn't want it getting out that the daughter of the perfect Samantha Cleaveland swallowed a bottle of sleeping pills and had to have her stomach pumped. When she shoved me in the car with her driver, she told me to tell anyone who asked that I was staying with family friends in Malibu. She didn't even bother to ride to the airport with me."

It was 8:20 on Thursday evening. The board of trustees sat nervously around the table in the recently christened Pastor Hezekiah T. Cleaveland Memorial Conference Room. The special closed meeting had been convened at the request of Reverend Kenneth Davis. The only item on the agenda was the selection of the permanent pastor of New Testament Cathedral.

Two armed security guards in full uniform were posted outside the door, with strict orders not to allow anyone to enter the room.

Kenneth sat at the head of the table as the convener of the meeting. Hattie Williams's wooden cane rested on the conference table. Her purse, filled with Kleenex, peppermints, and a pocket Bible, rested on her lap. Reverend Percy Pryce sat to her left, three chairs down. Despite his best attempts at appearing calm and detached, the moisture on his upper lip betrayed the churning in his stomach.

Kenneth nervously checked his watch. Scarlett Shackelford sat stiffly three chairs to his right. The pills she had taken before leaving her home that evening had effectively erased the remains of her shattered emotions.

"I don't think she's coming," Kenneth said, checking his watch again. "It's already twenty past eight. We were supposed to start at eight o'clock."

"Maybe we should start without her," Percy said softly.

"She'll be here."

All heads turned to Hattie Williams.

"How do you know that?" Scarlett asked coldly.

"Because she's already in the building," Hattie said. "I can feel her."

Scarlett rolled her eyes and said impatiently, "I say we call the meeting to order right now and get this over with."

As she spoke, the security guard swung one half of the double doors open and Samantha appeared in the threshold. Kenneth and Percy leapt to their feet, while Hattie and Scarlett remained seated. Before entering, Samantha made eye contact with everyone at the table.

"Good evening, brothers and sisters," she said confidently. "I apologize for my lateness, but I was attending to church business. Please sit down, brothers."

Kenneth walked to the console and poured a glass of water. "Would anyone else like a glass before we get started?"

A chorus of "No" and "No thank you, Reverend," followed, and he made his way back to the head of the table.

Samantha sat four chairs to the right of Scarlett, which placed her farthest from the head of the table. She crossed her legs and leaned back in the high-backed leather chair.

Kenneth placed the glass of water beside a single sheet of paper, five pens, a stack of index cards, and a small tape recorder. After pressing the RECORD button, he said, "I now call this special meeting of the Board of Trustees of New Testament Cathedral to order at 8:25 p.m. on this day of our Lord and Savior Jesus Christ. Thank you all for coming at such short notice. As you know, we are convened to decide an issue of the utmost importance. The sole agenda item is who will serve as the permanent pastor of New Testament Cathedral."

Samantha raised her hand and was immediately acknowledged by Kenneth.

"I would like to know what prompted this sudden need to appoint a permanent pastor," Samantha said calmly. "It was my understanding that I would be given ample time to demonstrate to this body and the congregation at large that I am fully capable of serving in that position on a permanent basis. Is one month the trustees' idea of 'ample time'?"

No one spoke as Samantha waited patiently to see who would lead the charge. Finally, Percy leaned forward and clasped his hands together on the table. "Pastor Cleaveland," he said, clearing his throat. "This is in no way a reflection on how we feel about your leadership during this trying time. I think I speak for us all when I say under the circumstances we feel you have done an amazing job in holding the congregation together and keeping the vision of Pastor Cleaveland alive and on track."

"Then what is this all about?" Samantha asked. This was punctuated by a flick of her French-tipped nail on the table.

Kenneth stepped in. "It's just some of us feel we may have not fully factored in your feelings when we placed you in the position. We . . . I mean I feel we may have acted too hastily, and selfishly, I might add. You just lost your husband, the center of your life. Reverend Pryce is willing to step in and give you the time you and Jasmine need to—"

"Reverend Davis, I am very aware that I just lost my husband," Samantha interrupted, "but contrary to popular belief, he was not the center of my life. God is the center of my life, as I hope He is yours. I loved my husband, but I also love New Testament Cathedral. I helped found this church when it was in a storefront on Imperial Highway. Before any of you ever heard of the Cleavelands or the Cleavelands had ever heard of any of you." Samantha leaned into the table. Her tone became firmer, and the words came more rapidly as she spoke. "Hezekiah and I built this ministry from the ground up, and now you think just because he's gone, you can snatch it from under my feet."

"Now hold on, Reverend Cleaveland," Percy said, jumping in and gesturing with both hands. "No one is trying to snatch New Testament away from you. We all recognize the significant contributions you have made to this church, and we all appreciate everything you've done to make New Testament what it is today. We're only thinking about what's best for you. That's all. This is not an indictment against you."

"You *appreciate* my contributions," Samantha said snidely. "I don't need your appreciation, Percy. It means nothing to me. Let me ask you something. How many millions of dollars have you brought into the ministry this year? How many new members have you brought into the church?"

Percy stiffened his back and said, "This isn't about money. It's about doing what's right by you. Hezekiah would have wanted us to look out for you, and by placing you in this position prematurely, we have failed him. You can wait a few years, can't you? Give it time, Samantha. You need time to heal."

"Let's be honest, Percy. This isn't about me at all. It's about you, isn't it? Did your wife put you up to this?" Samantha said, looking him directly in the eye. "Because let's face it, you don't have the guts to come up with a ridiculous plan like this on your own. Hezekiah always said you were a small-minded, weak little man, and I see now that he was right."

"That's uncalled for, Samantha," Kenneth interjected. "Please, I know this is a difficult conversation for us to have, but let's at least try to be civil with each other."

"Civil? You expect me to be civil when you jackals have plotted behind my back to steal my church. Well, let me say to you all, if you think you're going to pat me on the head and brush me aside, you are sadly mistaken."

Kenneth cleared his throat and said gently, "I'm afraid we do have the authority, Samantha. According to church bylaws section IIA, it is the responsibility of this body to select the pastor."

Kenneth reached for the single piece of paper in front of him and read it aloud. "A pastor shall be chosen and called whenever a vacancy occurs. A Pastor's Selection Committee shall be appointed by the church—that's us—to seek out a suitable pastor. The pastor's election shall take place at a meeting called for that purpose. That's this meeting. The pastor—for the time being, that's you, Samantha—shall be an ex officio member of all church standing committees, except the Pastor's Selection Committee."

Kenneth returned the paper to the table and said, "Because you are the interim pastor of New Testament Cathedral at the time this agenda item will be called to a vote, you will, unfortunately, not be allowed to vote on this matter."

"May I speak?" Scarlett said loudly.

Kenneth leaned back, relieved that someone else had entered the fray. "Please, Sister Shackelford, go ahead. You have the floor."

Scarlett spun her chair to face Samantha and said, "I'm not basing my vote on you or your feelings. I actually don't think you need time to heal. Do you know why? Because I think you're relieved that he's gone."

"Sister Shackelford!" Kenneth shouted.

"Let me finish," Scarlett said deliberately. "My decision is based on the fact that I don't think you are fit to be pastor. You are an evil woman who has demonstrated over the years that you are more than willing to destroy anyone and anything that stands between you and whatever it is you want at the time. New Testament Cathedral deserves better than that. God deserves better, and I know I deserve better. I'm ready to call this to a vote."

With her final words Scarlett spun her chair back to its original position. Samantha sat stunned and speechless.

Kenneth held his breath, waiting for Samantha to respond, but she remained silent. Kenneth then leaned forward and said, "We haven't heard from everyone. Mother Williams, do you have anything to add before we call for a vote?"

Hattie remembered the vision she saw in her garden of Samantha standing in the pulpit with thousands of lost souls standing at her feet, crying and raising their hands to the heavens. She clutched the handle of her cane and simply said, "I have nothing to add. I'm ready for the vote."

"Very well then," Kenneth said, reaching for the index cards and pens. "Please write your choice for pastor of New Testament Cathedral on these cards. Fold your card in half and pass it back to me when you're ready."

"May I ask a question before we vote?" Samantha said calmly.

"The discussion is over," Scarlett said. "Let's vote please."

"Hold on, Scarlett. Let her speak. Go ahead, Samantha. You have the floor," Kenneth said, leaning back in his chair.

Samantha looked to Percy and said, "Reverend Pryce?"

"Yes?" he said suspiciously.

"Do you know someone named Lance Savage?"

Kenneth jerked forward in his chair and lunged toward the tape recorder. He quickly pressed the STOP button and, in doing so, knocked over his glass of water.

"Oh God, I'm sorry," he blurted out. Water splattered down the center of the table, soaking the single white paper and forming a puddle around the tape recorder. Kenneth jumped from his seat and ran to the console for the cloth napkins. When he returned, the water had begun to drip onto his chair. Kenneth dabbed and blotted the table, the chair, and around the base of the tape recorder until much of the spill had been absorbed.

Samantha watched him curiously and noted the unexpected reaction to the name Lance Savage.

"I'm so sorry, everyone," Kenneth said with a shaky voice. "I'm so sorry. I didn't mean to do it. It was an accident. I'm . . . I'm sorry."

Percy retrieved more napkins from the console and wiped the remaining drops of water while coolly saying, "It's all right, Reverend Davis. Calm down. It was just a little accident. Calm down."

Kenneth sank back into the damp leather chair and said through labored breaths, "Samantha, I don't see what that has to do with the matter on the table."

Samantha returned her gaze to Percy. "Answer my question, Reverend Pryce. Do you know Lance Savage?"

Percy looked helplessly to Kenneth and then back to Samantha and said, "No . . . I don't believe I know anyone by that name."

"From Kenneth's reaction I think you do."

"You're stalling, Samantha. What does this have to do with anything?" Scarlett said impatiently.

"To be perfectly honest, Scarlett, I'm not sure. But I'm curious. You see, my assistant gives me a monthly report on the church telephone records. I like to know if anyone is making any un-authorized calls. We had a problem with that a few years ago. You remember that, don't you, Mother Williams? Anyway, in doing so," Samantha continued methodically, "she noticed two calls were made to a Lance Savage."

Samantha looked around the room and said, "Did I forget to mention Mr. Savage was the *Los Angeles Chronicle* reporter who was found murdered in his home on the canals in Venice."

She then looked back to Percy and said, "The calls were made from your extension to his cell phone and home. And, ironically, they were made on the very same day that he was murdered. Quite a coincidence, don't you think? I've been meaning to ask you why you called him, but I've been so busy burying my husband and running the church."

There was silence in the room. All eyes were now on Percy. Kenneth sat stiff in his seat. The remnants of the spilled water soaked the seat of his pants. Beads of sweat formed on his brow, and his heart pounded in his chest.

"Looks like you might not remember right now. That's okay, though, because you see, if I'm not going to be pastor any longer, I'll have plenty of time on my hands to solve little mysteries like this." Samantha leaned back in her chair and said with a smile, "All righty then, Reverend Davis, I think I have my answer. Now, let's get on with that vote."

Kenneth's hand shook as he passed the cards and pens to Hattie, Scarlett, and Percy. He kept one for himself. He used a dry napkin to wipe the sweat from his brow, only to have it be replaced by even more.

Scarlett was the first to hand back her folded card. Hattie was next. Percy's hand rested on the table, with the tip of the pen suspended only centimeters above the card. Scarlett, Hattie, and Samantha watched him as the pen finally began to glide along the surface of the card. He stopped and started several times before he finished. He then opened his fingers slightly, and the pen dropped to the table with a thud that echoed off the walls of the conference room.

Percy stared at the card without moving. All he could think of was his wife's final words as he left their condo for the meeting. "Call me as soon as it's over," she'd said, brushing imaginary lint from his lapel at the door. "And, Percy," she'd added, "don't screw this up."

Samantha leaned toward the table and said, "Fold your card, Reverend Pryce, and hand it back to Reverend Davis."

Kenneth's card was soggy from the droplets of water that remained on the table in front of him. He was the last to fold his card and add it to the stack of four.

"Thank you, everyone," Kenneth said nervously. "Here we go."

"Wait a minute, Reverend Davis," Samantha said calmly.

"Yes, Pastor Cleaveland?" Kenneth said humbly.

"I think it might be a good idea if you turned the recorder back on, for the record."

"Of course . . . yes, of course. I'm sorry. I forgot."

"No need to apologize, again," Samantha said.

Kenneth reached forward and pressed the RECORD button. "Okay, where was I?"

Kenneth opened the first card and read out the name written on it. "Samantha Cleaveland."

He opened the second card and said, "Samantha Cleaveland."

Scarlett looked bewildered and betrayed. The numbing effects of the medication began to wear off rapidly with the reading of each card.

Kenneth unfolded the third card and let out a gush of air. "Percy Pryce," he said with a hint of disappointment.

The last card seemed to levitate above the table in front of him. He reached for it, hesitated halfway, and then picked it up. He looked around the room at each person. Scarlett looked at him with a longing glare. Hattie's eyes were closed. She still clutched the head of her cane. Percy's eyes were closed, as well.

Samantha looked at him with the cold, clenched eyes of a woman who was about to lose everything.

Kenneth opened the final card and read it. "Samantha Cleaveland," he said, dropping the card to the table. He then closed his eyes and released a puff of air. "Let the record show that Samantha Cleaveland is as of this day the permanent pastor of New Testament Cathedral. Congratulations, Pastor Cleaveland." Kenneth slapped the table with his open palm and said, "This meeting is adjourned."

Samantha stood immediately and walked over to Kenneth. She reached over his shoulder and pressed the EJECT button on the tape recorder, and the little cassette popped up.

"I'll take this," she said. Without making eye contact with anyone there, Samantha spun on her heels and left the room.

The others sat in stunned silence, and then one by one they slowly exited the conference room. The last person to leave was Percy, who slowly turned the lights off.

43

Cynthia paced the floor of the condominium as she waited nervously for the call from Percy. A bottle of champagne chilling in a bucket of ice stood next to two glasses and a tin of caviar. In the bedroom she had placed twenty candles around the room and had laid an ivory-white negligee suggestively on the center of the satin-covered bed. It was already a quarter past ten at night, and she still hadn't received the call.

As she walked the length of the room, she gripped her cell phone in one hand and checked periodically to ensure the volume was turned up and the battery was fully charged.

With every step she took, she muttered a prayer. "Please don't let him fuck this up for me," and, "If you give me this, I promise I'll never do anything wrong again for the rest of my life."

Midway through one such prayer, Cynthia heard keys turn in the front door. Percy entered and gently closed the door behind him. He placed his keys on a table in the foyer and walked softly across the black-veined marble floor. Cynthia appeared beneath the arch that led to the living room before he could reach the hall to the bedrooms.

He could smell the perfume, a hint of sulfur, and burning candles in the air. He saw the chilled champagne over her shoulder.

"Why didn't you call?" Cynthia said, rushing to him and wrapping her arms around his barrel chest. "I've been going crazy waiting to hear from you. So what happened? Tell me everything."

Percy did not return her embrace. He changed his course and walked past her to the living room. Cynthia knew it was not a good sign that he had not spoken.

"Percy," she called behind him. "What happened?" This time she spoke more forcefully. "Are you the pastor? How did Samantha take it? She must be devastated. I'll have to call her tomorrow and reassure her we won't abandon her in her time of need."

Percy stood with his back to her, looking out the window. The city lights below looked to him like disapproving eyes all peering in his direction.

"You're scaring me Percy," Cynthia said, walking behind him. "Please tell me you are the pastor." She gripped his shoulder and spun him around. "You are the new pastor, aren't you?"

His silence and inability to make eye contact provided her with the answer. Blood rushed to her head, and time seemed to stand still. For a brief moment she thought she would faint. She clutched the arm of the sofa and braced herself. Her breathing became shallow, and the room blurred.

"I don't fucking believe this," she said in a pant. "Oh my God, I don't believe this."

"It's for the best, honey," Percy said calmly, holding her by the shoulders. "I didn't really want to be pastor. I'd rather spend more time with you. Honey . . . Cynthia, are you all right? Take a deep breath, honey. You look like you're going to pass out."

Cynthia straightened her back and pushed his hands from her shoulders. "Take your fucking hands off me," she shouted. "You didn't have to do a fucking thing. I set it all up for you. All you had to do was vote for yourself. Did you at least vote for yourself?"

Percy turned back to the window and did not respond.

"Oh my God," she said slowly. "You mean to tell me, you didn't even have the goddamned sense to vote for yourself? You stupid piece of shit! You fucking moron. You can't do anything right."

With her last words Cynthia reached for the bucket of ice and champagne and shoved it at the back of Percy's head. The metal made a loud clank when it connected with his skull, sending the bottle crashing into the window and spewing ice cubes around the room. This was followed in rapid succession by the chair she threw with such force that it shattered the window and plummeted twenty stories to the ground below. The cold of the city and the sounds of the night rushed in through the gaping hole.

Percy dropped to his knees from the blow and said, "Cynthia, what are you doing? Get a hold of yourself. It's not the end of the world."

Cynthia dropped the full weight of her body onto his back and began pounding his head with her fists. "You worthless piece of shit!" she shouted as she delivered blow after blow to his head and face. "I'm going to throw your useless ass out the motherfucking window."

Percy shielded his head from the blows. "Cynthia, stop," he shouted through the blood now dripping from his face and mouth. "Move away from the window. You're going to kill us both."

"I want to fall out. I want us both to fall out," she said, lowering her bloodstained fists again and again to his face. Her hair was tossed back and forth from each blow leveled with the full weight of her body. "I want us both to fall out the fucking window!"

Cynthia pushed the cowering man on his back. She then grabbed one of his ankles and began dragging him toward the gaping hole in the glass. "I'm going to throw your useless ass out the fucking window," she yelled through labored breaths. "You are worthless to me!"

"Stop, Cynthia. You're going to kill us," Percy shouted. He twisted and turned on the carpet, leaving a trail of blood as the two moved closer and closer to the window. "Stop, Cynthia, That's enough. You're going to kill us both!"

Percy grabbed the leg of an end table next to the sofa, but she pulled him harder. The table soon was on the same course as his sliding body. The lamp, the telephone, and the vase filled with flowers on the table came crashing to the floor.

Percy began to kick Cynthia with his free foot as they neared the hole in the wall. The first blow landed on her chest. The heel of his leather shoe struck the center of her howling, contorted face with the second kick. She continued to drag him, undaunted by the now vicious counterattack. He kicked her again and again, each blow harder than the one before.

The last jolt of his foot was delivered with such power that it caused Cynthia to lose her grip on his ankle and tumble backward. She landed with a crashing thud on the floor, with her head and shoulders hanging out the window and into the cold, dark night. Shards of glass scraped against her back as she squirmed on the floor, still screaming obscenities.

Percy rolled to his knees and quickly grabbed her waist, which was now at the edge of the building.

"Let me go!" she screamed, clawing at his bloody face. "I want to die. Let me go!"

Percy pulled the flailing woman away from the window with his last ounce of strength. When he reached a safe distance, he sat on the floor next to her and quickly wrapped his arms around her chest like a vise. "Calm down, Cynthia," he whispered repeatedly into her ear. "It's all right, honey."

Cynthia continued to squirm and wiggle to break free from his powerful grip and return to the window.

"It's all right, honey," he continued to say calmly. "Take a deep breath and calm down."

As she grew weaker, her resistance waned. The screams and rants gradually turned into wrenching whimpers and moans. "I want to die," she continued to cry. "Let me go. I hate you. Let me die."

"No, you don't, honey," Percy repeated over and over. "I know you're disappointed, but you don't want to die. You have everything to live for."

"I just want to die," were the last words Cynthia whimper before her twitching body fell limp in his arms on the living-room floor.

The sky was clear and blue above the translucent gray layer of smog that hung over the city. Danny lay by the infinity pool in the hot Los Angeles afternoon sun. Parker was curled in a furry ball near the water's edge. The yard was a page from *Architectural Digest*. Towering pine trees lined the sides, leaving the rear property line unobstructed to display the spectacular view of downtown. Los Angeles Jacuzzi at the end of the pool gurgled like a volcano threatening to erupt. From the vantage point of Gideon's home in the Hollywood Hills Danny could almost see the streets where he handed out condoms, socks, and clean needles to the homeless.

Wicker furniture and freestanding stone and artificially aged copper fireplaces were arranged throughout the wooded, grounds, creating numerous cozy nooks for intimate conversations, alfresco dining, or dancing the night away under the stars.

"Come and stay with me for a few days," Gideon had said the night they held hands on Danny's couch. "You shouldn't be alone right now. You can sleep in one of the guest rooms. I promise I won't try anything. Parker can come, too, to keep me in line."

Exhausted from grief and weak from loneliness, Danny had cautiously accepted the invitation. Although his visit from Kay Braisden had given him some respite from his isolation, she was able to stay with him for only three days before she had to return home to D.C. Danny had dreaded the thought of crying alone in his apartment another night.

Gideon had been the perfect host since Danny arrived two days earlier. The two men would pop popcorn and watch movies in his media room when Gideon wasn't working in his home office. They ordered takeout from Gideon's favorite little Chinese restaurant on Sunset Boulevard and sat in the middle of the living-room floor, eating shrimp egg foo yong and moo goo gai pan with cheap wooden chopsticks while sharing secrets, some of which they hadn't even told themselves.

"I haven't had sex in almost two years," went one such conversation. "It's just too risky. I'm afraid if I'm . . ." Gideon paused and stirred chow mein in a white box with his chopsticks before he continued. "I'm afraid if I'm intimate with someone, he'll go straight to the *Enquirer* and tell them everything, from how big my dick is to how I stutter like Porky Pig when I cum." Gideon raised his hands and stammered, "Tha-tha-tha-that's all folks."

Danny laughed and said, "You must be very lonely."

"You get used to it. I have my work. I have my friends, and I have my right hand," Gideon said, laughing. "But, yeah, I do get lonely sometimes. How about you? What was your life like before you met Hezekiah?"

"Strangely enough, it was very much like yours, except without the house in the Hills, the Mercedes, or my own television show," Danny said with a smile. "Before I met Hezekiah, I was almost a recluse. I had a small circle of friends and my work. That was it. I've always had a hard time with men. They were either only after quick sex, or they wanted to parade me in front of their friends like a mannequin."

"I can understand that. You are quite beautiful, Danny."

"Thank you, but I don't see myself that way."

"How do you see yourself?"

"To be honest, I didn't really see myself until I met Hezekiah. When we were together, every time I looked in his eyes, I swear I could see into my own soul. I could see how empty my life was. I could see how afraid I was. But I also saw how loving I could be. I saw how kind and compassionate I could be. But regardless of what I saw, he made me feel like it was okay. There was nothing about me that shocked or repulsed him. He made me feel like there was absolutely nothing about me that could make him stop loving me. He was an amazing man."

"You were very lucky to have him in your life, even for such a short time."

Danny looked away. "I don't feel very lucky right now. Sometimes I think I would have been better off if I'd never met him. At least I wouldn't be going through this hell."

"Do you believe in fate, Danny?"

"I guess. What do you mean?"

"I believe everything in life happens for a reason," Gideon said, looking directly at Danny. He could see his reflection in his eyes. "There are no coincidences, and wherever we find ourselves in our life, that is exactly where we were supposed to be at that time. There are no mistakes in the universe. Everything is perfect and as it should be."

Danny stretched his bare legs on the chaise lounge by the pool as he remembered the words Gideon had said to him the night before. He wore a pair of dark blue Speedos and sunglasses. The heat had caused his skin to shimmer in the afternoon sun. Dishes could be heard clanking and water running in the kitchen behind him. Danny stood and stretched his long limbs again, then made his way to the open French doors that led directly into the kitchen.

There he found Gideon, barefoot and wearing a yellow T-shirt and short khakis, standing at a green granite island, slicing peaches, a mango, and a cantaloupe. The kitchen was a stainless-steel shrine to food. A ten-burner Wolf range was against the wall; opposite it was a Sub-Zero refrigerator with double glass doors. The room was a series of red oak cabinets from the floor to the ceiling. Silver and black appliances and gadgets occupied almost every counter, and a flat-screen television hung from the ceiling. Pristine copper pots swung from a rack above the island where Gideon stood. "I thought you might like a snack before dinner," Gideon said, slicing into a melon. "Are you thirsty? There's Pellegrino, lemonade, beer, and juice in the fridge. Help yourself."

"Gideon, why are you doing this? Shouldn't you be interviewing some serial killer instead of making me a fruit salad?"

Gideon laughed and said, "I'm going in at four o'clock. I have to interview Tyler Perry. I'd rather hang around here with you, but hey, somebody's got to do it. I see the Speedo fits you."

"Yeah, just barely," Danny said, adjusting the tight briefs. "I didn't know anybody still owned these things."

"They were the only swim trunks I had that I thought would fit you," Gideon said and quickly looked away.

Danny laughed and replied, "Are you sure? I think you just wanted to see how I looked in them."

Danny would have seen him blush were it not for Gideon's amber skin.

"Nothing could be further from the truth," Gideon said with a smile. "But I do have to admit you look amazing in them."

"Gideon, you've been so kind to me and Parker these last two days, but I probably should be thinking about going home. I've been in your way too long already."

Gideon froze midcut but didn't look at Danny. "Don't be ridiculous," he said, resuming the slice. "You haven't been in my way at all. I've loved having you guys here. Besides, I think Parker's made friends with one of the raccoons. You wouldn't want to break them up."

"I'll promise to bring him back soon to visit."

Gideon began to arrange the sliced fruit on a tray. "I wish you would reconsider. I . . ." Gideon stopped and turned to face Danny. "I've kind of gotten used to you being here. The place isn't so lonely with you around."

Danny walked next to him at the island and said, "I know what you mean. For the first time since the day Hezekiah . . . since the day Hezekiah died, I've been able to sleep through the night."

"Then don't go," Gideon said, reaching for Danny's moist shoulder. "Stay until you know for sure that you're ready."

Danny leaned in and rested his head on Gideon's chest, and Gideon embraced him tenderly. The two stood in silence and luxuriated in their comforting, long embrace. After moments, Danny raised his head and looked into Gideon's eyes. Gideon slowly moved forward and pressed his lips to Danny's.

"I'm in love with you, Danny St. John," Gideon said through the passionate kiss. "Don't leave me. I need you."

Danny could feel Gideon's erection pressing through his khaki shorts as his own erection stretched the Speedo to its limit. Gideon slowly slipped his hand under the tight waistband and massaged him gently. Danny lifted Gideon's T-shirt over his head and kissed circles on his bare chest. He could feel Gideon's heart pound with each kiss. He lifted Gideon's hand to his mouth and kissed his palm and fingers. He could taste the nectar of the sweet fruit. With a flick of his finger Danny unbuttoned Gideon's shorts and slowly pulled the zipper, which allowed them to drop silently to the granite floor, forming a pool of fabric around his ankles.

The two made love for the first time on the cool granite floor in the house in the Hollywood Hills.

It was Saturday night at 11:55. Samantha drove her white Bentley sports coupe on Western Avenue. Even at that hour the street was filled with people going to or leaving their favorite nightclub, late-night restaurant, or theater. The duffel bag containing the two million dollars sat on the passenger seat.

While waiting for the light at Sunset Boulevard and Western, she looked in the rearview mirror to ensure David Shackelford was following closely behind. He had the gun in his pocket and passion in his heart. Samantha prayed he would use them both just as she had planned. As she continued driving, the gritty street gradually transitioned from run-down storefronts, hamburger joints, bars, and dollar discount stores to a tree-lined residential neighborhood of two-story houses with Spanish tiled roofs and circular driveways. Samantha turned left at the first entrance to the park. A canopy of trees covered the road and blocked the ambient light. Vintage streetlamps with glass globes provided the only illumination on the road.

When David veered onto the road, he turned off his headlights and slowed down to increase the distance between them. Samantha could see him only when he rolled under one of the few dim streetlamps lining the road. His car would disappear seconds after he passed each lamp.

There were no other cars on the dark road. Dense layers of trees lined each side as she drove deeper into the empty park. She could see traces of buildings in the dark as she ascended a hill, but couldn't tell if they were houses or public restrooms. Suddenly the entrance to the parking lot appeared on her left. She made a cautious turn, and the incline increased dramatically. When she reached the top, Samantha saw the parking lot sprawled out under the beams of her headlights. It was empty. Samantha immediately noted that there was only one way into the parking lot and only one way out of the large space. It was walled on one side by the sheer face of a wooded hill, and on another a steep cliff dropped down to the main road below. She parked the car so that it was facing the cliff and turned off the ignition and the lights. She could see only a few feet on either side, in the front and the rear.

David drove a safe distance past the parking lot entrance on the main road below and parked. His heart was pounding hard against the gun in his breast pocket. His hands were moist from perspiration. The darkness seemed to close in on him like the walls of a coffin. His breathing became shallow as he braced himself to exit the car.

David placed his hand on the door handle, then paused. "You can do this, David," he said out loud. "Samantha needs you. Don't let her down." The longer he waited, the shallower his breaths became and the more fiercely his heart pounded against the gun in his pocket. David reached over and frantically fumbled at the latch to the glove compartment. From it he pulled a half-empty bottle of distilled courage. He took one long gulp and then followed it with two more.

Samantha looked at her watch. It was now 12:08. "Come on," she said softly, tapping the steering wheel. "Where are you?"

Seconds later she heard a gentle tap on the car window. She looked to her left and saw the torso and hands of a man wearing a dark coat and standing at the window. The figure motioned for her to roll down the window.

"Hello, Samantha," the man said, bending down to the open window. "It's nice to finally meet you. I'm Danny St. John."

Samantha looked him in the eye and said, "I should have guessed. So you're the man that was sleeping with my husband."

"Yes. I'm also the man who loved your husband. Is that the money?" he asked, pointing past her to the bag on the passenger seat. "May I have it please?"

Samantha tried to look around Danny for David, but his shoulders were too broad. *Come on, David. Where are you?* she thought as she slowly reached for the bag.

"They don't come much lower than you, do they, Danny?" she said, stalling for more time. "Sleeping with a married man, then blackmailing his widow."

Danny laughed out loud. "This coming from a woman who killed her husband. You're in no position to judge me. Now, give me the money, and you'll never hear from me again."

Danny saw blackmail as his only way out. The only way he could move beyond her dangerous reach. *If she's evil enough to kill her husband, she's certainly evil enough to kill me,* he had reasoned in the grief-stricken days that followed Hezekiah's death. *Get the money and disappear. Leave the country. Move to a place where she will never find me.* He'd concluded that leaving Los Angeles was the only way he would be free from the paralyzing fear that every stranger he saw on the street was potentially a deadly messenger sent to him by Samantha Cleaveland. He also needed so desperately to be away from every inch of the city that reminded him of Hezekiah.

The two looked intently at each other and simultaneously understood why Hezekiah had fallen in love with the other. They saw pure, raw passion burning in each other's eyes. Two people who would stop at nothing to get what they wanted, whether it be love or money. In the dark of the night there was no need for pretense or defense. They spoke as if they were looking into a mirror.

"Was this your plan all along?" Samantha asked, looking in his eyes. "Was it always about the money?"

"This might be difficult for someone like you to understand, but it was never about money," Danny said. "I loved Hezekiah. Did you ever love him?"

"At one time I did," Samantha responded with a slight nod of concession.

"Then why did you kill him?"

Samantha paused but at that moment saw no need for caution. "It's the law of the universe, Danny. In order to get something you want, you have to give up something you love."

"Then I guess that law worked well for you."

When Danny said the last word, he felt a hand on his shoulder. He turned around quickly and found himself standing nose to nose with David.

Samantha shouted out loud, "He's got a gun, David. Shoot him! Shoot him!"

David immediately pushed Danny into the side of the car. The two men wrestled to the ground and rolled on the pavement, with arms and legs flailing in every direction. Samantha unlocked the car door, jumped out and screamed over the jumble of flesh and cloth, "Shoot him, David. He tried to kill me. Shoot him now!"

Suddenly a shot rang out, and the bodies went limp on the pavement. Samantha could see the gun in one of the hands lying flat on the ground. She rushed to the heap and snatched the gun away, took three steps backward, all while aiming the gun with both hands at the still pile of flesh. A chest was heaving, but she couldn't tell if it was David or Danny.

"David," she said, still pointing the warm gun at the heap. "David, are you okay?"

Suddenly the bodies moved, and David struggled from beneath Danny.

"Get up, David," Samantha said, directing the gun to the lone figure on the ground. "Is he dead?"

"I think so," David panted. "He's not breathing."

"Good."

David stopped breathing and looked at Samantha. "What are you talking about? I just killed a man."

"It was self-defense. If you hadn't been here, he would have killed me."

David reached into his pocket for his cell phone and began to dial 911.

Samantha grabbed his arm and said, "What are you doing?"

"I'm calling the police," he yelled. "We just killed a man. I'm calling the police."

"David, honey, wait a minute," she said. "Let me at least check to see if he's dead. He may still be alive."

Samantha walked cautiously to Danny's still body. She knelt down and first checked his coat pockets and then the pockets of his pants. She stood up and faced David and said, "He doesn't have a gun."

"What?" David screamed.

"You just killed an unarmed man."

"Oh, shit!" David said. "Oh, shit! Oh God, Samantha, you said he had a gun," he said, holding his hands against the sides of his head. "You said he was going to kill you."

"It looked like he had a gun in his pocket. I thought he had a gun," Samantha said curtly.

David began to pace back and forth in the parking lot, with his arms waving in front of Danny's lifeless body. "What have I done?" he said. "Look what you made me do!"

Samantha threw the gun into her open car window and grabbed David by his shoulders. "David, stop," she said, trying to calm the frantic man. "Listen to me, David. We have to leave. No one knows we were here. We need to just leave now and never speak of this to anyone. Do you understand me?" she asked firmly.

"Leave?" he muttered. "Just leave him there? Are you sure?"

"Yes, I'm sure. Everything will be fine. I want you to go home to Scarlett and not say a word about this to anyone. Ever! Do you understand me?" she said, shaking his shoulders. "Someone will find him in the morning. They'll never be able to link any of this to either you or me as long as we both agree that it never happened. Okay? Do you agree?"

"I . . . I agree," David sputtered. "Are you sure no one will find out?"

"I'm sure. Now, go to your car and wait for me at the bottom of the hill. I'll follow you as far as Wilshire Boulevard. Then I want you to drive straight home and put this out of you mind. Do you understand?"

"I understand," he said, shaking.

"And make sure you are at church tomorrow," Samantha continued. "I want to see you there with Scarlett on one side and Natalie on the other. We have to act like this never happened. Do you understand?"

"Yes," he said, shaking harder.

"Good. Everything is going to be fine, David. I'll call you in the morning to check on you."

David took one look at Danny lying face down on the pavement and ran sporadically to the edge of the parking lot, looking over his shoulder at Samantha and Danny. When he reached the edge, he took one step over the ledge and slipped in the loose dirt. His heavy body tumbled headfirst and rolled until he hit the road below with a thud. He scrambled across the dark road, covered in dirt and spitting dust. Once inside his car he reached into the glove compartment again and retrieved the almost empty bottle and guzzled the remainder of its contents.

Samantha did nothing as she watched the shadow of David's hulking body tumble down the hill. When she heard the thud of his body hitting the pavement below, she moved quickly to Danny and removed his watch. She recognized the dial of the Rolex immediately and said, "I assume Hezekiah gave this to you, so technically it belongs to me." She then removed his wallet and said, "Good-bye, Danny St. John. I'm glad we finally met."

In the car Samantha unzipped the leather duffel bag, revealing the jumble of cash. She placed the gun, the watch, and the wallet inside the bag and shoved it to the floor of the car.

Once on the road, Samantha followed David down the hill until they each vanished into the night as silently as they had come.

Samantha opened the door to her closet. It was three o'clock on Sunday morning. Etta was asleep in the maids' quarters. The house resembled a mausoleum with its dark, cavernous halls and lifeless rooms. Little green lights blinked on security devices throughout the house, and red beams guarded the most valued treasures.

When she opened the door, lights around a floor-to-ceiling mirror that stretched the length of the wall in the closet turned on automatically and flooded the elaborate windowless room with what appeared to be natural sunlight. Samantha stood in the threshold and admired the items that were so dear to her heart. Garments and shoes that had not been worn in years and would probably never be worn again were as admired as those she had just worn the day before. Some held sentimental value, while others were kept for their sheer beauty and exquisite craftsmanship.

Samantha normally took two hours early on Sunday morning to ready herself for church. But this was going to be another special Sunday. She needed more time to assemble the perfect image for her first Sunday as the permanent pastor of New Testament Cathedral. Samantha wanted to look her most radiant, while conveying an air of humility, with a backdrop of power. Her heels had to be just the right height. Her jewelry had to sparkle but not shine.

She had to select a look that would titillate the husbands but would not incense the wives.

Samantha grudgingly decided that because Hezekiah had been dead only a few weeks, she had to, for at least one more Sunday, wear black. After a lengthy search of the black dress section, Samantha selected.

She decided on Givenchy suit. Its color, shape, and easy movement suited her purposes well. The shoes she selected were not the pair purchased for the suit. Instead, she chose a pair with a slightly higher heel. The accessories were the easy part; the dress would tolerate only diamonds, a single-strand bracelet, and six-carat studs for her ears.

Samantha stood in front of the mirror to examine her final choice and was pleased. For a brief second the image of Danny's lifeless body flashed before her. "Give Hezekiah a kiss for me," she said out loud while surveying her figure from every angle.

***

It was now 7:45 on Sunday morning at New Testament Cathedral. The death of Hezekiah could still be felt in the air and seen on the faces of members as they filed down the aisles and into the pews. The entire length of the three steps that led up to the pulpit was covered from top to bottom with flowers left by thousands each Sunday. At the end of each Sunday the maintenance crew would remove the flowers, and the next Sunday there would be even more.

The pipe organ churned an upbeat hymn in an effort to elevate the mood as members took their seat. An eight-foot portrait of a smiling Hezekiah T. Cleaveland, draped with black cloth, hanging above the choir stand immediately reminded worshippers that a murder had taken place only a few Sundays earlier.

Cameras captured, for the two jumbo screens, the parade of colorful hats, mothers settling small children into the pews, and men escorting their wives down the aisles. The continuing saga of grief was felt not only in the sanctuary. People across America watched and cried along with them from the comfort and safety of their homes.

"Where are you, David?" Samantha asked, clutching her cell phone to her ear in the window of her office.

"I'm here, parking the car."

"Are Scarlett and Natalie with you?"

"Yeah, I dropped them at the entrance. She's getting our seats before it gets too crowded."

"Perfect. Did you say anything to her last night?"

"What was I going to say? Honey, guess what Samantha and I did last night?"

"Good, and make sure you keep it that way. Did she ask why you were out so late?"

"No. She was just surprised and relieved I came home. Stop asking me all these fucking questions," he snapped. "I told you I wasn't going to say anything, and I didn't. When am I going to see you? I want to hold you in my arms. I need to make love to you again. I love you, Samantha."

"Soon. Just be patient," Samantha said calmly. "David?" she continued.

"What?"

"You and I are in this together. Do not cross me, because as you now know, I can be a very dangerous woman."

When the clock struck eight, the side doors to the left and right of the pulpit swung open and the choir entered from both sides into the stand.

"We are on our way. We're on our journey home," the choir sang as they marched. "We are on our way. We're on our journey home."

The stage backdrop was an electric blue wall of light that periodically changed hues to match the desired mood of each moment during the service. The walls of the sanctuary pulsated from the brass instruments, drums, violins, guitars, organs, and pianos playing the rhythmic tune. Scenes on the two twenty-foot-high Jumbotron screens alternated rapidly between panoramic shots of the congregation standing, clapping, and singing and the two-hundred-member choir and orchestra.

Another door at the foot of the pulpit opened. All heads in the room turned to the door. After a dramatic pause, Samantha Cleaveland appeared in the threshold. The cameras rushed to catch every second of her entrance. As befitting a widow still in mourning, she wore the two-piece black Givenchy suit, which traced with precision each curve, bend, and twist of her hourglass figure. A sleek skirt sloped around her full hips down to the lips of a tulip shaped hemline just above her knees. The jacket was a cascade of satiny fabric, cinched at the waist and blossoming around her hips. The heels on her one-of-a-kind black Chanel sling-back pumps were the exact height necessary to mold her legs into the perfect female form.

Samantha entered the sanctuary with the gait of a woman straddling the line between courage and grief. Applause exploded throughout the sanctuary when the people saw her, and drowned out the singing of the choir. Samantha flashed her smile and waved triumphantly to the crowd. The diamond bracelet she wore twinkled like a cluster of stars in the midnight sky.

The image of Samantha Cleaveland standing at the front row, smiling and still waving to the crowd, filled the Jumbotron screens. The caption below read, "Reverend Dr. Samantha Cleaveland— Pastor and Founder, New Testament Cathedral." She repositioned her body with each wave to ensure everyone in the room got a complete view.

David Shackelford walked swiftly down the aisle and slid sideways into a pew two rows from the front. He stepped over shoes and purses until he reached Scarlett and Natalie. David scooped up the little girl and sat her in his lap and kissed Scarlett on her cold cheek.

Scarlett looked up at the screen filled with a twenty-foot Samantha Cleaveland. *God, what have we done?* she thought. *As usual, Samantha got everything she wanted, but at least she didn't get my husband.* Scarlett reached over and covered David's hand with hers. She found it hard to believe he was sitting next to her. *Thank God he didn't leave me for that bitch.*

When the applause subsided and the audience returned to their seats, the music gradually transitioned to a melodic and reverent tone. A soprano began to sing an operatic tune, and the audience followed her word for word. The melody from the crowd rolled from the front of the church to the top row of the sanctuary and filled the room as congregants softly sang in unison and looked upward to heaven.

The cameras followed Samantha as she walked along a path in the sea of flowers and up the steps to the center of the stage. Again, the audience leapt to their feet, and thunderous applause erupted. Samantha stood at the mic center stage, raised her hands in victory, and blew a series of kisses to the crowd.

"I love you, too, New Testament Cathedral family," she declared, her amplified voice rising above the cheers and applause. "I love you too." She beamed.

The outpouring of love and adoration went on for five minutes, until Samantha finally raised her hands and tamed the crowd into submission.

Cynthia Pryce sat on the front row with her husband, Percy. Dark oval sunglasses and a thick mask of Dermablend covered the black eye and the scars inflicted by the heel of Percy's shoe. A wide-brimmed hat and a collar that reached her chin provided ample cover for the bruises on her neck and back. Under the glasses her left eye twitched as she watched Samantha on the stage.

Percy reached for her shaking hand, but she pushed him away. "Don't touch me," she said under her breath. "That should be you up there, not that bitch."

"Good morning, New Testament Cathedral!" Samantha said to the rapt crowd. "Does anybody here know that God is still a good God?"

Thousands of voices responded with, "Yes, Lord," or "Yes, He is," and "I know it, Pastor. I know He is."

"We don't have anything to cry about this morning, New Testament. We have every reason to rejoice. God has seen fit to allow us to see another day, and I don't know about you, but I'm going to praise Him."

With that there was no keeping the masses in their seats. Hands flew up in the air, and shouts of praise swept through the room.

"There's a verse in the Bible that says, 'Touch not mine anointed, and do my prophets no harm.' Do you believe that, saints?"

"We believe it, Pastor," was the unified response.

"Well, I'm a living witness that it's true."

For the next thirty minutes the room hung on every word that fell from Samantha's glossed lips. Hattie Williams sat stiff on the front row at the end of the pew. Her arthritic knee throbbed with each pound of the drums. The head of her cane rested against her thigh, and the purse filled with Kleenex, mints and a pocket Bible sat on the cushion next to her.

Hattie looked up at Samantha in the pulpit and prayed silently, *Lord, have mercy on New Testament Cathedral this Sunday morning.*

Notes